What Is Visible

What Is Visible

A Novel

KIMBERLY ELKINS

TWELVE

New York Boston

Copyright © 2014 by Kimberly Elkins

"What Is Visible" first appeared in *The Atlantic*, March 2003, in a different version, and then in *Best New American Voices 2004*, and the 2005 McGraw-Hill college textbook *Arguing Through Literature*.

The prologue first appeared in a different version as "Laura Bridgman, Age Fifty-Nine, the First Deaf-Blind Person to Learn Language, Meets Helen Keller, Age Seven" in *The Drum*.

Chapter 17 first appeared in a different version as "The Letter" in "Printer's Row," the literary supplement to the *Chicago Tribune*, October 7, 2012.

Twelve
Hachette Book Group
237 Park Avenue
New York, NY 10017
www.HachetteBookGroup.com

Printed in the United States of America

RRD-C

First Edition: June 2014

10 9 8 7 6 5 4 3 2 1

Twelve is an imprint of Grand Central Publishing.

The Twelve name and logo are trademarks of Hachette Book Group, Inc.

The Hachette Speakers Bureau provides a wide range of authors for speaking events. To find out more, go to www.hachettespeakersbureau.com or call (866) 376-6591.

The publisher is not responsible for websites (or their content) that are not owned by the publisher.

Library of Congress Cataloging-in-Publication Data

Elkins, Kimberly.
What is visible: a novel / Kimberly Elkins.—First Edition.
    pages cm
ISBN 978-1-4555-2896-7 (hardcover)—ISBN 978-1-4555-2897-4 (ebook)—ISBN 978-1-61969-827-7 (audio download) 1. Bridgman, Laura Dewey, 1829–1889.
—Fiction. 2. Deafblind women—Fiction. 3. American Sign Language—Fiction. I. Title.
PS3605.L418W43 2014
813'.6—dc23
                            2013034399

To my parents, Paul and Linda Elkins,
for everything then and everything now

Acknowledgments

First off, a bottomless thank-you to Gail Hochman, my superhuman agent, a demi-goddess in my book; and to Deb Futter, my editor and an absolute dream sent from heaven. You two have provided such wonderful, heartfelt, and goshdarn smart guidance and support and hand-holding all the way through. And how lucky to have been blessed with the assistance of the brilliant Brian McLendon, associate publisher at Grand Central Publishing and Twelve; Twelve's publicity manager genius Paul Samuelson; and Libby Burton, Tony Forde, Carolyn Kurek, Kathleen Scheiner, and the rest of the amazing crew at Grand Central/Twelve. I am so happy to be one of the Twelve! A shout-out also to Jody Klein at Brandt & Hochman.

My mentors Bob Shacochis, Robert Olen Butler, and Ha Jin gave me the courage, the skills, and the wherewithal to write this book. I am also grateful to have studied with several other great teachers: Janet Burroway, Leslie Epstein, Mark Winegardner, Hilma Wolitzer, Jill McCorkle, Jennifer Belle, and Natalie Sandler.

My generous and needle-sharp first readers who helped me far more than they'll ever know: Rita Mae Reese, Kristin Ginger, J. Kevin Shushtari, Joe Connelly, and most of all my parents, Paul and Linda Elkins, who critiqued the work with amazing compassion, intelligence, and insight.

Much gratitude to all those who have encouraged and supported my dreams, early and late: my family, Toni, PJ, and nieces Bailey, Sophie, and Paola Elkins; Manny Azenberg, for nurturing me as a young playwright, and Harvey Weinstein, who employed me long ago as his assistant, for both proving that business can still be art; C. Michael Curtis, for publishing the story that begot the novel; dear friends Steve Bibko, Dawn Cardinale, Peter Cecere, Suzy Chamandy, Ben Coates, Cliff Cole, Natalie

Danford, Danny Depamphillis, Jeffrey Dersh, Gene DeSimone, Caimeen Garrett, Jeff Girion, Mark L. Gottlieb, Marni Halasa, Andrew Hollweck, Joan Ingber, Angel Khoury, Cindy King, Katherine Klotsas, Amir Korangy, David Krancher, Lys Lanctot, David Levinson, Tom Livesey, Melinda Marble, Michelle Mintzer, Randy Noojin, Noah Pivnick, Alden Richards, Page Richards, Mike Robinson, Jenny Schlossberg, Julie Shushtari, Judith Simonian, Monica Stordeur, Hal Stucker, Rebecca Webber, James Varner, and Tim Young; all my students, grad and undergrad, who teach me wonders; and Annie Ide, without whom this book would never have been possible.

For the two years of research necessary for the novel, I am indebted to the New England Research Consortium for providing me with fellowships to the Houghton Library at Harvard University, the Schlesinger Library at the Radcliffe Institute for Advanced Study, the Massachusetts Historical Society, and the Maine Historical Society; to Perkins School for the Blind, guided by expert research librarian Jan Seymour-Ford; the American Antiquarian Society, with special thanks to Joanne Chaison, Jim Moran, Jackie Penny, and Elizabeth Pope; the St. Botolph Society; and Marcia Trimble, for generous fellowships to pay for both my MFA at Boston University and a research trip to Italy.

To the terrific folks at the Kerouac Project, Blue Mountain Center, the Albee Foundation, and the Millay Colony who gave me time and space to write; and the Sewanee Writers Conference and the Wesleyan Writers Conference, where I was honored to be a Fellow.

To the books that inspired me in writing mine: Chris Adrian's *Gob's Grief*; Jean-Dominique Bauby's *The Diving Bell and the Butterfly*; and Valerie Martin's *Property*.

And to those of you who continue to inspire me daily, though you are gone from this place: my grandparents Lawton and Altona Walters and Clinton and Zelma Elkins, dear ones; Dawn Couch, Brook Thaler, Casey Nye, Clarence Pope III, Ann Gregory, and Chris Stewart. I miss you so.

Author's Note

The hand spelling used by Laura Bridgman was the manual alphabet, which augments current American Sign Language when spelling individual letters of a word as opposed to making signs that represent entire words. In the case of the deaf-blind, the letters and signs are performed directly into the hand. She spelled the letters into the palms of her teachers, friends, and others who had learned ASL to communicate with her, and they spelled into her hand the same way. This form of communication is now practiced as Tactile American Sign Language. In the case of those who didn't know ASL, a friend or member of the Perkins Institution staff acted as translator between them and Laura. She wrote on what was then known as a grooved French board to help align her block letters, and read from special raised-letter books printed by Perkins. Braille was not used at Perkins at that time, though it was used in Europe.

What Is Visible

Prologue

Laura, 1888

How little they trot me out for show these days, and yet here I am this frigid morning, brought down from my room to meet a *child*, and me not out of my sickbed two weeks. They're actually calling her "the second Laura Bridgman." The second, and I'm still here! What am I supposed to do, bow down to her? Set her on my knee? I didn't like children even when I was one, and now I think them worse than dogs. I've shriveled and so they've searched for another freak in bloom to exhibit and experiment on. It's taken Perkins decades to find one pretty enough, quick enough. Well, pretty is really the important thing, or at least not too strange or looking like what she *is*. Not looking like what I am.

"Just talk to her," Annie Sullivan writes upon my hand. "You have so much in common." Like two in the throes of the plague might share tips and grievances? Yes, little Miss Keller and I will rattle on about our lives in our respective cells, and since I can't taste or smell either—she's got that on me—she can tell me how the succor of roast mutton and strawberries and the odor of feces and chrysanthemums have opened enormous windows of happiness and universal feeling that I will never enjoy.

She curtsies, I feel the whoosh of her skirts as she goes down, and then she is on me, too excited for them to hold her back, if they are even trying. Her hair is heartbreakingly soft—I had forgotten this about children, this wonder—and her face round and warm as a meat pie against my leg, clutching at my dress, reaching for my hands. Too much! I raise both arms into the air. Annie always had bad manners, so this assault is no surprise. In the years she shared my cottage here, she acted the queen since she had partial sight, but really she was dirty Irish straight from the almshouse. After everything, though, I do miss Annie greatly, and she's done better than all right, it seems, as the teacher of this one. I taught Annie the manual alphabet, the finger spelling tapped out into the hand that is the only way to communicate with me and with Helen. Will she give me that credit, I wonder. And though Dr. Howe, Perkins' director, disavowed Braille, Annie says she is trying it with her charge.

The girl steps hard on my foot, right on the big toe that is bent with the rheumatism. "Get her off!" I rap into Annie's hand, and Helen is pulled back. We all breathe for a moment, and Annie takes the chance at last to greet me properly.

"Dear Laura," she writes, "you look well." Proof of her half-blindness right there!

"God tells me you are splendid also." She is no fan of religion, Miss Sullivan; that will get her goat. "Congratulations on your work with this—"

And then the little hand taps again at mine, insistent as a summer fly. "Thank you for doll. I love very much."

She is difficult to follow. "You're welcome."

"I'm almost nine. How old?"

What cheek to ask a lady her age, but then again, with my fame, it's no secret. "Fifty-eight." I try to walk away from her toward the heat from the window, but she grabs at my skirt.

"Please talk to me," she writes. "Please."

My presumptive heir is begging in my palm. And so I ask Helen my favorite question: "If you could have one sense back, which would it be?"

Her fingers go round and round in circles, and I can feel the girl actually *thinking* in my palm.

"Which do you pick?" she asks.

Though I have been deprived of all senses save touch since the age of two, while she is only deaf and blind, for me the choice is simple. "Sight," I tell her, all the glorious colors God has painted on lands and faces. Green is the color I remember with the most pleasure: green from the grass outside our house in New Hampshire. Blue still spills from that square of sky visible over the bed where I lay ill for almost a year, and Mama says my eyes were bright blue before they shrunk behind my lids. Red I have a strong and disagreeable sense of, from when they bled me with leeches. And black, black I know the longest and best because it is my constant companion. These are the only colors I can recall or imagine with any clarity.

"Choose." I tap Helen's hand.

"Still thinking."

What a serious one! The firmness of her fingers marks her as quite unlike other children I have known; she seems more like an adult in her faculties.

"Tell me," she writes. "Tell me about you."

My story? Everything? Heaven knows there are parts not suitable for a child. But maybe I could try, invoking the voices of others to join in, since much of the last fifty years is still a mystery to me. I fear this is my last season, so I will try. Yes. For Helen.

Chapter 1

Laura, 1842

"It is well for Laura Bridgman that she cannot read all that has been written and printed about her, for if she could, she would be very likely to be vain."

—*Youth's Penny Gazette*, September 26, 1849

"There she was, before me; built up, as it were, in a marble cell, impervious to any ray of light, or particle of sound; with her poor white hand peeping through a chink in the wall, beckoning to some good man for help, that an immortal soul might be awakened. Long before I looked upon her, the help had come."

—Charles Dickens, *American Notes*, 1842

I count to a thousand, bathing my hands in the bowl of milk I have begged from Cook, turning them over and over, kneading the warmth into each crevice of my palms, soaking my fingertips until they pucker. They must be soft, soft as the unlucky day I was born, to touch the world and be touched by it on this important occasion. I wonder what would happen if my hands blaze so brightly that all of the people who have come to see me are struck blind by their light.

With the fingers of my left hand I skim the raised letters of the page, while those of my right rest in Doctor's palm, as he waits for any questions I may have about my reading. The scratchy wool of his Sunday waistcoat sleeve tickles my bare wrist. Today, I have no questions because it's all for show, not study; I finished with this primer, *The Child's Fourth Book of Grammar and Spelling*, before Christmas. We host hundreds in the public hall for the usual Saturday Exhibition Days here at Perkins, but today we're in the front parlor, and Miss Swift, my teacher, says there are only about forty very special guests.

Doctor places my finger on a sentence, and I copy it onto the grooved French board: "After the children had exhausted their inquiries and expressions of admiration about the learned dog Apollo, William asked his mother if she thought, at some future time, there would be schools for dogs." So easy. Doctor holds up the board and the clapping drums through the soles of my shoes. Doctor had asked me if he could read out loud a letter I'm working on to send Mama in Hanover, but I told him no, not to the crowd. So I write a line now for him to read: "Dr. Samuel Gridley Howe rides all over Boston on his big black horse, then comes home to take care of Laura, his little dove." Doctor takes the page, but I don't think he reads it because there's no applause. I perform four arithmetics—one each addition, subtraction, multiplication, division—and on the division, which is quite simple, I pretend to make a mistake and slap my right hand with my left, the way Miss Swift does when I make a real mistake, which used to happen often, but not much now that I've been here five years.

Doctor writes "London" into my palm, his thumb and forefinger in the shape of an *L*, and taps me to get up. Exactly three arm's lengths down left from my chair I reach the embossed globe just as he sets it spinning, and the wooden continents rise under my fingers. I grab all of Europe, then trace my way to England and stop on its capital, the city of our guest of honor, Mr. Charles Dickens. The floor vibrates with the clapping, and I curtsy, which seems to generate more applause—they didn't think I could curtsy? I whirl the globe to Africa, fingering the wavy ridges of the Nile, and turn again to the crowd. I'm laughing at my trick because I know we have no visitors from Africa here; the slaves are all down South. No one claps this time; I guess they don't understand my little joke. Doctor pats my arm and pulls me down beside him at the desk. I'm not supposed to laugh hard, because Doctor says the sound scares people, but sometimes I can't help it.

There are too many people around me now, the air full of their heat. When there's a bigger crowd, the teachers push a row of chairs between me and them so they don't crush me. Miss Swift says I am puny and too thin, but Doctor says I am a little dove, which must mean that I am small in an excellent way, because doves are soft and, I think, very beautiful. Where is Doctor?

I walk the twenty-three lady's steps to my visitor's seat in front of the fireplace, and find rough worsted draped over the padded armrest. Tessy and her dirty shawl are in my chair! She is my best friend of all the blind girls, so sometimes I let her sit there to warm herself on very cold days like today, but *never* when I have visitors. Everybody knows that. I grab for her hand to tell her to get up, but she hides it in her sleeve, so I push her, just a little. I try to hold down the ugly sound I'm not supposed to make, the one I've felt from Pozzo, the Institution's dog, thrumming in the cords of his neck. Miss Swift comes suddenly between us—she's certainly wide enough to keep two armies apart—and of course, Tessy jumps up for her, but as soon as Swift moves away, Tessy sidles back and writes very hard, "You're not Jenny Lind, you know," and skitters away.

I start to go after her—I'm a very fast runner—but that's not how a civilized young lady of twelve should behave, especially at an afternoon exhibition. The blinds are all jealous because I'm the only one who gets to live in the Director's apartment with Doctor and his sister, Jeannette, while they sleep in dormitories and have to share everything, even soap. I know I'm not Jenny Lind, but I'm not just some silly blind girl either. I straighten my day dress, the green one Doctor picked to match the shade that covers my eyes, and settle back into the cushions to wait for the people to come to me.

My feet hear Doctor's boots at last. He is a very quick stepper and not so heavy on the floor as other men, like the one he's bringing with him. He leans down and writes that he is giving me Mr. Dickens, who I'm told is even more famous than I am. Mr. Dickens sits on the settee and Miss Swift tucks in between us to translate. I feel him pitching forward, too close, as he takes my hand. His knuckles are so hairy I pray he won't expect me to touch his face. I like to stroke the ladies' faces, their necks and hair, even the old ladies if their skin isn't too flappy, but Doctor's is the only man's face I touch, unless I'm requested to show my skill at identification. Doctor's eyelashes are as long as a woman's, as long as my whole thumbnail, and his sideburns curl around my pinkie. I have eyelashes too, but no one ever sees them because they might be frightened.

"He says you are the second wonder of North America," Miss Swift writes, and then adds that only the roar of Niagara Falls is more impressive than what I have achieved in silence.

"You write books?" I ask. "Good?" I would like to have the Perkins press raise one for me so I could form my own opinion.

"They sell," he tells me. "You remind me of girl in my last."

"Real girl or pretend?"

"Pretend. Little Nell."

Stupid name. I don't know if it's better to be a real girl or a pretend girl; that's something I'll need to think about. "Had scarlet fever like me?"

"No, but hard life like you."

"She can see and hear?" I ask, and as I thought, the answer is yes.

"Taste and smell?"

Yes again.

"Then she is not like me," I tell him. Everyone thinks Mr. Dickens is very smart, but I'm not so sure.

Miss Swift lays one of the purses I've knitted in my lap, and I present it: "For Mrs. Dickens. Carry her sundries." Then I lie: "Made it special." I hope he has a wife. I hope he realizes that people from all over the world come to pay half a dollar for my purses and crocheted napkin holders and handkerchiefs. I'm allowed to keep all my money, and I'm saving up for either a pearl necklace for Mama or a silver pen for Doctor to replace the one he lost last month, dear to him because it was engraved with thanks from the Greek Revolution he fought in before he founded Perkins. And he got Lord Byron's helmet from Greece too. I'm not sure exactly who that is because Doctor says his poetry is too hard for me, but he must be very important because the helmet is displayed in a glass case in the front parlor. Tessy says that Doctor gets trunks of money from rich folks to pay for our food and our clothes and our teachers. I asked him about that, but he said that little girls should not concern themselves with finances. Miss Swift doesn't know I didn't actually make the purse special for Mr. Dickens, but if anybody found out that I lied to the famous author, I would have to sit by myself in the schoolroom until I apologized, which sometimes takes me a whole day and a night. The good thing—probably the only good thing—about writing in someone's hand instead of speaking is that no one can eavesdrop. I don't know how regular people manage to have any secrets.

"Scrubbed everything for you," I tell Mr. Dickens. "Five floors. On my knees." I had to help; Jeannette is such a terrible housekeeper that I find balls of dust whenever I check the floor in my room. I can't see the dirt, but if you set me in a spot with a soapy rag and a bucket, I won't move until you tell me it's all spanking clean. I think one of the reasons Doctor keeps me in his apartment is because it would be a mess without me, and Doctor hates a mess, even more than Papa did. Miss Swift signs that it's time for Doctor to give a speech.

And so from Mr. Dickens one last thing: "God bless you."

"You also," I write. Then he pats my head, and I try not to flinch, afraid a crinkled hair from his knuckle might slip into my braid like an old spider. I plaited my hair myself in one long braid wound tight in a circle at the back of my head. It's very neat.

Miss Swift pulls a chair by mine and tells me that her hands are tired already, so she won't be filling me in on Doctor's speech, as she usually does. I don't understand how she can be so tired when we haven't even done much talking today, and heaven knows she never helps with the cleaning. I don't really mind, though, because I've gotten the Exhibition speech a hundred times: charity; education; how Doctor founded Perkins ten years ago; how Doctor doesn't like the Braille he saw in France and invented his own Boston type; and then he talks about me. I will sorely miss that part today.

I sit patiently in my chair until I feel the applause and I can tell everyone is rising to their feet, as they often do after Doctor, so I stand too. Then Doctor comes straight to my chair, but it pains me that he brings more guests, two stepping lightly who I know are women, and then one treading more heavily than a bear, Doctor's closest friend, Charles Sumner. Sumner is too tall; even when he bends down, he's my whole hand taller than Doctor. I was so scared of Doctor when he first came to see me in Hanover because he was the tallest person I had ever met until then. But I was only seven, so I didn't know anything.

He introduces me to Misses Louisa and Julia Ward, sisters visiting from New York City, who are staying nearby in Dorchester. The Julia one is standing so close to Doctor that his sleeve grazes me when I reach for her hand.

"Lovely little girl," Doctor says she called me, and then he is off to play with his other guests, leaving Miss Swift to translate.

The Miss Julia Ward is wearing a bracelet with huge triangles that feel like glass. "Diamonds?" I ask.

"Austrian crystals," but they are sharper than the crystals in Jeannette's jewelry. Maybe she is rich, like many people from New York.

I reach up to touch her hair. The women like me to play with their hair. They always invite me. Two long, crisp plumes stand straight on a tiny hat that feels like satin. It's not a daytime hat;

satin is what the ladies wear at night. And it has a jewel as well, a smooth, flat square. Definitely an evening hat. Her hair is pulled to the back much like mine, but I can still feel on the sides how silky it is—silkier than mine, thicker than mine or Swift's or Jeannette's or Tessy's or Mama's. I wonder if Doctor knows this. His own hair is almost that thick, and he isn't missing any on the top like some men. There's nothing more terrible than to explore a forehead only to find it goes on and on, especially if there are any tufted bits left sprouting like grass between stones. I check the front of Julia's head, because women can sometimes be missing hair too, especially the old ones, but no, Julia has it all. I trail lightly down the curve of her cheek—I want to get to know her face better—but she suddenly leans away from me. Very rude.

"Excited for Oliver coming?" she asks.

"Who is Oliver?"

Miss Swift's hand hesitates. "The one like you."

She's talking nonsense. I search the air in front of me for Doctor—where is Doctor? I stand and step on her foot. Sumner tugs at my upper arm, but I elbow him off and run through the room, cracking my knee against the corner of the chaise, grazing shoulders and backs as I circle toward the door, toward the bay window, the fireplace, and back again. Warm liquid spills down the front of my dress—someone's tea, I suppose—and then I find Doctor's coattail. He turns and shakes me by the shoulders, just like I'm trying to shake him, and then his hands go down and he writes on my wet palm, "Stop! Calm." I am behaving like a wild animal, and making the noises of one too, coming deep from my chest. I let them rip.

"Who is Oliver?" I write.

"Hush." He pats my back and guides me to a chair. "Little boy who is blind and deaf. Wonderful."

"How old?"

"Eight."

"Can taste and smell?"

"Yes. You'll help teach."

I shake my head.

"You'll love him, Laura, as we love you." I don't think he understands me as well as I thought. He tells me that he's off to town with Sumner and the Miss Wards.

He waits as I press my nails in. Miss Swift never lets them grow as long as I'd like; she cuts them every Monday morning.

"Let go. Now."

I allow him to pry my hands from his, and he goes. The last of the footsteps thud away, but still I sit, not even in my visitor's chair, but in a low, hard one by the bay window, letting the draft creep across my feet. I keep my hands shut, like a book with flat print that I'll never be able to read, maybe one of Mr. Dickens's, its pages filled with the joys and sorrows—no, the *adventures*—of someone like me. Oliver will come smelling flowers, sniffing Doctor's coat, tasting peaches and custards and boiled sugar syrup and sausages and turtle soup. He won't be like me. No one is like me. It's really true, and I don't know if that's good or bad.

Chapter 2

Laura, 1843

"The two [Oliver and Laura] presented a singular sight; her face was flushed and anxious and her fingers twined in among ours so closely as to follow every motion...while Oliver stood attentive...then a smile came stealing out...and spread into a joyous laugh the moment he succeeded, and felt me pat his head, and Laura clap him heartily upon the back, and jump up and down in her joy."
—Samuel Gridley Howe, "Tenth Annual Report of the Trustees of the Perkins Institution," 1843

Doctor pulls me onto his lap in the leather chair by the fire after supper; he is wearing his flannel robe, and I am wearing mine, because a shiver of winter runs through our apartment. He takes a walnut from his pocket—he always keeps some there for me—and lets me squeeze the nutcracker as his hand waits below for the prize. No other nuts please me like this one: the shell is the hardest to crack, and the meat is deeply ridged, each half different. Doctor says they are shaped like tiny brains, and like the nuts, each brain is different. Phrenology, the study of the bumps on the skull, is Doctor's favorite hobby, but he tells me that I am too young to learn it yet. He drops the nut into my open mouth. That is our agreement—if he lets me open them, I have to eat them—but tonight, he gives in, as he sometimes does, and takes the other half I tap against his teeth. He allows my fingers to travel over the face I know as well as my own: the strong, wide brow and bushy eyebrows; the straight perfection of his nose between the deep-set eyes; the bristly fur of mustache half covering his upper lip. And his beard, Doctor's beard—I could spend an hour curling each hair around my finger.

"Enough," he signs on the hand he pulls from his whiskers. "Oliver is coming tomorrow." I write nothing, as if I have no concerns. "Spending the night in town before they deliver him."

My parents did not *deliver* me to Doctor; he came to Hanover and took me. Papa did not even walk us out to the carriage; his last touch was when he pried my fingers from the doorframe.

"Your blue dress," Doctor says. I am dressing for a blind? "Invited the newspapers."

"Oliver isn't famous." Not yet, anyway.

"Historic, your meeting."

"Like you and Longo?" The first time Longfellow and Doctor met, they talked for eight hours straight.

"No," he writes. "A meeting between two of God's best creatures."

The newspapers are not coming because Oliver and I are two of God's best creatures, I know that. "Like General Tom Thumb and the Feejee Mermaid?"

He puts another walnut in my hand, and together, we crack it open. "You hurt my heart," he writes. "Barnum is a showman."

He sits so far back in his chair that I almost fall off his knee. I lift his hand from the arm of the chair to write my "sorry," but he balls both hands into fists. We sit still together for a moment, as we often do, but this time the stillness is full of Doctor's disappointment. He lets me uncurl one fist: "I will help with Oliver." He pulls me close to him then, my head settling in the familiar nook between his neck and shoulder, and I am his own little mermaid again, swimming in his warm waters.

The hall is crowded. The boy has come. For once, I try to stay back, invisible, leaning against the cold marble. Miss Swift writes that Doctor is pointing out the luxuries of our new Institution: the long, curving stairways; the carpeted, high-ceilinged rooms (Swift says you could stack five of me and still not touch the chandeliers). It's so fancy because it used to be the Mount Washington House Hotel. My first years, we were still in Mr. Perkins's house downtown on Pearl Street, but now here we are on Bird Lane in South Boston overlooking the bay. What a world away, Doctor tells the crowd, from the nearby House of Industry for Paupers and Orphans and the Boylston School for Neglected and Indigent Boys.

I figure he'll go on for hours with such an audience, but then Swift tugs me forward. Doctor writes "Oliver" and then places the boy's fingers on my eyeshade, and on my ears, and then upon his own. I can't tell from the child's movements if he understands anything at all—who knows? And then, without warning, Doctor pushes me smack into the boy's chubby arms, our faces so close that I feel the air sucked quickly in and out of his nostrils as he sniffs me. It is violent, it is rude, but still I wish I had that talent. I do not struggle, but I do not embrace him, either; I hold myself up as tall as I can, and I am taller than he is, his bangs swishing against my cheek. I tense as Doctor lifts my arms, but allow him to put them around the boy. It's like holding one of Cook's potato rolls risen with too much yeast and come to life. His hair is as downy as a girl's one hour out of the bath.

Suddenly, he drops to the floor, and I am afraid he is after my shoes, but he scuttles away from me. There is a jarring, and then Doctor pulls him up beside me, and everyone is jostled about. I search for Swift's hand, and she says that Oliver felt the warm air blowing from the grate of the furnace beneath his feet and knelt to inspect it with his tongue. It's true that there are no furnaces like the one Doctor had built especially for us, but it is not worth *licking*. I can't stop laughing; I don't care if his parents hear me. I was worried about a boy, and here they have brought me only a dog to play with. That's good then! I have long wanted a pet, as long as he is not too hard to clean up after. Poor Doctor—I wish I could see his face—does he show the embarrassment I am certain he is feeling?

He has recovered, though, and he puts my hand in Oliver's. I don't resist my pet. The fat, little fingers grip mine, and he trots forward, pulling me with him down the long marble hall, though of course he has no idea where he's going. He is off exploring the walls, the floors, jerking me this way and that, and he shakes with laughter at everything. Is Doctor sure the boy is not an idiot? No one in his right mind could possibly be this jolly about touching doors and walls. I remember the great terror that seized me when I first arrived, when everything and everyone was new and strange, and I had no way to *know* any of it, for good or for ill, except through my fingers. But Oliver doesn't even tremble, except occasionally with delight. Maybe he is not afraid of anything because his parents are here with him. Does he know they are going to abandon him within hours?

Swift and Doctor rein him in, and they are now beginning the official tour. Swift says they'll start with the boys' dining room. I rush ahead to brush each of the six long wooden tables for crumbs. I wonder if I should check with Cook to make sure she is presentable, if Doctor decides to show the kitchen. Thank goodness Oliver is a boy, and won't be at the table snuffling through his food between me and Tessy. Next I throw open the heavy doors of the gymnasium, and spread my arms wide so the visitors can take in everything: the climbing ropes, the ladders, the yardarms, and mats. Even the director of the Pennsylvania Institution for the Blind was shocked at the wonder Doctor created for us, and how rough-and-tumble we play in it. I'm not big, but I can wrestle most of the older girls to the ground, though I have been barred from such play temporarily for biting. I have excellent teeth. The people are moving around the room, and I would climb the rope all the way up for them and pose in the warmth of the sunshine from the top dormers if I had on my romp skirt and tights.

Doctor is behind me, his pocket watch thrumming through his waistcoat against my back as he presses close. "Tell the gentlemen from the *Herald* and the *Evening Transcript* what you think of Oliver."

Doctor offers me the slate to write on because there are too many hands to talk to, and I freeze: *he is a dog, he is a dog* is all I can think. Puppy? No, he is a boy, a good boy—what did Doctor say? He is a creature, he is God's creature. I remember something Swift's brother was going on about last week, and I think it might sound nice. "Oliver is the lamb of God," I write in big letters, and hold the board up for all to see. The floor vibrates—not applause, it seems, but low laughter—and Doctor grabs the board. I don't understand. Lambs are sweet and gentle; it is a much greater compliment than the boy deserves. Swift stops me as I try to go upstairs with the group. I know Doctor will be showing the students' rooms in the boys' wing, and I want to see if Oliver gets a room by himself like mine in Doctor's apartment.

"Doctor wants you to stay," she writes.

"Why?" I know I did nothing wrong, yet there is a little burr of worry beneath my skin.

"Wrong to call Oliver lamb of God."

"Everyone likes."

"Not a real lamb," she writes. "Bible symbol for..."

I wait, but she doesn't continue. Swift does not communicate well, like Doctor or like me. "Give me Bible like the blinds. I'll learn it."

Swift holds my hand more gently. "I try, but Doctor says no."

I won't be able to wait much longer, because God is the one person in the whole world that I have the most questions for.

True to my word, I am helping Miss Swift *attempt* to teach Oliver, but he is a very dull scholar, just as I forecast. A hundred times a day for the last month, I have moved his fingers from the metal raised-type labels for *fork*, *spoon*, and *pen* to the actual items, and back again. A few times he has been able to imitate my motions, but then he seems to forget and goes back to his fidgets. Doctor says that within two weeks, I'd already matched the labels of over fifty objects and was on to arranging the individual letters into words. Oliver didn't come down with the fever until he was three and a half, more than a year after I did, so Doctor thinks he should remember more from what he heard and saw. He was talking a blue streak by then, his parents said, and yet all he does now is make pantomime gestures. He finally does understand that, like him, I can't see or hear, so he pats my hand or my face when he wants my attention. He has different pats for *good, bad, stop,* and *hungry.* I am sure he will never learn real finger spelling. At first I didn't like it myself, but then Doctor told me that each hand-shape not only represents a letter of the alphabet, but also stands for a particular prayer taken from a book written by a Spanish monk over three hundred years ago. If a monk was too sick to re-cite a prayer, then he would just make the handshape for it. I like to think I am constructing words and sentences out of prayers, though I am still not sure that God receives them.

Doctor worked with us the first weeks, but then he got frus-trated with Oliver, and now he's gone to New York to raise money for the school. That's what he says, anyway, but I know he is vis-iting with Julia Ward. He used to say that New York City was only fit for vermin, but last week he didn't laugh when I made a rat joke about the Ward sisters. He has made more trips there in the last months—four, to be exact—than he has ever made before. "Are you counting?" Jeannette asked me, and I said, "Yes, ma'am, I am."

Before he left, Doctor told me that he is impressed, however, with how Oliver is taking to workshop with the other boys; he has already woven one manila doormat and is working on a basket. I wish the girls got to go all the way to the East Fourth Street work-shop every afternoon, walking holding hands along the water. I would tie the biggest, most comfortable mattress in the world for Doctor, and beat all the boys at chair-caning too. Instead, I must stay here with the blind girls knitting and sewing, washing and ironing, until supper at six. Those things are better practice to fit us to be good wives and mothers, I'm told. We are kept from the boys—or more likely, them from us—for everything except assemblies. I have only had occasion to meet with them then, and I am pleased with our separation because their touch is rough and their fingers grimy. Only Oliver is allowed to mix with us girls, and I help keep him very clean, going over his face and hands regularly with a wet rag.

Of course, I have my Laura dolls to practice mothering, all ten of them, the twelve-inch likenesses of me that are sold across the country, with their eyes poked out and little green grosgrain ribbons tied over the eyeholes. I sent Mama one for my baby sister Mary, and Mama wrote that the doll looks just like me. Pretty, Mama said, and well-formed. It is such a treat to touch myself, to run my fingers down my tiny nose and up and down my smooth legs beneath the dress. I wish that the fingers bent so we could have conversations, though I know they wouldn't be real. Still I write in my favorite Laura's hand sometimes, secrets and stories. I know which one she is because she is the only one whose hair I wrap up in a bun and tie with ribbon like a lady's; the rest have hair that hangs loose and straight down their back like mine. I can't wait till I can twirl it back and carry it on top of my head like Julia's. I used to let some of the older girls hold tea with me and all the Lauras, but then last month after tea with several of the girls and their dolls, I did the count and there were only nine Lauras. I understand the others would be jealous not just because I have more dolls than they do—most have only one—but that my face is so famous that little girls everywhere want to play with me. To show that I am generous, I gave Tessy a Laura on the condition that she not change her name and that she sleep with her every night. Sometimes I sleep with Tessy too, a Laura nestled between us. Every night before I go to bed, I brush each one's hair with a miniature brush the mayor's wife gave me, and on waking, I smooth their long white dresses. I ask Swift if any of their dresses are dirty from sitting on top of the armoire, even though I dust them with a feather duster every week, but she always says no. She's just lazy and doesn't want to help me with them. Swift asked if Oliver could join Tessy and me at doll tea on Sundays, but I said, "Of course not, he's a boy, he might break them." I am their mother, so I am responsible for their well-being.

Even though I won't let Oliver play with my dolls, I'm very careful with him, like a mother; I make sure he doesn't cut himself on the sharp edges of the metal labels, but today I slit the tip of my own index finger on the label for *book*. I tried to clean it up, but Swift said I was just making more of a mess. I wish I could have seen my blood, which Doctor says is red, dripping all over Oliver's desk, and maybe even splattering Oliver. I couldn't tell how much there was, but my finger was very wet, the bandage soaked through in five minutes. It doesn't actually feel bad to get a small cut. I think having my whole arm chopped off with a sword would be awful, but this little bit, this little hurt, fills me up inside in a way that is quite nice. I slip the metal label into my pocket.

I'm so glad it's finally recess. "Teaching is much more tiring than learning," I tell Swift as we straighten the classroom, and she agrees. Doctor doesn't like me to miss exercise, so I hurry to the gymnasium. Most of the girls are already here, and the floor shakes with their game. They skip one way, pause, and reverse, so that means it's Ring a Ring o' Roses. I love that one, even though part of it is singing, which I can't join in. The falling down part is good. I walk to the circle, and reach out when it stops, but these two, Susan and Mary, the oldest blinds, keep their hands locked tight—it is Susan, I think, who took my Laura—and then the circle spins again. When it stops, I find Tessy's shawl in my hand, but she skips away from me. Then to my surprise, it's Oliver's shoulder I touch, and then he is jerked away. The girls have never let any boys into their ring before. I back away from the circle and feel the heavy thuds as they all fall down, Oliver no doubt laughing and laughing among the tangled limbs. I rush in and grab Tessy's arm as they stand up.

"Why wouldn't you let me in?" I write.

"Susan says you smell bad." She walks away quickly with the rest of them. I've read that animals and foods can smell bad, but I didn't know that *people* could smell bad. What could I smell like—the bread and butter I ate for lunch? the pencil I used for lessons? my dress? Maybe it's the blood from my finger; maybe blood has a terrible, terrible smell. As the girls file out, I stand with my back against the wall, holding on to one of the climbing ropes. And then there's only Oliver, who has come over to tug on the rope, or maybe because my smell is so strong that he knows I'm here. I hold my bandaged finger up to his nose and let him get a good, long whiff. He doesn't move away, so I slide my whole arm back and forth under his nose, almost smashing his face into it. Finally he raises his head, and almost as if he knows what I am asking, he gives me his double pat along the cheek, his sign for *good*. I lift him up and help him climb the rope.

Chapter 3

Chev, 1843

Nothing was sweeter. He watched their hands: Laura's thin white fingers etched her thoughts on Julia's upturned palm, and then they switched, and Julia's fingers, plumper but even more dazzlingly white, responded. The last slivers of winter light made a halo of fire of Julia's red-gold hair, shining against the dark of Laura's braids as they bent their heads together. His beloveds, the sun and moon in his little heaven. Julia looked up at Doctor and smiled, as if she understood the pure delight he took in seeing them together. She didn't look the ten years older than Laura's thirteen.

Laura sensed the slight shift in her audience's attention and tugged at Julia's cuff, still writing. In her score of visits in the past year, Julia had mastered the mechanics of conversing with Laura as quickly as any he'd seen—far quicker than Longo or Sumner—but she was not yet ready for Laura on a tear. Finally, Julia raised her unpinned hand and waved.

"She's gone wild that I've called you Chev," she said. "I didn't know your nickname was a secret."

"It's not, but the children here don't call me that." He walked over to the settee and took Laura's hand.

"Thank you!" Julia shook her arm out. She could be very dramatic. They both could.

Laura pulled Doctor down to face her. "Why Chevalier? Leaving again to fight in Greece?"

"No. Chev a silly name."

"Like when I make noise for Oliver or Swift?"

"Yes."

"Are you talking about me?" Julia asked, leaning over Doctor's shoulders to watch his hands. Her breasts pressed against his back as Laura's nails pressed into his palm. He was sandwiched between one of the most acclaimed beauties of the Atlantic seaboard and the most written-about miracle girl in the world.

"Are you talking about me?" Laura asked. He freed himself from both of them and stepped away without an answer.

"Dr. Combe will be here in the morning," Doctor told Julia. "Let's get you back to the Misses Peabodys' before it gets late. I'll tell Brownie to get the carriage ready."

"You're serious about that? I really must have a phrenological exam before we can be officially pledged?" She sidled over and put her head on his chest, those auburn curls he dreamed of pulling rippling against the point of his beard. She only came up to his chin. In a couple of years, Laura would be the taller one.

"All my success here at Perkins is built upon phrenological principles, my dear. Combe is traveling all this way to meet you—how could I not let him believe his opinion is of grave importance? He is Spurzheim's protégé!"

Laura stood up and edged toward them, and Doctor broke the embrace before she joined it.

Combe was already set up in Doctor's office the next morning when he came in. Laura sat in the student chair and Julia perched on the edge of the desk. Julia wore a blue sprigged muslin that Doctor hadn't seen before. She would find that she wouldn't be buying new dresses every week when they were married, but that news could wait.

"You shall have your hands full of heads here, Combe," Doctor said. The phrenologist was almost seventy, but his handshake was still crushing. "Get your calipers ready!"

"Work Laura first, please," Julia said. "I would like to observe before I am examined."

Laura reached out to Doctor. "Have surprise for Julia," she wrote. Whenever she had a secret, she signed the letters more quickly.

"After the exam," he wrote equally as quick. It was their equivalent of whispering. She nodded and sat back in her chair, ready for the doctor. He had examined her annually since she arrived six years ago.

Combe stood behind Laura and placed one hand on each side of her head, but he spoke to Julia, who had come closer to watch.

"The brain is made up of congeries of organs," he said as he drew vertical and then horizontal lines on Laura's head with his index finger. "Each one corresponds to the thirty-seven innate and independent faculties of man. Each faculty, be it emotional or intellectual, has its seat in a particular region on the surface of the brain, and the size of that region shows the development, or not, of that faculty." He parted Laura's hair with the calipers and gently pinched the skin at the front of her skull. "The coronal, just above and behind the forehead, shows enormous growth since last year, especially in relation to her animal region, back here above the nape of her neck. The coronal is the seat of the moral faculty. Right behind her eyes, the organ of language, ah yes, continuing to grow, right on schedule."

Combe validated that Laura's brain was responding to Doctor's rigors and nurturance, just as he had hoped. Before his work with her, the world believed anyone this impaired to be doomed to imbecility, incapable of rational thought or the natural questing of the spirit for the divine. He had proved them all wrong. Not since Itard's progress with the Wild Boy of Aveyron had anyone created such a stir, and Doctor and Laura already had achieved far more than that feral child and his mentor. Doctor was now the foremost discoverer of the inner workings of the human mind and soul. Like William Parry at the Arctic, he had planted his flag on the farthest shore of the world, unexplored country.

Laura sat perfectly still. She seemed to be enjoying it. Combe continued his exam, stopping periodically to take notes on a small pad.

"Oh, Miss Ward," he said, "you should feel this. The bump of hope. On the left side below the braid. Very modulated. Do you want to touch it?"

Julia looked closely, but shook her head. Doctor moved Laura's braid. Yes, he was right. It was pronounced.

"You know, Howe, the girl started out with such a promising head—the contours have always confirmed naturally vigorous moral and intellectual powers—but my, what you've done with it!"

Doctor thanked him and tapped Laura to get up.

"My head good?" she wrote, and he told her the news of her growth. She clapped.

Julia sat down in the chair in front of Combe. "I'm a little nervous, I must confess," she said. She looked at Doctor. "There's so much riding on something I can't control."

"It will be fine," he said. "Let's see what she's got, Combe."

Julia closed her eyes as Combe picked and measured. "The anterior lobe," he intoned, tapping the right side of her head. "Very well developed. Knowledge and reflection. Self-esteem, love of approbation—you two share these things, Howe. And here"—he indicated a spot behind her ear—"quite the combativeness bump."

Julia opened her eyes.

"Almost as large as yours, Howe, if I remember correctly."

Doctor smiled at her. They would be fine; a little combativeness can be countenanced. Combe had found nothing terrible, no great aggressiveness or lack of order or causality.

"Dr. Howe has one of the largest affection bumps I've ever seen on a man. Most women don't even have them his size—like a walnut—though yours is close. I told him last year he'd better find a girl on which to exercise its benefits. The most eligible bachelor in Boston, over forty with no wife and that enormous bump. A sin, I told him!"

Doctor could have done without his friend sharing this particular knowledge. "That's not why I came knocking, my dear," he told Julia, though that wasn't entirely the truth.

"I'll take your word," she said. "Bumps and all." She laughed as she rose, and Doctor saw that old George was as charmed as most—dare he say all?—men were by his Julia. She laughed as much as any woman he'd ever seen, and yet managed not to be aswoon with frivolity. It must be the eyes, which had a way of looking smart even when her mouth was open. A rare talent for a female. If her laugh were too high, like a schoolgirl's, or too low, like a washerwoman's, or too long in duration, like a spinster's, or so short, like his dead mother's, God rest her soul, that it might be mistaken for a hiccup, then Doctor would not have been able to consider a life with her, no matter the light of devotion in those large gray eyes.

Laura tugged at his arm. "Julia's head like mine?"

"Almost exactly," he wrote, and it was true. They actually had far more in common than Doctor and Julia did.

"Dr. Combe, Oliver is waiting, and then the other children are lined up for you in the main hall," he told the phrenologist. "And I'd like you to take a look at my six teachers' heads too, if you could."

"Of course," Combe said and paused before Julia. "I hope to wish you the best in the near future."

Doctor showed him out, but as soon as he returned, Laura erupted in a low howl—"Whoowah! Whoowah!"—over and over again. She cast about for Julia's arm, but Julia moved quickly out of her reach.

Julia looked frightened. "Why is she doing that?"

Laura made the noise louder, and now he understood. "It's her surprise," he told Julia. "She's made a special naming noise for you." It was really quite good; she must have been practicing for a long time. "She has noises for everyone she likes, and each one sounds completely different. Well, not completely, but different enough to recognize, anyway."

Julia sat down in the chair farthest from Laura. "Oh," she said, "that's very sweet. It is. Tell her thank you very much, but could she please stop."

"Julia very excited," Doctor wrote. "Wonderful present." She howled again. "But stop now."

She quieted down and settled back into her chair, smiling, drumming her knees in satisfaction.

Julia said, "Well, that put a little damper on *my* surprise for you. I don't know how it will compare." She reached delicately into the front of her bodice with her thumb and forefinger, and Doctor was glad Combe was not there for whatever was coming. She pulled out a folded sheet and opened it, then arranged herself in front of the fireplace, resting one elbow on the mantel. She cleared her throat.

> *"A great grieved heart, an iron will,*
> *As fearless blood as ever ran;*
> *A form elate with nervous strength*
> *And fibrous vigor—all a man."*

Laura asked what Julia was doing.

"Poem," Doctor told her and signed the verses as Julia recited them. She was a slow but excellent declaimer.

> *"One helpful gift the gods forgot*
> *Due to the man of lion-mood*
> *A woman's soul, to match with his*
> *In high resolve and hardihood."*

He didn't finish writing the poem for Laura; he stopped at "lion-mood." She didn't need to know yet that Julia would be his wife. He would tell her when the time was right.

"Brava!" Doctor clapped. "Your poetry almost does your beauty justice."

"So we are matched then, now that Combe has combed my head for flaws?"

"In high resolve," he told her. "And so your lovely poems from now on, as we discussed, will be only for private consumption, yes? No more trying to publish, flying them out there in the world?"

"Yes, Chev," she said, but she wasn't looking at him. "Of course."

"I don't want a marriage of two minds, my darling, but only a marriage of two hearts."

"You have mine," she said, coming into his arms. Laura stood by her chair, her face turned toward them in rapt attention as if she were truly listening to every word. Doctor was not comfortable holding Julia with Laura this close, so he left the room and went to check on Combe's progress with Oliver.

Combe had just started on Oliver's crown when Doctor heard Julia shouting. He rushed down the hall and from the door saw the two of them locked in a strange embrace, Julia's hands on Laura's shoulders as Laura thrust her finger in and out of Julia's ear. He grabbed Laura's arms and pulled her away, her index finger still poking the air, and pushed her roughly back into her chair. Julia collapsed against him, her breath ragged. They were both breathing hard, and then Doctor realized so was he.

"Did she hurt you?"

"Scared me. I don't know what set her off."

Laura's hands pawed frantically at the air, signaling him. He helped Julia onto the settee and went to her.

"Wanted to feel bumps on her head," she wrote. "But ear—"

"You scared Julia. Like animal."

"She can hear you," she spelled with effort, and then Doctor understood. Through that sweet little maze Laura knew that Julia was able to hear, to let in the whole world, and most of all, his laughs and sighs. Nevertheless, he could not let her go unpunished. Julia was shaking, and this set-to would make the new arrangement of his world more onerous. Laura had slapped Miss Swift or one of the students many times, but never a guest, much less his beloved. She had grown accustomed, no doubt too accustomed, to asking for forgiveness from both the persons she had harmed and from God. Her friends always forgave her, and so too did God, but He absolved her only on the occasions when she was truly sorry. Doctor could tell from the set of her jaw that this was not yet one of those occasions.

He explained to Julia that Laura had only wanted to feel her bumps, and Julia seemed relieved, but when he asked if Laura could write her an apology, his fiancée quickly demurred and left the room. Laura sat in her chair, rocking back and forth, one finger bending the soft, pliable rim of her ear up and down, up and down.

Doctor was more comfortable in his dear Sumner's apartments than he was with the run of all five floors of Perkins. There he was the Doctor, the Director, while here he was just a man, a friend, a listener, a talker, maker of no decisions, bearer of no consequences. Sumner's landlady had installed precisely the right number of fat cushions for lounging, eight slung along the back of the divan. They didn't fall asleep in his rooms; they never fell asleep, even after six courses and too much sherry at Martin's with Felton and the gang. They always talked all night. Doctor had surrounded himself with women and children, of his own free will, but most days it was a hard bargain. He'd had the war, the wind, even the jail cell in Prussia, and now his most heroic act was guiding blind girls on horses down the beach.

Sumner poured them snifters from his finest decanter of brandy and lifted his glass in a mock toast. "Did you hear, Chev? Dickens's *American Notes* sold out the first print run in England in two days. You and Laura are all of chapter 4—got it in a letter from Robesey."

"And we come off well? Boz assured me the portrait would be favorable."

"Boz, is it? Didn't realize you were that close to the great scribbler." Sumner scattered the papers on his secretary, and a pile of law books tumbled to the rug. "It's here somewhere."

"You need a good wife or a better maid."

"We'll see if you end up with either," he said. "Here it is—'Paragon of Noble Usefulness,' that's what Dickens calls you, Robesey says. Do you feel like a paragon?"

"Yes, I do."

"And noble? And useful?"

"Yes and yes." It was true. "He's summed me up."

"Dickens is good for that. The book should be here in a few weeks."

"In time to impress the Astors at the wedding, I hope."

"The *Examiner* claims that you've stolen one of 'the three Graces of Bond Street,'" Sumner said. "It is madness, you're right, but the best kind, I suppose."

"Now, Charlie, Julia swears that I love you more than I will ever love her, but then I remind her that you were the one who brought us together."

"Yes, the 'rider on the black steed,' as Diva Julia has immortalized you in her girlish verse. And I am the dun-colored horse left grazing. I would whip myself if I weren't so tired."

"You were never dun-colored in your colorful life."

"If only I hadn't brought Julia and her sister to view the inimitable Laura Bridgman. It's actually Laura's fault, you know, because you've made her such a showpiece."

"She has been my own God-given, personal tabula rasa—how could I resist?"

"But with Julia, the slate is so full you'll be lucky to find room to sign your name. At the bottom."

"She's keeping the Ward—she'll be Julia Ward Howe—I made the deal with her brother in exchange for another thousand a year."

"Do you think, Chevie, that I'll ever be so blessed?"

"Of course," Doctor told him. "Maybe even snare one of the other Graces." But he didn't think Charlie would ever marry; he thought less of women, and more of men, than even Doctor did.

"Do you know what your fiancée said to me that night after I first introduced you—she said, 'Sumner, you and Dr. Howe are both so high-minded I'm surprised you can wear hats.'"

My darling Chevie,

If I have come to know you at all—and we are certainly doomed if I have not—I'd wager you don't want to hear all the gallivanting we've been up to with the ceremony details. So suffice it to say that I'll be exquisitely bedecked, as will the premises. All that remains of your duty is to ride that black steed to New York, or to poke along in a carriage with young goats Sumner, Felton, and Longo.

Your dear sister will, as we discussed, serve me at the wedding with my three sisters, but my family feels strongly that we cannot allow little Laura to be a member of our party. I pleaded, you know I did, Chev, but Brother Sam was quite resolute: if the Astors were gracious enough to host our wedding, we could not possibly repay them in such august society with the kind of interruptions the poor child would surely make. If my father were still alive to handle my dowry, things would not go so rough, but Sam feels he must act my fierce champion, especially since he settled with you on the house. And have you considered the glass eyes for her?

So please, darling, do forgive me on this one tiny point. I know you will.

Your soon-to-be-obedient—

Doctor folded the letter carefully in quarters, then in eighths, and finally into the smallest diamond he could make it, and thrust it into his waistcoat pocket. He was charged with the greatest philosophical and religious experiment of the century, and this was what his future wife saw—a mere nuisance? His blood was boiling to the consistency of molasses, and he knew he had to let it cool before he could even think straight.

After an agonizing week, he penned a note to Miss Swift instructing her not to tell Laura about the wedding until the day after he'd left for New York. He arranged for Laura and Oliver a tour of the Cunard steamer docked in Boston Harbor that he and Julia would be taking to England for their honeymoon. More than that he could not think about and stay sane. His life was changing, and he couldn't let this child—his feelings for this beloved child who wasn't even his—hold him back, paragon of noble usefulness or not. He'd have his own children, and Laura would too. No, she probably wouldn't, unless some violence was done, but she would have her own life. Perhaps. He had boarded her and fed her and taught her language and would continue in his loyalty, albeit with a fractured heart. What more could God expect of him?

Chapter 4

Julia, 1844

Her first glimpse of the RMS *Britannia*, the ship that would carry her into her future, into the whole rest of her life. The docked steamer presided serenely over Boston Harbor, flanked by two enormous paddle wheels, the late-day sun swatting the forty-foot steel funnel painted the signature Cunard orange-red banded in black. The *Britannia* would have dwarfed all other ships, but there were none with which to compare her majesty, because Cunard had constructed their own wharf when they'd launched her four months earlier.

Chev helped her from the carriage; he knew how tired she was after the long trip from New York after the wedding. They would have stayed over at Perkins, of course, but Julia was so loath to deal with Laura that she'd insisted they not stop the night there. Chev was irate until she showed him the letter that she'd received at her New York address from Laura the week before. *Dearest Julia,* it read, *I humbly ask your permission to hide in the closet to surprise Doctor after you set sail. I will be your maid for the journey, and you needn't even feed me.* It was signed *Your beloved sister, Laura.* Even Chev was shocked by the request, and so arranged that Laura and Oliver should tour the ship early in the day and be gone long before the happy couple arrived.

And happy they were, though they were saving their crowning

moment for their first night aboard ship. They had spent their wedding night, by agreement, not only in separate rooms, but in separate houses: Julia with her family downtown on Bond Street, and Chev at the Astors' mansion, where the reception had been held. The wedding had been all that the bride had dreamed of and more: hundreds of the best of New York and Boston society all watching her walk on the arm of her father down the long petal-strewn aisle of the church in her ivory Indian lace, the floor-length, seed pearl veil covering her face. But when she had looked toward her groom, regal in his bespoke morning cutaway, his hat high on his dark curls, all the glitter, all the eyes, fell away until his face was the only thing that filled her vision. She had never wanted anything more, and she was, of course, used to getting all that she wanted. The next hours passed like the gossamer currents of a dream, everyone touching her, telling her how beautiful she was, when all she wanted was his touch, his voice, now and forever after. Not until they finally stood on the foredeck of the ship could she really believe she was about to be his. She let the wind blow the spray into her face and inhaled the fresh salty smell of her life to come.

They had arrived early for the press interview, and the writer and photographer from the *Evening Transcript* took to their business immediately, arranging them against the railings, the silhouette of the harbor in the background. Then they took a picture of the new bride alone, and Julia lifted slightly the brim of her pale blue cottage bonnet, the traveling outfit she'd chosen from her ridiculously large—even to her—trousseau. She wanted that look, that radiance she knew she now possessed, to be recorded for posterity. Not that she didn't think it would last—no, it wasn't that at all—but today was the last glow of her girlhood. Any photographs hereafter would show a woman full in the knowledge of the ways of love. She left Chev to contend with the reporter's questions. Doubtless he would mention Sumner, who'd stood up as his best man, the only blot on the ceremony. He'd towered over them all in the moment when Chev should look the king, but the worst was his expression—not only did he not smile, even for the photographs, but he positively grimaced. Julia, of course, knew him to be of a naturally stern and even morose disposition, but on this, of all occasions, she believed he should have been willing at least to lift the corners of his thin lips. After all, she had been his friend years before Chev had ever met him, and he should be welling over with happiness for both of them. Instead he'd lumbered around like a kettle on low boil. She had thought she'd understood him, her Charlie, but now it was quite clear she did not. She was fairly certain that her husband—ah, the delight of that word even in her thoughts!—understood their friend more fully, and she couldn't place a finger on it exactly, but she was sure she didn't like it. Charlie had already taken up larking about the Institution far too much for her taste.

But Julia was in such a pleasant frame, she was willing to forgive Sumner. And maybe even Laura would not have ruined the wedding; it had been so perfect. The poor child—perhaps she should have allowed her at the reception, if not the ceremony, and then she wouldn't be so desperate as to suggest coming with them on the voyage. Julia could not identify with that level of desperation, and she realized the strange depths of the girl's longing were beyond her. Then again, Laura was young and impressionable, and it was quite apparent that she harbored some absurd, though harmless, attachment to her mentor. Julia couldn't imagine, even for a moment, what it must be like to be cocooned in darkness and silence, unable to experience the beauty and varieties of the world: the slap of the waves against the ship's hull, the crystal blue of the water mirroring the sky, matching Chev's eyes. Who was she, with all the treasure of the world before her, to begrudge such a creature a crumb of happiness? She would buy her a lovely present in Europe, a feather-bedecked bonnet, perhaps, something which she would enjoy touching. Yes, she would show Laura that not only was she not a threat to the couple's happiness, but that the new mistress of the house could open her heart, at least a tiny crack, to let the girl in, or at least not to completely exclude her. She felt better already just contemplating such compassion on her part, and she knew that Chev would be impressed.

Julia meandered down the deck, careful to keep her parasol aloft to protect her skin, and nodded at the seamen and the few other early arriving guests. She wondered if they recognized her; if they didn't, they would soon: Mrs. Samuel Gridley Howe. And though she had promised Chev otherwise, she fully intended to be recognized also as a poet, a major American poet, and sooner rather than later. There would be children, of course, but there must be far more poems than children, and she already had an inkling which one she likely preferred. She'd brought with her in her trunk her well-thumbed copies of Thucydides and Petrarch, both of whom served as inspiration for her latest work. She might have to write under the covers, but she could manage it by pretending to write copious letters home.

She thought she saw a familiar figure walking toward her from the starboard side. She shielded her eyes against the glare—yes, it was Jeannette, her new sister-in-law! What in heavens was she doing here—a surprise bon voyage perhaps? She didn't appear to be carrying any presents or bouquets, though.

Jeannette hurried down the long deck. "Oh dear," she said, "oh dear," taking Julia's hands in hers. "We didn't realize it had gotten so late."

"So late for what?" Julia asked, but the twisting in her stomach told her she already knew the answer.

"Laura insisted on counting the steps, the whole length of the dock. Eight hundred eighty-seven, I believe. And then Oliver, Oliver had to pet the cow in the hold. Quite remarkable really, one cow to provide milk for a hundred and twenty people." She seemed almost frantic that Julia be entertained by these facts, but she was not.

Julia removed her hands from Jeannette's. "She was supposed to be well gone by now. Chev promised. You promised."

"I'm so sorry, but Miss Swift and I—"

"Where is she now?"

"Well, she wanted— She dug her heels in and refused to leave...She's touring your stateroom."

Julia thought she might cry. Laura, of all people, in her room, the most special room that she'd been waiting for all her life? All her newfound goodwill toward the girl left her in a violent exhale. She grabbed Jeannette's arm. "Take me there." She glanced back at Chev, but he was still holding court with the pressmen. She pulled Jeannette headlong down the deck. "Which stairs?"

Jeannette pointed, and Julia dragged her along, almost colliding with a sailor who stepped out of the way just in time. To Julia's annoyance, Jeannette turned to gaze at the fellow. "At least we've gotten to look at some lovely seamen," she whispered. "Every outing with the feeble has its saving grace."

They walked down two flights of narrow steps and took a right into a long hallway. Jeannette stopped before an open door, and Julia closed her eyes for a moment before she could summon the will to enter. She had expected to be carried over this threshold in her beloved's arms, but here she was stepping over it alone, to find her palace occupied by the one person she had done everything to prevent spoiling this moment.

They stood in the doorway of the stateroom and watched as Miss Swift stood over Oliver, who was intent on examining the rug, thicker and softer than the carpet of the corridor's floors.

"Oh no," Miss Swift said and bowed slightly in apology to Julia. "I'll get them out in just a minute."

Oliver flopped down on his belly and rolled until he found a patch warmed by the sun streaming in through the twin portholes. Miss Swift gave him a nudge with her boot, but he didn't move, his face enraptured by the light. Laura skirted the corners of the room, touching everything with deliberation: the filigreed frame of the divan, the cubbyholes of the mahogany secretary desk, the brass faucets of the marble basin. When she reached the double bed laden with its silk sheets and eight pillows in brocade covers, she stopped and held out one finger, letting it sink slowly, inch by inch, into the plump damask coverlet of palest gold. She made a small, strangled noise in her throat; it was not her noise for Doctor or the new one she had mastered for Julia in approximation of her name, but a sound that neither Julia nor Jeannette had heard before.

Julia took a step into the room, a step toward the bed, and Laura turned, her finger still plunged into the linens. Julia was positive the girl knew exactly who she was, she could always tell. As if on cue, Laura swayed and then retched, spraying the bottom of the spread with vomit.

"Oh my," said Jeannette, but still she didn't move to enter. Miss Swift pulled Laura away from the bed, and the two of them sat down on the carpet with Oliver, who was engrossed in an examination of the armoire's lower handles carved in the shape of bulls.

"How in heaven's name did she get enough food in her to accomplish such a feat?" Miss Swift said. She plucked a handkerchief from her coat pocket, and wiped at Laura's mouth and the trickle of sick on her chin. To Julia's astonishment, Miss Swift began to giggle. "It's not funny. I'm sorry," she managed, but she couldn't stop herself; she laughed harder. She was helpless to it now, the fit overtaking her. Laura felt the convulsions in her teacher's arms and twisted away, ducking her head.

"You will pull yourself together and see that this mess is cleaned up," Julia said, holding her handkerchief in front of her nose. "This is...this is..."—and here she thought she might begin to weep—"my marriage bed." She could not bear to look at it. She grabbed Jeannette's arm and thrust her into the corridor.

"I am exhausted by the tour of this beast," Jeannette said, "and you are pale as your wedding lilies. Should we touch a tumbler in the ladies' saloon? It looks quite fashionable."

What a thing to suggest! Julia shook her head. "Just get me to Chev. Maybe he can have the room changed." She turned to take one last look at Laura, and she could swear the girl was staring at her, right through the green shade, though she knew, of course, that this wasn't possible. She realized she didn't know the color of her eyes—did it even matter?—but in this moment she pictured them glowing like fiery black coals, hot enough to burn holes clean through the cloth. She thought she heard Miss Swift whisper, "Bon voyage," as they whisked down the hall.

Chapter 5

Letters, 1844

May 1844, Laura to Dr. Howe

I know from your letter to Jeannette that you are landed and safe. I have had many nightmares about the sea swallowing you up. How is the weather in England?

I learned every inch of your ship. Did you walk all its 889 steps as I did? Did you go the top speed the Captain told us—9.5 knots? Your stateroom was like heaven, it was so beautiful.

Please remember me to Mr. Dickens and tell him that I have memorized the entire chapter about me from his wonderful book. Has he been asking for me? Jeannette said that Mr. Dickens got so sick on the same ship when he visited us that he had to go back on a sailing boat.

When you get this letter on the shore, you will probably get the three others I have already sent you.

May 1844, Julia to her sister Louisa

We are grounded at last: Liverpool—hideous dankness—and now London, an admittedly marvelous metropolis for which I am still trying to gain the proper rapturous appreciation. Six-

teen days on the Britannia, *and I spent almost half of them abed, until Chev brought down a thumping tumbler of whiskey and insisted I exercise my will over what he termed my "fancy." Stumbled on deck, half-fizzed, and my husband, as if we didn't know already, proved to be a genius. Again.*

Married life so far attempted between different beds in different cities, but he is my constant, and will remain so. Little one, I urge you heartily to try this state when we have found a fellow worthy. And we won't allow me to even think about anything that might upset my applecart six months down the road on my return! I know you have the gravest compassion for the unfortunate—we all do—but one's own living room need not be the asylum frolic.

The London season—we are already in the vortex—last evening at the Duchess of Sutherland's at Stafford House, we were served cake sent from HRM Victoria herself in honor of her new babe's christening. Invitations lined up: Thomas Carlyle; the childrens' writer, Maria Edgeworth; and of course, Dickens, who is apparently eager to show my husband every workhouse, prison, and nuthatch on the island. But of course, Chevie lives to be surrounded by the most grotesquely enfeebled, and it has occurred to me that my own wit, for whatever it's worth in our circles, is perhaps his least favorite of my charms.

Anywise, he is finding other charms aplenty, my darling. You will grow up and see!

May 1844, Dr. Howe to Charles Sumner

I have never missed your sweet society more than I do now to share in my deepest happiness. You complain, mercilessly, half ironically, of your cold lot, and yet you, with your boundless wells of humor and natural affection, would benefit most from leaping the bachelor fence.

I am so very happy that I am genuinely frightened: What does it mean? Is it some cruel illusion? Even if I deserve it, and you, dearest, would know whether I do—I never saw anything like it before. For all the happiness they tell you about in saturnine novels, it is humbug compared to this.

June 1844, Laura to Dr. Howe

Miss Swift has suggested that I visit my family in Hanover, but I don't want to in case you decide to race back across the ocean to be with your Laura. I think Swift would like me to go away so she can loll about and do nothing. The newspapers say that you speak of me wherever you go there and that everyone knows my name, but if I did not have someone to read the papers to me, I would swear that you had forgotten me. I would like to go to the Baptist church, as my family does, but Swift says no. She is too strict with me. Please write to her.

Please give my love to your wife. She has not replied to my letters either.

June 1844, Julia to Louisa

Chev heard tell of a woman, if you can believe it, even more God-slighted than Laura, and so of course, he had to visit her, though it meant a trip all the way to Portsmouth. Here is a ditty I composed in her honor which I thought might give you a titter:

> *I found a most charming old woman,*
> *Delightfully void*
> *Of all that's enjoyed*
> *By the animal vaguely called human.*
>
> *She has but one jaw,*
> *Has teeth like a saw,*
> *Her ears and her eyes I delight in:*
> *The one could not hear*

Tho' a cannon were near,
The others are holes with no sight in.

Destructiveness great
Combines with conceit
In the form of this wonderful noddle,
But benev'lence, you know,
And a large philopro
Give a great inclination to coddle.

July 1844, Dr. Howe to Laura

My dear girl, I cannot possibly keep up with your vast cor-respondence. I am so very glad that you enjoyed the tour of the Britannia *and that you are faring well in my absence. Help Oliver as best you can with lessons, though I know he is far from your equal. Remember to be at your tip-toppest especially on Ex-hibition Days as you are now known the world over!*

July 1844, Julia to Louisa

I have what one would consider the best of all possible news, and yet a great gift I'd wished for later rather than sooner: you will be an aunt. The honeymoon will extend itself into forever now, though with less honey. After being tea'd and pie'd all over Geneva, Vienna, and Milan, we have descended into Rome, a climate my husband has deemed optimal for my state. The city feels almost medieval—as do I at the moment—and we shall probably stay here to wait out my confinement. Impossible: less than a year ago, I was still a viable New York belle, holding court on Bond Street with you. I pray the child has your man-ageable chestnut locks, not my furlable red ones.

And the most I can say for my delicate condition so far is that my wits have gone a'woolgathering...

July 1844, Laura to Dr. Howe

I wish that I could have a cameo of your head to wear as a brooch on the lace collar of my day dress. And then at night, alone in my bed, I would push the pin of the brooch right through the skin in the hollow of my neck so that your dear face would stay with me the whole night long and I could run my fingers over your raised likeness and never sleep. Miss Swift says they do not make cameos of men, but I don't understand why not. Everyone says you are the handsomest man in Boston—who would not want you as an ornament?

And if I can't have that, might you please, please allow me the raised Bible like the blind girls? Do not tell God, though, that I would rather have your cameo to sleep with than His book. It will be our secret.

August 1844, Jeannette Howe to Dr. Howe

A request, dear brother, which I will trade you for a warning: Please write more often to Laura. She asks daily if there is a letter from you, and you have doubtless received bundles from her. She is becoming quite the lady in some regards—grown an inch, I'd say, since you left—and I hope that the money you left for her expenses will be enough to cover a new dress or two. She is, of course, too thin, but that is another matter. She sits sometimes addressing your chair, her hands out and fingers racing away, her head cocked at attention. We let her be, even when she laughs and rocks herself or cries a bit.

This religious business could split open, you know, with you away so long. On Visiting Days, the Institution crawls with all manner of misguided proselytizers, and many of the most orthodox seem to be the most vested in Laura's education, peppering us all with questions. I have never pretended to understand your choice of Miss Swift, an ardent Congregationalist with an even more ar-

dent brother, as Laura's chief teacher, and now that you are gone, I would feel remiss if I did not point it out to you yet again. She is a good teacher, but she is what she is and what she will be.

I miss you, sir, and look forward to the new family's return. It is heavy here.

August 1844, Charles Sumner to Dr. Howe

As Longfellow and Mann have kindly kept you up on the travails of my recent illness, you know that I was too weak to write, even to you. I hope you have not suffered unduly. My delirium, however, afforded me a vision. Why was I spared? For me there is no future, either of usefulness or happiness. I mock myself, and will doubtless be mocked, as I should be, but there it is.

And as I have often requested, out of modesty or fear—you choose—BURN THIS.

August 1844, Laura to Dr. Howe

Oliver misses you very much and cries every night because you haven't written. He asks me how God could let you leave us for such a long time. He does not understand about getting married, like I do. It is a shame that he is afraid of Julia. He says that her hands are colder and wetter than a fish.

Are you farther away from me now than God or closer? How far away is God?

September 1844, Miss Swift to Dr. Howe

I am sorry that I must inform you again that Laura's anxiety about religion is not at all relieved by my constant evasions on the subject, as instructed. She is becoming more difficult to manage, often flying into inexplicable rages. Yesterday, she threw a book across the room, and when I told her to apologize, she said she would only if she could ask God to forgive her, but she didn't know how. I told her, as I always tell her, that you will talk to her about God when you return. But she insists that if you are not here to forgive her when she does bad things—as she does frequently now—then the only other one who can possibly forgive and govern her is God. It's a fine bit of blackmail is what it comes down to, Dr. Howe, but I can't see my way clear of it.

I beg you to answer some of Laura's questions. I know she has been sending many letters. I am holding out as you have asked, but at this point, I fear that damage is being done to the child, if not to her immortal soul, then at least to her happiness and further growth.

I know you love her dearly, and all the best for her rests in your hands and heart.

September 1844, Dr. Howe to Laura and Oliver

I trust you are both behaving well for your teachers, and that I will find the Institution still in one piece when I return. We are hobnobbing everywhere, and all of Europe knows your names. Rome is hotter than Boston on the worst day—you would hate all the sweating, Laura! Julia and I are eating too much macaroni; our hands might be too fat to even fit in yours by year-end.

Keep up with your studies, and mind everything that Swift and Jeannette tell you, and who knows what treats I may bring back for you. I blow my love to both of you over the Atlantic like a strong wind. Can you feel it warm on your cheeks?

September 1844, Horace Mann, Secretary of the Massachusetts State Board of Education, to Dr. Howe

The evangelical zealots are digging my grave, Howe. In the legislature, the press, and from the pulpits, they batter me to put religious education back into the schools. Sometimes it is almost

impossible to believe that these Calvinists are our brothers in the Protestant faith; they often seem as far over the wall as the Catholics. We Unitarians still hold Harvard, of course, and most of the State House, but I am sicker with dread than you have ever seen me, friend. I cannot fault your being away at such a critical time in our long mutual fight against these Calvinists, but I must be assured that you are safekeeping Laura's soul from this mess. She is our living proof that children learn morality and reverence by example and inference, not through indoctrination.

There are many orthodox and Good News bearers about, even on the grounds of your Institution, and you must protect the sanctity of our best and brightest philosophical weapon. The public still weeps before Laura's goodness and purity, but once she is sullied with brimstone, we will have lost half the battle. Or more.

I care what is best for the girl, who is so dear to us all. What a perfect phrenological specimen, Dr. Combe tells me, as is your wife. My congratulations. I know no other man as lucky. The baby will most certainly sport the finest head in town.

September 1844, Laura to Dr. Howe

I don't want a letter to share with Oliver. He doesn't care. Miss Swift says that I cannot ask any questions about God. You have left me, so what I am supposed to do in a house full of silly girls?

I hope you and Julia are having a very excellent time.

October 1844, Dr. Howe to Miss Swift

I might long ago have taught the scriptures to Laura, and she might have learned, as other children do, to repeat line after line, precept upon precept, and to imitate others in prayer. But her enormous handicaps have proven a shield to protect her from being relentlessly subjected to the crude ideas and dogma with which other poor children are pilloried. God himself has given

us the purity of her consciousness to be spared from the masses'
metaphysical speculations. I do not ask you to sin, in your book,
but I will regard it as a sin in mine, if your Calvinist beliefs in-
terfere with the generous terms of your employment.

I am surprised that you imagine that Laura's eternal welfare
will be imperiled by her remaining in ignorance of certain re-
ligious truths for a few more months. You are only her teacher
in the seven subjects we have granted, nothing more. As the one
who rescued her from darkness, I hold the high responsibility of
the charge of her soul, at least for now. You may take it as sacred,
Miss Swift, that even from afar, I bear that gift and burden as
seriously as would the mother who bore her. I have been care-
fully preparing Laura's mind for religious consciousness for eight
years, and she will come gradually to understand every religious
truth that it may be desirable for her to know.

If she behaves badly, you have my permission to punish her as
you see fit; other than that, our accord remains the same.

November 1844, Julia to Louisa

I can't help thinking of Mother's death, of course. Maybe the
fear of childbirth is all that is shrouding my happiness. Chev,
archphysician that he is, has already pooh-poohed my apprehen-
sion. He swears it will be my finest hour. Actually, he says that it
is every woman's finest hour. Until now, my best have been those
spent on poetry, but that life is now undone, and in its place, I
have chosen a blended life. Forgive my grayness, darling. I am
getting old and foreign.

November 1844, Miss Swift to Mrs. Bridgman, Laura's
mother

It is not my place, but with the Doctor gone, I am the one who
must ask: please, Mrs. Bridgman, write to Laura. He is abroad

on his honeymoon until we don't know when, and she is very lonely. It's back to being hard for her to eat, etc. It is also clear to me that she is upset that she hasn't heard from you in several months, and it would do her more good than you know. She is smart as a lick, but she is more of a child at fifteen than your other children. She would no doubt like to come to Hanover, perhaps for the holidays.

Of course, we know that the Lord would prove the greatest source of comfort in her suffering, but Dr. Howe has forbidden me from giving your daughter even one page from the Good Book. I speak to you as a Congregationalist to a Baptist, and know that you and I are not far apart in our hearts and minds on this subject, unlike the radical Unitarians, so I tell you that I do my best to preserve Laura from harm. Give my kind regards to the rest of your family. God bless you and keep you.

December 1844, Charles Sumner to Dr. Howe

I am hurt to hear that all the Continent's bigwigs desire from you is the dreary decanting of Laura. Don't they know she is but the tip of your little finger? Pope Gregory XVI in Rome, the biggest wig of all, and he asks you only what Laura knows of God—how inhuman! What if you told them that your poor lawyer friend stopped by to check on the little package last week and that she bit him on the forearm? "You touched me too hard," she said. This is what they revere and write about in Europe these days, a rabid child?

I have been vigilant in keeping my eyes and ears in at the Institution as you have sworn me to, but the girl's behavior at this point is beyond the pale. And it so hard to tell the foxes from the chickens there at the moment, not to mention the snakes.

Good luck slipping off that mantle of fame you have laid across your too-broad shoulders, my Chevie.

December 1844, Dr. Howe to Laura

My girl, you have asked me so many questions in so many letters that I am dizzy keeping track. You are a threat to your Doctor's sanity. It would take very much time and reams of good paper to tell you all I know and think about the subject of religion, and you should be clear that I am very busy at the moment taking care of my wife. I shall try to tell you a little, because I fear that you might be receiving information from the wrong sources, which would be disastrous for us all.

First, it is the Christmas season, and you will no doubt be hearing much about the birth of Jesus, etc., but you are simply to enjoy the day and the festivities. God is a loving father, the most loving father, who has made the world and everything in it beautiful for us. You don't need to be told about it or read books about it to understand. Just take it in and be happy. That is as much as I can tell you for now, but that should be more than enough to hold you until my return. Your mind is tender, and the harder things I will explain when you are ready. All that heaven allows you shall have, my dear. Nothing more can be promised.

You have heard the joyous news that Mrs. Howe and I are having a baby. Not the Christ child, but a real live baby I will bring home for you from across the sea!

December 1844, Laura to Dr. Howe

Just one thing: Why didn't God let me die when I was sick?

Chapter 6

Laura, 1845

I'm glad Mama said it would be too busy with me home at Christmas. I don't like New Hampshire in the snow. Everyone says it's so beautiful and that each snowflake is different, but they certainly feel the same, though I do like to melt them on my tongue. The only good thing about winter is wearing my fur muff. And at home I probably wouldn't have gotten presents as nice; Mama doesn't even give us real stockings. Of course Doctor wasn't here to be my Saint Nicholas this year, but I did get an orange (I hate its seeds), a ball of yarn, and new crochet hooks. Some of the younger girls still believe there's a jolly old elf, but I never really believed that. Jeannette read Mr. Dickens's *Christmas Carol* to the six of us who stayed here for the holidays, but there was no one to translate for me. Thank goodness I am already familiar with the story. I feel an allegiance with sweet Tiny Tim, but at the same time, I'm not sure I want him to get all better and strong. Of course, I don't want him to die, but must every single thing turn out so well for him? What if Julia's baby is very frail, like Tiny Tim, and maybe lame? That would be very sad.

Now that it's April, Mama says I can come home for a month. The only terrible thing is that I won't be able to get Doctor's letters. I hope that I will have a pile waiting for me on my return to Boston.

I am so happy to see Pearly, our cat, though she still gives me a wide berth; apparently, animals have a memory as good as mine. When I was six, I tossed her into the fireplace because she'd scratched me, and though she was not dreadfully burned, Papa said her silky tail was singed black, and he stamped his feet harder that time than I ever remember. That's his way of letting me know he's angry, and it's very unpleasant to feel the wood floors shake so long and so hard, but it's still better than being cuffed on the head or slapped on the bottom, which is what he used to do until Mama stopped him. She didn't think it was fair to punish me like Mary and Addison because most of my sins were accidents. I was happy to let her believe that, anyway. After the fireplace, I wasn't allowed to play with the cat and had to content myself with the doll I'd made from one of Papa's old boots. I would untie the laces and pretend they were her long strands of hair, and touch the twelve tiny eyes that meant she could see more than anyone in the whole world. Caroline I called her, my boot baby, and I rocked her to sleep every night.

I ask Mama for Caroline, but she says she threw the boot out long ago. It has, after all, been three years since I've been home. Mama gives me the Laura doll I sent her, but I'd rather have my old boot, the leather rough against my chest. Mama can't believe how tall I've grown, though she swears I am more of a rail than when I left them. "What do they feed you?" she asks, and I tell her the truth: many days I eat only bread and butter and they leave me be. That is my choice. Doctor has given Mama strict instructions on my diet, that I am not to have salt or sugar or anything he considers *incendiary*—that's his word—he believes blinds must be protected from too much excitement. Of course in my case, it doesn't matter; she could dump in the whole salted pork barrel and I probably wouldn't know the difference. Still, I like to help with the cooking, and most of all, I like that Mama lets me. She trusts me to handle myself in a way that nobody at the Institution does, because she saw how I could get around and what I could do on my own here for seven years.

I limit my play so I can be the assistant cook and maid. Mama even allows me to cut up the vegetables for stew. At the Institution, they will never give me a knife, but the truth is I have only nicked myself twice this trip, and hardly at all, only bloodying one potato. I enjoy the precision of cutting one slice after another, stroking my way down the length of a carrot or sliding my finger into the shallow groove of the celery. And the funny little knots on the potatoes, I turn round and round and count them. Addison says they are called eyes, and I wonder that a potato, like a boot, can have a dozen eyes while I have none. I do not like to touch the raw meat, but I don't let on because I know Mama needs me. I sit on the back screened porch with Mary plucking the feathers from a chicken; it is awful work that almost brings me to gagging, but I continue, running my fingers over the bare, puckered skin until I can find no more feathers. I am glad I don't know what it looks like; I think if I did, I would never be able to eat it, or the beef or pork either. I have examined the shapes of cows and sheep and even a pig, but when they are cut up and turned inside out, I know they must look very different.

Since I look different on the outside than other people, I wonder if my insides look different too. I pluck a hair from my head like a feather and feel the tiny, wet bulb at its end. I wish I could feel all the inside of me; I admit I do try to get in any hole I can, and Mama often pulls my fingers away from my nose or ears. "Nasty habit," I am told again and again, but my self is all I have, since the girls I've tried to poke so far do not seem to like it much. Two of the blinds have bitten me this year when I tried to stick my fingers in.

I help much more than Mary, who is eight years younger than me, about the age I was when I was sent to live at the Institution. We hold on to each other's skirts as we move about the house doing chores, until Addison bursts in from school—I feel the air rush in as the door's flung wide and know it's him, since Papa barely opens it, almost as if he doesn't want to come inside. Addison takes us outside most days and plays at tumbling, then twirls me round and round until I fall down dizzy. He's hung a swing from the branches of the oldest oak behind the house, and that is my favorite thing: to sit in the rope seat with my brother's hands firm on my back and the sun and breeze light on my face. I try to decide if it's even better than sitting with Doctor after supper, and I decide that it is—for now—because Doctor has stayed far across the sea for over a year, and so I must open the doors of my heart to others, especially my own dear family. Addison is almost as tall as Doctor, with a bit of soft beard. Only he and Mama have bothered to learn the finger spelling well. He will be going away to study next year, but when he comes back, I think it is possible that we might marry. I can tell he loves me very much, and in my hand, he always writes, "My Laura," as if he has already claimed me for his own. Mama and Papa would be very happy, I think, though Mary would be jealous. And Doctor would probably be jealous too, even with his Julia. She is not half as celebrated as I am.

Mama also lets me knit and crochet without being watched. The only thing I'm prevented from going near is the spindle. She needn't worry; I am terrified of the thing. That I remember: the trip, the fall, the needle piercing my one good eye. If it had got the left one, no matter, it was already dried out, but the right one, a year after the fever, still held some light, a prism of colors on a bright day. Doctor knows, but that secret I tell no one else. It is too much, too horrible; it sounds like a lie, a bad joke that only God could tell. I've never had pain like that, most of all because it meant the extinguishing of the last glimmer of light, the last blade of green, the last patch of blue.

It's strange to think of how perfect I was born, how absolutely perfect with all my senses until two and a half. How I pray to remember those earliest years full of sights and sounds, tastes and smells! It must have been glorious. *I* must have been glorious. Doctor says some of those memories are locked inside my brain, and that's why I learn so well, drawing on those fragments that are buried somewhere deep down inside. I wish I knew exactly where.

Tonight Asa is coming for dinner. Papa says he's a half-wit, and it's true he can hardly spell in my hand and understands only the simplest words, but he has always been so good to me. Papa has never one time even tried to spell into my hand, and when I reach for his, he jerks it away. It would be so good to talk to Papa because he has some learning and reads the Bible more than Mama is able; he is a farmer but also conducts much business in town. He has been voted a selectman, Mama says, and that's very important and takes up his time. Papa asks me only one question on this visit, and I can tell Addison doesn't want to translate it by the way he doodles in my hand. "Write," I urge him, and so he does: "Papa wants to know why can't you talk yet."

That is an excellent question and one I mean to discuss with Doctor on his return. If he could teach me to read and write, I don't see why he couldn't teach me to talk. I can certainly make noise! If Asa can talk, then surely I should be able to master it. I don't mean to look down on him; Asa was a better friend and playmate in my helpless years than even Addison. Maybe that's because my brother usually had chores to do, but I don't think that's all it was. I think he saw me as a burden, like a blind dog to be watched after to make sure it didn't upset the churn or fall down the well. I think Addison still looks at me that way sometimes, though I know how much he loves me because he hugs and kisses on me so much. But no one—save Doctor—loves me the way that Asa does. Asa *enjoys* my company. I know he would marry me if he could, but he is too old.

He's waiting in the yard, and Mama says he's been there for hours, whittling me a stick pony. He grabs me up in his arms, and I pull off his old wool cap. As I pat his head, I realize that he has lost some of the hair he had three years ago. Asa's hair is like the last bits of roasted meat off the bone, spare, greasy strings, though the back is long and his beard as full as ever, hanging down to his heart. Mama's hair plays nicer on my fingers, and Mary's too, but I've never gotten to touch Papa's. I do forget a few things, like how to hold the mustard seed when I pound it, but I don't forget the features of any person. I wonder if Papa's head is mostly skin like Asa's. Mama and Mary don't have the skin mixed in with their hair, and I don't either. Both are nice, though. It is always the most fun to have many different things to touch on a friend.

Asa tickles me with the rough, tangled ends of his beard, but when he rubs it under my chin, I push his hand away. Now I realize he is dirty; I roll the grease and the grime between my fingers. Before, I never noticed, maybe because everyone at Perkins keeps so clean, as do I now. Hugging Asa has no doubt soiled my jumper, but that I will bear for my oldest friend. It is probably good that I cannot smell him, though. I can now understand why my family wasn't that keen to have the old man around; they let him come because he could take me off their hands, out to fetch the eggs or to skip stones in the creek down by the mill. He was my minder, this filthy, old man. No one seems to have any idea exactly how old he is. Papa said he's lived down the road in Hanover since he was a boy. And he's never had any family, as far as anyone knows.

He lifts me onto his stooped shoulders and falters beneath my weight. I was such a tiny thing last time he held me, and though I am still thin, I am full tall for a fifteen-year-old gal. I know to duck my head low as we enter the house, and I feel the shiver through him as Asa whoops his greetings to my family. Doubtless they do not whoop back. I insisted we have rabbit stew, Asa's favorite, and though little Mary refuses to eat it, dear Addison caught the hares and skinned and cleaned them. I admit I skipped that bloody task, but helped Mama roll the biscuits. I am a very good roller, though Mama says I always end up covered in flour.

Asa sits beside me at the table with Addison on the other

side—my two favorite men after Doctor! I feel very lucky, like a princess, so I even try to eat the stew. I feel my work in it: the potatoes and carrots peeled clean, and I'm proud. At supper Addison talks of training to be a Baptist minister or a doctor. I think I would like to be married to a minister, especially one with such thick and wavy hair, a cowlick that curls over his brow.

"But I am Unitarian," I remind my brother. Our whole family is pure Baptist but me, and this is something they apparently all worry about, even Papa. He is not concerned with anything about me, it seems, except my religion.

"Change to Baptist," Addison writes slowly, and I feel the biscuit crumbs in each letter. So he does not take my religion seriously. Is it because I am young or because I am so deficient?

"Doctor made me," I write, and it's true. He did not only make me a Unitarian; he made me in every way that matters. I left this family unformed, an illiterate creature less useful than a dog, and he has transformed me into one fluent with the language and with the world.

"Can't turn back," I say to Addison, and I hope he understands. He drops my hand and I know he is telling everyone at table. Papa shows his immediate displeasure by jiggling the whole table.

I lift my shoulders in a shrug and then point toward heaven, letting them all know that the matter is out of my hands and in God's. God gave me to Doctor and so I am Unitarian. I remember from when Mama would dress me up and take me to the little church down the road that the Baptists do more singing and clapping. My memories of those services are filled with a kind of joy that I admit I do not approach at the Institution's services, where there seems to be almost no noise, no tensing and shifting of the floorboards. But for now, I must trust Doctor.

Asa smears jam onto a biscuit and holds it to my lips. I don't think Doctor would like me to have the jam with sugar, but I take a little taste. I like the way it's sticky on my tongue, but basically it just makes for a wet biscuit.

Asa takes his leave suddenly right after dinner. Addison says he made a mess at the table, trying to fix things to tempt me to eat, and Papa asked him to leave. My own family doesn't care if I eat, and they throw out the only one who tries? I would've wolfed down every morsel, snuffled every crumb from the tablecloth if I had known. Addison feels my hand tremble in his and he knows how angry I am. He strokes my cheek and then pats my head over and over, and I know he is trying to comfort me—how I loved that touch when I was a child—but now I feel I am being treated like a dog. Pet the doggy and it will wag its tail and roll over and be good. No! I walk toward the heat from the fire where Papa likes to sit in his big horsehair chair after dinner and read the paper. I am not allowed on that chair. I kneel beside him and put my hand on his knee, and he shakes it in irritation. Papa doesn't like for me to touch him, but I am determined. I tap hard on his knee and point at the door and make my noise for Asa. I make the noise again, louder, and this time he nudges me with his boot. He doesn't kick me; only once he kicked me and that was when I'd wrapped myself around his legs and wouldn't let go. Poor Papa, he'd dragged me round and round the room before he finally got me off. I don't remember why I'd held on to him so fiercely. That was before Doctor came. Now he nudges again, and then Addison's strong hands are under my arms and lifting me away. His chest is hard and I feel his heart beating. How wonderful it is! I will let Addison and his heart take me away, though I am still angry with Papa.

Addison deposits me back in the kitchen and tells me that I must help Mama with the dishes. Usually I enjoy this task, but not tonight. Mama hands me the drying towel and then a bowl and I do nothing, just stand there, holding it, so she finally shoos me, gives me a marble to play with. Doctor let me hold a marble, a big one, to show me the shape of the eyeballs I lost. Think of that: pretty, round eyeballs with all their uses for good and evil, heated by the fever until they turned to liquid oozing down my face. I have never asked Mama, never held her accountable, but now she turns out my friend and gives me a *marble*. Does she care about me at all? I pull at her skirts until she gives me a soapy hand.

"How could you lose my eyes, Mama?" She twists away. Did you hurt them, did you mash them, did you know what they were, your baby's eyes, half her use and fortune in this world, or did you just wipe them away like snot? I fight for her hand. She won't let me write; she doesn't want to know. "Try to save them? Try to put them back?" I pound across her back until Addison pulls me off. I pummel his arms with truth: "Could've pushed them back in." Even if she had to hold me down, screaming, my head in a vise, and poke and plunge and stuff with her fingers; maybe if they could just have stayed in until the fever went down, even if they had lost their purpose, even if they had become a maddened swirl of blue and black and white like Doctor says the sky can be on a stormy night. Didn't you think that would be better than nothing, Mama, better than these tiny, wrinkled caves of bone? She tries to calm me as Addison holds me down, and I sign into the air: "Did you throw the mess outside?"

I cry myself into stillness as they both lean above me. I reach for my mother's face, trace one finger down her cheek. All my heartbreak, all my terror, all those terrible questions, and still my mother has not shed a tear. What's wrong, Mama, are you afraid you'll cry your eyes out?

Asa comes for me the next day, and I tell him I'm sorry they wouldn't let him stay. "Mama mean," I write, his crusted palm so wide that it holds both words easily.

"We play," he writes.

Papa is not rich, Doctor says, but he does have over a hundred acres here in the Connecticut River Valley. We can walk in any direction and it's still Bridgman land. Hand in hand, we walk to the creek, and Asa helps me find the roundest, smoothest stones for skipping. I can't enjoy the splash when they hit the water, but it gives me great pleasure to fling them into the air just so, just the way he has taught me. This creek was one of my favorite spots when I was little, and now I take off my boots and socks and dip my toes into the icy water. It is a tingle like no other, and then the squish of the mud between my toes, the jagged edges of the rocks that thrill me even as I know they can hurt me. I've cut my feet on them more times than I can remember, Mama getting so mad with Asa when he'd carry me back with a bloodied foot, me happy as a bird.

Slowly—it is always so slow with him—I tell him that Mama didn't cry about my eyes. He brings my hand to his face and shakes his head no over and over. He draws my fingers to his cheeks and slides them up and down, up and down, until I understand that he means Mama wept. He places my palm against his heart, and back to his eyes, and I realize how much my dear friend mourned also. After a moment, he writes, "2 babies die," and then, "before you." I rock back on my heels away from him, sit down hard on a slick rock. Mama had two babies who died before me?

"Fever?" I ask Asa. Yes. I have no memory of any babies dying, but then again, I was only two when the fever struck me.

"Boy and girl," he writes. No one has ever told me. Why? Did they think it would add to my burden? Or that I just didn't need to know, as they doubtless think that half the things of this world I don't need to know, information that even the slowest-witted possess, simply by virtue of seeing and hearing, by *witnessing*.

He taps on my hand again: "And your mam's mother too." My heart wells for her: the fever also took Mama's own mother from her; how does she walk upright with the weight of all this sorrow?

I wait a few days until Mama and I are alone shucking corn. I take the shock from her hands and brush away the stray kernels. "2 babies die?" I ask, though I already know the answer. Her hand squeezes mine so hard that it hurts, but in a good way. We sit at the table, holding hands amid the piles of corncobs, and I understand: she had no more tears left for me, and that is all right. I know she still loves me.

When the carriage pulls up to the front porch to take me back to Boston, everyone hugs and kisses me good-bye, and Addison writes one last message from Papa: "Don't come back till you can speak. Even the half-wit can speak."

Chapter 7
Letters, 1845

April 1845, Julia to Louisa

I have been too tired to write to you. Measure forgiveness by the heaping cup, I beg you, like we did when Cook let us help with the cake baking.

I am reduced to something less than human, while I remain married to one who believes himself divine.

May 1845, Laura to Julia

Here at Perkins, we all speak of nothing but baby Julia Romana. You have picked the most beautiful and perfect name. I can't wait to hold Doctor's baby. You don't have to worry; I will hold her very softly and be careful with her head. Miss Swift showed me how to do it with a doll, and I am practicing every day. Of course, I am too old for dolls! I am ready for babies. Julia Romana will be my sister, and you can also be my sister, and we will all live happily together in Doctor's apartment. And Jeannette too, if you would like.

I can't wait to hug you and kiss you and your baby. It is all I can think about for now. I promise that I will always set an excellent example for your children; I know the difference between right and wrong, as our dear Doctor has shown me. Please write to me, and I will know that you are keeping me also in your devoted heart.

May 1845, Charles Sumner to Dr. Howe

P.S. All that I may offer to you and Julia on the birth are the fruitless congratulations of a bachelor's heart, forever ignorant of the gardens of delight in which the happy parents revel.

May 1845, Julia to Louisa

Children are not like poems.

June 1845, Miss Swift to Dr. Howe

Congratulations on the birth of your daughter. We are looking forward to making her acquaintance.

I want you to be prepared: I found certain religious tracts in Laura's room, hidden beneath her pillow. They were not in raised letters, but if they're in her possession, it is possible that she found someone to read them to her. I don't know how this happened, because I have been very careful, as you asked, though my withholding on these matters has come at great spiritual expense to myself.

It was inevitable, sir, even if you didn't wish it.

June 1845, Laura to Julia

I am crocheting Julia Romana a pink cap, but I need to know the exact measurements of her head. Could you please send to me?

June 1845, Dr. Howe to Laura

I am told that you have been given certain tracts by those who do not know you, who do not understand you as I do. Believe me that God has appointed the day when you should know Him, but He will tell only me. Be patient, Laura, for Him, and for my return. Some things must change as we all adjust to my new life, but the important things will remain the same.

July 1845, Dr. Howe to Charles Sumner

Baby Julia Romana is the world's most compelling creature, as you will soon discover; her mother, however, does not seem to find her so. And the verses are gushing forth again—she actually leaves the papers about the apartment in Rome for me to stumble upon. I will not bore you with the effluvia of the Muse except to say that in one she rhymes dead *with* marriage bed, *and in another,* enfeebled blind *with* behind!

I thought I had chosen one whose spirits were nearly fireproof. I am more than a bit lost except for the child. And I yearn, more than ever, to touch your face. Very soon.

July 1845, Laura to Dr. Howe

Please, Doctor, I had a dream that your tiny baby was thrown into the sea and torn apart and eaten by a giant whale. I tried, but I could not save her. I am plagued with dreams, I can't sleep. It's always dark, but still I can't sleep.

July 1845, Dr. Howe to Jeannette

The time has come for you to do me a very large favor: Miss Swift is to be removed from her post well before we return in late September. I will send a letter, but it will need to be carefully written, so you must move ahead since it will take it so long to reach Boston. For now, simply tell her that she has disappointed me, and disappointed Laura. Leave it to her to decide if she has also disappointed God.

Miss Wight is my choice for Laura's new teacher. She is modest, articulate, and most of all, Unitarian. I was not wise in trying to see the best in human nature, regardless of creed, but I have learned my lesson.

And here is perhaps the more trepidatious task I set you, sister: please begin moving Laura out of the apartment. My private residence is no longer the right place for her now that I have my own family. I think if you carry out a few things at a time, while she is in classes, then she can be eased into the main wing. Nothing sudden or frightening, and the Exhibition and Visiting Days should continue as usual. But the last thing Julia needs is a scene the moment we arrive.

August 1845, Julia to Laura

Thank you for your kind words and many letters expressing interest in my welfare and that of my family. Please forgive me for not replying sooner; the travel, not to mention the multitudinous tasks of being Dr. Howe's wife and mother to his child, are sometimes quite exhausting.

You sound very well and very eager, as always, to join with us in our joy. I look forward to you meeting little Julia Romana, but we must be careful with her in ways that might prove difficult for you, Laura. A baby is far more delicate to play with than a dog, and I remember the howls of poor Pozzo as you stepped on his tail more times than I can count.

I was sorry to hear about dear Miss Swift. She was as good as she was large, as is often true of broader persons generally. I think perhaps it is we leaner ones of us who are more viperish.

The Institution is spacious and beautiful, and I am sure we will all be happy there over time. We will all be fixed very soon, to the best of the abilities God has bestowed upon each of us.

Chapter 8

Laura, 1845

I have spent all afternoon entertaining Governor Briggs, and I am fairly tuckered. Over five hundred today in the hall, so many that my feet shook constantly from the activity. I wish that the Institution would limit my visitors to a reasonable number, perhaps a hundred at a time. Much is expected of me, and much I deliver—today I topped off the show by devising a poem on the spot and writing it out on the board. At least on days such as these, I do take in a fair bit of money from the sale of my lacework and purses, working away like one of Mr. Dickens's heroines, though in much nicer surroundings. I thought I should keel over by the time all was done, and then there was the governor at me again, begging that I write out the verses I'd composed to take to frame and hang in his mansion.

Miss Wight, my new teacher and companion, has stuck fast by me the whole day, even filling my palm with descriptions of the visitors, more than I could glean from their fingers. She is quite good at such portraiture, describing the governor's head as an ostrich egg and his wife's as a quail's. But she also reminded me, more than once, that I am meant to be an Inspiration to Others, that that is God's plan for me, to show how much can be achieved in the face of greatest adversity. I know that Doctor has told her to say that. It is very tiring to be an Inspiration, and I'm glad now we just sit together in the back parlor alone. I am so thankful that Doctor picked her for me; it is more than proof that he was thinking about me and my studies all the time he was away. Miss Swift rode hard on me, and so I reared and kicked; the problem was to be found in both our natures, though the world seems always to fault the student. But for sweet Miss Sarah Wight I will be the nicest filly ever for her to lead where she pleases. She is only twenty-two, just seven years older than me, so we will be great friends.

Wight doesn't wear a lace collar. It's good to be plain, I'm often told, but I do like nice things on ladies to touch. I will tat her some lace and she will wear it for me. Oh, what plans I have for my new teacher! She will be my very own Wightie, three fingers spread for the *W*. She has let me touch her face before—she's been here at Perkins going on a year riding the little blind girls, working her way up to me—and her skin is smoothly pleasing except for a few tiny bumps on her chin which must be changeable with the weather because they're not always there. She doesn't have Swift's plump cheeks, though. I will miss those cheeks, for certain. Wight's face is long, a little longer than mine, over one and a half hands' lengths, and when I make her stand with our backs together, she measures in full about three inches taller. So she is tall and reasonably soft, with fine hair that Doctor says is so blonde it's almost white. It's stuck very close to her head, a little slick even in its braids. I wanted a teacher with curly hair, very curly hair, so I could spring it and bounce it, but Doctor said that curly hair is hard to find in Boston, and also that it's not important what kind of hair a teacher has. Doctor's hair is curled sometimes over his ears or around his collar, tickling at my fingers when he lets me hug his neck. I have not touched him for eighteen months, and at my worst, I believe he is gone from this earth. We will find out in two weeks. And the baby? I am not sure it exists. I am sick of cradling the doll in anticipation, but at least the doll doesn't wriggle or vomit. Maybe Julia won't come back. Doctor thought my Julia noise was the best one of all, but Jeannette told me that Julia hated it. I give her my best and she despises me. Sometimes I think she even fears me.

When Tessy was angry that I let Oliver play with the Laura dolls instead of her, she told me that the newspaper warned against pregnant ladies coming to the exhibitions to see me lest they swoon in fright and their babies be cursed with my afflictions. How might just one look at me brand another human being for life? I cried for days after Tessy told me that, until finally she hugged me in bed for a whole hour. I realized that is probably why Julia has stayed in Europe while she is with child: the fear that it could turn out like me. I wonder if Doctor is afraid too. I cannot let myself think about this or I will run screaming into the Charles.

I'll try to say my new teacher's name out loud now. I'm not supposed to, but I'll bet she doesn't know that. "Wightie! Wightie!" I call, and she is tapping my hand, so she heard me. Did she hear her name, her real name, or just a sound, an ugly sound? I make it very small, very tiny, like a mouse practicing in a little hole in the floor, and she lets me. She is a good woman, and I promise for her I will be a good girl. I will try to be a good girl. Well, I'll do the best I can.

All right, I can't speak or sing—for now—but I can do a little dance to celebrate my new teacher. Come dance with me, Wightie; give me your hand—ah, I've got one finger to pull. Come on! Doctor says exercise is good for me, how can you resist me one spin? I tap my foot on the floor, *tap tap*, the way I've felt the beats reverberate from the cabinet piano played in the parlor. Today I make my own music—*tap-tap-TAP, tap-de-tap-tap*—and I pull Wightie's hands up and over my head, in a twist, in a twirl that I memorized from the raised pattern in the Institution's one dance book. We will have to do a waltz since there are only two of us. The Viennese waltz is the one I learned, and I write that on Wightie's other hand, including the sixty measures a minute with a clockwise rotation.

"A what?" she asks. "Sixty what?" And I realize that maybe she doesn't know dances, maybe she is not that kind of young woman, perhaps she is too plain to be asked to dance, or maybe she is too religious and strict to indulge. I don't care. I'll make her dance. I have waltzed three times with Doctor, and for a summer party we did the Virginia reel with six ladies and six gentlemen in rows. Jeannette says that I'm an excellent dancer. I can see the patterns in my brain shooting straight down to my feet, and my feet in turn relay the calling of the music through its vibrations for a certain type of movement. Oh, the dancing I would do if I were a normal girl: I would jig home to Hanover and back—no, all the way to Africa, where I read the Negroes beat crazily and loud on enormous drums with sticks. I would love it in Africa with all the drums talking to my feet. I wonder do they have pianos there and flutes—"W, do they have pianos in Africa?"

What a stalling she does, this one; she is just going to have to get used to my questions, what Dr. Combe labeled my "pathological curiosity." But why have a brain if you don't want to fill it up with things? Miss Swift wouldn't answer but a tenth of my queries, and only the most stupid, boring ones. I hate waiting for answers, and it seems most people definitely do not think as fast—or even as much—as I do. Is this arrogance or just the truth?

Finally, W allows: "Only pianos in Africa if a missionary brings."

Still she is resisting me on the waltz. Arithmetic is finished; geography is done; I have signed fifty silly autographs, until my hand aches, including one to send to the President's wife, Mrs. Polk, though she has not yet deigned to visit me, and now it's time. Wightie can't seem to follow the count, so we'll just try twirling. I've got her arm up and it's over my head, but my shade seems to be caught on something. It's yanked upward, and I try to stop her arm. The ribbon is riding up the back of my head, but now Wight's tapping too—*tap-te-tap*—she is in the mood at last, and my face is caught in the crook of her arm, as if she is protecting me. It must be the buttons on her sleeve that have caught the ribbon, and as her arm goes higher still—*TAP-TAP-TAP*—she yanks with it some hair from my braid, and I cry out, I mouth her name, but she doesn't stop, she is tapping away, and I'm trying to stop the spin, all in one or two seconds that are sprinkled with bright lights in my head, and then I'm turned—*tap-te-tap-tap-TAP*—she has turned me most the way around—*tap-tap*—and the shade pulls clean off my eyes—*TAP*—and Sarah Wight stops completely, stumbling back a little when she sees, I guess, what has happened, and taking my shade with her.

I have lost her arm's protection, and I go down at the end of my twirl, my dance, crouching on the floor with my hands over my face. Doctor has made it a rule that I am never to uncover my eyes for anyone but a physician in private, and he certainly brooks no argument from me on that point. It is as far from my desire as Boston is from the North Pole to offend my friends' sensibilities, to frighten or disgust them.

Stop touching me! Miss Wight is all about me, hands and arms, patting, poking.

"So sorry." Waiting. "We'll put it back."

No, I am comfortable making my ball here on the carpet, with its beveled tufts against my cheek. Jeannette told me this pattern is roses and angels in blues and golds. How beautiful to behold roses and angels together. Sarah Wight is practically lying on top of me, causing us both to sweat, in her what—grief? anguish? embarrassment? I am the one eyeless, revealed, naked in the face in the cruelest way of all nakedness—why should she be aggrieved? If the eyes are the windows to the soul, as one of Doctor's poet friends recited, then what kind of soul do I have, Wightie? What did you see of my soul before I went down, cowering on the floor like the wild child, the beast, I used to be? You have ruined the dance, you have ruined the day, with your sweaty hands and your big arms. You can't even do a simple turn! What kind of lady are you? Leave me be on the soft carpet with these roses that will never die and the angels who might protect me. You cannot protect me even from your stupid self.

"I won't look when I put it on."

I slide one hand out of my position. "Did you see me?"

"No." The response too quick, and so I know she lies.

"You did," I stamp on her arm.

"I saw nothing." Her hand falls away. Now she is telling the truth, she saw *the nothing*. So the first day teaching, my new role model, this package of Unitarian virtue and womanhood, and we find she can't dance, as a lady should, and that she lies, like a Christian should not. This is what I'm stuck with.

If I could stay like this, exactly like this, frozen, for days, weeks, without a thought to any bodily needs, would I waste away or might God give in to my demands for another life? Would He let me die rather than grant me even one wish?

I start. I must have drifted off. Wight is still here beside me, and dozing too by the slight rise and fall of whatever I'm poking. She is good to stay with me; I'm sure there are a hundred things she'd rather be doing than lying on the back parlor floor with me. I was too rough with her today; she probably thinks I'm a mad creature now. Maybe she won't even want to teach me after the wildness of this afternoon. That would be terrible. I let myself go galloping off in my head like I do, not taking time to explain what I want, what I need. But would she understand if I did try to explain?

Ah, well, let me touch Sarah Wight's tears. I know they're there. I can make a grown-up weep just at the sight of my eyes—isn't that a hoot and a holler?

"I'm sorry, Wightie," I write onto her outstretched arm, and she's stirring, sitting up, though she doesn't reach for me.

"Time for tea," she writes as if nothing has happened, and then she's slipping the shade over my eyes, tying the ribbon tight above my bun, tucking in the ends.

"Will you still be my teacher?"

"Of course," she says—it seems without thinking—and helps me to my feet.

"I can teach you to dance," I tell her.

Chapter 9

Laura, 1846

I have tried to fatten myself for Doctor. He will be here in a week. My bones poke through my skin, and I think it is much nicer to touch the soft pillows of Tessy's hands than to feel my birdy bones. But I must remember to eat, to eat more; I vow to chew and swallow all three meals every day. It is so hard, though, when I taste almost nothing. I move my jaws and grind my teeth and pass my tongue over the lumps of whatever it is that slides from the forks and spoons, but it seems a meaningless exercise.

I would much rather dip my fingers into the warm pond of the soup and plumb its depths for legumes, rend the slick skin from the chicken and peel away the sheaves of muscle until I reach the hardness of the bone, tear the bread into a hundred tiny pieces and roll them into buttered balls I juggle over my plate, squish through the pliant mounds of the potatoes, ravage the soft pulp of the baked aubergines, and burrow both fists into pie I will never know the sweetness of. Soak the whole feast in milk. The only delights of food for me are in its destruction, and it so disappoints me that I can no longer indulge my play now, not at my age and not at my station in life as the world's most famous woman, second only to Queen Victoria (second only to *Julia*!).

Today, today, Doctor arrives today, and I am ready! I have eaten all my meals this week, even asking for seconds on several occasions, much to the surprise and delight of Wightie and Cook. I feel very cheerful and plump, no little bird, but a downy hen. All night I stayed up, unable to sleep, tiptoeing from my bed to the closet to pat down my new dress for wrinkles. I know it is clean because I have been saving it for Doctor's return. I asked Jeannette for a yellow muslin, but when I showed it to Wight and asked did she like my yellow dress, she said it was brown. Brown! Jeannette said she couldn't get yellow muslin for a good price, and besides this one matches my hair. I think I will look like a dung beetle when I wanted to look like a butterfly, fresh sprung. Green would have done, pink, or even red, but when I started in, Jeannette said, "If you pitch a fit, I won't let you stand in reception for Doctor and the Missus at all." Wight said brown is better for me anyway because it won't show the food I drop as much as a lighter color would. It is very hard to let others make the decisions about one's appearance. I learn a lot about the fashions from touching the ladies' clothes, and I would like a ruched silk bonnet. I asked Doctor to bring me back a blue one in the French style. I hope he didn't forget.

It's the least he could do after he's moved me out of his residence. Jeannette said he needed room for Julia and the baby, but I wrote to Doctor—I am your family too. You always said I was your dear daughter. "There are different ways of having children," Jeannette says, "different kinds of families." I know that. I am not with my own family; Doctor made me his daughter when I was seven, and now I'm being pushed aside by a mere babe, when I offered to be her sister as well? It is clearly Julia's doing. If I believed in witches, which I don't, I would say she'd cast a spell on Doctor. When I wrote to him, he said that Oliver and I were both his children out of love, but that baby Julia Romana was his child out of marriage. Then Jeannette said I could be her daughter too because she doesn't have any children. None of it makes sense to me, but the more I ask, the more confused I become. And anyway, Oliver's gone back to Maine, lolling, tongue out, like the fat and beloved family dog that he is.

My room in the Institution is not nearly so nice as my quarters in Doctor's residence. There I had three big pillows, where here I have only one, and there I had a deep, soft carpet I could stick my littlest finger all the way in and that fitted to the edges of the wall, but here there is only a thin rug by the bed. But the worst is the bang and scamper of blind girls up and down the hall, and I have no lock on my door so they can sneak in any time, though Miss Wight told them not to bother me. Most of them I have no time for, no wish to know.

Tessy has grown taller than me, and other parts too. She says I will get bigger parts as well, but I'm not sure I want them. Doctor might not even recognize me, his dearest daughter! I have collected all his letters from Europe, tied with a ribbon with tight loops, hidden beneath my mattress. It's not a large parcel, but I still wore out Swift's fingers having her read them to me again and again. Now I have them all memorized, and so to open them, I pretend to turn a key in my ear, and then I mouth the words. I sent Doctor over one hundred letters, and I shall ask my new teacher to read them to me. I know Doctor will have saved them and carried them back with him over the ocean.

I have also written many letters that I never sent, letters that were secret, only for me and for God. Those I wrote in blood, though I was never sure if there was enough blood to write out all the words, so I had to keep making more little cuts with the metal label along my inner arm and thigh. It doesn't hurt. I actually like it because it is the sharpest feeling I know. I push beyond the barriers of myself, and I am bigger for a moment, flowing out into the world. For me, it is not mutilation, but *experience*. Before Wightie came, Swift had asked me about the blood on my sheets, and then she hugged me and congratulated me that I had started to bleed. I was very surprised that everyone did this, but then she gave me rags to stuff between my legs and told me it would happen every month. I didn't cut myself down there, but I didn't tell her the truth. I asked why does the blood come out there and she said, "It is how God shows you that you are growing up." It turns out that God loves blood too. I thought He did, and that is why He fills me with such joy every time the metal slices through my skin.

Swift said it was time for a corset after she'd found the blood. At first, I hated it—how tight she pulled its laces!—but after a couple of weeks, I began to thrill to its pinch. The more parts of my body that I can feel at once, the better. I certainly don't fill it out like Tessy, but I enjoy the extra petticoats I get to wear over it. Before I wore only one or two in the winter, but Swift claimed that some ladies wear as many as ten, some of them corded, to achieve the right base. I only have three, though. Who would have thought I'd ever own three petticoats? Chemise, corset, crinoline, petticoats. The crinoline is my least favorite of my new accoutrements, like standing in a steel-hooped cage, a trapped sparrow. My waist is only one-and-a-half hands' widths when I'm corseted, and then the dresses bloom outward with all the layers of flounces and furbelows beneath them. Every time I walk up or down the stairs, I must hold up my dress with one hand. Becoming a lady is hard work, but I am ready.

In the great hallway, waiting to receive Doctor, Jeannette has lined us up, but when I walk down the row, touching the shoulder of each person, I can tell immediately that she has not put us in the right order, so I move everyone about. Jeannette, me, the teachers, then Cook, nine of us. I'll bet no one else is wearing *brown*. Sumner has brought them from the pier; he'd better not try to touch me with his giant, clumsy hands.

I know that Doctor is not here yet. I can always tell when he is in a room—the air warms and condenses almost imperceptibly and its weight tilts me gently in his direction, as if I were borne aloft on the high end of a seesaw, but losing balance, sliding slowly toward him on the ground. Julia does not bring warmth, but a coiling chill about my chest, while Sumner blocks all heat and wind. As for the child, we shall see. The floorboards tense and the heat circles. Doctor. After an agony of minutes, his hand is on mine, trying to write, but I wrap my arms around his waist, press my head against the buttons of his frock coat, and feel his great heart thudding against my ear. He is so happy to be back home with his Laura, it tells me! And then he has me at arm's length, and I let him write, but I don't even try to follow it, my head is still alive with the joy his heart has shared. He moves from me to the teachers, and I wait for the stiff caress of Julia. She is here, the floor shudders with the *plot-plot* of the solid heels of her traveling boots. There is a great rustling as Jeannette greets her, and then nothing. She has not greeted me. I start forward and Jeannette tries to stop me, but I shrug her off and hold my arms out wide, completely open to welcome Julia and the babe. The air is empty, but I stand my pose, waiting. Finally Julia's ungloved fingers take mine, and she leans in to kiss me upon the cheek. I allow my arms to encircle her, but keep her bosom held away from me.

"Give me the baby," I write.

And then her nails tap lightly, "Too small."

For me, who has held a tiny kitten in my arms, and nursed it through sickness? Is the child a meringue that will crumble in my hands?

"Let me," I say, and a moment passes before a delicate bundle is laid in my outstretched arms. I draw her slowly toward my chest, more careful than I have ever been, and press the tiny face against my cheek. It is cold and hard. The child is rigid in my arms. It is a doll! I don't throw her; I just let go, and I feel her hit my feet and roll away.

Jeannette grabs my arm roughly and writes, "Laura doll."

Oh, well, then I shouldn't have thrown myself to the floor. Another Laura doll from far away. Another little me to add to my menagerie. Does Doctor believe me so stupid and vain that I want to spend my days hosting tea parties for all my mock selves? Is the baby being given to everyone else down the line, even to the teachers? My hands are much cleaner than their ink-stained ones. I hold one arm out into the air, my palm cupped downward, and I am content to wait. Minutes go by, and then there is a downy tuft beneath my palm, and I have only time to stroke the soft skull once, never reaching the face of my sister, before she is taken away. I rub my fingers together, the electricity of Julia Romana's hair between them.

The dinner tonight is only for grown-ups, I am told, and Doctor says he will see me in his chambers in the morning. I am banished to eat with the blinds, who pester me for news of the happy couple. Julia has gotten very stout, I say, while Doctor is lean as a pistol. Perhaps she steals his food. The baby, the baby, they all want to know, and I stand and show them how I held her in my arms, nuzzling her angel face against mine. The girls grab at my elbows as if I really do hold the child. "She is a fairy baby," I sign to them. "I felt her tiny wings concealed beneath her traveling gown. We are fortunate to have such a creature among us, but none of you are allowed to touch the child. Only I can hold my fairy sister, Julia Romana." Tessy and the older girls laugh and say they don't believe me, and caution the others that my words are not true. But they are, and the best of the children will know that in their hearts.

Tessy grabs my hand and writes, "I will tell you the secret."

What secret? Who is she to know more than I?

Late that night, after everyone is asleep, I slide along the wall to Tessy's room and slip into her bed. I touch lightly the back of her neck and she stirs, turns over. She gives me her hand.

"Tell me." I feel her stretch and yawn, the breasts beneath her cotton gown rubbing against me.

"Sure?" she writes onto my palm, held close to her face, and I tap her hand.

"Doctor put his thing in Julia to make the baby," she says.

"What thing?"

Her silky hair whips across my face. "Down Pozzo's belly. Big thing on some of the horses."

I have scratched low on Pozzo's belly and also accidentally touched on a horse that fleshy, unnatural hose, but Wight said it is how they relieve themselves.

"Animals," I remind Tessy. "Different."

"All men have," she writes and traces a long shape down my wrist. I shake my arm to rid myself of the tingle of the loathsome drawing.

"Animal!" I tell her again. Doctor has no such thing and I should know better than anyone; countless hours I have spent in his study, sitting on his lap, my arms around him, and there was nothing of dog or horse on my dear Doctor!

"Foolish," Tessy says, and I want to slap her, but at the same time, her hand is so warm in mine, her chin nuzzled against my neck. How I wish I could sleep with her every night! Or any of the girls, for that matter, even the ones with lank hair or those I do not like, but Doctor won't allow it. How could he understand how endless the nights are, how terrified I become in the complete stillness that I will never again feel the touch of another human being. I do not believe Tessy's story, not for one second, but I cannot resist the sweetness of this moment for my body's sake. Maybe I am an animal too.

The next morning I prepare for Doctor. I choose the blue dress, his favorite, though it's grown a little tight. I keep my dresses in careful order by color so I'll know which one I'm picking.

He makes me wait outside his study door, and I lean my head upon the frame, and as the minutes go by, I begin to knock my temple against the wood. *Doctor is back! Doctor is back!* is the rhythm I tap into my skull, harder and harder, until he opens the door and I almost fall in.

"What on earth?" he writes and pats at my head.

I apologize and take my usual seat, moving my chair up close.

"You are well?" he asks.

"Very grown."

"I see. Proper young lady."

It must be the corset; nevertheless, I am pleased that he sees that I am so different from the colt he left nearly two years ago. He fills my hand with his travels as he mouths them, allowing my fingers to float in front of his lips so that I can feel the different forces and velocities of the puffs of air as he exhales the names of places I will never touch: "London," "Rome," and then in a warm fluff of breath, "Paris." "Paris," he says again—he knows the exquisite pleasure that the rushing air of any *P* gives me—and in my excitement, I rub my fingers against his lips. They are slightly dry and chapped, maybe from riding in the wind. I am pulling open the lower lip with two fingers when he grasps my wrist firmly and pushes my hand down into my lap. I am too bold today; I have never tried to open Doctor's mouth before. I can tell from the movement of his arm holding mine that he is leaning back and away from me.

"Happy?" I ask him, and his fingers hesitate.

"Of course," he writes. "My family."

"I am still your daughter?"

"Always."

My heart is full to bursting, but my temple has begun to ache. "Baby my sister?"

"You can call her that."

"Play with her."

"Very tiny. Mrs. Howe will decide."

Mrs. Howe? I'm not calling her that. "Practiced with dolls."

"Baby not a doll. Very careful." He pats my hand, and I know we are finished with this subject. For the moment. "Like Miss Wight?"

"Very much. Very good."

"Excellent," he says, and then pauses. "Swift talked about God?"

"A little." Not a tenth as much as I'd have liked.

"Wrong," Doctor writes. "You were not ready."

"Ready," I write emphatically.

"I am the judge, Laura."

"Thought God judge?"

His fingers waver. "God trusts me."

"Blinds read Bible." Anything I know I've gotten secondhand from Tessy or one of the others. Like the ridiculous idea that Doctor is a horse or a dog. I am tempted to ask him about that as well.

"But you are special," he writes. "You inspire others."

It always comes back to that. "Want God to inspire *me*."

"When the time," he taps, but I push away his fingers.

"He speaks to me." This is not completely true, but when I try to pray, there is a voice that I am sure is not mine, that is louder than mine, except maybe when I'm angry. Then mine is very loud. "He wants me to know Him."

Doctor drums his fingers; he does not know how to argue this, which is what I've counted on. A long moment passes before he writes, "Make a deal."

I nod vigorously. Any deal should be worth this.

"Mrs. Howe says noises scare baby."

I don't understand.

"Your noises."

Yesterday I allowed myself to yelp at Doctor's return and to make all my naming sounds. I thought they would be happy.

"Made baby cry."

That's what they do all the time anyway, isn't it? "Then teach me to speak."

"Deaf don't speak," he writes. "Too hard."

"I'll learn." I know I can. "What makes you speak?"

"A tongue," he tells me, "lips, vocal cords at the back of the throat." Mine obviously work since I can already make noises. I trace the perfect heart of my lips, and then reach inside for the slick curl of my tongue and pull it. Good and strong and very quick. It even has the bumps on it that Doctor says help you taste, though mine don't work; otherwise it is fine.

I reach for Doctor's mouth. "Touch tongue?"

"No," and he pushes me off.

I only wanted to see if it feels the same as mine, so I'll know mine is really working. That's all right; Wightie will let me in her mouth later, I'm sure. But then Doctor says I need ears, ears that can hear. "Why ears?"

"Need to hear yourself to speak properly."

I don't think so. I would *like* to hear myself, but I don't need to. I can't hear my naming noises, but I can feel their vibrations in my throat. "No deafs speak? Ever?"

I can tell he is impatient, but I keep tapping, and finally he explains. Many years ago, Reverend Gallaudet, the founder of the Connecticut Asylum for the Education of Deaf and Dumb Persons, went to Europe to learn their methods of teaching. Only the British and Scottish had found a way to teach the deaf to speak, but they said it was a secret and would not share it with him. I know that Gallaudet married a student, and she was just a boring deaf girl. If I had been sixteen as I am now, I think Doctor might have chosen me instead of Julia. But I was only thirteen when Doctor's affection bump forced him to choose an object, and we all know whom he chose: Julia Ward, known for being in possession of all five senses and then some. And anyone who has eyes to see confirms that Julia has not lost the weight from the child. Gossip flies into my hands as easily as it does into the ears of others, and lands buzzing on my palm like flies.

"So nobody here can teach me?"

He pats my hand. "Perkins is school for the blind, except for you."

"But will inspire more children if I speak." That's the truth: if I can learn language *and* speak, then I will prove an even greater example. One would think that every effort would be made to assure that I'm accomplishing all that I'm able. After all, if the deaf are talking it up over there in the British Isles, then I should be able to grace our republic with speech.

"For your noises," he writes, "need a private place."

"What place?"

"Closet in kitchen."

I know that closet; it is small and dank and couched with bags of flour. He has this whole thing figured out, and I'd thought I was being the clever one. "Bible?" I will trade my silence—for now—for the chance to meet with God.

"Genesis I will give you."

It isn't much, but it's a start. I laugh and put my hand to his face. The beginning! It's the beginning of everything.

Chapter 10

Sarah, 1847

Sarah Wight had a headache; she got them frequently. Laura stood over the settee where her teacher lay, dipping a rag into a pan. She tried to wring the cloth, but water dripped onto Sarah's forehead, and then in tiny rivulets down her cheeks and chin onto her collar. Sarah had given up wiping it away; she was now fairly soaked by her pupil's frenzy of attention. She should never tell Laura when she had a headache.

Jeannette brought a vase of fresh-cut lilies into the parlor and surveyed the scene. "At least she didn't dump the whole pan on you like last time," she said.

Laura reached down and felt the wetness, and began to pat wildly with the rag. She covered Sarah's nose and mouth, and Sarah pushed her hand away more roughly than she intended. The girl's anxiety was telegraphed through her fingers, though Sarah knew it would be even worse if she sent her to her room. Relieved of her duties as teacher's nurse, she would spend the night in an agony of retribution. Nothing made Sarah's headaches worse than the sound of Laura's keening in that frightening, guttural way of hers, unaware that her sorrow made her far less sympathetic. Sarah had delighted in teaching Laura the Bible, knowing how long the Good Book was kept from her, but she had to admit that the introduction to religion had made the girl much more highly emotional, and worse, even harder on herself than she was before.

"You'll be drowned if you let her keep on," Jeannette said and tried to take the rag from Laura's hand. A tug-of-war ensued, during which Sarah got even wetter. Jeannette finally wrested the cloth from her, and Laura turned round and round in near panic. Her fingers quivered on Sarah's arm until Sarah wrote that she was the best nurse ever and that she was all better.

"You spoil her to bits," Jeannette said. "I've warned you. Tell her it's supper, if you can get her to eat."

Sarah pried Laura's arms from her waist. "She'll likely skip table entirely in this state. She's wasting under my care."

Jeannette snorted. "She's always been a terror to get fed, worse than a two-year-old. She used to throw half the food down the table and spit the other half out on her plate. A mess to clean, every blessed day. Only reason she's up to eighty pounds is to impress Chev. Stuffed herself for weeks before he came back."

"Dinner," Sarah signed into Laura's palm and the girl shook her head vehemently. "Doctor wants you to eat," she tried again.

"Doctor eat with me?"

"No, but I will."

Laura smoothed the front of her dress, considering. "Feed me?"

Sarah cast a despairing glance at Jeannette, who laughed. "Ladies eat on their own."

Laura stood up straighter. "I use fork better than blinds," she wrote, and Sarah agreed. She took her arm to escort her to the dining room.

"How's the spell?" Jeannette asked. "You still look peaked."

"I'll be lucky not to lose my soup," Sarah said, "but it will be worth it if she eats hers."

"My brother has found an angel."

"Send that birdsong into his ear then because he finds me far too human."

"Heaven help him, he rarely gets the worth right." Jeannette walked with them down the hall.

"You mean Julia?" Sarah whispered.

Laura poked her teacher in the arm. "What talk?"

"Worth her weight in gold or coal, I cannot say."

"You tempt me with such palaver and deliver nothing," Sarah said. Laura poked her harder in the arm. "We say how nice Julia's having another baby."

"Stay fat," Laura wrote.

"She's sick most every morning," Jeannette said. "Says the house full of blinds bodes ill for her laying-in."

"All this time, and I think she's still actually afraid of them," Sarah said. "Or afraid she'll birth one herself, God forgive me."

"Afraid of that one most of all."

"As well she should be." Sarah helped Laura into her chair at the head of the first table. Laura pressed her teacher's arm to sit beside her.

"You'll catch your death, still half-drowned," Jeannette warned.

Laura held Sarah's hand tightly and banged their twined fists upon the table. When the dishes were served, Sarah found she could only manage a few spoonfuls of soup, which was nothing more than hot water afloat with a few limp vegetables. Since Doctor believed that any spices added to the food would be too stimulating for the blind, Cook was not allowed to use even salt or pepper, and no sugar for tea. Fruit was never served raw, but cooked for so long you sometimes couldn't tell if you had an apple or a pear before you. Desserts only on Christmas, when the girls devoured them and, sure enough, were often sick. Maybe Doctor was right—maybe they were too sensitive—but Sarah missed sweetness most of all, a good chess pie, even a fry-up dusted with sugar. Of course, it was all the same to Laura. Sarah ended up spoon-feeding her half the bowl of soup, but Laura removed from her mouth each of the beans and placed them around her dish. "Like bugs," she said. It was always something.

She twisted her bread into a sort of animal shape—it had four legs anyway—and galloped it up her teacher's sleeve. She'd mostly broken her student of playing with her food by constantly reminding her of her age—seventeen!—but this often led to a discussion of what other girls her age were up to—walking out with beaux, going to balls in carriages—and Laura usually ended up weeping at the bleakness of her own life. It was one thing to admonish her to act like an adult, and then another to refuse her any adult activities. Sarah wondered if this disparity could ever be resolved; might Laura at say, twenty-one, finally accept her limitations and be able to fashion some sort of real life for herself in the world? As difficult and heartbreaking as it was for Sarah, she hoped to stay at Perkins long enough to find out. Sarah finally popped off the head of the bread animal, which by now had lost a leg anyway, and pushed it into Laura's mouth, caught open in a laugh. The girl chewed the bread, but complained that Sarah had destroyed her dog. In moments like these, Sarah found it almost impossible to reconcile the Laura who devoured the Old Testament and pelted her with incisive questions with the petulant, crumb-covered child before her.

The blind girls chattered loudly in the hall, and today Sarah wished they were all deaf-mute as well. She offered up a quick prayer as the milksop was served, asking God to forgive her for such terrible thoughts. Usually she ignored the girls, so occupied was she with her one demanding charge, but today she heard something that pricked her attention.

"She got up in my bed again last night," said one of the older ones, gesturing at Laura. "Kept me awake all hours, petting me."

A pigtailed girl across the table nodded. "Just push her out. That's what I do. But then she makes that awful noise, like a horse dying." The girls instinctively inclined their heads in the direction of Laura's table in case her teacher could hear. "I never push her hard, though," the girl said loudly.

"Doctor would have your head," the first one whispered. "You must not injure the star of his shows."

The girl with pigtails said, "I think I'll put a bag over my head so she can't get at my hair," and the table was overcome with giggling.

Sarah was accustomed to the blinds discussing Laura right in front of her. Sometimes it was useful, but often it was cruel, and Sarah wished that she herself couldn't hear. As much a trouble as she was, Laura was the beneficiary of all of her teacher's stored-up love, for which she had no other object, with the exception of her family out in Wayland.

Girls routinely slept together at the Institution, just as they did at home with their siblings. Only Laura had a private room, and though her teacher's room was beside hers, Laura managed to sneak out quietly enough that Sarah missed it half the time. Whenever she did hear the patter of Laura's slippered feet inching down the hallway, she roused herself from her bed and collared the girl. Sometimes Laura was so startled that she let out an alarming yelp, and then everybody woke up. No matter how many times she'd been reprimanded, Laura thought her midnight larks were funny, and so she was in high spirits for an hour before Sarah could settle her down again. Sarah knew exactly what the blind girl meant; her own hair seemed to be a source of endless fascination for Laura, who alternated between stroking it gently and pulling. It was only when her hands strayed down Sarah's neck and began exploring below the collarbone that she firmly pushed Laura's fingers away and back up to her head. Sarah was constantly in a state of rearranging her bun as Laura dislodged it. A teacher must always be a model of modest perfection, even if her students couldn't see her. "You can play my hair too," was Laura's open invitation, as she tickled Sarah's nose with a stray lock. Sarah did play with Laura's hair, brushing it, braiding and unbraiding, but she stopped short of the rougher work that the girl asked for. Why would anyone want their hair pulled? But then again, on the occasions when she helped Laura dress or bathe—she did most of her grooming herself now—she saw tiny lines of dried blood on the insides of Laura's thighs and upper arms.

At first, she'd believed Laura's explanations: "Fall down," she'd say, or "Pozzo scratch," or "Blind play hard." But after finding a very precise trio of cuts on her inner thigh, Sarah knew they couldn't be accidents. "Who's hurting you?" she asked, but Laura only shook her head. Perhaps it was retribution for the higher status bestowed on Laura—her own room, famous visitors, private time with Doctor—or maybe because Laura simply annoyed the living daylights out of some of the girls. Laura was plenty capable of protecting herself, however, as her ferocity in gym games had proven, and Sarah couldn't imagine her being that abjectly passive. She certainly wasn't with her teacher. Maybe it was some perverse adolescent game; she herself had never engaged in such activities when she was at school, but there had been a group of girls who fancied themselves some sort of secret society with strange rituals. Sarah shuddered at the thought of blind girls playing with razors. Maybe she should tell Doctor, but she was afraid to even ask the other teachers or Jeannette if any of their students suffered similar wounds. If they didn't, she would only arouse suspicion about Laura, and goodness knows the child had enough on her plate as the only deaf-blind since Oliver left. But after months of finding the tiny incisions, Sarah realized that Laura herself was doing the cutting, though so far Sarah hadn't been able to find the instrument. When she asked Laura why she did this, the girl denied it, her face a mask of pure innocence, not even the sly expression she usually wore when caught at something. Sarah held Laura in her arms and told her that she didn't have to punish herself for anything.

"Not punish," Laura said. "God punish. Doctor punish."

Sarah lived in fear that her charge would cut too deeply one day in her quest for whatever it was and seriously wound herself, but she still didn't dare tell Doctor. She considered taking Laura's hatpins, but then how on earth could she secure her hats? It was a conundrum she couldn't see her way clear of, so until she could come to some logical conclusion and solution, she kept Laura safe from prying eyes and prayed for guidance, for answers.

Thank the Lord, Dr. Howe didn't pay much mind to Sarah. He respected her, she thought, but he kept his distance and, at this stage, rarely inquired after Laura's progress. Jeannette said he used to demand a daily report of her, which then dwindled to weekly, and now he merely asked offhandedly if he happened to pass Sarah in the hall. Now that he'd given in to Laura's demands for the Bible, he seemed to regard her as a lost cause. Sarah knew from reading the papers, even before she had arrived at Perkins, how important a pawn Laura was in the battle that Doctor and Horace Mann waged against the Calvinists. Doctor insisted that the girl was a blank slate who would come naturally to God, proving man's innate religiosity and spirituality and refuting the idea of original sin. But the crumbs he dropped were never enough for the voracious Laura, and though her moral sense was well developed, she insisted on learning the tenets of Christianity and studying the minutiae of the Good Book, contrary to general Unitarian beliefs. Sarah herself was a Unitarian; her father had been the first Unitarian minister in Wayland, but she still found herself leaning a bit dangerously toward Calvinism with its more concrete view of the Holy Trinity. Her father had once spanked her for going to services at a Baptist church with a friend. If he were still alive, he would have gotten along famously with Dr. Howe.

When Doctor summoned Sarah the next week, she knew it would not be good news. Doctor didn't take interest enough in the teacher or the pupil for it to be good. She came to his office at the appointed time and knocked repeatedly, but no one answered. Then she heard the low rumble of male laughter from within. She was ready to leave when the door opened and Charles Sumner emerged. Generally he was one of the best-kept gentlemen that Sarah had ever seen—white shirt collars starched, even a velvet riding jacket once—but now his wide cravat was askew and his dark hair tousled. He must have been riding.

He bowed. "Good day, Miss…" And Sarah curtsied and supplied her surname. She didn't expect the great Sumner to remember it. He extended his arm with a flourish, indicating the room within.

"The Chevalier is all yours," he said and smiled his thin smile.

Sarah made it a rule to at least attempt not to think uncharitable things about anyone, but she could never summon anything but distaste for Doctor's famous friend, probably because Laura disliked him so strongly, more than anyone. She claimed that Sumner was rough with her, and she wouldn't let him even try to write upon her hand. Sarah had heard from another teacher that Laura had actually bitten him once, but she couldn't believe the girl would go that far with Doctor's dearest friend.

"Come," Doctor said and motioned toward the straight-backed chair in front of his enormous cherrywood desk. The desk was piled with newspapers and loose sheets and a teetering stack of books, and Sarah felt the itch to tidy everything up; that or sweep it all away. Didn't he let the maids clean in here? She wondered how Julia felt about the office's disarray. There was definitely not the slightest hint of a woman's touch anywhere in the room. Sarah had to remove a book from the chair before she could settle herself. Her palms were sweating, her anxiety made worse by the fact that Doctor was not saying anything, only watching her with a slight frown and that wrinkle between his eyes that somehow made him even handsomer.

"Miss Wight, it has come to my attention... It's been reported that..."

Sarah realized he wasn't angry, just terribly uncomfortable.

"It seems that Laura has been, um, bothering some of the girls. At night, that is. Were you aware of this?"

"I heard a girl mention it at table, but I didn't think..."

"You sleep in the room beside Laura, correct?"

"Yes, sir, but she can be very quiet when she's determined."

"Determined to what?"

"Well, to seek... to seek affection." Sarah felt the color rising in her cheeks and knew it would not go down.

"Do you not give her enough affection?" Doctor asked.

"I think I do, sir. Yes, I do. I care for the girl very deeply, but she seems to require more affection than I can provide." If only you would give her a bit, like when she was younger, Sarah thought, if you could bring yourself to take her in your arms the way you used to. Sarah remembered her first year at Perkins teaching the other girls, the year before Doctor married, how he and Laura would walk hand in hand down the halls, how she'd run to him whenever he entered the room, and he'd gather her up and kiss her. Once she had seen him carrying the girl on his shoulders in the garden, her face turned upward toward the sun, lit with pleasure as she fingered the leaves on the trees. But she was no longer an adorable little girl, but a difficult and, yes, strange-looking adolescent. Sarah recalled her own early years; they had been trying enough without Laura's heavy load. Sarah had been plain, was still plain, but at least no one had ever ridiculed her for that; instead, she was ignored, almost invisible, she sometimes thought. An invisible woman teaching blind girls—how perfect!

Doctor particularly had never paid her the least notice, but now he stroked his beard and gazed at her with those penetrating eyes. He was so fine that even Sarah sometimes found it hard not to stare. She looked down at her lap.

"Do you think it's necessary for you to sleep with Laura? Miss Swift always—"

Sarah shocked herself by interrupting him. "No. No," she said, perhaps too vehemently. "Miss Swift cared for Laura when she was a child. Now that she is seventeen I don't believe she needs her teacher sharing her bed." Oh, Lord, please, if she had to sleep with Laura, she would never catch a wink, she knew it. The girl's hands would never leave her.

"Then it is up to you to make sure she does not crawl into the beds of others. The girls do not need to be harassed, and her behavior is unbecoming at this stage."

"But many of the girls snuggle in together, Doctor, even some of the older ones. Is it possible they are singling out Laura because—"

"They are singling out Laura because apparently the extent of her...affection exceeds that of the other girls."

Sarah dared not think what he might mean, but she knew there was something to what he said, something she could not quite put her finger on, or didn't want to. "I will mind her, Doctor. It won't happen again." How she was going to accomplish that Sarah had no idea. Tie Laura to the bed? Lock her in?

"Miss Dix will be arriving this afternoon. Make sure that Laura is clean and at her best."

Sarah was stung by the remark and realized she was being dismissed. Laura adored Dorothea Dix and was always on her best behavior for those visits. The reformer was nearly as devoted to Laura's cause as she was to helping the insane. Nearly ten years had passed since she'd brought about the changes to Massachusetts' asylums. Before her graphic reportage, the poor lunatics had been tied up, kept in pens, lashed, starved. Sarah read in the paper that Miss Dix was now establishing hospitals in Illinois and North Carolina.

Dorothea Dix didn't look like a reformer, not like Elizabeth Cady Stanton or Lucretia Mott of the coming Seneca Falls Convention. Miss Dix appeared to lack the robust constitution necessary for such demanding work; she was as pale and nearly as thin as Laura, and the two could have passed for sisters. Miss Dix had the consumption, and it was rumored she'd had it for years, but every time she went down for the count—this last time in isolation for six months in Chicago—she bounded back and took up her causes again with renewed vigor. Of all Laura's celebrated visitors, this lady was the one whom Sarah most admired. Here she was barely able to handle her one charge, and Miss Dix was off wrangling armies of the insane, some of them violent, drooling maniacs. She put even Doctor's great enterprise to shame, and when they were in company, he looked like his collar was too tight; after all, he had advised her, assisted her in her early endeavors in Massachusetts, where she'd started, and now her work—a woman's work, for God's sake—far outshone his.

He'd apparently been very supportive of Florence Nightingale too, when she came to him for advice in England on his honeymoon. Julia told Sarah how furious she'd been that he had encouraged the young woman to work while insisting that Julia herself not even publish her poetry. "Miss Nightingale is not married," he'd told his wife. Neither was Miss Dix. Of course, neither was Sarah; perhaps she should embark upon a crusade for which the great man would trumpet her. No, all he wanted of her was that she keep Laura Bridgman out of the blind girls' beds, and heaven knows, that was task enough for Sarah. She might truly rather tackle the bedlamites.

As soon as Miss Dix arrived, she insisted they take Laura out for a walk on the beach. She was a big believer in getting everyone outdoors, if possible, and though it was raining lightly, Sarah acquiesced. Laura delighted in the rain, though it was bad for her to be out in the wet, especially as sickly as she often was, so Sarah rarely allowed her this pleasure. But today, and for Miss Dix, anything. Sarah held the large black umbrella over the two as they walked and talked along the water's edge, Miss Dix just barely keeping Laura out of the foam as it surged and retreated. They both knew that if she let her go, even for an instant, she would be up to her knees in the surf. She loved all water, warm, cold, no matter. Laura would bathe every day if her teacher would let her, and only the admonitions by Doctor about the potential damage of too much bathing kept her away from the taps.

Another wonderful thing about Miss Dix was that she always included Sarah in the conversation, unlike many other famous visitors, like Longfellow or Thomas Wentworth Higginson, who held private court with Laura, while her teacher had no idea what they were discussing, unless one of them required her assistance with communication.

Miss Dix looped her other arm in Sarah's. "I was telling Laura that

I'm petitioning the federal government to set aside five million acres for the care of our lunatics. And the rest for the deaf." She patted Laura's hand. "It is doubtful, however, that Congress will accede to my plan, though I have been winning them over state by state."

Laura grabbed at Sarah's palm. "But I stay here with you."

Miss Dix laughed. "She is concerned about being trapped with the maniacs."

"As she should be," Sarah ventured.

"But some of them get better," Miss Dix said. "It is astonishing, but I've witnessed it many times. With the right care and compassion, the madness can be lifted, or at least held at bay, especially for the melancholics."

Sarah watched the waves roll in and out, pinholed by the drizzle. Her own dear brother was of such disposition, but sometimes even he was seized with gaiety, if not a complete reprieve. Her own temperament tended that way, Doctor had warned her, and this offhand diagnosis was not a complete surprise to her. She knew that she must keep her spirits up for Laura, even when in the midst of one of her spells, which she felt sure were of a physical, rather than a mental, nature.

By the time they'd walked down to the pier and back, all three were fairly sopped, but in an excellent frame nonetheless. Miss Dix kissed them both on each cheek, the way she said it was done in Europe, and went to meet with Doctor.

After Miss Dix left, Laura was in high fodder, so Sarah seized the moment, though it took a while to get her inside. Laura twirled around, bumping into furniture, trying to get her teacher to dance with her. Usually Sarah obliged, but today it seemed unwise, given the intended subject of the conversation. Finally she got her down.

"Important," Sarah wrote, but Laura interrupted her.

"Music still playing," she said and then pressed a finger to her temple as if to turn it off. Sarah waited patiently, but apparently the tune had started again, because Laura was still rocking and tapping her feet.

"Talked with Doctor," Sarah wrote, and that got her attention.
"Me?"

"Yes." She struggled to put it in terms that would brook no argument from the girl, so she skipped right to Doctor's mandate, because while Laura might debate the abstract, she still very much wanted to please Howe. "Doctor wants you stay in own bed," she wrote. "Not bother girls."

"Not bother," Laura wrote. "Play. They like."

"Doctor doesn't like."

"But blinds sleep together."

Sarah had known this was coming; even she often slept with her sister or cousin at home for warmth. She took the only tack that worked with Laura: "But you are special." This almost always did the trick, and frankly, it was true.

"Doctor said?"

"Yes."

"Special good?"

"Of course. Doctor worries. Says sleep better alone."

"But I like..." Her fingers trailed in Sarah's palm, and her teacher was grateful for once that she could not articulate exactly what she meant. "Stay alone always?"

Though she could not see the tears behind the shade or hear them in the girl's voice, Sarah knew that she was beginning to cry. Without the usual cues, it had taken her a while to figure out when Laura was crying, unless she was going full out—nose dripping, shoulders shaking—which only happened maybe once a month lately. Now the corners of her mouth turned down and her fingers faltered.

"God with you," Sarah wrote. It was the best she could do.

"God not warm."

Well, Sarah couldn't argue with that.

"You sleep with me?"

"Grown ladies sleep alone," she wrote emphatically. "Jeannette alone. Cook alone."

"Julia alone?"

Oh dear. Sarah scrambled. Ah— "Julia sleeps with baby."

Laura nodded slowly. "If I have baby, can sleep with me?"

"Yes." Sarah felt no qualms making this promise because she knew it would never happen.

"When does God give baby?"

Oh no, it was backfiring. Think. "When two people love each other, God gives them a baby." This explanation seemed to satisfy Laura, and to Sarah's surprise, it satisfied her as well. She hadn't known she was quite so wise.

Chapter 11
Julia, 1847

Julia had found Sarah to be a good companion, the best at least that the Institution offered. No society belles here, no great minds with which to discuss philosophy or the latest poetry. Chev, of course, was capable of these things, but he refused. He was all action, little thought, her husband, though she'd long ago realized that that was a choice and not necessarily a character trait. And deprived of his animal rights, he granted her very little attention, though he doted on the children and the students. She knew that if she burned out her eyeballs with a fiery poker, he would be all tens and elevenses again. Sarah was decently educated, respectful of Julia's position, and thoughtful in her opinions, if a little dull, though her slavish devotion to Laura was beyond Julia's comprehension. She herself was not that rapt in her attentions to her own children, even with a third on the way. She loved them all dearly, especially her first, Julia Romana, who, at two, was turning out to be as beautiful and sensitive as her mother. They were all her little planets, revolving around her sun, while it was clear that for Sarah, Laura was the center of the universe and all revolved around her. But still she found herself searching out Sarah's company, especially in these last months of her confinement. Her own dear sisters were far away, and letters could not look back at you and give you the sympathy you craved. And so the price for

Sarah's company was allowing Laura to play with Julia Romana, though she kept baby Florence well out of her reach. Florence was a good child, much sweeter than her sister, but the sting of being forced to name her after Chev's protégé, Miss Nightingale, had not yet lost its venom. And soon there would be another one! She was still aghast that her body had produced three children in as many years. Though she loved her husband and even the physical side of their relationship, she had been thoroughly unprepared for this relentless onslaught of nature. And what toll it had taken on both her body and mind: she found herself unable to bring forth the quotes and aphorisms for which she was noted, and unlike some other women with child, her complexion suffered, no longer pink and rosy, but pale and drawn, though she knew she was still counted among the loveliest of Boston's blooms. Chev had criticized even the way she walked, not cradling the precious treasure of her belly the way most pregnant women did, but instead with her arms rigidly at her sides.

Julia was still quite wary of Laura, the way one would be around an unpredictable dog. The girl vacillated between jumping on her, patting and petting, overwhelming her with physical affection, which she did not return; and blatantly ignoring her, pretending she wasn't even in the room. Julia knew good and well that Laura could always tell who was in a room; she couldn't explain how, especially without a sense of smell, but she had an almost unfailing knack for knowing who entered and who left. "Air changes," was her only explanation, though she was clearly proud of her ability. And Julia had to admit, the children seemed to enjoy playing with her; perhaps because she was, in some ways, on their level, and they regarded her as a playmate in kind.

Today Julia and Sarah sat over tea in the playroom, supervising Laura as she attempted a game of tops with the girls. It was these drowsy afternoons, spring sunlight from the latticed windows dappling her children's extraordinary curls, that she felt she could unburden herself, just a little. After all, Sarah was the perfect confidante; she apparently spoke to no one but Laura and a bit to Jeannette. She was not close with the other teachers, whom she'd confessed she found somewhat frivolous and low-minded, and Julia knew that out of respect for her Sarah would never repeat anything to Laura. Still, Julia shocked even herself when she confided that while Doctor was thrilled with the pregnancy, she felt uneasy, occasionally despondent. "I am much happier producing poems than children, while my husband insists on the reverse."

Sarah blushed. It seemed to Julia that she had already accepted the edict of spinsterhood from the Lord and that it didn't bother her, perhaps because she was dead on her feet every day from taking care of one of His children whom He'd amply slighted.

"I wouldn't know much about that," Sarah said. "The truth is I probably never will."

It was true she was quite plain with her fine whey hair and pale gaze, the kind of woman a man's eyes never lit on first in any room, but still there must be someone, equally slight, to match with her. Julia took her hand. "I doubt that, my dear. You would be an excellent mother, though you are too hard on yourself, and far too soft on your charge."

"I can't be anything but soft with her," Sarah said. "She has so little, and she tries so hard for love."

"Whose love?" Julia asked, her eyes narrowing, thinking of the girl's ridiculous attachment to her husband.

Sarah turned to her. "Anyone's."

After that conversation, in spite of her queasiness about the blind, Julia began to thaw toward Laura, giving her more playtime with the tots, and as Laura sensed this shift, she too became warmer to her former rival. She began insisting on serving Julia tea, and though it was a potentially dangerous mission, Julia allowed it, and to Laura's credit, she only scalded Julia once. And when Laura asked, as she had with Julia's other pregnancies, if she could touch her stomach, Julia surprised herself by consenting, even helping Laura to kneel and situate her hands. Then Laura pressed her whole face into the dome of Julia's belly, and they both let out a yelp as the baby kicked once, hard. Laura pulled away and stood up, then wrote on Julia's palm: "Boy." What cheek the girl had, and yet Julia felt instantly that she was right. How could she possibly know?

On one occasion, Chev popped his head into the nursery, and he looked as if he'd suddenly come upon the three witches of *Macbeth* toiling and troubling over his children. He actually stammered, and when he left, Julia began to giggle, and then Sarah started in too, and soon they were both nearly doubled over.

The next afternoon, Julia brought a pamphlet and handed it to Sarah. It was about the ocularists who'd set up shop in New York. She'd found it in her desk last night when she was looking for a new ink blotter, having forgotten that she'd picked it up in New York.

"I mentioned this to Chev years ago," she said, "getting the eyes for her, but he didn't seem interested. I think he believes himself too much a purist to adorn Laura with artificial devices. The Germans were making mostly enamel eyes—very easily damaged, I'm told—but now they're blowing beautiful glass ones in all colors. I met a young lady on the train to New York last year who had perfectly lovely green eyes. They looked almost real in a certain light."

Sarah nodded. "I had considered bringing that matter up to Doctor, but I'm afraid I lacked the courage."

"He can be a lion," Julia said, "but I will help you tame him, just enough. Tell her. Go ahead."

"I hesitate to incite her with the prospect because she will be so disappointed if—"

"I will make it happen," Julia said, and she patted Sarah's arm and then Laura's, suddenly as confident of her great powers as she had been before her marriage.

As Sarah wrote into Laura's hand, the girl's face brightened with joy, as if she had just been given the greatest gift of her life. "I'll get big blue ones," she wrote to Julia.

Julia warmed to the girl's excitement and to her own compassion and generosity. After all, what a boon eyeballs, even the facsimile of such, would prove to the girl's countenance. She might come to look almost normal, and that would certainly make her much more pleasant to be around. Aesthetics were nothing to be slighted. Early in her husband's courtship, when she had been sure he would grant her every whim, Julia had asked to see Laura without the shade and had been shocked by the violence of Chev's denial. It was as if she had asked to see the girl stripped buck naked. Now her youthful curiosity had abated, and she was thankful she had been spared the sight of those blighted sockets, which would probably have given her nightmares.

After this news, Julia didn't think Sarah would be able to get Laura to settle back down, but Laura sat quietly at their feet, her head inclined upward to the left the way it was when she did her deepest thinking. Finally she reached for Julia's hand, and Julia spoke the words as they were written.

"She asks if I remember when she hurt my ear. She says she only wanted to feel the bumps on my head." Did she *remember*? How could she ever forget those fingers, thin as pencils, jammed into her ear. It had felt as if Laura was trying to tunnel straight through to her brain, perhaps to remove it. Julia recalled with pride how well she'd handled that assault in Chev's presence, but afterward, she was reduced to shaking and crying in her room for the afternoon, and the memory pricked at her still. Julia smiled at Sarah. "That was before your time. She did have a go at me, but the truth is I don't much believe in the science of phrenology, as my husband does."

She could tell from Sarah's expression that she wasn't a believer either, but she was clearly afraid to voice her opinion on a topic so sacred to her employer. But as Julia wrote of her doubts in Laura's hand, she saw that Laura was shocked, her mouth open in an O. Then she nodded and signed rapidly into Julia's palm.

"She says she thinks phrenology interferes with free will," Julia told Sarah. "Exactly. If we are born with bumps that govern our character, then how are we to grow and change?" She'd had no idea the two of them shared this sentiment. Laura had far more depth and independence of thought than she'd given her credit for.

Julia laughed as Sarah watched them converse. Both of them could have been knocked over with a feather. She'd had no inkling that Laura could be such a compelling creature, under the right circumstances.

Julia made an appointment for the three of them to speak with her husband about the ocularists. She and Chev had been on good terms lately, and so she felt reasonably sure that she could convince him. And wouldn't he be delighted that she was not only spending time with Laura, but was actually trying to do something for the girl. Julia had given the pamphlet to Sarah for a good study and suggested she accompany Laura to New York for the fitting. It would be nice for them both to visit New York since neither of them had been. Julia briefly considered going with them as a guide to her beloved city, but she couldn't, after all, take them to any of her old haunts or to meet her friends or family. It would be unfair to all to expect too much of the young women and a breach of taste and imposition to expect her friends to readily accept them into their houses. Of course, there was the fame card to play with Laura, but seriously, could she bear the girl's strange company for a week? How did Sarah do it? She had thought of giving Sarah some of her old clothes for the trip so that they might at least have dinner somewhere reputable, but the poor dear could never fill out the bustline without much retailoring. What a blessing to have round and perfect bosoms; as a matter of fact, she might have to use them today to gain the advantage with her husband. The pregnancy had near doubled them, and he had not been allowed a squeeze since her third month in, so she chose a much lower neckline than a woman in her state would generally advertise.

"I don't have much time," were the first words out of Chev's mouth before they had even installed themselves. Right out of the gate, he was using that brusque tone in front of Sarah. "I have a meeting with Mr. Mann about the prison system."

They'd agreed that Julia would do the talking. "Chev," she started and saw that she had already misstepped as he winced at the use of his nickname in front of the help. She began again. "A wonderful opportunity has come up for Laura. Apparently, some German ocularists have set up in New York, using the latest techniques to—"

"Glass eyes?" he asked incredulously. "That's what you're on about?"

"Yes, I have here a pamphlet..." Julia handed it to her husband.

"It's fascinating to me, my dear, that you have turned from mocking the feeble in verse to standing as a mighty champion."

Julia looked down. "That was *one* silly poem, sir. And people do change." She leaned forward so that he might get a good look at her décolletage, but he appeared as dismissive of her breasts as he was of the girl in this instance. What *was* the world coming to?

"Do they? Now that is a matter indeed for phrenological consideration." He skimmed the pamphlet while Laura wiggled in her chair, reaching for Sarah's hand. "I know all about this, of course, and if I'd thought artificial eyes were a good and useful investment for Laura, she would already have them."

Julia was surprised to hear Sarah speak. "But why..."

Chev sat on the edge of his desk and looked at her as if she were a recalcitrant child. Julia could tell he was dying to say, "Because I said so," but he forced himself to give an explanation.

"Glass eyes are newfangled, at least in this country, and are known to be hideously uncomfortable. As a doctor, I can assure you that the procedure is certainly not as simple as popping a marble in and out, regardless of what that tract says. Laura has an especially low threshold for pain, given the nature of her one sense, and so the eyes would not at all be in her best interest, which is what I always have in mind, of course."

Laura was tapping insistently on Sarah's hand to translate, but Julia saw that Sarah merely squeezed her fingers tightly, knowing she would need a little time to soften Chev's speech for the girl. Laura held her head at attention in his direction, as if she were following every word.

He wasn't finished, though. "The other and perhaps more important thing is that I have long observed that Laura is overly vain, a common unpleasantness with blind girls. As if glass eyes would really help her presentation anyway, bag of bones that she is, as unnatural as she has come to look. And yet she is so concerned with appearances, and with trying to appear 'normal,' that I have seen her more than once sitting with an open book, a regular one, before her in the parlor, pretending that she could read it."

Laura often insisted on this charade; Julia had witnessed it several times herself. "But she isn't actually trying to fool anyone. She knows—"

"But such acts serve as a grave exacerbation of her affectations. I can only imagine what enduring damage a pair of big blue eyes might do her character."

Julia stood up, her hands on her belly. "So her character is more important than her happiness?"

Chev slid off the desk and faced his wife. "I must make decisions for the good of the entire Institution and all my charges. If I allow Laura the artificial eyes, all the blind girls will be begging for them. A riot of vainglorious children popping their marbles in and out while their teachers crawl beneath beds and tables chasing these ridiculous apparatus. No, I will not have it, so you and Miss Wight might as well tell her and get it over with."

Sarah uncurled her fist so she could write, but Laura almost immediately interrupted her teacher. "She says the pain is fine," Sarah told them, "and that she'll pay."

Laura had made quite a tidy sum recently from sales of her crocheted doilies, called antimacassars, used to protect furniture from being stained by the Macassar oil men were now using to slick back their hair. But Julia knew it wouldn't make a difference if Laura paid or not; the emperor's mind was made up.

"I'll just tell her that you say no, that it's simply not possible," Sarah said, and Laura's hand shrunk away. Before Sarah could stop her, Laura went down, kneeling in supplication, her upended hoopskirt a bone-limned half-moon behind her. Julia stood her ground and Sarah stood beside her. They were two strong women and a weeping child to confront him.

Chev stepped forward and addressed Sarah. "Miss Wight, while it is commendable that you are keeping company with Mrs. Howe during her lonely and apparently unbearable confinement, please remember that your allegiance must always be sincerely pledged to your employer, and not to my wife, who has absolutely nothing whatsoever to do with the running of the Institution."

Julia forced herself, just for a second, to meet his eyes, which were large and beautiful and shining and completely resolute, before she swept out of the room.

He didn't speak to her for a week after that, dinners suffered in silence followed by his reading the papers. He knew that this punishment caused her the greatest agony, to be abandoned by his company. It was not an unusual practice for him, but rarely had it lasted this long. And to think she was enduring this treatment on account of Laura, of all people! After the first two evenings, she gave up on any attempts at conversation, met as they were by grunts. And then Friday and Saturday nights he stayed over in town at Sumner's, not even sending word where he was, though of course she knew. When he returned on Sunday afternoon, she resolved to regain his favor, if for no other reason than that she had no one to talk to besides Sarah and Jeannette, who was even duller than Sarah. Chev came in sweaty from riding, and she followed his scent, most beloved by her, into his bedroom. She wished that she could have gone riding with him, but her condition prevented strenuous exercise. She doubted she would even be capable of mounting a horse this far along. He did not acknowledge that she had entered the room, and she watched him strip down out of his riding clothes. His hair shone almost black with dampness, curling in tendrils around his neck; he needed it trimmed, a task she was sometimes allowed and that she performed with pleasure. She stared at the dark, matted V of his bare chest, her favorite place to nuzzle in all the world. How well she remembered the first time she had seen him naked that night in the swaying bow of their room aboard the ship. No great sculpture—not Michelangelo's *David* in Florence or the Discus Thrower in the British Museum—had ever moved her so well or so quickly. Now he turned away from her, standing in front of the armoire in only his breeches and riding boots. She tiptoed up behind him and rested her head against his back—she only came up to his shoulders— and slowly slid her hands down his abdomen and toward his waistband, feeling the tightening sinew beneath her fingers. She was acutely aware of her belly rounded against him, but she brought with it all of her warmth, her femaleness, and yes, in this instance, her humility.

He turned so suddenly that he had to grab her shoulders to right her. "What do you think you're doing?"

"I thought...I thought you might want me," she said.

"When you are this far gone?" he said, releasing her and stepping back. "You would endanger your child for a moment's wantonness? You are long out of season."

"It's not wanton," she said. "I just thought...It's out of love that I—"

"The things you would do for *love* are nearly as strange as the things you would not do for it."

And still she stood before him, her breath rising, willing him to want her, even out of season, but he strode past her toward the armoire.

"I must dress for dinner," he said. "Sumner and I are meeting up with Longo."

"But you spent the last two nights—"

"What do you want to hear? You should be happy for me that God in his mercy has granted me one person who is always aligned with my wishes. Would that it were my wife, but we both know it is sadly otherwise."

"He is always in season," she murmured, though even as she uttered the words, she was not quite sure of their meaning.

"What did you say?"

"Less than nothing." And with that she left him and crossed the hall to her room, where she buried herself in the satin pillows and wept until she came down with hiccups that lasted for hours, depriving her of her solitary dinner. Finally she slept, with both hands folded between her legs as if in prayer for her helpless and thwarted desire.

Julia had fashioned for herself a nest at the top of the stairs on the landing leading to the attic. Just enough room for a child's desk, which she'd carried herself up six flights from the schoolroom in the dead of night, stealthy as a robber in her own home. But no one caught her that night, and so far no one had discovered her hiding place. It was here and only here that she could devote herself wholly and completely to her writing and the readings. And it was here that she could ride out her melancholia, sometimes weeks or months afflicted. "The old black dog," she called her doldrums. She had met the dog long before her marriage; however, she had been capable of calling him to heel then, and now he ran amok, unleashed. He howled loudest when she was in rowing season with Chev or when she was pregnant, though the joy at the birth of her children released her in an instant. She felt grateful that she wasn't doom-laden after childbirth, as she knew some women to be. She couldn't suffer through these spells in her own bedroom, as she desperately wanted to do, because being abed attracted Chev's attention and scorn. And if she stayed downstairs at her desk in her room or even in the library, she was sure to be nagged by one of the children or Cook or one of the housemaids asking her direction on some household matter: Should we have powder biscuits or plain tonight? Would she like the blankets washed completely after Florence's accident or just the spot attended to? Would madam be requiring the seamstress next week or would she be going to town for her fitting?

The only time she cared about attending to these ridiculous and myriad details was when she was planning a party or when someone she liked or needed was coming for tea, such as Reverend Parker (or Teddy, as she called him in private), with whom she could discuss the Greeks, so different from the usual stuffed-shirt churchman. Except for her darling sisters, away in New York, Julia hadn't much use for the female sex, preferring the company of learned men with whom she could wage battle through debate, banter, or if all else failed, the batted eyelashes or the demure hand on theirs. She was known as a flirt as much as a wit, both of which her husband despised. One would think he'd been tricked into marrying a belle instead of a cook and nursemaid.

Also matched as a running battle was her willingness to hand the children over to their nursemaids more often than he thought healthy. It was true: Chev was the dotingest of fathers, and while she loved her babies with all the considerable power of her heart, they did little enough for her brain, to the point where she felt it had nearly atrophied during each of her three pregnancies. Between that and the sickness (which only a man could have described as "morning") from which she now, in her sixth month, had only begun to have respite, she would be over the moon not to bear another child. How she wished, how she had argued, for the kind of companionate arrangement that Harriet Beecher Stowe was rumored to have worked out with her husband: alternating years devoted to her work and the sharing of her bedroom. And yet here Chev berated her for the loss of affection even when she was weaning and raged against the publication of each bouquet of verse, small and delicate though they were. And as great as his seemingly endless compassion and genuine fondness for his enfeebled pupils was, he was indifferent to his wife's isolation from the gay society to which she had been accustomed since birth. Not only did he keep the divine nightingale caged in the Institution, far from Boston's social whirl (it could never rival New York, but Beacon Hill was a glittering beacon indeed compared to the mundanities, and even indignities, of life among the blind), but half the great house was left unlit to save on expenses because the children had no use for light! At least that helped Julia creep about in the shadows, hiding her from those who would dog her with inanities.

But most hurtful was Chev's complete lack of sympathy for the fears that held her captive with each confinement—would she die giving birth this time, as her mother had of puerperal fever when she was five, and as nearly half of all women seemed to, especially the poor? He was a doctor, for God's sake, and yet he would not stay in attendance at her bedside during labor until the last possible moment, the moment when he could wrench *his* child from her womb and behold the glory, which he seemed to believe he had achieved without her help, as if she were the mere vessel for his lineage. Oh, how Chev loved his children, even with two out of the three girls, a fact that would have appalled many men. And yes, yes, and yes, she had to admit that he loved her too, because no man could possibly be capable of greater ardor or attention to his marital duties when he was allowed. And yes again, despite herself, she was captive too to that ancient bond, though her husband didn't believe how much she adored him physically. But was it worth all the trouble? She was constantly torn, and so the fabric of their marriage. She didn't know how other women did it, gave in and stayed pregnant and half-brained until forty, with the nippers pulling at their filthy skirts.

Only here, in her aerie—which had for her become as enchanted as a fairy tower, though it lacked any natural light and she fought the good fight with the wasps who'd built their nests in the eaves, the spiders and dust mites that crept across her couplets by the light of her one purloined candle—did she find peace and solace from her lot. How she longed for the bright yellow-curtained room of her girlhood. Often she stopped, pen in midair, and imagined what her life would have been had she chosen one of her many New York beaux, those planets around her fiery sun, but the dream would vanish into the ether when she remembered when she'd first beheld Samuel Gridley Howe, riding in on his black stallion straight out of a fairy tale the day Sumner had brought her to the Institution to meet Laura. There were no eyes like that in Gotham, none she'd ever seen, that sharp and fathomless blue that had held her attention from the first moment, and still did, when she allowed herself to really look at him, which was not often because of the power he held over her, even now at forty-five to her tender twenty-eight. Those eyes, which never left hers as he panted above her, still open even at the moment of release. Ah, tarnation, she did not climb these steps to think about her husband! Swedenborg was calling to her, and Hegel, her dear ones, who kept their hold on her higher faculties even while Dr. Howe maintained his grasp on her lower ones.

The next weekend, when she'd assumed Chev would again be spending his nights in town, he showed up well past the dinner hour with Sumner.

Julia was flustered. "You could have sent word ahead," she told her husband, as he and Sumner draped their jackets over the dining room chairs.

"Ah, but Charlie here got it in his head that he had to see you, it had been too long," Chev said, and Sumner made an elaborate bow and kissed her hand.

"But I would have had Cook fix a proper service and I would have dressed—"

"Diva Julia looks as lovely as ever," Sumner said.

He knew how she hated that nickname; after all, he was the one who'd given it to her during her courtship. And she knew she did not look her best—she was wearing a simple sprigged muslin festooned with the drying stains of baby spit-up.

"The children are already in bed," she told them. "I hope Cook is still about so she can—"

"But my darling," Chev said as he took his seat at the head of the table, "surely you can whip up a small repast for two starving gentlemen."

Julia felt her cheeks flaming. He knew good and well she didn't cook; as a matter of fact, he regularly abused her for that and for other domestic failings. Have mercy, she'd grown up without a mother to school her in the proper management of a household and the disciplining of the help. Of course, she also had no interest in learning to eviscerate a duck or a piglet, to stew tortoises and hares, to labor for hours over making sure the tea cakes were frosted just so.

"A simple hasty pudding would be fine," Sumner said and actually winked at her. "I do remember you pulling off an almost creditable blancmange years ago, so you must have some magic."

"And should I rouse Laura to entertain you, Charlie?" Julia knew how the two detested each other. "It must be ages since you've seen her."

"The always titillating paradox that she can be seen and yet cannot see," Sumner said. "It never grows old. So thank you, but I think for this evening, you can leave the Eighth Wonder be."

Julia was too furious to speak, so she left them for the kitchen, and found it dark and empty. She hurried down the back corridor to Cook's room, but there was no light under the door. The woman was nearly seventy and the rheumatism was making her job difficult, so Julia knew it would be wrong to wake her for the Doctor's caprices. A hasty pudding, yes, she could do that, blast them both to Hades. Did it take oats or cornmeal? She racked her brain. Eliza Leslie's famous cookbook—where was it? Maybe it was flour. In the enormous open pantry, she found the cornmeal first. She dumped some out into a large iron pot with salt and lit the stove, then looked round for the mush-stick she'd seen Cook use to stir it to prevent lumps. The worst thing about hasty pudding was that although it was relatively easy, it actually couldn't be made in haste or it wouldn't thicken properly. So Julia stirred and stirred until her arm grew numb, but the mush still had lumps the size of doorknobs, which she finally beat down to the size of buttons. She checked her watch—it had been well over half an hour, so that would have to do. She pulled some cured pork from the larder and scraped the pudding into matching bowls.

The mistress of the house entered the dining room bearing the tray and set it down with a clatter. Chev glanced at Sumner with obvious amusement.

"Looks most worthy," Sumner said.

"Yes, well, it is what is," Julia said, "so eat."

Chev said a much longer grace than usual, taking care to bless the abundance of the feast before them.

"A toast," Sumner said, tapping his spoon against his goblet. "To Diva Julia, South Boston's hostess *sans pareil.*"

Julia almost bit clean through the rim of her glass. Of course, South Boston was a virtual wasteland with no prominent houses or hostesses. "Charlie, you know how much I admire your cleverness, but also how much I dislike that ridiculous name."

Sumner raised his glass again. "Diva Julia lives up to her sobriquet, though she still objects with *but* and *yet.*"

Chev laughed so hard he almost choked on his pudding, which was probably choke-worthy anyway, and Charlie grinned from ear to ear. It was unusual to see him so happy, she'd give him that. Why were they so bent on the task of humiliating her this evening, and in tandem? Had they come specifically for that purpose? "Gentlemen, I am tired and so I'll take my leave." She stood, but Chev grabbed her hand.

"Darling, please stay. It's been such a moon since Charlie's seen you. And here I thought you'd be pleased that we came here instead of dining in town."

Julia sat back down and poured herself a second very large glass of sherry, a very rare thing for her, especially when she was this far along. As usual, her husband and his friend delighted loudly in their inside jokes, their endless arguments over political and social issues, which gave them both such obvious pleasure even when they violently disagreed. All this Julia was forced to endure from her corner of the table, and to wish—not for the first time and surely not for the last—that she, Julia Ward, one of the endlessly desired Graces of Bond Street, had been born a man.

Chev was circling back to a topic that would needle her. "Do you remember last year when Fanny Longfellow's cook went down with the pleurisy, and she plucked all the chickens herself and came up with those ravishing five courses for the dozen of us?"

Julia had heard this story recounted endlessly.

"How could I possibly forget?" Sumner said. "And by the way, this pudding is a masterpiece."

"And when might you be blessed with a wife of your own, Charlie, to cook for you?"

Julia had attempted to play matchmaker several times, since after all, with his money and connections, he was considered an excellent catch. Yet her ladies to a one reported back to her that while his manners were impeccable, his conversation consisted solely of monologues, and while that could be put up with in a gentleman of his station, his complete lack of interest in their charms could not. "What a slippery one you are! My cousin Charlotte swore you didn't seem to notice she was even in the room at luncheon last week. She is so lovely, isn't she, Chev?"

Her husband nodded, unsure of how to counter this attack.

Julia wagged her finger at their guest. "When a man waits too long to find a mate, his meat grows cold upon his plate."

Charlie set his glass down. "In the jungle, they say, it's to be deduced, when the lioness denies, the lion will be—"

"Stop it, both of you!" Chev stood. "What are you, children in the nursery?"

"Very clever children," Julia said.

"Very playful children," Charlie agreed.

Chev sat back down. "True combatants do not use rhymes for battle."

Sumner took a long sip of port and pushed back his heavy forelock. As the years passed, he'd come to resemble nothing so much as an overstuffed horse, and probably a Trojan one to boot. "I thank you both, as always, for your continued attention to my poor bachelor state, but I have yet to find a lady who might live up to the memory of my dear mother, or even a helpmeet so satisfactory as Mrs. Longfellow."

Chev sighed. "The wrong choice, I assure you, can doom you to a life of misery."

Julia knew that her face was probably as red as her hair, but she couldn't stop herself, not this time. "As for the brayingly domestic Fanny, she's good for a dollop of gossip over tea, but the chicken was half-raw. One must never confuse the duties of the wife of a great poet with the duties of a great poet who is also a wife." The world would probably never uphold the distinction, but for now she could be happy that she'd hushed two of Boston's biggest mouths, the grand orator and the almighty humanitarian. She left the room knowing that she might not be able to sleep for replaying this small triumph in her head, but that it would be well worth it.

Chapter 12
Sarah, 1847

For weeks Sarah had hardly slept, staying vigilant for the slightest sound from the adjoining room. She was even more concerned than usual that Laura would seek comfort in the night, given her latest disappointment. At least she had stopped talking about the glass eyes, though she swore to her teacher that when she was "grown" she would get them in spite of Doctor. Frankly, Sarah hoped so. She rose at least three times a night to check on Laura, but every time she appeared to be fast asleep, her fingers signing against the quilt as they did when she dreamed. In the daytime, they continued easily with their studies, the only difference in their routine occurring at mealtimes, when Laura asked to switch from her usual table with just the two of them to the table of the oldest blind girls. Of course, she didn't know that some of them were her complainants; she must have thought they missed her nighttime company and sought to make it up to them. She reached across the plates often to grab at the girls' hands, usually Tessy's. The girls allowed her play in the dining hall, but although Laura couldn't hear their groans and giggles, her teacher could. Sarah made a point of not listening to their whispered conversations, and only when she heard Laura's name spoken loudly did she admonish them. Tessy had been her student last year, and though she was intelligent and generally well behaved, she had a mean streak. Sarah thought she would have been very pretty if her general expression were less of a sneer. If only she could have seen her own face.

The truth was that Sarah had never felt for any of her students anything like the affection she maintained for Laura. It wasn't pity, though, of course, a large dose of that came naturally, but a true love of her curiosity, as annoying as it could sometimes be, and an admiration for her stubborn optimism and self-regard, neither of which her teacher could fathom in the girl's ridiculously pathetic circumstances. Sarah, on her best day, could not compete with Laura in sheer strength of spirit. The Creator had, in His one stroke of mercy, graced the girl from within. Sarah knew that if she were afflicted with Laura's deformities, she would probably have been dead long ago, never having left her bed. Some days now she could barely leave it, what with the spells, which Doctor seemed to think were a symptom of her weak emotional constitution rather than her physical one, though she was hardly robust. Maybe he was right, though she'd cried for days after he'd told her. His eyes had not held even the smallest light of empathy on that occasion, but rather a steely glint of reprobation. Sarah thought of herself as a shadow, as blanched as her surname suggested, a woman never completely there, who might fade at any moment into the very air. If she was white, then Laura was a bright, blinding yellow or a shocking blue, some glorious hue of rapturous sky.

On a night when the humidity wouldn't allow her to sleep, when she stuck to her dressing gown, which stuck to the sheet, Sarah rose at midnight to check on Laura. Good, she was there, but Sarah thought she would get too warm under the coverlet pulled up over her. When she went to turn it down, she found only the lumpy goose down pillow. Oh Lord, Sarah wondered, had she pulled the same trick the other nights? Sarah stalked down the hall, tiptoeing from one room to another. Each room held four to six beds; only Laura had a room to herself. Sarah had to bend down over each bed to see anything, though, because the rooms were kept pitch-black. No need to light the night lamps for these students. One of the girls woke up and Sarah quieted her. It was frightening for the blind to wake to someone standing over them, with no idea who it was. Perpetual night. Sarah didn't think she'd ever have been able to get used to it; she supposed old age might force her to find out, and she dreaded it, perhaps even more so because of her experience. She expected to discover Laura in Tessy's bed, but no. In the first bed in the last room down the long corridor, she found her, one leg thrown over one of the new students, both hands tangled in the girl's long blonde curls. They were both asleep, and though Laura had probably hurt the girl, playing with her hair, she was new and would have been afraid to cry out or go for a teacher.

Sarah shook Laura's shoulder and she stirred. The girl woke too and asked, "Who's there?"

"Laura's teacher," Sarah said. She shook Laura again, but Laura brushed her away and turned back over, spooning against the girl. Sarah had no choice. She grabbed Laura's arm and tried to pull her up, but she resisted. She hoisted Laura from the bed with all her strength, and the girl struggled, kicking against her. The new girl jumped out of the bed on the other side. Laura began to yelp, the most terrible of her noises, something between a wolf howling and a baby bawling, and fought Sarah as she was pulled onto the floor with the bedclothes. Several of the students had woken and stood bunched in the doorway. Sarah almost laughed at the idea that she was being *watched* by a bevy of blind girls.

Suddenly Jeannette pushed her way in, her long stocking cap askew over her gray braids. "Shoo!" she told the girls. Jeannette was tall and broad-shouldered like her brother, and within a minute, Laura had been tamed and lay motionless on the floor. The new girl cowered in the corner while two of the older ones patted and soothed her. The women tried to pick Laura up, but she kept her limbs completely limp, as if dead, except for the low whimpering sound she now made. Sarah took her arms and Jeannette her legs, and they carried her down the hall to her room and lay her back in her own bed. She moved only to pat her shade, making sure it was still in place, then locked her arms rigidly at her sides. She knew what was coming.

Jeannette got the gloves from the bottom drawer of the tallboy. Sarah hadn't even known where they were kept because she'd never had to use them. Jeannette held them out to her.

"You should do it," Jeannette said.

"I know." But still she hesitated; Laura would know instantly that it was her beloved teacher punishing her. She turned to Jeannette. "Are you sure—?"

Jeannette nodded emphatically. "When she gets that way, she needs to know there's a consequence. It's your job to make sure she conducts herself like a young lady, not a wild beast."

"And she won't just pull them off?"

"No, this is a bitter pill she takes when she knows she deserves it."

Sarah looked at her ward; she was absolutely still, so small and defenseless, barely breathing it seemed. But then she saw it: Laura's lower lip was protruding the way it did whenever she was defiant, and Sarah could see now that the girl's jaw was set firm. She wasn't sorry. It had to be done. Sarah took the gloves. Oh no, they were not soft cotton as she'd expected, but a coarse, scratchy wool. They would be awful in the heat. And they were dark gray; she wished for Julia's light silken church gloves, pale pink or creamy mint.

She lifted Laura's right hand gently and eased the glove on, pushing down in the valleys between the fingers to make sure all was snug. She resisted the urge to write any comfort or apology, but as she gloved the left hand, she began to cry, though Laura herself didn't appear to be crying. The protruding lower lip didn't tremble. It was the cruelest thing Sarah had ever done in her life. With the gloves on, it was nearly impossible for Laura to communicate with anyone. Though her punishment was deserved, it seemed worse than the solitary confinement with which they punished criminals, because not only would she be cut off from all human contact, she would also lose all but the roughest impressions of the world itself. Touch, her one intact sense, and now it was thickened and furred almost to nullity by the gloves, an item that on other young ladies her age would mean they were going out for a stroll.

"There, there," Jeannette said, patting Sarah's back as she stood up. "You're a wonderful teacher, but sometimes you must be hard."

Sarah wiped at her eyes. "How long, do you think?"

Jeannette sighed. "Well, if she doesn't have to wear them daytime so she can't talk to anybody, it's not much of a punishment, is it?"

"Tonight and all tomorrow then."

Jeannette nodded. "Let's go round and get them all tucked back in. Then we'll have a nice cup of tea."

Sarah looked down at the girl on the bed: the hair wild, escaped from its bun, the white cotton dressing gown hiked up, revealing one painfully thin leg, and the hands, still rigid at her sides, now isolated in gray wool.

Dawn found Sarah still awake, and she rose to meet the day with fresh tears, knowing that last night's scene would unfold again and again.

Chapter 13

Laura, 1849

Mr. Edward Bond is here to see me—again. The third Sunday this month! I knew it wouldn't be long until I had a proper suitor. I am fair to pleasing, I think, dark-haired and pale; my features regular, only my nose a little long. "Petite," I have had spelled into my palm many times, and Mama says I am like a little bird. Who might not love a little bird, I am hopeful, even if it is locked in a dark and silent cage?

But then, of course, the question: Does the little bird desire to be stroked by any hand that reaches into its cage? So far, I haven't taken any special care with my dressing for his visits, but now is time. I put on my green muslin and the bonnet to match my shade. It's last year's dress, but Miss Wight says I look fresh as springtime, perfect for our walk in the garden. I asked for my usual new spring dress, but Doctor said that the Institution couldn't afford such a luxury this year. A luxury? One new dress a season for the second-most-famous woman in the world? I'll wager Julia is decked out in the best from Paris, straight from the pages of *Godey's Lady's Book*.

In the drawing room, Mr. Bond is waiting, and when I enter, he kisses my hand. His lips are a bit dry, and his touch slightly clammy, as always, so this does not endear him to me. He is taller than I am, but not by much, I can tell, and the bones of his hand and wrist are slight.

Miss Wight walks between us to handle our conversation, because at my age, Doctor has deemed it unwise that unmarried men might hold my hand for the time required for real talking. He is right, I'm sure; I want no liberties taken, and yet I'm tired of Wightie's fingers always as interlocutor. The novelty and variety of different touches has always been one of my greatest joys, and now I am allowed only the fingers of women, children, and old men, just at the time when a young man tickling my palm might interest me.

So Wight converses with him, and relays the information back and forth. I trust her to give me, mostly unvarnished, the truth of what my visitors say. When charged with the same simple task, Jeannette will deliver to me only what she believes will do me good, an astonishing rudeness, which she freely admits. Doctor apparently agrees with her that sometimes I am to be "protected," from what I am not exactly certain. Surely not from the spiritually enriching words of a Harvard Divinity student such as Mr. Bond? I have had to reprimand Doctor for opening my letters before he gives them to Wightie to read to me. I have a vast correspondence, from the First Lady Mrs. Polk down to the most pedestrian of devotees, and he has no more right to monitor my letters than I have to read his. He did not take that very well, of course, and we shall see if he honors my request.

On Mr. Bond's first couple of visits, the conversation was dreadfully dull, so I try to liven it a bit today by asking him which dances he prefers, but Wight says that's not a proper question for a man I hardly know. Mostly we just walk the grounds, and I take care to point out the wisteria bushes, the chrysanthemums, and the rhododendron, all of which I know by touch. "Sniff," I urge him, "and tell me what they smell like."

In reply, Miss Wight writes only, "Sweet."

"No, exactly how they smell," I ask, but again all I get is "Sweet." Not a poetic soul. I must ask Longo the next time he's by to see Doctor. I would eat the flowers if I could.

Later, as she helps ready me for bed, I ask Wightie if Mr. Bond is handsome, but she demurs from stating an opinion and gives me instead only the concrete details I request. Hair, blond and fine—much like her own, she says—but hardly a whisker on him, and him twenty-eight! I like thicker hair, wish I could get my hand in his to test it. Maybe I can arrange a way. Eyes, hazel, she says, a color name with which I'm not familiar. Wight, poor darling, tries hard, and finally comes up with a description: "a patch of dirt lit by sunlight." I try to imagine this, the sun-glazed brown of his eyes, which must be regarding me so carefully. Has all his teeth, she reports, and the clothes befitting a young Unitarian minister-to-be, shabby but very neat. She assures me he is absolutely refined in all his demeanor, but I can tell she can't muster the passion with which she has described a select few other gentlemen, such as Julia's brother, Sam Ward.

"Favorite book of the Bible?" Mr. Bond asks on his fourth visit.

"Revelation," I answer because I know this will be the most shocking. Imagine the young lady who desires the company of the Four Horsemen of the Apocalypse! The truth is I've only heard bits of the more awful details of that book, since Doctor won't let me read it; it's the one book of the Bible that the Institution press has not presented. "A detriment to young minds," Doctor says, but he obviously knows little of what really transpires inside my head. If the world is indeed going to end, I deserve to be as prepared for it as everyone else. I believe that in that last glorious blaze, I will finally be able to see everything—for good or for ill—all things bright and beautiful and terrible, and to hear the children wailing and the angels singing and the devils gnashing their teeth.

Miss Wight pats my hand in exasperation, and I know she's told Mr. Bond that I have not indeed read Revelation. Heaven knows, if Wightie can handle it, with her meek and gentle disposition, then I am well equipped to do so. Mr. Bond then asks which book I actually cherish, and I decide to give him the truth. Easy: the Psalms. The Psalms are beautiful, most of them, though for all his poetry, King David whines incessantly, as, of course, does Job. I tell Wight this, but I don't know if she relays it to Mr. Bond. She is perhaps censoring me, though not, of course, to the extent that Jeannette would or that Doctor would probably desire.

My suitor says he approves of my choice. It is refreshing to have someone interested in my spiritual progress and opinions, since Doctor does nothing but try to quash them. In turn, I ask his favorite, and he says that after the Gospels, which he thinks are the most important, he would choose Proverbs. He is wise; I am lyrical. We might make a good match, after all, even with the fine hair.

Genesis I have often pondered, and I wonder if I should share my thoughts with my suitor. Michael, the archangel, was thrown out of heaven for challenging God. Dare I consider that might be how I lost my senses, thrown out of the ordinary and essential garden of man, where all the senses are thoughtlessly indulged, out into the blackness beyond Eden's gates, left only with the feeling of my fingers scraping at the gate, scrabbling about in the endless dark.

"Mr. Bond," I write, "if I were Eve, I wouldn't take the apple."

"Why?"

"I cannot taste and I hate snakes." I can tell he is impressed and is now contemplating how the world might have turned out very differently indeed if Adam's mate had been a clever but fever-crippled girl like me instead of the sense-full and silly Eve. Oh, I *know* that the apple represents the hunger for knowledge, but it is too delicious to take a wee poke at a theologian.

Since we are now in the mood for gardens, I lead Mr. Bond to the rosebush by the entrance gate, which I'm told boasts the reddest blooms. He picks a rose for me, which even I know is an established sign of courtship, and presses it carefully between my fingers. I hold the tightly closed bud to my cheek—why did he not give me an open flower?—and rub the petals against my skin, back and forth, back and forth, imagining the hand of a friend, perhaps even Mr. Bond. I revel in the softness upon softness even as I know I am destroying the flower. And then I can't help myself; I lower the stem and rake the thorns into the hollow of my neck. What ecstasy! What proof of God.

Wight grabs the rose and dabs at my neck with a handkerchief. "In front of Mr. Bond!" she writes. Well, if a minister can't manage blood and beauty, then he is in the wrong business.

I have read in all four Gospels about the crown of thorns nettling Christ's head, the nails driven through His precious skin, His side pierced by the sword. It is all terrible perfection. Julia has given me a crucifix she bought in Rome, and the knowledge that she truly cares about me is nearly as precious as the object itself. I spend hours tracing the lines of His body: the long, writhing limbs; the beard like Doctor's; the splayed palms and feet. I have begged Doctor for a cross, even a small one to wear around my neck, but he won't give in. Unitarians don't take well to the violence of the crucifixion. "Think of the ascension, not the suffering," he says, but the transfiguration I can't imagine, while the crucifixion feels like second nature.

"Dress spoiled," Wight spells. I loathe having even one crumb of dirt or food defile my clothes, but the red blood on the green cloth sounds quite lovely. If Mr. Bond is a true man of God, he will find it lovely too.

I began to bleed below last year. So that was what Miss Swift was talking about. Since I have never cut myself there, I didn't understand. Wight said it happens to every girl and it means that you are a woman. "What does it mean to be a woman?" She told me it means you can fall in love and have babies.

"You bleed? Jeannette? Julia?" Yes, yes, and yes, she tells me. I can't imagine the dark blood pooling between Julia's legs beneath the fine silk petticoats. Does Doctor like it?

That night I ask Wight if Mr. Bond was upset by the events of the afternoon.

"He's fine," she says, and so I think maybe I will consider him as a possibility, though it would mean going off to the Sandwich Islands where he plans to be a missionary. Wightie would miss me unbearably, and, of course, so would Doctor, for all his grumbling.

"Bond likes me?"

"Yes, he likes you."

"I'll wear blue dress next."

"You don't need..." Her fingers trail off. "He isn't..." And again she doesn't finish. Dear Wightie. She is concerned that this little man of the cloth is not good enough for me, but I will be the judge.

"Don't worry," I say, "understand," and she holds my hand long in hers, as if she is making sure I'll have no regrets. Of course, a woman as celebrated as I am must be extremely careful to choose well for love.

So this night I allow myself to think a bit of Mr. Bond as my hands go down. I imagine surprising him on our wedding day with my glowing blue eyes, and then that night he gives me Revelation at last, scoring fire and brimstone and apocalypse into my palm. It is working; I feel the beginning of wetness. Usually I think of sitting in Doctor's lap, or about Tessy rubbing against me. I am very careful, though, to wait for at least an hour after going to bed before I begin, when I know most everyone on the floor should be asleep. Last year, I was on my stomach (Tessy let me in on that trick) since of course I can't hear anyone coming, and if I am mightily preoccupied—as I am tonight—then I won't feel even the slight vibrations from footsteps on the wooden floor. That night, I was shocked from my trance by a sudden smack on my upper arm, and I pushed down my nightdress and turned over, my hands up, waiting for the intruder to write upon them. Instead, a fist came down on my forehead and "*no*" was rapped across my brow by hard knuckles. I pulled the blankets up under my chin, and a minute later, a cold, dripping washcloth was flung at my face. Every night for the next month, the gloves were left on top of my pillow and taken away again the next morning. I made sure that the gloves were spotless, unspoiled, but it was a struggle. At least they were cotton ones, not the scratchy wool with which I'd been gloved before. I am still not sure whether it was Wight who found me or Jeannette, or to my greatest horror, maybe Julia, who was staying here because the Institution was short of help. It wasn't the first time, and it certainly wasn't the last, no matter how many times they gloved me.

No one can comprehend the multitude of pleasures I receive from my fingertips, the hours I can spend stroking Pozzo's wiry, tangled fur, careening my fingers down the long whip of his tail, rubbing the softness of his firm belly. And the ladies' clothes! Their silks and satins, even the roughness of the out-of-towner's cotton broadcloths; the deep crush of velvet collars and the short, nappy rub of their felt hats. And I am never more stirred than when I find the sharp quill of a plume on a hat and can surrender myself to the feather.

I have devoured the scriptures—I am a very fast reader—and have never found anything that I believe speaks against my explorations of my body. I contend that the unique condition my Maker has forced upon me for His own unintelligible reasons might also grant me an exception—a special pardon, if you will—when it comes to touching. The sensitive, peaking nipples of my breasts and that whole silken netherworld are God's gifts to me. My universe is manifest only through my fingertips, and I refuse to be a stranger to it.

Mr. Bond has done well by me tonight, and I am pleased. I kneel and offer a prayer to my Lord who has favored me with such raptures.

Chapter 14
Chev, 1849

Chev supervised the placement of the hundreds of skulls around the Institution's Exhibition Hall, even dusting some of the cases himself. Less interesting were the busts and plaster casts of famous heads, though he was happy to have the bust of Voltaire, which clearly showed the bulges of language, mirthfulness, and vitality. The skull of an Indian, bullet hole notwithstanding, made concrete the combativeness, destructiveness, and secretiveness inherent in that race's nature as a whole. As the president of the Boston Phrenological Society, the preeminent American arm initiated by Spurzheim himself on his trip from Germany in the late '30s, Chev was responsible for the country's largest collection of phrenological specimens. The maids had set up tall vases of red roses between every few cases, and the contrast between the crimson petals and the ivory patina of the shining skulls pleased him immensely. It would prove a grand day for the Perkins annual fund-raiser with the Chevalier at the helm, where, of course, he always preferred to be. Governor Briggs and most of Boston's society were coming, even some bigwigs from New York and Providence, all ready to dig deep into their pockets and purses to help those less fortunate. And Chev's friend and ally, Horace Mann, who in addition to being the secretary of the state Board of Education was also an avid phrenologist, planned on making the gala the upcoming feature of his popular *Common School Journal*, which had already faithfully documented Laura's progress over the years. It was important for Chev to show his solidarity with Mann and to open more keenly the eyes of New England's elite to the true basis for his internationally lauded work in education. To that end, besides displaying all his finest specimens, he had invited Dr. Combe to give the opening demonstration and lecture.

Chev was well aware that many of the guests would be there for the explicit purpose of seeing and, if possible, meeting Laura, but at this stage of croquet, he dared not give her any real platform. At the last two exhibitions—fairly small ones, thank God—she had not only answered questions about religion, but had continued to expound on her increasingly Calvinist views until he rushed the stage and took away the French board on which she was writing. For the fund-raiser, he had come up with a beautiful plan to exhibit his "crowning glory," as he often ruefully still thought of her, while keeping her opinions from polluting the crowd, though he admitted that her evangelical leanings would actually prove of great appeal to at least half of them. The problem was that Laura knew that too. Chev wanted to sway the crowd his way—the right way—not merely to persuade them to hand over their money based on purely philanthropic interests. He and his fellow enlightened Unitarians had waged the battle so long and so hard to showcase Laura as proof that the young and pure would come naturally to God without having the Bible crammed down their throats in the Calvinist fashion, so he wasn't about to give up the fight now. And so she would sit only as Combe's subject, while he traced her history and accomplishments on her very skull. He had told Laura that she and Combe would open the ceremony, and though she was not that warm on phrenology anymore, she always liked to be the center of attention, and so she eagerly agreed. When she asked, "Then I talk?" he told her that this time the schedule for the event was packed tight, with the blind girls giving a chorale and the boys displaying their woodworking, not to mention his own speech, and a tour of the facilities. She wasn't happy, but she'd acquiesced and coquettishly added that she would arrange her hair in "spaniel's ears" for the occasion, that style being the height of fashion. Again, her vanity preceded her moral capacity. Perhaps he could get Combe to batten down that vice as he worked her over. Just imagine what a preening bird of paradise she'd have become with false and gleaming colored eyes.

The hall was full, the air scented with lavender and sweet French wine. The overflow, which Jeannette had made sure were the more pedestrian of folks, was corralled into the marble foyer, some even perching on the stairs. The blind girls were all dressed and ready in matching sky-blue jumpers, the boys hatted and suspendered. Chev rushed to and fro overseeing last-minute details—did Combe have his spectacles, his gold-plated calipers instead of the silver? Chev finally took his place on the dais beside his wife. Julia had never looked more lovely, he thought, rosy in the glow of new motherhood, still plump from the pregnancy the way he liked her, his son swaddled in her arms. Chev knew the baby's tiny skull was still developing, and yet he sometimes couldn't stop himself from fingering his way around his soft spot, from which he knew great potential would manifest. To his surprise, even Laura had managed to look reasonably inviting for the occasion, dressed in a simple white gown that highlighted her ethereal features, making her look the part of the angel in the cage, which was what he still called her on good days. On bad days, he referred to her as a squawking emu, but only to Sumner, the one person with whom he could truly and openly share both his soul's delights and its travails, however petty. He hazarded a quick wink at his friend, who smiled back from his gilt chair in the front row.

The pianoforte thrummed, and the audience clapped enthusiastically as Laura made her way carefully, unassisted, to the stage. She was holding something behind her back, probably a bouquet for Dr. Combe. But as the phrenologist pulled out the chair for her at center stage, she brought forth a foot-high wooden crucifix, intricately carved and so brightly painted that Chev was sure the oozing streams of blood could be seen from the back of the hall. Chev recognized it immediately; it was the hideous souvenir Julia had insisted on buying outside the Vatican, a garish relic of propaganda. And here it was being displayed for all to see as Laura cradled it gently in her arms like a child. A damnably convenient day for Sarah Wight to have suffered one of her spells. Combe clearly didn't know what to do; he hopped from one foot to the other behind Laura's chair, the calipers paused in midair. Chev's instinct was to jump up and grab the thing away from her, but what would look worse than the Director of the Institution struggling with his most celebrated pupil? That would make news, all of it bad, though the cross itself was sure to be mentioned in the broadsheets anyway. He had to sit calmly, not make it worse. He glanced at his wife and saw that her mouth was twitching, contorted, and realized to his horror that she was trying not to *laugh*! Samuel Gridley Howe and *his* God would not be shown for fools. It was no longer worth wearing the mantle of Laura's creator, if she chose to act so brazenly against his wishes and his beliefs. Besides, in truth, he was tired of having his name tied forever to hers because he suspected that hers got top billing. His work with Perkins and his many other causes should provide ample laurels. He rose slowly and motioned Combe to the side of the stage, away from all ears, and spoke with him in a low whisper for a moment only.

Combe nodded and returned to his subject. After the preliminaries, the doctor stopped and then began again. In a somewhat strangled voice, he said that while Laura's chief intellectual faculties remained intact, there appeared to be some disturbance at her crown, where the bumps associated with spirituality and moral rectitude reside. The animal regions at the base of her skull also seemed to be rather engorged, which would help explain the degeneration of her higher proclivities. This was a frequent occurrence in the brains of the severely enfeebled, he concluded.

Chev saw to his great satisfaction that his wife now kept her head down, looking only at his child, who continued to sleep peacefully.

All the while, Laura sat very still, her head erect as Combe tapped away at it. Only her fingers moved in and around the crown of thorns, stroking the head of the Christ as if trying to read in the notches of the wooden skull the very nature of His divinity.

Chapter 15

Laura, 1850

I know that Doctor was not pleased by my showing at the fund-raiser last month, and I could tell that Combe seemed to be troubling over my head. For the first time, his touch was fumbling and hesitant, but I have asked both Julia and Jeannette, and they said all was fine. What a pity Wightie could not leave her sickbed that day. I could trust her for a full report. But she and Julia are both treating me so kindly of late that I could never complain. Doctor left the day after the event, and so we have not spoken. He didn't even say good-bye. But I will patch the rift between us, as I always do, because if Doctor will not accept Mr. Bond, then he must find me a suitable young person, soft-skinned and well-spelled, from among his vast acquaintance for the commencement of the new life for which I am exceedingly ready.

And just in case Combe has in any way disparaged me phreno-logically, then I will endeavor to appeal to Doctor on his terms, however misguided I find them. Clearly, the way to his heart is through my head. First I will fatten my affection bump so that the enormity of my capacity for love will be impossible to miss. I tried once before to elevate its standing at the top of my head by beating on it with the ends of my knitting needles, but that in-creased it hardly at all. Now I have a whole week, and this time I will not shy from employing the best tools at my disposal: the heels of my Sunday lace-up dress boots. I will make certain that

Doctor will not perceive my faculties as greatly changed, but only rendered more pronounced by his acute perception on the matter.

I take the boot with me to bed and pull up the blankets, leaving only the top of my head uncovered. I hit myself hard on the spot I have studied from the raised charts he has given me. Harder, harder, and it hurts, yes, it hurts, but it will be worth it. While I do not believe that my character, especially my ability to love faithfully and well, is sealed within the physiognomy of my skull, Doctor does, and so I rally my cause—*To Love! To Love!*—with each shuddering vibration through my temples and down my jaw. I move the heel of the boot closer to the front of my head and strike at the positions of benevolence and veneration, because I know that these are the qualities that impress Doctor most and are his own largest visible faculties.

I have been careful, ever so careful, to wear my cotton bonnet all week so that no one might observe the heightening of my bumps. I have used the excuse of helping to clean and scrub the premises for Doctor's arrival, because I always wear my bonnet when I clean so that no strands of hair might escape and be dirtied. Miss Wight was pleased because I am an excellent cleaner. If you sit me down and give me some good rags and a bucket of soapy water, I will scrub and scrub until you tell me everything is spotless. This quality will also prove me a good wife; the only bad thing is wearing the heavy cleaning gloves, but they are necessary to protect the softness of my hands, which Doctor will soon be touching.

I run the duster over the top of my armoire and let the feathers stroke the heads of my Laura dolls. As I tickle the tiny molded toes, it occurs to me that if I am to have a *real* life—the *realest* life—then I must no longer allow myself to quicken with these constant reminders of my fame. The little girls who cuddled me are all grown up, and most of them probably have their own babies to play with now, as I intend to. Carefully, I take the dolls down from the armoire and place them in a heap on the bed beside me.

One at a time, I rock each Laura to sleep, humming a tuneless lullaby I'm sure would make a real baby cry, and before I push the dolls into the dark beneath my bed, I untie the ribbon from the sightless eyes of each porcelain head. I braid the ribbons into a thick, soft plait, and then fold it beneath my pillow because Mama says the color green will bring me luck. But it is yearning alone that glimmers in my darkness, and the shades of my deepest desires cannot be described, just as I am certain that the color that is God is not known to any man.

I pat the hands of my clock's glassless face over the armoire—it's almost time! The bonnet comes off and I check the bumps. They are raised and sore, the veneration one, especially. I hope they are not red. I've woken every morning with a headache from the boot's work, but the pain is nothing compared to gaining my share of life's affections. I part my hair in the middle, then make two braids and coil them into buns above my ears so that the bumps are shown to their best advantage. I have even taken the additional charge of plucking a few hairs from the tops of each of them, so that they might be seen more clearly. I change into my best Sunday dress, my only silk one—a rose-pink *robe à l'anglaise* that Miss Wight says gives me color—and lace up the boots that have nearly knocked me senseless. I slip the shade over my eyes and go to meet Doctor, as nervous as I have ever been.

I sit in my chair by the hearth, pinching at my cheeks to redden them, and wave away Wightie's attempts at conversation. I am almost faint with worry when suddenly the air shimmies with heat and I feel the floorboards tense and then shift heavily—Doctor at last! But he doesn't come near me for a good ten minutes, probably talking with Miss Wight, and I force myself to wait patiently for him like a lady. Finally, the chair beside me is pulled out, and his hand takes mine.

"L," he writes, "you're looking very well."

Ah, he has forgiven me already. He lifts my hand to his face so that I may feel myself how well he is looking.

"And you," I write as I limn the familiar perfection of his profile. "How was your trip?"

"Good. What happened to your head?"

"Nothing," I reply. "Fine."

"Looks like a woodpecker got loose. Banged on bed frame?"

That is what he sees—an *accident*—when I want him to see my future? So I am not forgiven. "Still angry about the Jesus?"

"You know it was wrong."

"Calvinists have money too." I'd wager that I actually helped further the causes of the Institution with my display.

"Yes," he says, "but you hurt me very much. And Combe."

I struggle to say I'm sorry, but instead my thumb strays across the beloved hairs on his knuckles. Is it possible that being grownup means one is not forgiven, except by God?

"Dear L," he writes, as if composing a letter to me, as if we were corresponding from across the ocean, though I am trembling right here in his hands. "Made special trip back just for you." His fingers stiffen, as if he's finding it difficult to write, and I worry that he might have contracted the rheumatism. Mama has it, and she can scarcely bend her fingers to converse with me. "Went to see your family."

"Mama and Papa well?"

"Of course," he spells. "Miss you very much, and we all think..." His fingers stop, only the warmth of them hovering above my palm, and then he etches the words into my soul, firmly and furiously. "It's best if you go home."

"For visit?"

"To stay."

My fingers panic; they scrabble all over his palm, paw at his arm. I am squeezing his hands, reaching for his face. Doctor pulls away until I stop moving and sit still, my hands shaking, but folded in my lap. After an eternity, he reaches for me again.

"Education finished here. Nothing left to teach you."

I write as deliberately as he does, though usually we are both so quick with each other that no one else could possibly keep up. "Don't you see I am ready?" I will have to say it. "Ready for love."

"Of course your family loves you," he says, and I realize that he does not see me at all.

"Mr. Bond," I write. I don't really want him but he is what God has presented. I wipe at the wetness soaking through my shade.

He pats my arm. "Don't worry for Wight."

What does Wightie have to do with it? "Wight leaving?"

"Work with you finished."

He has got things all wrong. The heat of the whole house presses down on me, setting alight the useless bumps on my head, and the disembodied eyes of all the blind girls circle me, strung on garlands. Now I shiver with cold, and the high laughter of Julia and her children freezes into icicles that plunge from the ceiling but do not shatter. The slop of all the soups and puddings rises, and a thousand roses prick me all at once.

Doctor's fingers thorn again the hollow of my palm, but I am thinking about my favorite Bible passage, Mark 7:32–34: *And they bring unto Jesus the one that was deaf, and had an impediment in his speech; and they beseech him to put his hand upon him. And he took him aside from the multitude, and put his fingers into his ears, and he spit and touched his tongue. And looking up to heaven, he sighed, and saith unto him, "Eph-phatha," that is, "Be opened."*

Every night before I go to sleep, I put my fingers in my ears; I spit and touch my tongue, and looking up to heaven, I sigh and write the ancient word upon my hand. I spell it across my forehead; I open my thighs and write the letters down that slope, against that place, the only place, that is as dark and silent as the cave inside my head.

I pull my hands away from Doctor and stand up. "Eph-phatha," I write across the width of Doctor's forehead, and I laugh through my tears because I have finally spelled a word that he does not know.

Chapter 16

Laura, 1850

I love to ride in carriages, even over patched and bumpy roads in an April thunderstorm, which was the state of things all the way to Hanover. I opened the window and let the cold rain lash my face. Sarah probably got drenched as well, since we both had to kneel on the carriage floor because of our crinolines. I had told off Doctor, I had told off Sarah, there was no stopping me, for if I stopped, I might fall into despair. And so I continued in high form, even allowing my voice full rein. I laughed, giggled, shouted, and let loose with as many rude or merry noises as I could conjure. The coachman must have thought me an imbecile, but I am done with worrying about what others think. Where has that gotten me, after all? I kept my music box in my lap, the prize that Doctor gave me for my twelfth birthday, and cranked it over and over, the three songs it plays dancing on my thighs. It must have driven Sarah to distraction, and while that was not my intent, nor did it serve to deter me. She has told me again and again that she does not want to marry Mr. Bond, that she never did, and that she has refused him. I no longer care. I am for me, all for me, and I am full of it; I am ripping at the seams, a Laura doll that walks and barks and bangs ahead. My family will find me changed, I'm sure, and not to their liking, but so be it.

*   *   *

Papa told me not to return home until I could speak, but I had no choice. He has only hit me once this time; Sarah's presence probably ensures his probity. My dear old Asa comes for me in the mornings, and I stay out with him all day, playing in the woods. Mama scolds me for being filthy, but now I only wash once a week, and I stay in my favorite blue dress, even in bed, having flung my corset and crinoline and petticoats across the room as soon as I arrived. I hope they throw them in the fire. I have no use for such frippery, so why continue the charade of posing as a lady? One might as well put a ball gown on a pig and a silk stovepipe on Asa.

I invite Asa in for tea or supper every night that suits me and serve meals of my own creation, which only he and I eat: raw sliced potatoes with onions, soaked in milk; porridge with fatback and apples. I eat with my hands and dust the crumbs onto the floor. I bring the dogs into the house and roll on the floor with them, letting them lick me all over. I carry a robin's nest Asa found for me in the big oak into my bed and wait for the babies to hatch, so that they can sleep with me, their downy fluff against my cheek. I am middling careful, but I wake one morning with bits of shell pricking my backside and tiny feathers mixed with ooze down my bare legs. Twice I knock over the bucket in the night and leave the contents to despoil the rug. Someone will clean it up—it doesn't bother me—I can't smell the stench. I play between my legs whenever I want and read from my Bible, occasionally at the same time. I moan with delight, and Sarah reaches up from her pallet on the floor to stop me, but I will not be stopped.

"Think of little Mary," Mama says, but I am no example. I am no longer an Inspiration to Others. I am the creature that I am, and finally I am free, not in peril of pleasing anyone. Not Doctor, not Papa, not even goody Miss Wight.

She insisted on coming, though I did not want her. She should go to the islands with her Mr. Bond, convert the heathen, dance naked with the natives. No word from her when it was warranted, not one, that Mr. Bond was courting *her*. Foolish is a small package for how I feel. I am careful not to step on her head when I get up for the bucket, but I do not converse with her unless absolutely necessary, and spend much of my days slapping away her hands. Doctor dismissed her as my teacher—what is she waiting for?

I have been here almost a month, and though the days of freedom are long, I have ceased to find joy in my wildness. I have written letters to my friends all over the world, pressed with pansies or violets, asking if I might visit them. I am certain to hear from Miss Dix any day, and others too. Something that had been hidden from me has come to light and has brought my spirits lower than ever before. When Doctor turned me out, I had some understanding of his logic, though I prayed that his devotion would win out over any rational argument. To love me is not rational, I realized long ago, and so I prize those who do so highly.

Doctor no longer loves me, and he ordered Sarah to bring with her the proof, Perkins' "Fourteenth Annual Report," to give to my parents. Doctor's Annual Reports about me have circulated the world all these years, been pored over by the philosophers, and detailed in the papers. He has sung my praises to the rooftops and detailed every aspect of my activities, my progress, my learning and growth. Though he has always claimed that my moral and intellectual senses have triumphed over my physical limitations under his guidance, in this latest report he wrote that I am "very liable to derangement." My volatile disposition he now attributes to disturbing forces within my very constitution, which I have inherited from my parents. Miss Wight did not plan to tell me, and my dear mother was apparently suppressing her deep humiliation so as not to cause me further grief, but neither of them could contain my father's rage. Doctor had written that Papa had a small brain and that Mama's "though active was not much bigger." He even decided that this temperament of mine, this "dash of the scrofu-lous," had predisposed me to the fever in the first place. So I am blamed for my condition and for bringing shame upon my family.

"Small brain!" Papa shouted and forced Mama to rap his out-rage into my palm. "Because of you," she wrote, people all over the world had read about his faculties so mightily insulted, along with those of his family. I don't believe Papa has a small brain, though perhaps a less than average-sized heart. "Asa is the small brain," Papa yelled, and blamed him for my present wildness, threatening to throw me out into the wilderness with only my beloved half-wit to care for me. Papa barred the door against Asa, and Mary says he pounds upon it for hours, then sits outside and howls for me, and also for the penknife that I slipped from his pocket while he lay snoring in our favorite meadow. Bereft of Asa's company, I start to talk to Wight again, in the blind hope of understanding Doctor's denial of all that we have accomplished over the years, his denial of my very self. The one true thing he reported is that I am indeed subject to derangement; many have seen that aptitude and even its consequences. And in the month here in Hanover, I have nourished this propensity until even I can't stand the beast.

Wightie cries in my arms. Perhaps she is becoming a bit de-ranged as well. She repeats that she does not want to marry Mr. Bond and go to the islands, but I know that anything must be bet-ter than her place here beside my bed. Doctor has disparaged her also in the report, blaming her for allowing my grosser tendencies free rein and hinting that she was perhaps too melancholy to be inspiring as a teacher. How wrong he is, but the best I can do now is to comfort her, to assure her that she has been, and will always be, my darling Wightie, and that without her, I probably would not have survived at all. In the tin bath, I scrub myself sore.

I have my family, for the time being, but it's as though I am bor-rowing a family, that I do not own one like other people. Addison has gone away to school, so there is no one to make me laugh. Little

Mary, nine now, sticks by me like a shepherd with a lamb and pets me like one as well. We pet each other, and in that I find great solace. Her hair is long and straight and silky, and I entertain her by pulling it across my upper lip like a mustache or draping it round my chin as a beard. I would like very much to finger Papa's beard—he has muttonchops—but he pushes my hand away, not gently. I know he does not want me here. Though I am hardly an extra mouth to feed, I still must be watched and taken care of. The food they needn't worry about because I am down to a few tablespoons of milk and gruel a day. I am not trying to starve myself, I keep telling Mama and Sarah—who will not leave because she is afraid for me—but what I don't tell them is that I will not try to stop it if it happens. For once, I finally feel free to refuse food. I do not want it; I do not suffer pangs of hunger. Would they not be better off if I starved? I am not feeding on pity with that sentiment; I think it is a cold, hard fact. I am even too tired to whittle away any more of myself with Asa's knife, though the slanting cuts on my thighs still sting. Blood, they must've thought, from the dead chicks or from my monthly, which I've ceased having. Mama and Wightie don't bother to poke and prod and check my body like they did when I was a girl. No doubt they are afraid of what they might see.

Last year at Perkins, a Back Bay society belle about my own age came to visit with her mama and papa. She allowed me to touch her clothes, even the damask camellias on her hat worn to the side and tied with a big satin bow under her chin. She opened and closed her parasol and let me twirl it, scrunch up its ruffled edges. "Pink," she told me, and I imagined myself all swathed in pink, flowers on my hat, bow beneath my chin, mincing about in dainty velvet slippers with kitten heels. I was beautiful, shining, in my head. She enlisted Tessy to tell me she'd give me her parasol if she could ask me one question, just one. Of course.

Tessy's fingers hesitated, and then she wrote, "Why haven't you killed yourself? I would."

I tried as hard as I could, but I couldn't think of a single answer to that question, so I gave back her parasol. Why indeed? This bilious femme was perhaps my most erudite visitor, asking the question, the most important question, that all the acclaimed philosophers and poets dared not ask. I have kept the memory of those words scalded in my palm until they have burnt through the flesh, into my heart, where they will reside forever. The brilliant girl with the pink parasol.

I lie in the same little bed in which I writhed with fever all those years ago, the bed in which I saw my last sights, heard my last sounds, maybe Mama saying my name or Addison laughing. Maybe my own sobs. I tasted my last sweetness here, porridge with sugar or a hard butter candy. I inhaled the last scent of my mother, talcum powder and grease and coffee. I dream almost all the time—sometimes terrible dreams where giant birds tear at my limbs, other times lovely ones about going on a honeymoon to Europe with Addison or Tessy, or flying high above the earth, seeing all the wonders down below. Mama comes for my hand, and little Mary, and of course Sarah, and I wave them away, or sometimes do not move at all, but let them tap until they give up. Papa finally allows Asa back to visit, and he comes every day for a while, but then he stops because really he only enjoys me when we can go outside and play; he has no use for a girl in a bed. Papa is relieved, I do not doubt, that I have ceased to terrorize the household, and he never strays near my tiny alcove, not even when I stop eating entirely.

"70 pounds," Mama says after she forces me up to weigh, and then it seems only a few dreams later that I wake to her writing, "60. Please." She's put a pan in the bed, but I'm too tired to be ashamed. I still read my Bible when I can muster it, and the Psalms grant me my only pleasures. Psalm 139: *O Lord, thou hast searched me and known me! Thou knowest when I sit down and when I rise up; thou discernest my thoughts from afar.*

Sarah reads me a letter from Doctor saying that I can come back to Perkins, if I'd like. She has obviously written to him that I am wasting, appealing to his vanity, if not to his moral sensibilities, that

I will perish without him. There is even a short note from Julia inquiring about my health, but I can't concentrate on her dither. *Thou searchest out my path and my lying down, and art acquainted with all my ways. Even before a word is on my tongue, lo, O Lord, thou knowest it altogether.* I no longer wish that I had wrought a cameo of Doctor's head to lie on my pillow because I finally understand how hard and lifeless it would be. He was never mine; no one was ever mine or will ever be mine. Darling Mary, with her soft hair brushing across my face, her sweet, wet kisses on my cheek, her tears on my bony breast, and yet still she is not mine. Addison comes home, or maybe I dreamt him, but he appears at my bedside and my fingers brush the grizzle on his chin. They seem to orbit me now—my family—as if I am a dying planet. Not a sun, never a sun; any light I had to give is dying with each day. *Thou dost beset me behind and before, and layest thy hand upon me. Such knowledge is too wonderful for me; it is high, I cannot attain it.*

I am in and out of the hours, days, and nights cut from the same cloth. *Whither shall I go from thy Spirit? Or whither shall I flee from thy presence? If I ascend to heaven, thou art there! If I make my bed in Sheol, thou art there!* Over and over Sarah pulls my hands from the bedclothes and opens my palms. *Tap-tap-tap.* My last connection with this world. *Tap-tap-tap.* Once I am awake for a bit and up to a spoon of gruel, when I realize she is writing about Miss Dix. I force myself to attention, struggle to focus on her fingers. She reads me a letter: Miss Dix has raised funds for a companion for me. For life. For my life. She has written to Doctor. I ask Sarah to read it again and again until I understand that it is true. I must lie back and rest now. The news overwhelms me. When I wake, I am certain that I have imagined this wonder, but Sarah assures me that the offer is a fact. I hold the paper in my hands and feel myself begin to stir.

If I take the wings of the morning and dwell in the uttermost parts of the sea, even there thy hand shall lead me, and thy right hand shall hold me. If I say, "Let only darkness cover me, and the light about me be night," even the darkness is not dark to thee, the night is bright as the day; for darkness is as light with thee.

Hungry. Mama brings me soup, and I let Mary spoon it to my lips. It tastes of nothing but warmth, but that is enough.

More letters from Doctor. Julia has given birth to another daughter, and they have named her Laura Elizabeth after me. I wonder what he promised Julia to make her consent to such an extraordinary thing. I will have to go soon to hold her, the little Laura. In my head I add her to my collection of dolls. And the blinds: I am often dismissive of them, even facetiously so—my God-given singularity my defense—and yet I know that my very life offers proof to them that if I can accomplish some, then they can accomplish more.

The girl twirls her parasol and is gone, at least for now.

Chapter 17

Sarah, 1851

Sarah woke in a panic, thrashing the netting above her. She cried out and Edward jumped from the chair beside the bed, throwing his blanket on the floor.

"It's all right," he said, trying to untangle her as she struggled. She shook her head and shrunk away from him. "It's for the mosquitoes. I put it up after you fell asleep."

She tried to rise from the low rush bed, but his arm stopped her. "You're making it worse," Edward said. "You're confused."

Sarah stopped moving. "I know where I am," she whispered. She was still wearing her good dress, the one she'd married him in yesterday, but it was wrenched up on one side, leaving one calf visible. She saw the darning tracks in her stockings and the large hole that had not been darned, through which her skin shone pink. She had rubbed herself almost raw when she took a much-needed proper bath at Reverend Carpenter's house between getting off the *Morning Star* and getting married. A hundred and twenty-seven days of grime accumulated aboard ship from Boston to the Sandwich Islands.

Sarah covered her legs and let him pull the netting from her limbs. Their fingers touched for an instant through the tiny holes in the silk.

Edward backed away from the bed. He had taken off his dark

waistcoat from the ceremony, but still had on his white shirt and suspendered trousers. "I'll let you get yourself fixed. There's the basin." He pointed to the ceramic bowl in the corner. "No looking glass to be had." He left the room, but there was no door to close.

There were no windows either, not one in the house, unless you counted the outside door, which he opened in the central room to let in the light and the breeze. Sarah had kept her surprise to herself last night when Reverend Carpenter drove them home in his brougham; she thought Edward's house would be like the minister's, except less grand—a regular frame house with low stone walls—but it was little more than a thatched hut. She slid off the bed and craned her neck to make sure he couldn't see her; no, but she could hear him humming and the clank of a spoon on metal. She splashed water on her face and smoothed her pale hair back into its bun. Her trunk sat against the far wall, unopened.

She bumped her head on the low opening of the room, but not hard enough to really hurt. Her boots crunched against the thin layer of gravel on the floor.

"You can buy rugs," he said. "I haven't fixed it up yet because I wasn't expecting... Here, sit." The sun floated in, illuminating the small wooden table, but not the corners of the room. He set a bowl in front of her. "Breadfruit, like you had at the Carpenters', but raw. It's good."

She took a piece and nodded. She looked at the stone fireplace, the one pot slung on a hook.

"You can let me know what you need for cooking. I have a few things here—tea, sugar, salt pork—but make a list and I'll pick up everything in Lahaina."

He had given her a tour of the town's one street the night before: the dry goods, the stable, the butcher, the smith, with the Methodist mission at one end and the Congregationalists at the other, all surrounded by swaying palms. The Methodists and Congregationalists had been here for thirty years, he told her, but the

Unitarians had only arrived two years ago. Edward had come to be part of the fledgling Unitarian mission.

After she washed the plates in the basin, Edward took her outside and showed her the yard: the chicken coop behind the house where she would gather eggs, the bench he'd built to sit and read, the twelve-foot ti plant waving over the house made from its own leaves, and the pili grass of the fan palms.

"When the winter season is over next month," he said, "those yellow-and-red flowers will turn into berries. They're not much for eating, but you can use them for digestives."

Sarah smiled at him. "You might find that necessary with my cooking."

"I had forgotten how funny you are," he said, but he didn't laugh. "It's good to have you here." Together they watched steam rise off the grass. "Well," he said, "I'm sure you have a lot of unpacking or resting, or whatever you'd like to do. I'll be taking Regina." He gestured to the bay horse tied up at the gatepost. "Past her prime, but you will come to love her."

"What if I need to go somewhere?" Sarah asked, moving closer to him.

"You'll have to walk the six miles into town, one more to the Carpenters'," he said. "Unfortunately, we have only the one horse and no prospects of another. I can ask the reverend to check on you perhaps or send his man."

"Is it safe here? The door doesn't even have a lock."

"It is as safe as I can offer. You can push the table against the door when you're in, if you'd like, but you'll shut out the light."

"But the natives? They look like yellow Negroes, but wilder. And half-naked!"

"And more than half-Christian, at this point. In most ways, you are safer than you were in South Boston." He patted her shoulder and walked across the wet grass to his horse. He mounted easily and looked down at his wife. "Except for the mosquitoes. The story goes a Mexican sailor fell in love with an island girl, but was refused. He sailed home to Mexico, brought back a barrelful of mosquitoes, and released them on his beloved's shore."

"And let her be bitten too?" Sarah asked.

"Revenge, I suppose. The sting of love."

"I'll be fine," she said, squinting up at him through the glare. She noticed how blond the line of his hair waved against the tan of his high forehead. In Boston, he had seemed to her like a pale child, if a child could be balding.

He bowed his head slightly and clicked his heels against the horse's flanks. She watched him until he disappeared on the path through the dense foliage. Then she walked around the yard bounded by trees whose names she had yet to learn and kicked dirt into the chicken pen. The birds treated it as an offering and pecked through it for anything worth eating. She kicked more dirt at them, harder this time, and ran into the house. She left the door open while she inspected the kitchen—two pots, a pan, a few utensils, three cups. She stood in front of the table, scooting it toward the door with her foot, but then left it in the middle of the room.

She unpacked all the clothes she owned in less than half an hour, folding them to fit on the low, narrow shelves by the bed. There were no closets, but his clothes took up only one shelf. Her books and undergarments she left in the trunk. She touched his pants, the waistband first and then the leg, fingering it slowly. She unfolded them and held them out in front of her. Though he was shorter than she was, he still seemed much taller than she remembered. She thought of him strolling by her side with Laura on the grounds at Perkins, fidgeting, always fidgeting. Half-bowing every time she came into a room or left it. Though she was considered virtually a spinster at twenty-eight, she had never had any other serious suitors, and the truth was she didn't expect any, plain-faced, plainspoken woman that she was, but she had had no great struggle of heart or conscience saying no to him just eight months ago. He had not seemed like a man really, not like Dr. Howe, or even

Cook's husband or Sumner. Maybe he appeared taller now because she had been looking up at him on a horse, or maybe because there were no other men around with whom to compare him.

She picked up the blanket from the floor where he'd thrown it. The wool was scratchy and stiff; he'd given her the softer one. She lifted the netting and arranged his blanket beside hers on the bed. She stared at it for a long time and then took it off and moved it back to the chair.

The heat wasn't terrible yet, more like a moderate New England June than a dog's day August so far, but enough for her to take off her long-sleeved broadcloth dress now that she was alone, and slip her day shift over her petticoat and corset and chemise. She had decided she would wear her crinoline only when they ventured into town. She unwrapped the daguerreotype of Laura and set it on the top shelf. She had written to Laura and Julia and to her sister Elizabeth while she was at sea, but the letters weren't mailed until she disembarked on the Big Island three days ago. Those letters had been full of shipboard misery—the food, the illness, the doubts—though she had tried to leaven them with anecdotes about the other passengers, like the redoubtable matriarch who'd tried to marry off both of her enormous daughters in the course of the voyage. She had succeeded in the engagement of the larger one to a ship's mate, which Sarah viewed for the girl's station and sweet character as a worse match than none at all.

She found her letter box and pen and settled herself under the mosquito netting. The table might be more comfortable, but as Edward pointed out, the mosquitoes were something she could at least spare herself; they weren't a serious malarial risk here, the ship's captain had told her, but they could carry other diseases. She would write first to Laura, who needed her most.

Dr. Howe had allowed Laura to return to Perkins from Hanover, but only because she was at the brink of death. The endless carriage ride back to Boston haunted Sarah still, Laura shivering in her arms, too weak to write more than a word or two.

Sarah had been sure she would not make it through the two-day journey. Doctor was waiting at the door when they arrived, and he lifted Laura from the coachman's arms, clearly shocked at her condition. In his eyes she'd hoped to see guilt or at least contrition, an awareness of his part in her downfall, but she read only alarm and curiosity in his flickering gaze. He had banished Laura on the pretext that he had nothing left to teach her, that he saw no need for a paid companion, much less a teacher. He promised Laura that he'd find her another companion, but when Sarah asked outright about Dorothea Dix's offer, he told her that Miss Dix had specified that the woman hired could not be an Irish and that he would not have her telling him what to do. What a joke; Sarah knew he'd never hired an Irish for a serious job anyway. Turn the sum over to him to use for the Institution as he saw fit, he told Miss Dix, with none of your restrictions. She had declined, being nearly as bullheaded as he was. It didn't matter; the money would not have gone to Laura. Doctor had turned his face from her, just short of letting her die. Without someone always beside her to translate the world and its comings and goings, she was left utterly alone, in a vacuum, at the mercy of those who happened into her palm, or not. Laura had ardently declared that she would never love another teacher as much as her dear Wightie, but Sarah could not bring herself to tell her that there would be no one to replace her, though she knew it was probably more cruel to leave the poor darling strung out with hope. Laura's and Sarah's fates both changed at the snap of Doctor's fingers, and worst of all, they were banished from each other. With Sarah's parents dead, there was nowhere for her to go. She should feel blessed that Edward had accepted her with a dowry of only twenty a year, even though she had declined him when she had a position.

She hadn't seen much of the Sandwich Islands yet, but she described for Laura what she could: the almost nauseatingly sweet smell of the orchids and plumeria blooming along the road from Lahaina that Edward had pointed out from the barouche; the briny tang of the ocean and the raw fish and whale meat piled on the docks mixed with the sweat of the shirtless yellow-brown men swarming them, crying out in singsong to help load the bags. Laura would thrill to all these words, as she did to all words, in trying to share her teacher's experiences, but Sarah knew that the only thing Laura would be able to completely understand was the weather—how something *felt*—so she took great care to detail the warm and gentle play of the breeze inland, where the house sat, compared to the wild assault of the wind at the shore when they'd arrived, and the great variations in the heat from the night to day. She finished the letter and thought she should try to make something from the salted meat Edward had shown her.

She woke in the dark to Edward's low snores from the chair beside the bed.

The next few nights he also slept in the chair, and so in the second week of her marriage, Sarah told her husband that he looked awfully tired.

"You're yawning over breakfast," she said. "I know I haven't yet mastered the fine art of cooking poi, but it's not that bad, is it?"

"No," Edward said. "Very well done."

She looked down, brushing the crumbs from her lap. "You don't have to sleep in the chair, Edward."

He waited to finish chewing. "I am so grateful for everything. You knew me and you came here anyway." He rose from the table. "I have to ride across the island today to Kihei. The mission is looking to purchase a plot to build the church."

"And will you preach there when it's done?" she asked.

He patted her cheek. "You are too good to me."

That afternoon, she named the old rooster Dr. Howe and pelted him with pebbles when he harassed the chickens.

Sarah dreamed of writing on Laura's hands, having Laura write on hers with those endlessly moving fingers. She had considered it a nuisance then, all the touching that the girl required, but now she realized how much she longed for it.

Edward wasn't in his chair, squirming and snoring, as he'd been the other nights. He must still be in the other room at prayer.

On Sunday, they rode into town for services. Rather than worship in the churches of their Protestant rivals for the islanders' souls, the small band of Unitarians—fewer than twenty, including the families—met in the parlor of the Carpenters' frame house. Sarah hadn't seen anyone but Edward since the wedding a fortnight ago, so she was happy to be among people. Only the reverend and his wife had been at their ceremony. Edward had wanted them wed as soon as she arrived, so they wouldn't have to inconvenience his employer by having her stay more than one night.

Reverend Carpenter delivered a sermon from Ecclesiastes and the group sang hymns together. Afterward, the women retired to the large terrace for cold jasmine tea and pineapple, while the men stayed inside to talk church business. At first Sarah didn't know who Mrs. Carpenter was speaking to when she said, "Mrs. Bond, please pass the sugar."

Sarah laughed. "I'm not used to my new name," she said to the other ladies, but no one made any mention of her marriage to Edward. And not a soul had asked her about Laura, though the Carpenters knew she'd come straight from Perkins. Had Laura's fame really begun to dim so quickly after the last terrible report? How lonely she must feel, her hands bereft of the hundreds she was used to clamoring for hers, and now not even a companion. And even if the people still wanted to see her, Sarah knew Doctor had cut back on the Exhibition and Visiting Days. Laura had spent most of her short life being celebrated, performing and being praised, and now she was left to her own thoughts and her darkness. Sarah prayed that she kept up her spirits enough to eat.

She mentioned Laura to the women and they nodded politely; of course they all knew who she was, but they asked her nothing.

She'd never met anyone who wasn't brimming with a thousand questions about her former charge. Sarah wondered if the oppressive heat made folks less talkative than in Boston, but no—soon the women were chattering on about everything, especially the indolence of their servants, even the converted ones. It sounded like everyone had servants but she and Edward.

Mrs. Carpenter asked if Sarah knew the story of the island's chiefess, Kapiolani.

She shook her head.

"Kapiolani was one of the first converts in the islands. The Methodists accomplished it, but nonetheless. She was already a grown woman, married to her own brother, and still cavorting with half the population."

Sarah gasped. She knew that the natives were unschooled, but she'd had no idea that they behaved that unnaturally.

The ladies tittered, and Mrs. Carpenter nodded knowingly, pleased at the effect of that scandalous tidbit on the newcomer. "Kapiolani was won over gradually—if I knew exactly how, I'd tell my husband and we'd capture them all that way. Her family and most of her own subjects were stuck fast to their old gods, but she figured a way to show them the power of our almighty Savior."

Mrs. Carpenter's baby began to cry and she shifted the child in her lap.

The girl was pretty, but Sarah could already see in the too-round cheeks the promise of the mother's corpulence. And Reverend Carpenter was so fat that his bulk had exceeded the width of the homemade pulpit by almost a foot on each side. Sarah had a sudden horrible vision of the sweaty, rolling flesh of her hosts attempting union. Thank the Lord she and Edward were fit specimens. Their children would be perfect. To make up for thinking such awful things—and right after church, no less—she held out her arms toward the querulous child.

"I'll take her," Sarah offered. "I'm good with babies." Julia had certainly let her help out every chance she got.

Mrs. Carpenter pulled her daughter closer against her bosom. "That won't be necessary," she said, and gave the baby a sugared finger to suck on.

She continued her story. "Kapiolani walked thirty miles barefoot up the black lava tracks to the mouth of the mightiest volcano, Kilauea. Hundreds of her subjects thronged around her as she stood on the lip of the smoking rim and called on Jesus to challenge the volcano goddess, Pele. Kapiolani descended sixty feet into the flaming crater, carrying only her spelling book and her Bible. The crowd scattered, waiting for the lava to spew, the volcano to swallow her up. But of course it didn't."

"They all converted on the spot," one of the women chimed in.

Mrs. Carpenter leaned back in her chair, the baby quiet now. "God will always win out, that's what you have to remember. Even here."

"Have you met her?" Sarah asked.

"She died ten years ago," her hostess said. "Pity."

When they got home, Sarah asked Edward which volcano was Kilauea.

"Right there," he said, pointing to the largest of the mountains they could see in the far distance.

"Is it very dangerous?"

"It hasn't erupted in more than twenty years. Only smokes a bit."

She studied the mountaintop for a moment before she followed him into the house.

Three days later, Edward took her to Kaapalani Beach north of Lahaina. She rode sidesaddle behind him, her arms tight around his waist as he galloped, the fern-covered cliffs rising above them. They spread a blanket on the black sand and ate the lunch she had packed—boiled sweet potatoes, fried taro, slices of baked ham, and papaya. Afterward, they walked barefoot along the beach, dipping their toes in the water, the waves several feet higher than any she'd seen in the Atlantic. Sarah caught her husband staring at her ankles, and lifted her skirts a bit higher on the next wave, flashing a shimmer of white calf.

At first, Sarah told him, she'd thought it was completely different from the Massachusetts shoreline, but now she realized it was almost the same. "The feeling," she said.

"Identical," Edward agreed and reached for her hand. Just a touch, two fingers, before he let go. "Look!" he shouted. "Jellyfish!" And they ran to examine their find.

On the ride back, Sarah let her head press into his back, happy she'd washed her hair that morning with the *aupa* oil he'd given her as a wedding gift. It smelled like lilies sprinkled with cinnamon.

It was late when they arrived home, so they skipped their reading and went straight to prayers, kneeling beside each other in front of the fireplace. Most nights, they prayed only for about half an hour, but tonight Edward seemed deeply absorbed. Sarah kept opening her eyes to check, but he didn't budge, his back ramrod straight, his hands joined in front of his bowed head. She saw that the back of his neck was sunburned, and she knew when he opened his eyes that they would look even bluer than usual.

She stood up quietly and went into the bedroom. She held up the small gilt hand mirror and what she saw pleased her. For the first time, her blonde hair, bleached now almost white, seemed to glow against the fresh tan of her skin. She even liked the freckles on her nose. Sarah changed into her dressing gown and dabbed a bit of the *aupa* oil on her neck and wrists. Just a little—it was very expensive, he'd told her, and he seemed to be earning much less than she'd thought a Harvard-educated minister, even in this corner of the world, would be due.

He didn't come into her bed that night either, and the next afternoon, she wrote to Julia: *Did your husband extend you a prolonged period of kindness and ease when you were first married? How long?* Of course, by the time she might receive an answer back—it could take months on the packet steamers winding their way around Cape Horn—the problem would doubtless be solved.

Sarah was feeding the chickens when Edward rode up at dusk.

"The *Artemis* arrived today with the mail," Edward said, swinging off his horse. "You haven't been here a month, and already it's the biggest packet I've ever received." He held the parcel above his head, out of her reach, and made her jump for it.

"Give it here!" she said, and he let her have it, laughing. She rushed inside to light the lamp. She unstrung the packet, and pulled out the letters. Edward stood in the doorway, watching her, smiling.

"One from Laura, Julia, my sister, my sister, Laura, another Laura," she recited. "And another from Julia...no, she's written over this one." She brought it closer to the flame. "It says, 'This arrived after you left.' It's from you, Edward." She held it out to him, surprised.

Edward hung his hat on the hook behind the door. He walked to the table and took the letter from her, turning it over and over as if he couldn't believe it was his, or that it even existed. He rubbed the envelope between his fingers, traced each line of his handwriting in the address.

"What is it?" Sarah asked, but he walked out into the yard, still holding the letter. She followed him. "Did you write and tell me not to come?"

He shook his head, his back to her. The tips of the ti leaves above them glowed pink in the setting sun, and the shadows played on his shoulders. Finally he turned around. "Here," he said, offering her the letter. "Read it."

She took it from his hand, trying to read instead whatever was in his eyes that she hadn't seen before. She went into the house and settled into her chair. He pulled his chair to face hers, a few feet away, different from the way they sat reading at night with their chairs beside each other. She opened the letter.

October 1850, Lahaina

Dearest Sarah,

I am so sorry to hear about the way that Dr. Howe has treated you. You have always been the most affectionate and sincere friend and champion of Laura, and it is a shock and a pity that he doesn't recognize your goodness. My sad thoughts go out to Laura also, that she is not only losing you, but her home, and perhaps even her place in the world.

My offer of course still stands, but my circumstances have altered since I made it. There is no way to tell you but straight out, as I have always spoken with you.

A month after you declined me and I set my path on missionary work, I was given a physical examination in Cambridge to ascertain my fitness for the voyage. What Dr. Barber found made me unfit, it was decided, to pursue the ministry, even with my graduation from the Divinity School. The French disease, some call it, or the Italian, it doesn't matter. Now it is mine, and someday I might lose my sanity because of that one dark, untempered moment of my youth. I have already lost my real vocation, though the Foreign Missions Board allowed me to come here to assist Reverend Carpenter with legal and administrative matters. He was apprised of my situation, and he has welcomed me as well as he is able. I will never preach the word of God, nor minister to the sick or heathen, and I should not.

So you, my darling Sarah, must be the judge of your future and of mine. I want you to come, I want you to be my wife, even if it is in name only.

I will try at least to prove worthy of being your life's best companion.

Sarah raised her head and looked at her husband. His eyes were closed, and he sat rocking a little in his chair. She stood and put the letter on his lap, but still he didn't open his eyes. She walked into the bedroom, lifted the netting, and crawled under it, keeping her arms folded tight across her chest, hugging her shoulders. She didn't weep for almost an hour, but when she did, the sound of it drove him out into the yard.

Hours later, she heard him come into the room to get his blanket and drag it out to the other room. When she woke in the morning, he was already gone.

For three days, they barely spoke, aside from the necessities. He came home after dark, shoved down whatever she'd prepared, read for an hour or so, and then went down on his knees to pray alone in front of the fireplace until she went into the bedroom. He slept in the main room, or maybe he didn't. Maybe he prayed all night. She didn't know.

On the fourth evening after dinner, she fixed his tea, a quarter cream, the way he liked it, and watched him sip. "You're having the mercury treatments?" she asked him.

He looked at her full in the face for the first time since the letter had arrived. "Once a month when I go in to the island." He waited, as if trying to gauge whether he should continue. "But there's no way to tell...in the future—"

"I understand," she said and returned to her knitting.

The next night as soon as he came home, Edward grabbed the ax from behind the door and went out into the yard. Sarah watched him swing wildly at the small koa tree at the edge of their clearing. The puffballs of yellow flowers trembled on its delicate branches.

"What are you doing?" she said. "It just started blooming on Sunday."

He swung again, barely making contact with the wood. "Are you staying?" he asked, without turning around. She watched him throw his weight into the next stroke, and it connected. He did it again, and she saw the wood was dented at least an inch. She looked at the peak of the volcano silhouetted in the distance, rosy gold against the gathering night.

"It's too dark to chop wood," she told him. "You'll lose a finger."

He swung harder, and small pieces of the red bark splintered against the grass. "If you're staying, I'm building a bed," he said. "For myself."

He kept working, shoulders moving, half-bent over the tree. She could see the sweat beginning to soak through his shirt, limning a faint, dark line down his backbone.

"Come inside," Sarah told her husband. "We'll pray."

Edward stopped, and after a moment, he turned and walked toward her. The sun was behind him and she couldn't see his eyes. He still held the ax in one hand, dragging its blade through the grass until he dropped it outside the door. They entered the house and knelt, a foot apart, in front of the unlit fire.

For the first hour, there was no sound, no movement, except for their breathing. Then Sarah reached across the divide between them and loosened one hand from the steeple of his prayers. The sweat of her palm slid against his, and the dampness sealed their hands together.

Chapter 18
Chev, 1851

Chev read with interest the article in the *Boston Evening Transcript* about the Great Exhibition taking place in London. Prince Albert, Queen Victoria's consort, had overseen the construction, in only nine months, of the Crystal Palace in Hyde Park. Beneath the soaring glass dome, all the civilized nations of the world, including the imperial colonies of India, Australia, and New Zealand, displayed their contributions to nineteenth-century industry and manufacturing at its halfway point. The crowds lined the ten miles of the pavilion to see India's Koh-i-Noor Diamond, England's adding and cigarette-making machines, and the sumptuous textiles of France. Among the more than ten thousand objects, half of which were British, were such frippery as the stiletto umbrella, the leech barometer, and foldable pianos for yachting. Chev's interest was piqued, however, by the "tangible ink" for the blind, which allegedly produced raised-letter type automatically. Why hadn't he thought of that? And the first public conveniences in the Retiring Rooms, charging one penny each for private cubicles—another step forward! But oh dear, now the article got round to reporting on the American exhibit: a giant eagle draped in the Stars and Stripes, a model of Niagara Falls, a few sets of false teeth, McCormick's reaping machine. Who could have put this mockery together?

Thank goodness Mathew Brady had at least won a medal for his daguerreotypes, sparing Americans from total disgrace. He had done portraits of both Chev and Laura years ago for his *Gallery of Illustrious Americans*. But not Julia; Brady had not considered her illustrious enough apparently. Chev thought his own particularly good, though Laura, even with Brady's skill, betrayed some of the strangeness that now marked her: her head held too rigidly, her face lacking in animation. She had been a well-enough-looking child, but at this point he could barely stand to look at her. She was grown and peculiar, and she reminded him of nothing but both their early promises. She had failed him on every front, both those she couldn't help (the way she looked, the way she bore herself) and those she could (her embrace of religion; her stubbornness; and those godawful noises, which he had once trumpeted as evidence of her profound and innate desire to communicate at all costs).

At the close of the column, the paper proposed a remedy for America's poor showing at the Exhibition: to send posthaste to London the showpiece with which no nation could compete, the new republic's finest accomplishment, Laura Bridgman. Chev's jaw dropped; he wondered if the writer had had a good look lately at this gem, this pearl beyond price. And his last report on her had been written up in the very same paper.

He folded the paper slowly. Then again, it was he who had effected this transformation, this miracle of philanthropy and education, and it was his creation that was being proposed as the highest achievement of his nation. Two hundred fifty thousand tickets had sold out the opening day of the Exhibition, and up to six million were expected over the nine-month run. It could be Laura's—and his—largest audience by far. He allowed himself a smile in the privacy of his study. If Laura were the *pièce de résistance*, then he was certainly the godhead. He wondered if Julia had read the piece yet; surely her heart too would swell with pride on his account. But wait—now the public would no doubt rally for Laura to actually be sent to the Exhibition. The broadening acclaim, the acknowledgment, was one thing, but the idea of sending her out to the greatest show on earth was frightening. The only time she'd ever even been on a ship was when she'd toured the *Britannia* before their honeymoon voyage, and look what had happened then.

Good Lord, what if someone had already told Laura about the paper's proposal? She would no doubt think it grand, but without a teacher or companion for her, he was the sole decider of her fate, a role he had once, but no longer, relished. Should he abandon all in his hands now to accompany Laura to London? Perhaps if he could extract a promise that she would not speak on the subject of religion. Nonsense, of course the press would ask her. They would field questions to her like sugar cubes to a horse. And she would gobble. She believed only what she believed now, and set her God—who was not Chev's God (though he was no longer sure if his God even qualified as a "who")—as a higher authority than her mentor. Better that she had never grown up or that he had not exhibited her to the world so steadfastly in the past. He would have to blame his own pride and ego for that.

But if he did accept the herculean challenge and go to London, would Julia perhaps accompany them? Would it make her happy? At this point, he cared more about his wife's happiness than his ward's, even if Julia was not the nation's greatest and most peculiar wonder. Actually, sometimes she was, to his mind.

He crossed the hall to Julia's room. For a year now, separate bedrooms. Four children, and she said she couldn't bear more. As a doctor, he knew damn well she could, but that she simply didn't want to. So here he was, the Chevalier, denied intimate companionship in his own home. He didn't know what to do about this most delicate and absurd predicament. He'd tentatively broached the subject with Sumner, but Sumner had seemed somehow pleased rather than vexed and offered absolutely nothing useful. Of course, Charlie wouldn't know his way around a woman;

as far as Howe could tell, his dearest friend had made no inroads on any female territory whatsoever.

He knocked, but didn't wait for an answer before entering. She was dressing, the milk of her shoulders and upper back visible, her eyes staring up at him from the oval of the vanity table mirror. She turned and crossed her arms, and he wondered if this was because she believed that the mere sight of her uncorseted breasts swelling above her linen chemise might prove too enticing for him. She might be right. He adjusted his gaze upward.

"Did you read the editorial on the Exhibition?" he asked, brandishing the paper at her.

"Of course. You and Laura are quite the *cause célèbre* again. You don't seem pleased."

"It's a bit late in the game; the Exhibition is already under way." Julia shrugged. "Six weeks at sea."

"You actually think I should go? After what I said about Laura in the last report?"

"No one will remember if you hoist her up again on those broad shoulders."

Was she flirting with him? She still hadn't put on her dress.

"You could hire a companion. You've promised her that already."

"She's fine without one. I don't see the need."

"Then why the promise, Chev?"

He put his hands lightly on her shoulders as she dusted powder over her face and décolletage, speckling his fingers. "Don't tell me how to manage her, Julia. You know better."

She shook herself from his hands. "Then don't ask my advice."

"Would you go—would you consider making the trip to London?"

"You are in a funny mood," his wife said. "Here, help button me up. You, me, and Laura crossing the Atlantic? At least one of us would go overboard in the first week."

"She's not that bad."

"I didn't say she was. My dear, you have disparaged the girl to the entire world. Don't look to me for any help at this point."

"You were never any help with Laura." There, her dress was buttoned all the way up, thank God, so he'd be spared that distraction in an argument.

"And you are never any help with your own children, probably because they are not idiots."

"Are you ill, Julia? Your color is as high as your temper."

She faced him, and her eyes met his fully for the first time. "I'm going to Rome, Chev, to spend the season with Louisa and her husband. And I'm taking the children. You should go to London with Laura, if you'd like."

She swept out of the room before he had time to formulate a response, and he was left with nothing but the sweet scent of her powder. He raised two fingers to his nose and inhaled deeply. He looked around the room. He felt utterly lost, a very unusual state for Dr. Samuel Gridley Howe.

Dash it, someone had told Laura about the *Transcript*'s proposal. He figured it must have been Dorothea Dix on last week's usual prying, doting visit. Laura refused to say who told her, but whoever it was, they'd read her the entire editorial.

"Priceless art," Laura told him first thing. "Me."

If so, she had been his canvas, and God knows, at the moment he regretted his brushstrokes, both broad and narrow. Ah, what respite it would be to deal with one of Vermeer's pale beauties rather than some scowling oddity from Mr. Bosch!

"Why not go?" she asked, and when he didn't answer, she wrote it again and again until he swept her hand away.

"Much trouble," was all he could think.

"You love London. See Boz and others."

And they would see her, that was the problem; they'd see how he'd failed with her, how charmless she'd become as a woman, how opinionated and singular in the very worst way for a lady.

"Busy here."

"Julia Rome."

How the devil did she know that already? Did everyone know? He'd only told Jeannette and Charlie. Wonder who Julia had announced her grand intentions to. Bragging, no doubt.

"Paper says I'm best of America."

At the moment, she wasn't even best of Perkins, as far as he was concerned. "Vanity a sin," he wrote.

"I don't say. Paper say."

"Silly idea."

She slammed both hands on his desk. "I want to go."

He'd had enough. "Then go."

She stood still, thinking. "No Wight. Can't go alone."

"Then find someone."

"Who?"

"Don't care."

"Not proud of me anymore," she wrote slowly. "I'm deranged, with small brain."

She had never mentioned the Annual Report, but he should have known someone would have gotten to her; after all, both Wight and the Bridgmans had been furious.

"Not small...different than I thought."

"My bumps?"

Chev felt himself struggling for an explanation that would make sense to both of them. "Tried to make you something you're not." There, that was the truth.

She remained standing, a rigid column before him. "A disappointment."

"No—" Why was he still so soft on her whenever her hand was in his?

"I knew that," she said, her fingers surprisingly cool on his own. "Knew when you sent me away."

"But you're back," he said helplessly.

"My brain's fine," she said. "My heart also. But you—"

He waited for her to finish. How often he'd judged her, privately and publicly, and now she was finally ready to render a judgment on her maker. But after a few seconds, she simply removed her hand and left the room. To her credit, she did not collide with any of the furniture. Chev realized his hand was still out, palm open. What had she been going to say? At least she hadn't tapped something unintelligible across his forehead like the last time they'd fallen out. *Eph-phatha?* He still didn't know what that meant, or if it were something she'd made up in the boil of the moment to confound him. Maybe it was a curse. He groaned. He was feeling cursed, indeed. All the women turning against him, when they all used to be so tangled in his beard he could scarcely breathe.

Chev wrote a brief letter to the editor of the *Transcript*, thanking him for such an excellent and complimentary suggestion, but explaining that a trip of such duration would not betoken well for Laura's present health. Or for his own.

Chapter 19

Laura, 1851

A new girl," Jeannette writes. "Kate O'Boyle."

An Irish. I am surprised Doctor is taking another one; we already have half a dozen, and they are wild as cats. And she's hardly a girl: her hand is nearly one and a quarter the length of mine, and the fingertips as callused as any I've ever had from a female. Too much pressure with the thumb—who doesn't know how to shake hands? I withdraw but not before I'm scraped by a ragged nail. Jeannette pats my shoulder to calm me; if this one is an actual idiot, she should have warned me first. I believe she sometimes thinks it funny to spring them on me. What she sees might be comical; what I feel, however, is not.

"Not blind," Jeannette says. "Orphan. Helps Cook."

"Girl's hands disgrace," I tell her.

"Had more than her share."

Oh, we get shares, do we? Then I own the entire Institution, thank you.

The girl is standing far too close; her heat is overwhelming. I back away, but Jeannette pushes me toward her again.

"Don't take yourself so serious," she says. What does she expect? I've no teacher of my own—not that I need one, though Doctor had promised me a companion if I came back from the dead—and I spend half my days helping with ignorant and disrespectful blind girls. I hate it when Doctor leaves Jeannette in charge.

She tries one more time. "Friend for you. Schooled."

How grateful I should be that they've found me a new *friend*, fresh from the almshouse, from rolling around with the destitute and the insane. I hope they scrubbed her down.

I feel her lowering herself, her hand in mine. Ah, she curtsies. All right then. I curtsy in return, and Jeannette takes her away, satisfied I am behaving.

The sun is full out today, so after I help with the maths, I perch on the stone bench by the stable to write.

> *My darling Wightie,*
>
> *I was so thrilled to hear you had your baby. Thomas is a lovely name, though of course I did want you to have a girl so you could call her Laura, as you'd promised. Can you blame me?*
>
> *I must admit to you now that I had doubts if you had made a good match in Mr. Bond. I didn't think you truly loved him and wanted to go to the islands. But you said that when two people really love each other, God gives them a baby, and so now I know that your joy is real and complete. I am filled with happiness for your family.*
>
> *I wish that I could be there on the beach to play foots with Thomas, as I play with Julia's latest...*

Someone's leaning over me—what, trying to read my letter? I shield the page and then reach backward, snagging a rope of hair. What a strong braid! I can't get more than a fingernail between the plaits. I don't know this hair. Down it I go, two hands' worth tight as a paintbrush, to the tiny band holding the ends. Who wears no ribbons at all? But then, oh, the surprise at the end of the plait: a good two inches of curls that coil around my finger. How difficult it must be to force those curls into submission. I tug hard and down comes the head attached. I turn the letter over and raise my other hand to the face, employing the braid like a pulley.

The chin juts a bit; mine does too, but this one more. The bottom lip yields to my fingertips, but it is ridged and cracked. Generally, only men have such lips, like Doctor after a long ride in the wind. Before I can scale the cheeks, the person takes advantage of my lax grip and jerks away. I frisk the space on both sides, but she is gone—not just a few inches out of my range, playing a game, I pray, the way so many students have mocked me. I pretend to be occupied with my letter, and then *ha!* I lunge from the bench, wheeling around in a wide circle. Nothing but air. The ladder of hair is gone. I settle in again with my page, dozing in and out. Climb the rope; pound on the door of that dry, closed mouth; peel away the flakes of skin until all is smooth and wet, like mine.

Today is horses, my favorite. To think, all those years ago riding Asa's shoulders that I would one day sit so proud on a mount of my own. I am not allowed a gallop or even a slow trot unattended, though, and I am never given the reins by myself; someone is always at the end of those reins, pulling me along the path they have chosen for me. From the saddle, there is no way to communicate my wishes except through noises, but these are never heeded unless I continue with great force.

"Why does it matter where you're going?" Doctor once asked me, so angered by my noises that he'd stopped and pulled me off the horse. "You don't know the difference." But I do: toward the sea we race the fastest, and the wind slaps my face and pricks at my nose; toward the forest, branches scratch my arms, leaves nest in my hair, and warmth becomes coolness; through the gardens, we move slow as a waltz as the horse is guided between bushes and flower beds; and out the gates and on to Boston, we fly, and then heel, waiting for others to pass in the street, and the jarring of the hooves on the cobblestones hurts my head.

I am tasked with helping the new girls, so I won't be riding. A shame with the late August breeze so brisk, as real as rough hands at my back. Doctor believes in breaking students in fast, going straight to the exercise most of them have never tried, helpless as they are. Visitors can scarce believe it, all the blind children rushing about the yard, and when they see the gymnasium they are amazed—sightless little ones swinging from the bars! But it is the horses and fresh air that are Doctor's genius; for me in particular nothing provides more sensate variety than the weather, the act of simply being out of doors. The air inside the house rarely moves and changes, but outside I am constantly delighted by even the slightest shifts in wind or the angle of the sun or shade.

I brought two sugar cubes in my pocket for my favorite horse, Wightie. I'm told he is almost pure white with one small black spot on his head and so this name is particularly apt, though I would've named him after Sarah Wight anyway. He is a wonderful beast, even if he is male. That was a grave disappointment. Wightie's mane is tangled, and I give it a good, hard brushing. He recognizes me as always and nuzzles my neck.

Here is my girl—Jeannette tells me it's Kate, Cook's assistant. Better her than a clinging, frightened child, I guess. But why is she so special that she gets lessons when she should be cooking us lunch?

"Learned finger spelling," Jeannette says. "To talk with you."

"Why?"

"Lonely, blinds too young." Jeannette puts the girl's hand in mine. "Try her."

"How old?" I spell out with excruciating slowness.

"17," she writes back, much quicker than most new to the signing.

She's only four years younger then; none of the rest of the girls are more than thirteen now. Even Tessy finally left; her family took her to New York for glass eyes, and *voilà!* a husband soon appeared. Apparently, artificial eyes are just the ticket to a normal life, though Doctor still claims I would never get shut of the discomfort. "There are different measures of discomfort," I told him, and I should bear a Job's load for blue and shining eyes to greet my public. They all leave, except for me.

"Like horse?" I ask her.

"Big," she writes. "Ugly."

Ugly? I might not be able to see Wightie, but I can tell an ugly horse when I feel one, and Wightie is magnificent.

"Wightie beautiful."

Kate spells "Whitie" into my hand.

"Wightie," I write again.

"White," she raps emphatically. "And ugly."

"Not color. Named for teacher." I punch each letter so I don't have to do it again.

"Here?"

I start on "The Sandwich Islands," but of course she would not have heard of them. "Far away."

"Sad?"

What cheek. "Pet." I take the girl's hand but she pulls back. I remember my months of fear; horses are enormous, the largest creatures I have met, yet the gentlest. Do I share this information with her? She's probably angry at being paired with me; with anyone else she wouldn't have to finger spell—she could speak. Maybe she *is* speaking. I feel her turning away, kicking grass. I don't blame her. I take both hands firmly in mine.

"Here one year before I rode."

"Fall?"

"Never."

"Fell bad." Kate hooks her right thumb into my palm. The second joint crooks oddly, the knuckle humped. I bend her other thumb and rub the tough pads against my soft ones.

"Pet Wightie together." And we do, first her hand over mine, and then mine over hers until she stops trembling. What a thing to hold a girl's hand bigger than mine and yet it still trembles.

"Smooth," she writes, and I allow her to stroke by herself.

"Left Ireland famine?" I ask.

"Born here."

She's not boat Irish then. That's good. I've been told the English and the Irish have funny accents, but they don't translate with the finger language. "Now the nose," I say as we move to Wightie's front.

"Bites."

"Won't."

I reach into my pocket for one of the sugar cubes I was saving to feed Wightie myself, and give it to Kate. I lift her hand toward the horse's mouth until Wightie's breath is warm on us, but still the girl resists.

For two more weeks Kate stays afraid, stubborn, and sulky. Finally, I tell her, "He will love you," and it's that simple: for this affection, she puts herself in harm's way. She tenses, and then a giggle shakes her as Wightie snuffles the sugar. Kate's hair tickles my nose. This is the hair—it was her in the yard, looking over my shoulder, teasing me with her braid. Today it is unplaited, and I slide one finger into the mass. When she doesn't recoil, very slowly my whole hand enters, fingers first, an inch at a time, until it is suspended in that soft forest.

She doesn't move away from me, though she doesn't move toward me either. I can tell from the thrust of her shoulder that she is stroking Wightie's mane. My hand in Kate's mane, hers in Wightie's; nothing has prepared me for the perfection of this moment. I am careful not to pull, though I want to, and am ready to bury my whole face—the tip of my nose already in, my lower lip so close a tendril vibrates in my sharp exhale—when my arm is grabbed and wrenched away. My fingers tangle in Kate's hair, and she twists against me.

Jeannette has made me hurt the girl. She grips my forearm and shakes it free of all that beauty. We are separated, and when I put my hands out in front of me, there is nothing but briny wind against my palms.

*　　　*　　　*

By the last week of September, Kate is riding. I ask Jeannette if I can mount with her, but she says that two ladies sidesaddle is begging for an accident. One of us could ride the way men do, I suggest, but she swears Doctor won't allow it. He seems much more ill-tempered with Julia away in Rome than he does even when she's here. Jeannette lets me lead Wightie on the beach with Kate astride, but I know she watches. Of course, I don't have the true independence of the lead, but it's nice to pretend. These twice weekly lessons are our only time together, and when she is atop the horse, I can't have her hand for talking. Cook drives her from dawn until past teatime, and she is so exhausted that she goes straight upstairs. I feel bad that she must share a room with three blind girls. Last year, Doctor moved me into a cottage of my own at the back of the main house.

Today when she jumped off Wightie, she said, "Read poem about you."

"Which?"

"You're angel."

"In the cage."

"Famous," she says.

I'm one of the most famous women in the world, but I decide to be modest. "Doctor's famous," I tell her.

"Famous for *you*."

"Not like before. And young ones don't like me."

"Blinds," she says. "What do you expect?"

Lydia Sigourney and all the best poets have written poems about me, except for Doctor's wife. Julia writes hundreds of poems, yet here I've sat for years, right in front of her, apparently the ideal helpless Muse, but nary a word from her stingy pen. She did try to get me the eyes, though. "Julia has red hair like you," I tell Kate. She can't believe that I guessed her own color correctly, but the truth is most red locks have a certain memorable coarseness that gives them away. Her eyes, however, I guess wrong. Blue, I thought, but she says green, my favorite.

Kate is allowed to ride on her own now, and I am left with the children. For weeks I meet her only in passing, with time to write only the simplest greetings. Then yesterday outside the stable, she grabbed my hand and held it.

"Tonight. Your cottage."

"No visitors allowed nights."

"Yes." She slapped my palm. "Bring treat. To thank for teaching." She patted my arm and ran off to make supper for us all.

I have straightened everything in my one room and swept the floor three times. I comb it inch by inch on my hands and knees to make sure I haven't missed anything, but then my hands get dirty again. I crank the music box on the table by the bed and stay close to the door so I won't miss the vibration of her knock.

At eight she comes. She hands me a plate.

"Smell," she says.

I inhale deeply and make an appreciative noise.

"Biscuit with jam. Blackberry."

I eat with what I hope is gusto, smacking my lips. "Delicious." Why spoil it for her? Let her believe I'm *only* deaf and dumb and blind.

"Little bird," she writes. "I'll fatten you up. Like me."

It's true she is quite plump; whenever I help her on or off the horse, I grab a quick squeeze of whatever softness I can find. She must sample while she's cooking.

Over the next two weeks, she brings me something nearly every night, which I force myself to swallow. She steals for me; I eat for her and pray she won't get caught. How can I tell her it's all for nothing, all a show just for her?

*   *   *

This time it's meat pudding, apparently.

"Like?" she asks.

I nod vigorously and force down another gelatinous spoonful.

She stops feeding me. "Your face bad liar. Hate it."

I am so tired of pretending, of eating all this food. "Can't taste it."

"Not enough kidney?"

"No, I can't *taste anything*. No taste, no smell." She would have found out sooner or later.

"Impossible."

"Everything about me is impossible."

"Serious?"

"The fever."

"Cook says no seasoning. If you—"

"Doctor's orders."

Finally she says, "I can make you taste."

"Only God."

"We'll see," she writes. She walks out and takes the pudding.

She doesn't come the next night as she promised, but the night after. I am almost asleep when she creeps in and sits down on the narrow bed beside me.

"Open," she says and drops tiny flakes onto my tongue. I wait, and then I feel it: a warmth that is different from heat, that is actually coming from my tongue, and then a sharp stinging. My whole mouth burns. Is this *tasting*?

"You taste it!"

"Yes," I write after a moment. It's too much to comprehend. "What?" I finally manage.

"Red pepper."

"You eat," I tell her, and her laughter jolts the bed.

"Too strong. Only you need strong."

"Just touch it on my tongue," I beg her, and she reaches one finger into my mouth. I hold it there, sucking. I can't help myself. And then it is her mouth on mine, and I am coating her tongue with pepper.

After what feels like hours, we return to ourselves. My heart has taken captive my whole body, and each thud shakes me with fear, with delight.

"Tomorrow," she writes. "Surprise."

All I can do is nod. I can't imagine what could be more surprising than what has transpired tonight, inside and out.

All day I can hardly breathe. I go up to the main house early and tell Jeannette I'm ill. It's true. I do feel ill. Light-headed, my heart still struggling. I lie on my bed and relive the kisses again and again until she comes.

I am expecting her mouth on mine, but it is metal she holds to my lips. A liquid burning, different from the pepper, suffusing my chest, coursing down into my stomach. I try to sit up but I am dizzy. She tries to force me to drink more, but I stop her.

"What?"

"Whiskey," she says. "Blood of the Irish."

I have tasted wine, a few sips, at table when Doctor and Julia have hosted fancy dress parties, but it was nothing like this. It had no taste for me. Actually, this whiskey doesn't exactly have a *taste*, I don't think, but more of a *feeling*. And what a feeling. I allow her to give me more, and we pass the flask between us. I giggle and make my whole menagerie of noises for her. Is this what it's like to be Irish?

"Tell me about Tewksbury." I have been waiting for the right moment to ask her because I know it's a sore subject.

"Can't tell you. You're too soft," she writes, and I feel both the pride and the dismissal in her touch.

"In my life, nothing surprising. What did you do there?"

"Cooked. Played in the deadhouse." The children's only playroom was where the corpses—and apparently there were many—were prepared for burial.

"All terrible?"

"Not all," she says.

She asks if she can try on my dresses, though I know none of them will fit, not even close. Nevertheless, I am excited to help her out of her corset. It is far inferior to mine, with stays of wood instead of whalebone. And I am even more shocked at the fact that she wears only one petticoat and that her crinoline is made of scratchy horsehair. She must have gotten it second- or third-hand because horsehair went out of fashion over ten years ago. She gives up on the dresses and tries on my bonnets instead. I imagine her standing before me in just her shimmy, my white straw bonnet framing her ringlets, the lilac velvet ties hanging between her heavy breasts.

The warmth of the whiskey spreads, and I take off my dress too. Kate unhooks my corset, and then my petticoats and crinoline are dragged to the floor until I stand shivering in just my chemise and pantalettes. Her mouth is on mine, and I slowly lift the linen over her silken thighs and slip my hand into her drawers. Ah there, a garden of curls. My finger slides in. Her finger slides in. I see flashes of light behind my eyelids. Salty, sweet, sour, bitter: I can taste everything.

Chapter 20

Julia, 1851

How different Rome seemed, seven years after Julia's honeymoon visit. It certainly wasn't that the ancient city had become more modern, even with the country up in arms over the recent liberalization of Pope Pius IX. No, it was that the first time she had come to Rome a blooming bride and had left it a burdened mother. Still, if somebody had told her back then that she'd be overjoyed to return sans husband, and with only two of her brood of four, she wouldn't have believed them. But now that Louisa had settled here with her husband, the sculptor Thomas Crawford, Julia was provided entree into the Roman-American intellectual and social circles, most necessary since she was not a known quantity in Europe. She had high hopes this stay would change all that, perhaps even elevating her to the status of the late Margaret Fuller, that paragon of female achievement who had famously flowered in Rome in the decade before.

Julia set up house in an apartment on the Via Capo le Case a mile from Villa Negroni, where Louisa and Thomas lived. It was not the most fashionable or prestigious of addresses, but it was in the hub of the artistic scene, which flourished in Rome. As soon as she found a grand piano and had it delivered, Julia felt she was home. The piano was the kind of detail that Chev would have deemed a ridiculous extravagance, so thank heaven she had retained a trickle of income from her brother Samuel's trust, though her family had unwisely bargained away the majority of her interests over the years, giving her husband almost total control. She hired a young Italian nurse for the children, a lovely girl who also spoke a bit of English. What a pleasure to be able to hire youthful and attractive help, which she had had to give up on entirely at Perkins due to her husband's shocking willingness to cross the lines of respectability with the servants. Amiability was fine, preferred even, but outright conviviality with the help? Absolutely not, a point that had been hammered home to her when she'd heard the last nubile housemaid actually call him "Chev"! She now made sure that only women either over the age of thirty-five or in possession of some gravely unattractive feature were installed in key household positions, even if that meant a loss of efficiency and vitality. She'd employed a new assistant for Cook, a pock-faced young widow, before she left, as the old one had gone down with the cholera. Chev still insisted on doing his phrenological exams of any potential staff, which most of them took for a lice check. Luckily, he had found nothing untoward on the widow's graying head, though Julia knew that he well might fire her as soon as she was gone, as he often did, rationalizing the shrinking or ascendance of some bump or another rather than ever admitting he'd been just plain wrong. Of course there was nothing Julia could do about the teachers he chose for the Institution. He seemed to use good judgment there, however, favoring the somber over the well-endowed, cognizant as he always was of getting the best for his blinds, even if they were not a treat for his own eyes. It wasn't that she actually considered her husband capable of having an affair; she knew he was far too high-minded and self-righteous for that, especially with a female so far beneath him. Look at how long it had taken him to choose a wife, so exacting were his standards, though at this point they both realized that in some respects he had chosen admirably but not well.

For her cook here, she'd hired a wonderful old *nonna*, who came in for a few hours a day and left them prepared with feasts. Ah, the joys of garlic! Julia could never get enough, probably because Chev loathed it and never allowed Cook to use it at home, though he gave her free rein with more moderate spices, unlike the tasteless meals he had prepared for the students. Julia couldn't understand how he'd come to the conclusion that a bit of salt or pepper might cause an uprising. Julia was perhaps one of the only Boston elite who greeted the recent influx of Italian immigrants with anticipation, in hopes that the otherwise derelict South End might soon be awash with little trattorias, not that Chev would probably ever take her there.

As the chill of October set in, Julia ordered firewood for the short Roman winter, which was delivered by donkey. She wrote by the fire in the mornings while the nurse kept the children at bay, and if there were no social engagements, again by candlelight when the babies were tucked into the *letto matrimoniale*, or marriage bed, as all full-sized beds were called. Little Laura was just a year and a half, but she'd weaned her already, far younger than she'd weaned any of the others. She'd kept Florence at her breast until she was past two to keep Chev out of her bed, dangerously fertile as they both appeared to be. The poems were coming along, but they lacked a theme, save marital discontent, which had to be finessed with nearly impenetrable metaphors and aphorisms, much like the eight poems that had recently been published in a well-received anthology. And to think she wasn't paid a red cent for any of them, only given one free copy—one! She was hoping that the Eternal City would soon provide her with greater inspiration, even of a religious sort. To that end, she had acquired, through a recommendation, the services of a well-known rabbi to continue the study of Hebrew she had taken up long ago, before the children. He came twice a week to the apartment, clad in the long black robes required of all the Italian Jews, and always left well before dusk to be back behind the ghetto walls by six.

And here she had lots of exciting new friends. Why, just upstairs

from her lived an artist and a composer, Edward and Augusta
Freeman. Julia and Augusta would go on long walks together,
without the children, often ending up at one of the cafés that
ringed the Piazza del Popolo or the Trevi Fountain. With Mr. Freeman, they toured the house where Keats had lived and died in the
shadow of the Spanish Steps. And on Sundays, she and Louisa attended services at the Aracoeli and then took long afternoon drives
in the Campagna.

The pope had been forced to flee to Naples, but the fat, old fellow
was back, and Julia soon found that it was considered unwise
to speak against him among the Italians, and even found herself
glanced at sidewise when she brought up the issue at the American dinner parties. It was difficult because she was, after all, the
wife of the man who had helped bring about the Greek Revolution and had been named a Chevalier, a fact she became fond of
mentioning, though it had never brought her much pride in the
States. But here in Italy it gave her, through marriage, a frisson of
international intrigue and even cachet. She had never been one for
political caution, but she didn't want to offend any of her hosts
and ruin even one day of her glorious sojourn.

Through Thomas Crawford, she had also befriended the Strattons, whose reputation rested largely on their celebrated friendship with the late Margaret Fuller. It was the perfect social
mechanism for Julia to exploit, and so she was delighted when
they invited her to a ball, more of a soiree actually, though they
called it a ball on their beautifully engraved invitation. Her first
opportunity to wear one of the two gowns she'd packed carefully
in the steamer trunk! Of course, she didn't have any of her good
dresses made in Boston, where the scene was still fairly provincial
in terms of fashion. Instead, she scrimped and saved for her trips
into New York to visit her favorite salon there, or if she were
desperate, even sent a list to Annie of things she needed, which
her sister would bring on her next trip: a blue silk sash, perhaps,

and slippers to match, or a white rabbit muff to match the collar of her winter coat. At Perkins, she had finally given in to sometimes wearing plain washable muslin dresses, the type worn by the students and teachers that she would never have dreamed would touch her skin, but she had to admit they were good for when one of the babies spit up on her before she could hand the child off to a nurse. In Boston, there were infrequent occasions to showcase herself, and for the few grand events that presented themselves annually, Chev usually found some reason not to go and to try to prevent her from going. This past year, it had been headaches, terrible raging headaches, that he'd used to keep her at home by his side, though he proved the most irritable patient imaginable. How she wished he'd let Jeannette nurse him or even Laura, though Laura had nursed poor Sarah Wight nearly to death.

For the ball, Julia chose the pale yellow Indian silk gown and accompanied Thomas and Louisa to the Strattons' villa near the Colosseum. What she would give to live in such splendor! The courtyard boasted a fountain with a ubiquitous centaur entangled with a nymph, from whose mouth gushed the clear water. Ancient cypresses dotted the grounds in clumps, their dark green heads bent together as if in gossip. The dinner was properly served by waiters, all Italian, and *grazie, grazie, prego, prego* trilled round the long table, set for twenty. Julia was seated between an Italian writer and an Umbrian count. Though they both spoke some English, Julia endeavored to practice her Italian—she had studied the language from the age of fourteen with Mozart's former librettist—and they were predictably charmed by the results, correcting her mistakes gently with the tap of a finger upon her hand. She enjoyed the slight physical contact as much as the conversation, but only the count she found attractive, though his hairline had reached the middle of his shiny skull. How thick and dark Chev's hair still was, even the widow's peak still intact. What bourgeois folly that she was thinking of her husband when these two men of the world were hanging on her every word, however mangled. And then the question was asked that she had come to dread: What was Laura Bridgman like? She couldn't believe that people on this side of the Atlantic were still so fascinated by the girl. At first, she had tried merely shaking her head in mock sorrow and saying that Laura's star was in decline, without specifying the who or what or why of it. But she soon found that was not enough. "Why hasn't she come on a European tour?" they'd pepper her. They all wanted to welcome this prodigy, to see her in the flesh and be amazed by her knowledge. So at this point Julia had resorted to, well, lies.

"*Cara mia* Laura," she had started calling her, her hand on her heart. She described how she transcribed the latest poetry into Laura's hand, how she guided her horse down the beach at dusk; how she and the girl took turns braiding each other's hair while exchanging views on philosophy. "*Siamo come sorelli*," she told the gentlemen—we are like sisters.

"And so you have written poems to celebrate her?" asked the writer, and Julia was caught off guard.

"Of course," she said quickly, though in truth she had written poems on every conceivable subject, from roses to heartbreak to grand cosmologies, but never about the *miracle* that she lived with, day in and day out. In her quietest moments, she was willing to concede that perhaps Laura actually was a miracle, and as such, more than Julia could understand or put into words. But she knew that both her husband and his pupil would draw inordinate pleasure from having her immortalized by the lady of the house, and she could not bring herself to give them this much pleasure. As it was, nearly every poet, major and minor, had written about Laura already. What she would add, if she were truthful, would be a description of the strange way she cocked her head as if listening to conversations, the too-sharp scratch of her nails—deliberate, Julia was certain—on the palm, the way her fingers would linger on Chev's long after the words had run dry. Julia knew the world did not want to read these things about its peculiar darling, and so she refrained. But now she was lying through her teeth, and she saw

Louisa glaring at her from across the table. Louisa knew very well that no such verses existed, but then again, Louisa was a prig and always had been, so Julia would not worry about her sister's opinion, as long as she kept it to herself.

"Why don't you recite one of your Laura poems?" Louisa asked loudly, raising her wineglass.

"Hear, hear!" said the writer and the count at once, and suddenly Julia held the rapt attention of the entire table.

She placed her knife down dramatically across the plate of osso buco. "The poems, two of them, will be prominent in my next collection. Please forgive me that I have not yet committed them to memory."

There were murmurs of sad assent, but the silence was buttonholed by Louisa: "We all await these *grandi poesi sulla cara* Laura."

Julia couldn't believe her sister was being so nasty. As the oldest, Julia was not used to being challenged by Louisa, of all people, but perhaps her sister felt that she somehow reigned in their current circle. Well, she'd see about that. And yet Julia surprised herself that she actually felt *guilty* regarding her little lies about her intimacies with Laura, and pledged to buy the girl a scarf or a hat, perhaps, with many textures to give her fingers the greatest joy. Gloves, she knew, would not please Laura, but remind her of the punishments she had endured years ago, which Sarah had confided to Julia. That must have been awful, and here again she felt a twinge of communion with Laura because she herself had spent many nights with her hands between her legs, in the full knowledge that her husband slept in the next room and could well answer her desires. But somehow this perverseness—his presence so close and her ability to control it—made the quest for fulfillment more urgent and the release more gratifying.

Though in the month since the dinner party at the Strattons', Louisa's temperature toward her had run from tepid to frigid, she still asked for Julia to play the piano for their Christmas party. Besides being the most literary and intellectual of the three sisters (as well as arguably the loveliest), Juila was also the most musical, a fact that Louisa's request acknowledged. They all attended Christmas services at both Santa Maria Maggiore and St. Peter's. For the party, Julia changed into her dark green velvet gown, sashed with gold, and an emerald necklace given to her by her father for her sixteenth birthday. She splurged on having a girl, recommended by Mrs. Freeman, to dress her hair, roped with tiny garlands sparkling among the red corkscrews. She felt like a present, ready to be unwrapped, as the Crawfords' brougham trotted through the winding streets sprinkled with the sugar of a light snow.

When she arrived, one hour late as planned, although she was providing the entertainment, she found thirty or forty guests already gathered in the grand hall of the villa. The place looked splendid, she had to admit, with her brother-in-law's sculptures of virile naked youths each pooled in its own spotlight of brass-sconced red candles. The enormous crystal chandelier was wreathed with garlands of pine, and cast its soft light on the fifteenth-century murals that Thomas had spent endless hours and much money restoring to their original beauty, though the ravaging of nymphs hardly fit with the gay holiday theme. She wished there were murals at Perkins, but she had to fight with Chev to even get him to hang paintings, given that the residents of the place had no appreciation for them. Louisa's glory stood in the corner of the hall: a twelve-foot-high fir tree strung with satin ribbons and tiny biscotti, which the guests were encouraged to take down and nibble along with the flutes of prosecco handed out by the tuxedo-clad waiters, handsome young Italian boys all. Most of the guests were grouped around the tree, which was a great novelty since Italians did not celebrate *Natale* with trees. Thomas had fashioned a shimmering ceramic star for the top, though, and had also sculpted several small but perfect angels for the mantel of the ancient marble fireplace.

After greeting her hosts with apologies for her lateness, Julia made her way to the grand piano opposite the tree and took her seat. It didn't take long for the spell of the music to overtake her, though she would much rather be playing Bach cantatas or Beethoven concertos than Christmas carols. At least she got to play tunes for dancing after the initial few, but within half an hour, her feet were tapping wildly in her new golden slippers and she wanted to be dancing, not playing!

Thank goodness for the dinner break at last. Julia was surprised they hadn't served dinner sooner, since the Italians had been fasting for the last twenty-four hours, a ritual that Julia had definitely not observed. Louisa's cook had prepared the traditional *Natale* meal called the *cenone*: spaghetti with anchovies, an assortment of fish, fresh broccoli, fruits and sweets. No meat was allowed. The American she was seated across from looked very familiar, and when he leaned across the table to take her hand and introduce himself, she remembered: Horace Binney Wallace of Philadelphia, whom she'd met years ago at her sister's country home and who had displeased her by repeatedly remarking on Boston's backwardness compared to the City of Brotherly Love. She had disagreed with him at the time, being new to her husband's home, but in retrospect she saw that he had been entirely correct. She probably also hadn't recalled him at first because he gave no great physical impression: rather slight, with curling ginger hair and a polite but reserved bearing. But as he engaged her in conversation, proving much more interesting than the dinner companions on either side of her, she fell a bit into his eyes, which were a soft doe brown, and his bone structure was really quite fine. He was a lawyer, but taking a year away from his profession to soak up European culture— a common thing, though not that common for one of his age, which she estimated to be about thirty-five, just three years older than she was. What interested her most was that since their last meeting he had published two novels, *Stanley* and *Henry Pulteney*, along with several stories, all under different pseudonyms.

"But why so many pseudonyms, not just one?"

"The private man versus the public person," he said, "much like the public person versus the private woman."

Julia thought of some of her latest poems about her marriage, desperately disguised as pastoral odes, and found herself blushing in agreement. She had already realized she would probably have to publish as Anonymous to placate Chev.

"Now I must read your books," she said, and he told her that he would bring them to her if she would favor him with her address.

"But," he warned her, "they are, for the most part, quite violent and morbid, not necessarily to a lady's taste. I was a friend to the late Mr. Poe, and we brought much to each other."

"What a contrast indeed to your demeanor!" Julia said, though she realized that might not have been polite.

"I believe that ideally what art draws from us is not what the world would expect," he said.

When it was time for the dancing to resume, Julia took Louisa aside and prevailed upon her sister to play so that she could dance. And dance she did, from the polka, which had come crazily into vogue in the last decade largely because the turns allowed women to keep their hoopskirts out of the way, to the new five-step waltz, which she stumbled through.

After the last dance of the evening, when the sherry had been passed, Mr. Wallace lifted his glass and proposed a toast: "To redheads, for it takes nature's highest efforts to produce a true *rosso*."

Julia clinked glasses in full and grateful agreement. A true *rosso* indeed.

They soon fell into a pattern: every morning, after they had both had time to write, Mr. Wallace would stroll over from his pensione on the Via Felice, always dapper in his bespoke suits, though he cut an almost boyish figure, and stop to buy her a nosegay of violets from the vendor on her corner. Fresh flowers every day—how he spoiled her! Then after a cup of strong Italian coffee, which they had come to enjoy, they would start out walking, weather permitting. Julia carried her lavender parasol, unfortunately the only one she'd had room to bring with her, and Mr. Wallace wore his felt derby so that they could protect their equally fair complexions from the winter sun, even if it was deceivingly weak. Mr. Wallace joked that they could both freckle and burn in a snowstorm. Julia had visited all the major monuments on her first trip to Rome, and several of them this time as well, but it was never the destination that was important with Mr. Wallace's arm in hers; it was the company, the intellectual conversation. He was as bright as any man she'd ever met and nearly as sensitive as any woman, a combination that she was surprised so attracted her. Chev, after all, was the epitome of the dashing and masculine ideal.

Their favorite spot was the Forum, situated in a valley between the Palatine and Capitoline Hills, where they wandered in and out of the shells of the temples and the House of the Vestal Virgins, sitting on the pocked pigeon-sprinkled stones beneath the shadows of the columns. On their second visit, Mr. Wallace had told her he had discovered a surprise, fit only for her. He led her to one of the standing curia, or meetinghouses, the lower part of it covered in slabs of marble. Inside, the building was fairly austere except for the beautiful floor: rosettes and cornucopias in red and green against a background of yellow and purple. Julia had never seen anything like it.

"Numidian yellow and phrygian purple," Mr. Wallace read from his guide, and told her how the original construction on this meetinghouse for the senate had been interrupted when Julius Caesar was assassinated at the Theater of Pompey.

"It's stunning," Julia said, "but why is it so special to you?"

"It is the Curia Julia, the meetinghouse of Julia."

She was touched, almost unbearably so. "I have never been the first Julia." She told him how her mother had given birth to a baby named Julia, who died at one of whooping cough. Just two weeks later, she herself was born and given again the name Julia.

Mr. Wallace handed her his handkerchief and then said, "Perhaps you have been granted the blessings and abilities for both of you. The second Julia, bestowed with twice the beauty and the grace." She was delighted, and so it was here, on the broad steps, that they discussed philosophy; by unspoken agreement, more frivolous subjects were left for coffee at a café before they returned to Julia's apartment, with Mr. Wallace leaving her to lunch with her children.

Mr. Wallace was a student of Auguste Comte, the founder of positivism, which recently had become popular. He spoke ardently of the ideas and of the man himself, whom he had visited twice in Paris. Julia was unfamiliar with Comte, save the name, but she soon felt herself drawn to his theories of progressivism, and she in turn shared her thoughts on Hegel and Swedenborg, though Mr. Wallace knew a fair amount about them as well. Even more fulfilling than the philosophy, they could discuss poetry, most specifically hers. Though Theodore Parker and Longfellow were supportive of her work, neither was willing—or perhaps capable—of giving her the grave and direct criticism of Mr. Wallace. He could spend an hour on one stanza, and Julia respected his opinions as well as his taste since he proclaimed his great admiration for the majority of her verse. She even showed him the latest poems, camoflauged plaints of her marital discontent, and he uncovered the very heart of them straightaway. How he could see through her, or perhaps more correctly, into her. She had never encountered a soul like him. And it wasn't as if they didn't laugh—oh, they did—and Julia found herself sharing stories about Chev and Laura and life among the enfeebled. Mr. Wallace did not seem to judge her, even when she confessed how she had fibbed about writing odes to Laura as they finished their hike to the top of the Tarpeian Rock overlooking the Forum. As she climbed the steep hill, Julia deliberately lifted her skirts a bit higher than necessary and gave him a flash of her stockinged ankles; they weren't near as lovely and slender as before her pregnancies, but she knew they were still comely.

Mr. Wallace had read that during the Roman Republic, the rock was used as an execution site. Murderers, perjurers, and runaway slaves were thrown to their deaths, as were those with severe mental and physical disabilities since they were believed to be cursed by the gods.

"Forgive me," he said, "but the company of a blind-deaf-mute must be quite boring."

Julia looked down at the sheer hundred-foot drop and thought carefully before she spoke. Laura, she guessed, would have been flung over the cliff. "No, it's not that Laura is boring. She has the spirit of a bobcat matched with the curious affection of a kitten." There, she had summed her up so aptly. She must remember this description to tell Chev; surely even he would be pleased at her insight. She went on to tell Mr. Wallace how Laura had despoiled her marriage bed; assaulted her ear; slapped various teachers; and generally wreaked havoc at Perkins with her caprices. She didn't mention how Laura had embarrassed the great Dr. Howe on the religious front, mostly because she herself viewed his long battle against the Calvinists as slightly absurd.

"But you named your last daughter Laura," Wallace reminded her. He'd held little Laura himself in recent days, once even rocking her to sleep. The children appreciated his gentleness, his calm.

"When she became too much for even Chev to endure, he sent her home, but then she tried starving herself to death. So the naming of my child was an offering."

"You were very kind to agree."

Yes, especially since she'd been afraid that the name itself might jinx her daughter for life, cause her to trip into a spindle or go deaf. But so far, she was a delightfully average—no, above average—child. And in exchange for the name, Chev had moved Laura into a cottage on the grounds on her return, no longer to haunt Julia in the main house.

She told Mr. Wallace about the stench of the Institution's water closets; the drafts that kept her swaddled in layers even in late spring; the eerie walk through a gauntlet of oncoming blind children, dodging their spidery hands, their arms out, groping like ghouls, meeting the blank green-masked gazes again and again until she thought she would go mad.

What sweet relief to be unthrottled by the ruff of philanthropy, the ill-fitting mantle of forced humanistic feeling! And so with Mr. Wallace, in his accepting and perfectly *simpatico* company, Julia felt the most comfortable since she was a girl with her beloved tutor Cogswell, who had applauded her high spirits and strong opinions, which the rest of society might not have gallantly received. "A truly independent thinker," he'd praised her, not, she knew, what her father or her husband wished her to be. But now she had been granted this unexpected gift of Horace Binney Wallace, who, she had begun to feel, had given her back her true self.

Julia was more surprised than alarmed when, after six straight weeks of daily friendship, Mr. Wallace didn't show up one morning. It was raining—that must be it—and on ill-weathered days they had to stay inside, in Julia's small parlor, their talk constrained by the presence of the nurse and children nearby. But the next day was sunny, and still he didn't come, and so she sent a letter to his residence. By the fifth day, she was considering going there herself, though she feared she'd get lost among the tiny winding streets, as she always did when she was alone.

It did not help her mood that an irate letter had arrived from Chev, a long tirade demanding her return and mentioning Mr. Wallace not once, but several times. He seemed to think himself the butt of a scandal, a possible cuckold. Perhaps the recent success of Mr. Hawthorne's *The Scarlet Letter* had inflamed him; though Chev didn't read novels, he doubtless knew about the passion-blind Hester Prynne since the book had sold over twenty-five hundred copies in its first ten days. Did he wish to brand his own wife with a scarlet *A* upon her return? Julia was incensed; no line of propriety had technically been crossed. Louisa had intimated, however, that something untoward had happened, or was happening, though Julia assured her that the couple had never even passed an unchaperoned dinner together, only eating out a few times in the company of others. But when Louisa and Thomas had shared a supper with them at Antonio's, Louisa appeared scandalized that Julia had ordered—had said out loud!—spaghetti *puttanesca*, the so-called sauce of *puttane*, or whores. The heavily garlicked and pepper-laden dish was Julia's favorite. Afterward, Louisa had chastised her for not only that, but for her "too intimate" rapport with Mr. Wallace.

Julia knew better than to allude even obliquely to her sisters her feelings for her new friend, though she had confided in letters to Sarah a bit about her romantic longings, not only because she trusted her, but because she was thousands of miles away. Julia missed Sarah's sensible but pleasant company, but at least they were both freed from beneath the Chevalier's iron fist. Sarah had written her a couple of quite peculiar letters, however, that seemed to hint at some unmentionable discord with Mr. Bond. That would be such a pity, Julia thought, since she had secretly matched them in the first place, one of her greatest social triumphs. When Sarah had told her before she left that Laura had thought the minister was courting her, Julia had first laughed out loud and then felt instantly sorry. Was it possible that there was someone out there in the wide world for Laura Bridgman, perhaps some other gravely injured or God-slighted creature? She would keep an eye out, she told herself sternly. Of course, she'd realized long ago that Laura was, in some strange way, in love with Chev, but she was sure now, though she had not always been so, that it was an unsexed devotion, more that of a daughter for a mercurial and ambivalent father than that of a woman for a man. Still, such longing must be very painful for her, even now. Julia remembered how close the two had been at the time of her courtship and early marriage, and she was not proud of how she had done everything in her considerable power to drive a wedge between them. Though letters flew back and forth across the oceans between Sarah and Laura, Julia was confident her friend would never mention anything to the girl. And even if she did, Laura would have no real understanding of what it meant to actually be in love, or of what was at stake.

The oddest thing—Laura had written to Julia that she had recovered her sense of taste. Julia was sure this wasn't possible, but in her reply said only that she was glad for the girl.

Obviously, it was Louisa who'd written to Chev, or, clever gossip that she was, probably to her dear friend Sumner, who would of course go straight to Chev. And that was the other thing that prickled her: her husband had Sumner, with his peculiar and annoying attachment, to stroke his monstrous ego. He was the perfect mate in that regard.

Shortly before she left, Julia had discovered, quite by accident when she was looking in Chev's desk for a new pot of ink, a cache of letters from Sumner tied with a red silk ribbon. Since when did her husband buy ribbon? She'd untied the packet and skimmed each letter quickly, mostly for unfavorable references to herself, of which there were many. But aside from expected insults and the tittle-tattle of politics and yawning social reform, she was more than a bit unnerved by the fulsomeness of the endearments, by the sheer number of times Charlie spoke of longing to touch her husband's face, his hands, any part of him, it seemed. And at the bottom of the last page of nearly every missive, in bold capitals, the words *BURN THIS*, a request that her husband had obviously not obliged. Why did he keep the letters, over ten years of them? She considered confronting Chev about what she'd found, but really, what was there to say that would make any sense? It was all too confusing for her to even formulate a plan, and she didn't understand the heat of her own reaction. After all, most people, Julia included, wrote letters full of affection to their dearest friends. What did Chev's letters to Charlie say? She decided she preferred not to know, even if that had been at all possible.

But she was more than a bit frightened that her husband seemed on the verge of actually bringing up divorce in his letter to her, especially when their circle was still abuzz with last year's trial of Edwin Forrest. The famous actor had sued to divorce his wife of twelve years after catching her with another man, a circus covered daily in the papers. She would never subject herself or her children to such a frenzy, and so she would have to go to great lengths to make peace with Chev when she returned, whether she wanted to or not. All this tortured her as she waited for Mr. Wallace to return. She had taken to wondering if perhaps their very propriety was what was now keeping him away, but then again, he had never touched her, except for her hands. If he did want to take her, she decided she would let him, though she knew how easily she fell pregnant. If there were to be a consummation, she would have to rush back to Boston immediately to cover any possible consequences, but the truth was she thought it would be well worth all the trouble.

She tried to lose her worries in her work. Through her discussions with Mr. Wallace, the collection had taken shape and she could finally see a real book in it. She wrote to Longo for publication advice, enclosing a few of the poems, and promised herself that on the voyage back, she would dig in and begin the wrenching process of revisions. The poems would be by far the most candid and emotionally revealing of her career, but Mr. Wallace had helped her to realize that their hard-won authenticity was what made them true art. Still, she didn't have a title for the book.

One week later, he arrived at her door, violets in hand, but his angelic face was haggard, dark circles beneath his lovely eyes. She thought for a moment that he might collapse in the foyer, but he made it to the settee.

"You have been ill?" Julia asked and felt a little twinge of satisfaction that he had not stayed away from her on purpose.

He nodded and then began to talk of a new opera, *Rigoletto* by Verdi, and would she like to see it with him? She had to tell him that an evening out, even in the company of others, was impossible at the moment due to the mongering of her sister. Mr. Wallace suddenly put his hands to his face, and Julia realized he was sobbing. Her instinct was to put her arms around him, to comfort him, but she knew she couldn't. She wasn't the kind of woman who could ever throw herself at a man. Instead, she patted his hand.

"It's just an opera," she said, "and not even the premiere. That was in Venice last fall." She waited. "You're still ill, aren't you, poor thing? Is it your head again?"

He raised his face to hers and laughed, but it was a low and bitter laugh. "Yes, it is my head again."

She rose. "I'll get you a cup of tea and a cold cloth—" But he reached out and took her hand, pulling her back down onto the settee.

"I was praying I wouldn't have to tell you the truth," he said.

Julia couldn't breathe. Was he in love with someone else?

"I am afflicted with spells of melancholy, many years of misery. You don't deserve to be brought low by my moods, even for one day."

Julia couldn't help it; she too began to weep, but with relief. He did love her, after all, and also here, piteously revealed, was another thing they shared.

"A confession," she whispered as he wiped at his face with a handkerchief. "That black dog is one of my oldest companions."

He looked at her as if she were joking. "But you...," he started. "But you are always sound, always bright. The light of..."

"Not always, dear Mr. Wallace. I don't think it is my natural disposition, but I have my spells in despair over my marriage and," she whispered, "my childbearing state, which renders me useless."

He nodded. Finally he smiled. "At least yours is brought on by circumstance, while I fear mine is entirely constitutional. Here with you I have been as happy as I have ever been, and yet it has overtaken me once again. The ancients would have flung me from the Tarpeian Rock for certain."

She made him happier than anyone! "You should have come to me sooner."

He laughed, a real laugh this time. "I couldn't get out of bed."

"Ah, that is the difference. When you have children, you must get out of bed. We will blow that smoke away together." She stood up. "The old stones await."

"What a fine pair we make." His eyes, still gemmed with tears, were steady on hers as he rose and they left the apartment. The nosegay lay abandoned on the table, the violets without water.

Over the next three weeks, they resumed their daily walks. But Chev had sent another letter, this one telling her to stay in Europe, that he didn't want her back. More than that heavy news, though, was the knowledge that they would soon part; long before they met, Mr. Wallace had already made plans to return to Paris to spend more time with Comte. Julia was in anguish at the idea of going back to America, which now seemed the country of her ex-ile, a land of the new, the modern, the ill-considered, everything utterly lacking in timelessness and fascination. So they made a plan to meet in New York at the end of spring when Julia would go there to visit her sister Annie.

On the day of Mr. Wallace's leave-taking, Julia stopped him in a side alley several streets from her apartment, its only resident a gargoyle spewing water into a small basin. Like the French, the Italians decorated even their drain spouts.

"I can't bear to have you leave me at the door," she said. "So here."

He said to her only two words—"passion flowers"—and then took her face in his hands and pressed his lips to hers, just for a second, but she felt his sweet breath enter her, and for a while, this would have to be enough. Beneath the upturned brim of her bonnet, she stared into the unblinking eyes of the gargoyle, his smile twisted into a salacious grimace.

Chapter 21

Chev, 1852

Your wife is frolicking on the Spanish Steps, and here you spend your dark winter's eves with me," Sumner told him, though Chev knew that his friend was inordinately pleased to have him all to himself lately, especially for the recent New Year, this alleged beginning.

"Are you merely needling me with your sharp prong or do you actually have something to tell me?" They were cozied in Sumner's apartments, suspenders loosened, feet and fire up, fourth brandies in hand.

Sumner closed his eyes and rested his leonine head against the pillows, as if he were seriously considering. Chev was used to his dramatic silences as much as his dramatic monologues, both of which he held ridiculously, inestimably dear for reasons he could not explain, even to himself.

Sumner opened his eyes and sighed. "There are certain whiffs of an inopportune nature blowing over the Atlantic," he said, his words breaded with sympathy.

"There always are," said Chev. "That is why we still secretly delight in Europe, but you have already apprised me of Julia's friendship with Mr. Wallace, Esquire."

"I have been told that Mr. Wallace encourages and critiques her verse, so much so that Longo says she'll soon have enough for a book."

The poetry, always back to the blasted poetry. "And has he read any of it?" Chev knew Longfellow held an equally strong allegiance to both Julia and himself, though he trusted him entirely with Julia, even in the delicate bower of poetics.

Sumner lit both their cigars, the finest from Cuba, a holiday treat from Horace Mann. "Yes."

"And?" Sumner possessed the natural storyteller's gift of drawing out any tale to enhance the suspense, something that served him well in the courtroom, but tonight Chev was tired of it.

Sumner grasped his hand as if to prepare him. "The poesy seems to be all about the rigors—'dues,' I think she calls them—of marriage versus the state of natural love and freedom."

Chev allowed his friend to continue to hold his hand. He knew Julia had written a few poems about marriage and that they might be of a more personal nature than he desired, but he had not considered that she might be selfish enough to offer them up for public consumption. Especially with a young lawyer loitering nearby.

"She wouldn't be unfaithful to me," he said.

"Except in verse," his friend countered, and Chev detected a decided relish in the pronouncement. He moved his hand away and concentrated on the soothing scent of his cigar.

"Perhaps," he finally allowed. "But it is all rumor, and rumors from across the Atlantic often acquire a tsunami's worth of dubious detail in the translation, as we both know well."

"Or they become diluted." Sumner tapped him emphatically on the knee, leaving his fingers to rest there.

Chev stood and did his *de rigueur* round of pacing in front of the fire. "If there were actually a book, I would know. I would definitely know."

Sumner lounged back against the cushions like an enormous house cat. "The title is *Passion-Flowers*. By Anonymous."

Chev exhaled long and hard, and sat back on the sofa, his head on his dearest friend's shoulder. He knew Charlie would tell him everything, whether he wanted to hear it or not. Sumner stroked his hair, and he let him.

"*Passion-Flowers*," Sumner repeated. "Do you think she means *flowers* as a noun or a verb?"

"It's not good either way. The verb is worse, I suppose. But at least she has the strength of character and respect to publish anonymously."

Sumner tugged at Chev's dark forelock, a bit harder than he would have liked. "Until the wits and wags of Beantown devour and regurgitate it, picking through for clues. It shouldn't take long to finger the authoress, from what I've read in the past of Julia's work. She seems to take everything most personally, an almost deviant quality in a wife."

Chev shook himself. "And what would you know of wives, Charlie? What you've read in books? Seen at the opera? Gleaned from my conversation and Longo's and Mann's?"

Sumner's color rose. "I know—"

"What you know could fit in a thimble. Have you ever advanced past the stage of polite discourse with even one lady?"

"I have been impolite with many. You do not know every inch of me, Chev."

"Meaning you've what—paid for a woman?"

"No. I mean...No." He put his great shaggy head in his hands, and Chev felt instantly, deeply sorry for his interrogation of his friend.

"It's all right, Charlie," he murmured. "Whatever it is, however it is, it's all right."

Charles raised his head and looked up at him. "Whatever it is, however it is?"

"Yes, my dear. Of course."

And before he could move to stop him, Sumner's lips were on his own, tentatively at first and then with a greater urgency than he'd ever felt from a woman. He put his hands on his friend's chest, and for the briefest instant, allowed his mouth to soften, his shoulders to relax into the embrace. But then he collected himself violently and pushed Sumner so hard that he half-fell from the couch, landing in a position of supplication, down on his knees. Chev snapped his suspenders and stood over him. Sumner did not bend his head; instead, he matched him look for look: helplessness, curiosity, revulsion, amiability, and then the smooth, impenetrable veneer of the public man.

"Find a wife, Charlie," Chev said. "I mean it. Nothing will serve you better."

Charles laughed until he almost choked. "As yours serves you? No thank you, sir."

"Then make the best of your...nature." Chev threw on his jacket, did not look back. As he reached the door, Sumner whispered, "Passion. Flowers."

Chev slammed the door, wondering if he ever dared cross that threshold again.

So Julia was living again the life of a belle, a diva, free from his rules, far from his bed. He'd never enjoyed the type of socializing of which his wife was so fond, where charm passed for character and witticisms for truth. But he trusted her to be faithful, he thought, if for no other reason than the possibility of pregnancy, the state she so dreaded. Her mother had died in childbirth, it was true, but that shouldn't make a lifelong coward of a woman, a betrayal of the natural order. Of course, he'd found a soft nest in which to seek comfort, to have his feathers smoothed, his nature attended to. He had been remarkably gallant during her first two pregnancies, until he realized she was deliberately weaning the babes for months longer than necessary, a strategy he was sure she employed solely to keep him from her bed. How could he impose himself with his own little poppet pressed close on her mother's bosom, sleeping away the night while he paced? He felt made a fool of, and never more so than at this moment, with Mrs. Samuel Gridley Howe loose at the Colosseum. And so he'd now bestowed upon himself the gift of a young redhead, but not so young as to be innocent of the world.

His last letter to his wife had not been full of titter and gauze. His pen had trembled over the word, but he dipped it again in the ink and forced himself to write "divorce." A possibility. A scandal, though if Dickens could do it, so could he, and unlike Dickens, there'd be no other woman officially involved. Yet. The redhead would never do for a wife, miles below his station. He needed a young, firm one from a good family with a naturally pliant domestic nature. And that would mean more little ones! God love him, he adored his children—well, most children—especially all his sweet, blind darlings racing about the place, laughing and hugging his knees. He doubted seriously if he could ever go through with a divorce; he probably couldn't because he did love her, damn her, after everything, but she had pushed as far as he could suffer, and he needed to put the fear of God in her. To think back to those gray eyes cast down demurely as she'd promised at their engagement that she would not publish her work. Obviously, her desire for fame, for blatant display of pure ego, was stronger than her womanly instincts. *He* had not chosen fame; it had chosen him through the vehicle of Laura, but his own acclaim was also born naturally from the humanitarian instinct, the gravely large bumps of ideality and compassion that God had engendered on the grid of his skull. He thought back to Dr. Combe's prenuptial examination of Julia, and how little he'd allowed the diagnosis of her self-regard and combativeness bumps to bother him at the time. Had he betrayed even phrenology for a woman? He ran his fingers over his own finely shaped head to see if there were any slight changes, any faction more pronounced. No, there was his affection bump at the back, large and healthy and deserving as ever. Combe insisted that no man he'd ever met had been given a gift so Brobdingnagian, and always cautioned that he must honor that most distinctive sign of his nature and all that it portended.

Chev received a letter from Laura's mother, telling him that her old friend, Asa Tenney, had died. She didn't know the cause; as Howe understood, the man had never been right anyway. Didn't matter, Laura loved him. Her first friend. He dragged himself out of his own wallowing long enough to tell her and did not flinch when she fell into his arms. So strange to be holding this grown woman, usually so straight and brittle, now soft against his chest. All the times she'd sat on his lap after supper, those dreamy hours they'd spent together when she'd lived with him in the residence. He let her stay in his arms as long as she wanted and was surprised when that privilege was not enough to allay her sorrow. So he told her that she didn't have to partake of any of her usual duties for as long as she needed, and didn't have to help with the blind girls. The funeral was over; there was no point in her going home. He dried her face with his handkerchief, patting the eyeshade gently.

"Asa watching?" she asked, biting her lip.

"Yes," he told her, "always." She nodded and left him. He wondered if she felt as bereft as he did.

Chapter 22

Laura, 1852

She comes to me almost every evening, especially now that I need her comfort more than ever after the news about Asa. She tells the blinds in her room that Cook is making her work nights to prepare for breakfast, so they pity her, and she steals back to her bed while it is still dark. No one guesses our delirious secret life. Some days Kate swears she is so tired that she's put carrots in the porridge, cream into the roast. When she can't come, I am in agony. It's icy out, so we're not riding the horses. The only chance I have to see her is the kitchen, but every time Cook catches me and rushes me out. I save the weekly cup of milk Cook gives me to bathe my hands and surprise Kate with it, rubbing the liquid into each crack and crevice of her palms, soaking her fingers in my special bowl until the calluses begin to soften.

Tonight, she brings bread sopped in something. The taste is not pleasant—it actually makes me wince—but it is, after all, a taste. Vinegar, the only truly sour thing she could find. "The next time will be honey," she says, so pure she swears I will understand sweetness.

"Don't tell anyone you taste yet," she writes.

I agree, though I have already mentioned it in letters to both Sarah and Julia. I am bursting to tell Doctor. He will be so proud, so excited! Kate lets me brush her hair, and tomorrow when she is gone, I will collect the coiling strands from the floor and add them to the store in my pillowcase. She tells me how she went to town to see the exhibition of Julia Pastrana, billed as "the World's Ugliest Woman" because she is covered head to toe with thick black hair. I think she would feel very nice, but Kate says I wouldn't think so if I could see her.

I pull the shimmy over her head and find her nipples. Her breasts are more than twice the size of my little bumps and seem to have grown even larger under my ministrations. But it is not the pillows that move me; it is the hard stiffness of her nipples in my mouth, the way they change as I suck and her moans shake against me. But now she smacks me lightly on the shoulder, and then again. I raise my head, lost.

"No biting," she says.

"Don't like it?" I like it. The kissing and touching are wonderful, but those are only the soft beginnings of any *real* feeling. The truest pleasures lie in all that the teeth and nails and fingers can accomplish, especially after a few sips of whiskey.

Kate sits up. "You mark me," she says, bringing my fingers up to the side of her neck and shoulders. "Bruises."

"That's bad?" I ask. I've been told I had bruises on sore spots when I've hurt myself.

"Colors on the skin. Hide with shawl."

"What colors?"

"Blue, black, violet. Fade to yellow or green."

"So beautiful." I pat her neck, but all I feel is the slightest of welts on one spot, nothing of texture. How I'd love to see the colors I've given her. Maybe when I become more proficient, I can employ the bruises to write upon her body: first wrapping an *L* around one nipple, and then imprisoning the other within the *B*. What will I engrave on the high roundness of her stomach? Maybe I will stamp my entire name all over her, covering the soft meat of her thighs and buttocks with my letters. I don't know if she'd enjoy this, but I would. She is certainly more gentle than I am; perhaps most people are.

"Next time," I tell her, "only green to match my shade." I scissor my legs between hers, chasing joy.

In the dining room at meals, I am careful to act as if nothing is different; it isn't that hard because the food is far too bland to reach the threshold my sense requires. Sometimes I think I detect a belt of salt, or even pepper, in my meat or soup, and I wonder if Kate has found a way to deliver a special dish to me. When I ask, she only laughs. She thinks that now my taste has begun developing, it will continue, though it might take years, she says. I'm not sure if I'm getting any better at it, but I trust her experience. No one, not even Doctor, has ever given me so much. Maybe one day I will even be able to smell her. "If I could smell only one thing in the world," I tell her, "it would be you."

"Not flowers?"

"No."

"Not ocean?"

"No."

"Not Doctor?"

"Only you." She says some parts don't smell good, like feet and bottoms, but I know it would all be delicious to me.

Tonight she has brought me not food, but a book, *The Age of Fable, or Stories of Gods and Heroes.* She borrowed it from one of the teachers, but promised we'll only use it late at night and she'll return it by morning so no one will notice. I am excited because I read that most myths have to do with transformations; these are the things I dream about. Kate flips through the pages and summarizes the stories for me. I'm not sure she can really read that fast or if she's making some of it up. Either way, I love it: a nymph turned into a tree, a god into a swan, a woman into a spider. She tells me about Semele and Zeus, Psyche and Cupid, tales of mortals blind to their heavenly lovers who come to them in darkness. Would I explode into flames or be changed into showers of gold if Kate were ever revealed to me in all her glory? Would that I could be transformed by the piercing of an arrow or the lightning of a god. Most of the metamorphoses seem to be for the worst; however, if I could be given one hundred eyes like Argos or roam the earth as a seeing, hearing, tasting cow like Io, that wouldn't be so bad. My God is not keen on metamorphoses, though, except, of course, Christ's transfiguration, and so it appears predetermined that I should stay trapped in this diminished form. On days when I am feeling particularly wise, I think of myself as Athena, shot straight from Doctor's forehead like a cannonball. And Julia of course is the jealous Hera, Kate the magnificent Aphrodite. The goddess of love comes to the bed of the blind seer, and mortal and immortal are joined, however briefly.

I lie awake waiting for the slight shudder of the door. My door has no lock, though I have asked a dozen times. Doctor claimed it is more likely that I would be a danger to myself locked *inside* than that anyone might come to harm me. "Privacy?" I asked, and he said, "Never wanted to be alone before, even when you should."

I know he is remembering the years when I crawled into Tessy's bed, or sometimes another girl's, only to be discovered and reprimanded, or worse, gloved. All I wanted was to curl myself around them, to kiss their hair and maybe the backs of their necks. A rule I made: no rubbing, the way I did in my own bed. I liked touching Tessy's skin and Wightie's cheeks, but I did not wait and hunger, coil and uncoil, in anticipation as I do for Kate. Maybe it's because Kate returns my longing, while I see now that the others only suffered my caresses out of kindness.

The damp rushes into the room, and I know she is here. She doesn't sit on the bed yet, but raps her knuckles lightly against my lips as if asking for permission to enter. I open, and she places something small and wet upon my tongue. It fills my mouth with a not unpleasant tang.

"Strong, wonderful," she writes.

"Want to spit."

"Italian! Garlic!"

"Doctor went to Italy. Doesn't eat."

"Cook at Tewksbury Italian."

"Friend?"

"Taught me everything."

I wonder if she got the garlic from this Italian. She won't tell me where she gets the things Cook doesn't stock. I suppose she has her ways, probably some useful tricks learned from the hard life of an orphan.

After a moment, she says, "Stop. Breath smells."

I pull the bulb from my mouth. "Made me smell bad?"

She kisses me. "Now we're same."

She touches my eyeshade, and I try not to flinch.

"Off," she writes. "I want to see you."

Only one person has seen me uncovered since my childhood besides Doctor: Sarah Wight, and that was an accident. But then again no one's ever seen the rest of me the way Kate has.

"No light," I tell her. She leans over me to douse the lamp, though I realize I won't know if she's really extinguished it or not. I sit astride her and slowly untie the ribbons from my shade, letting it fall onto her stomach. Her hands reach for my face, but I grab her arms and push them down over her head. With my green ribbons I tie her wrists together. The air feels likes cool breath on my face. I trace the empty sockets of my eyes and begin to move.

I wake in the night with our hands entwined and write softly upon hers: "Will get glass eyes for you." I think she is asleep because her hand is still for a long while, but then she writes, "No. Windows to soul open." It is the most beautiful thing anyone has ever said to me, and I will try to think of my defect in this new and unexpected way. It will be hard, though, no matter how much she loves me.

I am surprised after lunch when Jeannette tells me that Doctor wants to see me in his office right away. I am even more surprised that I do not rush to him as I always have. I let him wait for almost an hour while I stroll around the back by the stable, hoping to find Kate, but she's probably still washing up. No doubt I have food on my dress, as I usually do after lunch, but I don't change it when I stop in at my cottage before going to see Doctor. I splash cold water on my face, and that's it.

"You must be very busy, L," he writes instead of greeting me properly.

"Women are busy," I write. "Children are not."

"True," he says as he helps me into a chair. "Looking like a lady. Plumper. Eating well?"

"I can taste." I hadn't planned to tell him, but there it is. "Taste food."

"What?" His touch is rough.

"God," I say. "God gave me taste."

"God," he says. "Very generous of God so late."

"Serious."

"Taste everything now? Eggs, pies—"

"Only strong. Vinegar. Garlic."

"We don't even have garlic. Ridiculous."

"You haven't tried," I tell him. "Here, gruel, toast, boiled meat."

"I begged you to eat. Almost starved at home, and now you say I don't feed you well? Ungrateful girl."

He is right. He let me come back because he thought I might die, even if he put me in a cottage instead of letting me back in the house. How far I've come from starving! Why can't he share in my joy? I thought he would be leaping for the chandeliers.

"Not ungrateful," I write. "Happy."

The floor trembles as he paces. Finally, he stops.

"All right. A test."

A test? Doctor must always test everything: my word, my happiness; the health in my cheeks is worth nothing to him without science. Without documentation. For years, I sat in this room, early evenings after supper, letting him quiz me for hours just to have the chance to stroke his beard.

"As you wish," I write and stand to go.

"Down," he says. "Called you because of problem with new girl. Cook's helper."

I squeeze the chair's cushion until my fingers begin to go numb. "Know her?"

I nod. I don't want him to speak her name.

"Irish, but clever. Thought I'd done the right thing."

I think of the friction of skin on skin. There is nothing else like it in this world, not even close. Regardless of what happens, he has done the right thing.

"She's been in your cottage?"

"No," I write. Then, "Maybe. Don't remember." It's all right if she's been spotted coming in or out; I'll say I was helping her with lessons.

"Jeannette caught her with your music box behind stable. Tried to bury in hay."

I don't understand. "You gave me that box."

"Kate says you gave it to her."

"You talked?"

"This morning."

"She sat in this chair?" Was her bottom, marked with the prints of my fingers, pressed into these cushions as she answered all your questions? Was she frightened?

"Don't remember which blessed chair. You didn't give. She stole."

I imagine Kate squatting in the hay, humming, holding the box in her lap. Such pleasure she takes in its three tunes, especially "Johnnie My Boy."

"Should've checked bumps on her head more carefully when we checked for lice."

I want to scream. My darling's head is even more perfect than Doctor's.

"I gave," I write. "I forgot."

"Thought you loved it."

"Can't hear music, can I?"

He puts the box into my hands. "You begged for this," he says. "Twelfth birthday. Your initials carved into its bottom."

I trace the delicate cuts in the wood. "Still there."

"Girl did nothing wrong?" he asks. "Sure?"

"Nothing." I rise. "Much reading to do."

He bends to kiss my hand. The stiff hairs of his mustache bristle my knuckles, and I wonder if Julia misses the feel of it against her breasts.

I lie on the bed with the music box on my chest. Each time it finishes its cycle, I wind it again. Twenty-seven times and still she hasn't come. I must have fallen asleep because suddenly the box is being lifted. I grab for her wrist.

"Stealing again?"

She scoots onto the bed. "Would give it back." She's certainly very calm for a criminal. Probably not the first time she's nicked something.

"Why?"

"When I'm not with you, it reminds me."

I don't know if I believe her. Kate raises my hand to her cheek, and I feel the tears there. "If I give it, you'll get caught again." Slowly, I crank the music box and nestle it between her thighs.

After a moment, she stands and the rough cloth of her work dress falls against my stockinged feet.

"Bruise me anywhere," she writes.

And so I do.

Kate comes tonight, but only to tell me that she can't stay, not even for half an hour.

"Three miles' walk to Saint Malachy's before breakfast."

"Just talk to God in your head." He is my closest friend besides Kate.

"Need help from saints."

"Saints stupid. God right here," I tell her, holding out my arms.

Why would anyone communicate with the Lord through a third person when they could have direct access? It was like *choosing* to be blind and deaf, and relying on somebody else to carry your news back and forth. Talking to a saint or even Mother Mary when you can speak to God directly—what a waste. What do these Catholics think they're doing?

She folds my hands into my lap. "My God not here."

"Talk about me?"

"Confess everything."

"But only wrongs. I am not a wrong."

"I'm full up with sin," she writes, trailing the last word onto my wrist. I start to reply, but she won't have it; instead she pushes my palms together in the attitude of prayer. She sweeps her curls across my face, back and forth, back and forth, the way I like it. She tries to stand, but I snare a ringlet between my fingers. She pulls away, and I know I'm hurting her, but still I hold on until she bends down and kisses me on the cheek, gently adjusts my shade. I let the hair uncoil from my finger, one ring at a time, and then she is gone.

Kate hasn't come to me for two nights, and so I try to sneak into the kitchen after breakfast. Cook takes me by the arm and walks me back out immediately.

"Where's your girl?" I write.

"Irish gone," she spells and then brushes me away. I force myself to put one foot in front of the other until I reach my cottage. I pull the pillowcase stuffed with her hair from beneath the bed, and bury my face in it.

Generally, I stay clear of the gossip of the schoolgirls. I used to love it, but now that I am the eldest by far, it is beneath me to indulge their silly stories. But today at lunch, I do not close my hands, and they peck at me like chickens. I know, just as I know that the mash I'm eating is not going to stay down, that these dirty, little fingers will spell out "Kate."

"A baby!" one girl writes, and in my other palm crashes the news that they threw her out in the street.

"Who?" I ask.

"Doctor," taps one, and another adds, "Jeannette and Cook." They write many things about my beloved that I can't bear to repeat, even if they are mere opinions, not facts. The only thing that sticks is that we're having a baby.

Two weeks have passed, and I keep my hands away from the gossip about Kate. I am sure she is the subject of much ridiculous speculation, given the nature of servants and blind girls, but words tossed into the air, even if they reach heaven, cannot hurt us. She is out there, out in the life of Boston, just beyond the glowing circle of my world here at Perkins. Her belly grows fatter, our baby grows bigger, and they're both strong as cows. I understand why the Lord in His wisdom gave the baby to Kate instead of to me; certainly nature has ill-equipped me for motherhood. I think it takes about a year for babies, but the child will arrive with curling hair and my blue eyes, and Kate will bring her to see me. She will test me to see if I recognize the girl right away. As soon as I touch her, I will know that she is ours. I can wait for this day. I smile as I dust and clean and help the young ones with their reading and maths. It's only a matter of time. I am so glad she took the music box and also the white straw bonnet with the lilacs. She wants to keep me with her always.

Chapter 23
Chev, 1852

Julia was back. He'd known it wouldn't take long after his letter; within two weeks of receiving it, she'd booked her westward passage across the Atlantic, macaroni and lawyer be damned. He was ecstatic to see his children, and yes, ecstatic to see her too. He hadn't realized how much he'd missed her until he gazed again upon that lovely face, that radiant oval he preferred above all others—still—and the fact that it did not betray any trace of sulkiness or resentment made her homecoming all the more perfect. That first night, once she'd gotten the children down, she shyly invited him into her bedroom, and he knew that his threat had won him back everything. At least for now. First, she told him the most important thing: she would agree to publish the book anonymously. It was, after all, not her own glory that she sought, but only to celebrate the inspiration of both God and her muse, Poetry. He reveled in the warmth of her embrace and took his rightful place beside her, on top of her, behind her, once again. As the weeks went by and she allowed him virtually unfettered access to the delights of her chamber, he found himself hoping that she would not get with child particularly soon, because although he'd wished for another, he wished for the continued sweetness of her company even more.

Two months passed in relative bliss. She worked on the edits of her book almost daily and took excellent care of the children, with help, of course. She had never really cooked or enjoyed any of the domestic duties except hostessing, but he forgave her that now. She was once again his true mate. She was so overtaken with passion one night that she broke down and cried in his arms as they lay in bed, and he comforted her like a babe, finding that he enjoyed her at her most vulnerable, those hot tears upon his neck. Then it happened again, a couple of nights later, a veritable flood, and this time he asked the cause, to which she murmured only that her nerves were bothering her. She had always been high-strung, so this was no great surprise. But then he came upon her at her desk, her head bent low over her pages, weeping as if her heart were broken. He was a doctor; he should have guessed it already! She was in the family way again; apparently, nothing could stop his hot-blooded course to fatherhood. He tiptoed out and left her to her womanly tides. She would soon be fat and happy again, he knew it.

But the crying and dark moods continued, and so he finally asked, and she said no, there was no child, nor did she want there to be one. Yet still she kept him in her bed, though he now found it more difficult to perform if she was weeping. And the little hiccups after the sobs, which at first he'd found endearing, now vexed him no end, each little pop a reminder that there was something he did not know. He woke several nights to see her standing at the window, hands upon the sill as if about to jump, her narrow shoulders shaking from behind.

Chev knew that Longfellow had been to the house several times to go over pages with Julia, but he had not stepped into the office once, not even for a greeting. It was clear that Longo, one of his oldest and dearest and his friend long before he became Julia's, was avoiding him. He knew why, of course, but what kind of man would he be if he did not confront it? Longo was being weak, a puny snake in the grass, and so he called him out, sending a letter asking him to the club for a Saturday night, the way they'd done a hundred times, with others, or alone. Thank God, the poet was still upright enough to agree to meet.

The main room of the club was glutted with overstuffed sofas and chairs, but Chev preferred the smaller smoking room, where the furniture was burnished mahogany leather, the walls wood-paneled, and the lights low. Longo hurried in late, as was his habit, but his dark eyes were lit with their usual intensity and curiosity. He must know why his friend had asked to meet, so Chev got to it after the cordialities and a requisite amount of hobnobbing.

"You have been avoiding me, sir?" he asked.

Longo looked down, fingering the ivory buttons on his fine bespoke jacket—he'd had an excellent year for a poet, been able to retire from teaching at last—then met his gaze square on. "I know you well enough, Chev, to know that you are nettled by me, and that's putting it mildly, for my support and encouragement of Julia."

"You are as wise as you are wise." Long sips of brandy on both sides.

"She is a delightful poet, a natural lyric sensibility and a tether between the earthly and the divine, which is unusual, especially in a woman."

"I stand informed that my wife is a very unusual woman."

"Yes, and I thank God that I am wed to a more usual one. Fanny is as simple and well-serving as they come."

"And you have the six to show for it, while I merit only four."

"Well, my friend, the stallion must do his part as well."

This was his old friend, the old teasing, the challenge of tightrope-walking between high and low humor. And it was true that Fanny was his second, after his first had died of a miscarriage, and Fanny Appleton had taken seven years of courting to secure! How he had poked Longo mercilessly about that. Seven years' worth of barbed pleasure, but always with the undertow of empathy, something that he also felt from his dear friend in the moment.

"So the poems are really so good that they merit a book?"

"Yes, the title one particularly."

"Ah, yes, 'Passionate Flowers.' I heard."

"Sumner's mouth is as wide as his feet. But it's 'Passion-Flowers.'"

"A significant difference, I'm certain."

Longo leaned forward, earnest for the first time. "She told me she has agreed to publish anonymously to placate you, and I believe that is all you can ask, even of a woman."

"You would allow yours to do as much?"

"Mine cannot rhyme *hot* with *pot*, for which I thank my Benefactor every day."

"You are a lucky sot." Chev waited. "Rhymes with..."

"Ah, the wit entire." Longo's saber sharp as ever.

"You don't think that any of the poems are of such an unguarded nature that they might lash me outright to the mast?"

"Will the wags guess her identity? I don't know, Chev. I can't say for sure."

"Then there is cause for concern, you admit."

"The truth is that under the dire emotional circumstances she suffers, I believe that you should allow her this one thing."

"What circumstances? Surely she does not report her return to life with me as that horrendous."

"I thought you knew. I thought Charlie surely would have...or Julia herself..."

"What?"

"Wallace, her friend. He committed suicide in Paris a month after her return. Slit his throat. Grisly business."

For once, Chev was speechless. He reeled with possibilities. "Did he...Did the man do it because of Julia?"

Longfellow patted his arm. "How can one discern that deeply within a stranger's heart? I have no idea."

"So he left no note? Nothing to tie her to the scandal?"

"Not that I have been told. Wallace was known to have a melancholic nature. I believe you have nothing to worry about."

"No," said Chev, but he didn't meet Longo's eyes. "I suppose not." Should he tell his dear friend the truth, that she wept all hours, both in his arms and out?

"Simply a worldly lady's chats with a worldly man. Now an otherworldly man." Longo was notorious for his puns, even at the worst of times, something that Julia enjoyed, but Chev fairly loathed. "Let's move on to port and toast to your wife's book. Can you manage that?"

Chev raised his hand for the waiter. "I can as long as she is never known as my wife."

"To the private heart of a public woman." Longo raised his glass and Doctor clinked a bit too heartily.

"That would be a far better title than *Passion-Flowers*," he said.

"Ah, well, chalk that up to Mr. Wallace."

"He gave her that?"

"If that's all he gave her, we'll be of good cheer. Now drink up, my man. I have a wife to get home to."

They walked along the Charles, the road to the bridge over the dark river goldened by streetlamps every fifty yards. At the bridge, they embraced and parted, Longfellow across the river to Cambridge, that delightful house on Brattle Street, bubbling with domestic warmth and affection; Chev rambling, a bit drunkenly, toward South Boston, wondering what he would say to Julia when he returned, if anything. Maybe he would swing round the Back Bay to Sumner's for a late-night shot of comfort. Charlie was always and ever on his side.

When he arrived home just before dawn, she was sleeping, this stranger, this woman, this wife, her hair wild, undone, both arms flung over her face as if in self-defense. He watched her from the door of her bedroom for a moment, the bile rising in his craw. He would not be bothering the lady tonight. Chev didn't know if he could sleep, but he damn sure wasn't going to try it in her mourning bed. Let her wake and wonder why, if she had offended or displeased him. Let her lie and dream of her poet, reciting gibberish through the bloody gash in his throat.

The next day he thought about mentioning his conversation with Longo, but couldn't figure out how to bring it up. Then a week passed and she seemed to be getting better, a little gayer, a little warmer toward the children. He only caught her weeping once, as she climbed the stairs to their rooms. Her coming up, him coming down, and his eyes searched hers for any sign of the truth: had she really been in love with Wallace? It was not unheard of for a woman to cry over a friend's passing for months, and Julia was a more sensitive flower than most. She never offered any explanation for her tears, nor did she acknowledge that he had suddenly left her bed. He tried very hard not to return, but that resolve melted within the month, and a bit sheepishly, he appeared in his dressing gown at her doorway one night after they'd thrown a small dinner party. He said nothing, his hand on the doorsill, until she looked up from writing in her journal and nodded, such a small movement that it was almost imperceptible. But it was enough for him.

He realized, of course, that he could simply read her journal; he knew where she secreted it, in the smallest hatbox on the top shelf of her closet. Yes, he had found it—that was long ago when she had banned him from her quarters the first time during the weaning—and yes, he had retrieved it again, actually three times, each time exploring its red-and-gold brocaded cover, fingering the tight slew of pages, flipping the tiny lock, which he knew he could break and then repair in an instant. Would it be worth it? What if he found the evidence of her love for another man that would throw their marriage into eternal damnation? What if the threat of divorce were forced to be made real? In the pit of his stomach, which irritated him more and more these days, he felt that Julia had not been physically unfaithful to him and decided that would have to be enough to soldier on with her. He himself had crossed that bridge long ago, and she was none the wiser for it, or at least he thought. If she had shared her heart, however briefly, with another man, then he would take that, must take that, and spend the rest of his life with a woman with only half a heart to offer him. And from Laura, regardless of how she sulked at him now, he would always have the other half. Many had fared far worse.

Chapter 24

Laura, 1852

Doctor holds the spoon to my lips, and I open just enough to allow it. The first offering is heavy, sticky, familiar. I tongue the residue from my front teeth. Enduring sweetness.

"Honey, of course," I write on the pad Doctor has set in front of me for the benefit of Dr. Combe, whom he has invited to witness. Too easy.

Doctor pats my hand and offers me a sip of water. Then another spoonful, this time like grains of sand. I remember this, the sensation of the sea upon my tongue.

"Salt!" I write and hold my glass out for Doctor to fill it again.

Twice more, he feeds me, and then I wait as he and Dr. Combe confer.

"Not as well as you'd hoped," Doctor says.

"Tell me."

"Knew you couldn't suddenly—"

"If you give me right food—"

"No. It is as always. You are as always."

I stand, registering the vibration of the crack as my glass falls from the table. "I am not as always. I can taste everything." Footsteps shake the room; he must have asked Dr. Combe to leave. He is embarrassed that I am making a scene. I hold out my arms until he takes my hand again.

"Should I lie?" he asks.

"No." But I know that a lie to him might be the truth to me.

"Got one right. Only—"

I crush his fingers in my fist. "You want me to fail. Great Doctor wrong? Don't know anything about me."

"Knew you'd guess by texture, so—"

"I know what I know."

"Used pepper jelly instead of—"

I drop my hand before he can write another word. I brush the front of my dress for crumbs and walk out the door. It was honey. Honey, I'm sure of it. The rest doesn't matter.

Chapter 25

Chev, 1856–1860

Oh, Charlie, what have you done?" Chev changed the bandages on his friend's head as the blood seeped through the gauze. He'd given him laudanum twice today for the headaches, but Sumner still complained. It had only been two weeks since he was beaten almost to death on the Senate floor by Representative Preston Brooks. Brooks claimed Sumner wasn't even gentleman enough for a duel after what he'd said in his three-hour speech, raving against the Kansas-Nebraska Act, which gave settlers of those territories the right to choose slavery or to abhor it. For the assault with his gold-headed gutta-percha cane, Brooks was fined a measly three hundred dollars.

"I have to go back," Sumner said, his words slurred from the slice through his lip.

"Not now," Chev told him, wiping the sweat from his face. "In time." He regaled Sumner with the tenderness he usually reserved for only his youngest patients. He drifted back to sleep, woke yelling from a nightmare, his words indistinct.

"What was it?" Chev asked.

"I don't know. Chasing me."

He soothed him by telling of the thousands who had attended rallies in his support not only in Boston, but in Albany, Cleveland, Detroit, New York, and Providence.

"Cleveland?" he said, and for the first time since the accident, he laughed, a low, gurgling sound. Chev employed the nightstand as a podium and repeated the rousing speech that he himself had delivered at the Faneuil Hall rally, defending his friend. He reminded Sumner about the million copies of his now famous Senate speech that had been distributed all over the North, but didn't mention the hundreds of new gold-headed canes that had been sent to Preston Brooks from all over the South to replace the one he broke on Sumner's head.

"So I got the whole country riled?" Sumner asked, attempting a smile that looked more like a grimace.

"Yes, indeed." Chev held his tongue regarding the repercussions he felt sure would come, and quickly, from this event. The republic had never been so polarized. Charlie had made sure of that. But slavery was an abomination, and it was probably true that there would be no other way for it to meet its end than with violence.

"Cleveland." Sumner laughed again and closed his eyes, glad, Chev thought, at what he had wrought. Maybe that was because he'd always been a man who could only fight with words. He'd claimed he was channeling Demosthenes and Cicero, but the truth was that the "Crime Against Kansas" was three hours of vulgarity, far crasser and less noble than Charlie had ever been in his five years in Congress. His lowest note was mocking South Carolina Senator Butler's speech and mannerisms, which all knew were the result of a stroke. Chev was disappointed in his closest friend, though of course the blight of slavery was far more disappointing. A duel would have been more manly, and God knows Sumner needed to be presented to the world as manly.

Even Julia was so concerned that she came to help out when she could spare herself from the children and the writing, and poor Laura had offered her services as well, though she'd always loathed Sumner and God knows Chev wouldn't wish such a nurse on anyone. He recalled how she tortured Miss Wight with good inten-

tions when she had her spells. Julia was as wound up about abolitionism as he was now—a tie that finally helped bind them—and
the time had come for him to act. With the help of their dear
friend, the Reverend Theodore Parker, the abolitionists, the Free-
Soilers, and the former Cotton Whigs had united to supply the
new band of seven hundred and fifty Kansas settlers. They'd raised
almost six thousand dollars, most to go for Sharps rifles, revolvers,
ammunition, and Bowie knives. Chev could not lock up his principles any longer, living in fear of contributing to the havoc; it
was too late for that after Bleeding Kansas and bleeding Charlie.
He had been approached by a man intimately involved in settling
matters in those territories, sometimes in the direst of ways. But
these were the direst of times, and so he charged forward, not dar-
ing to look back.

The day before Sumner's speech, the country had thundered
with news of the Border Ruffians' sack of Lawrence, and then the
retaliation on the Pottawatomie by Chev's new compatriot, John
Brown. Atrocities on both sides, with Brown and his sons cutting off the arms and butchering the remains of the Ruffians they
thought were responsible, though these men did not themselves
hold any slaves.

By January of the next year, 1857, John Brown had arrived in Boston. He met for the first time with his most loyal New England
supporters—Chev, George Stearns, young Franklin Sanborn, and
the two ministers Theodore Parker and Thomas Wentworth Higginson. But not Sumner; his psychic wounds were deep, and Chev
didn't know that he should return to the Senate at all, though he
swore he would. Already his enemies were accusing him of cow-
ardice.

With his cropped graying hair and streaked beard, Brown
looked as if he'd stepped straight from the pages of the Old Testament, a prophet blessed with great self-possession and natural
gravity. Everyone looked quite ordinary compared to Brown. For

a man in his late fifties, how could it be that his eyes gleamed so electric, a beam as focused as the light that shone on Calvary? If Sumner was the Negroes' greatest friend, then Brown was their deliverer. The group all agreed instantly that Brown was their man and cobbled together money for his expenses, a letter of credit, and one hundred of the Sharps rifles. Chev gave him a rifle and two pistols himself, placed them directly into those powerful hands that would wring such justice from the world. Gerrit Smith of New York joined them, putting his entire vast estate at the disposal of the abolitionists.

Chev brought Brown home to Perkins. He had told Julia all about him, and the man was so extraordinary that he wanted his family to meet him. They had had guests from Boz to the governor in this house, but he had never felt such reverence in introducing anyone. He could see in his wife's eyes that she too beheld the singular greatness in the man; Julia rarely, if ever, became flustered, but she acted like Moses himself had stepped over the threshold. She declared him a Puritan of the Puritans. Cook had outdone herself, serving up a feast of roast mutton, tortoise soup, baked doves, and a layered huckleberry cake. Chev had made a point of not inviting Laura to dine with them because he knew she would prove a distraction, and yet at the last moment, she wandered in, brought no doubt by the great preparations rocking the first floor. He couldn't keep her away from anything. Brown eyed her, and she was the first person who had appeared to interest him.

"Laura Bridgman," Chev said.

Brown nodded. "I have heard much of her. One of our Father's miracles, I'd say."

Chev tried to explain quickly to Laura just who the man was as he led her to Brown, in the hope that she would behave accordingly. Every night, the students were read the *Transcript*, with one teacher appointed to translate for Laura. So although she was reasonably kept up with the news and politics, so far she had displayed a disappointing lack of interest in the slave question and the civil strife it promised. She curtsied, and upon standing, offered her hand to Brown. He held it firmly but with great courtesy, and yet she suddenly jerked her hand out of his grasp. She backed away and into Chev, who shook her for her rudeness.

"What's wrong with you?"

She spelled back in near frenzy. "Mad. He is mad."

"Please excuse her," he told Brown, who didn't look concerned. "Sometimes she skitters like a frightened horse."

"Put in the bit," Brown said quietly and walked away.

She must have felt the immense power emanating from his hands, so that was actually a good sign. Chev trusted her to act as his barometer for the extraordinary. But he still didn't want her at the dinner table, so he sent her back out to her cottage. For once, she seemed glad to go. Brown hardly spoke during the meal and left far earlier than the Howes had hoped. He simply wasn't a brandy and cigars kind of fellow.

The next week, in one of their many discussions on the abolitionist platform, Julia suggested that Laura could actually be quite useful in the grand scheme of things. Chev was not so sure she would volunteer to be of help; her ardor for her dear Chev had quite noticeably cooled. When he walked into a room, she sensed it immediately and usually took her leave forthwith. That was the thanks he got for rescuing her from death, a death she was hellbent to bring upon herself. At least she'd never brought up again her alleged ability to taste and seemed to be eating enough, presumably satisfied with the provided victuals. If he were made of weaker stuff, he would've patronized and encouraged her delusions, which he was certain would have proved more damaging to her in the long run.

When he and Julia sat her down in the parlor, Laura held herself ramrod straight, her head cocked to one side like an inquisitive parrot. She clearly knew it was a serious matter if they were both meeting with her.

"Angry about Mr. Brown?" she wrote before they could begin.

"No," Chev told her. "But why?"

"Brown not blind, but—"

"Of course, he's not blind."

"Only one big eye, like Cyclops."

Chev couldn't believe it. "Where in the world did she get hold of Homer?"

Julia laughed. "No worse than the Bible for her."

"Mr. Brown has two eyes," Chev wrote.

"Sees only one thing," Laura countered. "Mad." She fidgeted with her eyeshade, and for one frightening moment, Chev was afraid she was going to suddenly rip it off, which would be too much of a shock for Julia, who was not accustomed to such awful sights.

"She says he's mad," Chev told his wife.

"Well, she has held the hands of many maniacs and idiots. Perhaps she feels something—"

"You're doubting the man now? Based on Laura's assessment?"

"You're the one who's always claimed she could tell more from a person's touch in thirty seconds than the rest of us could in thirty years."

Chev looked disconcerted for a moment. "She does have her way, but I have no doubts whatsoever that Brown is willing to devote his life to the redemption of the colored race."

He took Laura's hand again, though her expression was obstinate. "We are helping Brown fight slavery."

"He's bad."

"Slavery is bad." Chev couldn't believe he felt the need to explain himself to her.

"L," Julia wrote, "surely you care about slaves."

"I am not free," Laura wrote, pushing down so hard that Chev could see the prints of her fingers in his wife's palm. "I am not free to even be a woman like you."

"Of course you are," Julia said.

Chev noted that both women's palms were sweating. Strange. Laura's hands almost never sweated; she used a dusting of powder to make sure of it.

He tried again. "On Exhibition Days, help by writing against slavery to visitors."

"What exhibition? You hardly show me."

"I will then. You can write about Negroes. Have great influence."

"You are all black to me," Laura wrote. "Everyone is dark. Think it is the same for God."

Julia was excited; she grabbed Laura's hand again. "You could write exactly that."

Laura sat for a moment, her lips twisted as if in exasperation, then tapped Chev's arm and gestured at the door. "Go?"

"Yes," he told her, and he and his wife were left alone. "You'd think she'd feel for the slaves, see that they are held captive as she is."

"Why don't you have the press raise *Uncle Tom's Cabin*? It's been out five years already, and none of your girls have read it. If only Laura could see one of the 'Tom' shows running. Two on right now in Boston."

"I keep meaning... But that Stowe woman, she just rubs me—"

"Harriet is not my favorite model either, but I think the atrocities of the book will impress Laura, even if it's not particularly well written."

"That's the other thing. I've always made a concerted effort not to overstimulate her. Those who are merely blind are subject to a much greater disturbance of their faculties when confronted with such horror, but with Laura the sensitivity is severely heightened. Who knows what she might do?"

"I think you're more afraid of her getting started on religion again."

"Even if I ordered the press to start tomorrow, it would still take a couple of years for the full print. And we have several other important books pending."

Julia sighed theatrically. "I've tried to rile Laura up on women's rights, you know, but she takes no interest in that either."

His least favorite subject. Thank God Laura still had some sense, Chev thought, but shook his head in mock conciliation. "I'm surprised. She has perhaps lost her tender streak with age."

"It can happen to the best of us," Julia said quietly, then stood and left the room.

October 18, 1859. A day Chev would never forget. John Brown had been taken alive, but seriously wounded, at Harpers Ferry, Virginia, by Col. Robert E. Lee and company. Brown's small band of eighteen, including two of his sons and five Negroes, had held the government arsenal for two days. His sons were dead, and none of the Negroes he'd been expecting from neighboring plantations had joined the rebellion. All this time the South had cowered in fear of a slave uprising, yet even the slaves Brown had freed voluntarily returned to their masters. For the life of him, Chev didn't understand this; none of the abolitionists did.

He'd known old Brown was planning something, and the Secret Six, as they'd come to be called, had kept sending him money, Sharps rifles, and pikes. Brown was indicted exactly one week after his capture for treason and murder, and Chev immediately formed a committee to provide for his defense. True to his word, Brown refused to implicate the Northerners, but the authorities found letters and other papers incriminating the six at his farm just over the Maryland border.

Rumor had it that a federal warrant might be issued for the arrests of the Secret Six and they could be extradited to Virginia, where they could end up being tried for conspiracy. The Chevalier had never panicked in his life, but now he did. The month he'd spent in a Prussian prison in 1832 had hardened him against any real martyrdom. It had been soul-killing, and he'd only been in his early thirties then; now at almost sixty, he would fear for his life and his sanity. Let Brown be the holy martyr. Chev left nothing to chance; he composed a letter to the newspapers, disclaiming any prior knowledge of Brown's plans. Of the assault at Harpers Ferry, he wrote, "It is still to me a mystery and a marvel." By the day the letter appeared in print, Chev was on his way to Canada, telling his family and close acquaintances that it was a long-planned trip to recruit Canadians to teach the blind. He tried to get the others to flee with him, but only Stearns went.

Chev had made a point of avoiding Laura since the raid, but as he carried his bags down the stairs, there she was, waiting in the main hall.

She grabbed at his hand. "Where?"

"Don't need to know."

"Told you. Madman."

Who was she to lecture him? He put down his bags. He channeled all of the nervous exhaustion and anxiety to strike at her palm. "He was a saint. Should pray for him." He knew he was hurting her, but he couldn't stop.

She managed to twist one hand out of his. "Pray for people he killed."

"Slavery is evil, Laura."

"Murder is evil, Doctor."

"I regret nothing," he said, though at this point, it wasn't entirely true.

Then of all things, she patted him on the back as if he were a child. It had been gut-punch enough that his wife had said, "Just go," and only halfheartedly hugged him good-bye, her belly big with child against him.

"I need to find teachers in Montreal," he'd told Julia, and she'd laughed. She'd actually laughed in his face. Yes, of course, she was worried for him, but she'd stopped just short of calling him a coward. Higginson, however, had not held back and made a point of informing his longtime friend that he considered his present actions ignoble. And the greatest slight had come from Sumner, who had not even replied to his messages.

On December 2, Brown mounted the gallows and the North fell into mourning. By then, Chev was already in Montreal. The time there was torturous, but three weeks after the hanging, he got word that the danger of extradition to Virginia was past and arrived home just in time to see his son born on Christmas night. Samuel Gridley Howe Jr. As he held the child safe in his arms, he dared wonder if perhaps the fiery spirit of John Brown, just departed, might have found its way into this new soul. He didn't mention his strange hope to anyone, least of all Julia. It was a secret wish he would keep to himself.

In January, a congressional summons was issued, and the Secret Six appeared before a Senate committee investigating the raid. But the last thing the committee wanted to do was blight the lives of these fine New Englanders, and so they all returned to their homes, their explanations and denials having quickly satisfied their peers. Chev could breathe again, though his wife would barely look him in the eye, much less let him in her bed, for months. Once again, she used the nursing as an excuse. How much he loved his children, and yet the irony was that the making of them prevented making more of them, at least for now, and for that he was in a constant state of distress. If Julia were a man, she would understand. Then again, Sumner didn't understand. But if Sumner were a woman—no, he would not play out the thought. Even Laura had not touched him since his return; she refused to so much as acknowledge him when they passed in the hall. In what strange, new world was it possible for Laura Bridgman, of all people, to act morally superior to Dr. Samuel Gridley Howe? A strange, new world in which brothers turned against brothers, and the country split into bloody halves, flies buzzing over the tender flesh despoiled. A real war was on its way, he was sure of it.

Chapter 26

Julia, 1860–1863

Before Sammy's birth, Julia would have sworn she had no favorites among her children, but he quickly changed that. From the moment he was born, when she first saw the downy red of his hair, she was smitten. Her only redheaded child! It was as if the spirit of her beloved Mr. Wallace had descended through the ether and passed into the child, and so as the baby lay swaddled in her arms, she breathed into that tiny rosebud mouth the sweet breath that had entered her only once. She nursed Sammy for thirteen months and let him sleep in her bed well after that. Though she had previously valued her time in her attic nook above all, now she studied and wrote in the nursery while her son played. He was rarely out of her sight; she bundled him up and took him with her on walks and carriage rides into the city. Though her other children were well and truly beloved, Florence and Julia Romana never seemed to have forgiven their mother for leaving them for her hiatus in Rome, and now sided with their father in all domestic disputes. Julia realized that she had long thought of her children as background to her intellectual pursuits and personal preoccupations, but now for the first time motherhood was the foreground of her life. Funny thing, though they already had a son, Harry, this one proved even Chev's greatest little fellow, and so the parents spent much more time together, bound by their love for the child. They tried not to compete for the boy's attention, but it was a constant struggle, and therefore, he was the most spoiled of their children.

But life outside the home bore the beginnings of a national hell. Fort Sumter was attacked, and the war became a foregone conclusion. Both Julia and Chev applied their efforts to the cause of the Union. Julia was one of the founders of the Women's Central Association of Relief for the Sick and Wounded of the Army, a title she felt was far too long, but a great venture nonetheless. Chev campaigned to head the Sanitary Commission, a supply and relief organization supporting the Army. In late 1861, the couple headed off to Washington to further their efforts, and to the surprise of the older children, they took Sammy, who was almost two, along with them.

While Chev politicked, Julia did some rambling, always in a carriage and always accompanied by either Massachusetts Governor Andrew or James Freeman Clarke and his wife. She was surprised that the city of Washington seemed more like an unruly village than a true city, much less the capital of the nation. The wide avenues were still unpaved, and ambulances, soldiers on horses, and orderlies on foot trailed up and down Pennsylvania Avenue. Most of the federal buildings stood only half-finished, and the Capitol itself had yet to be crowned with its dome, another project put on hold for the war effort. The grand Army of the Potomac surrounded Washington, their brown tents pitched like molehills all along the outskirts to protect the city from the Johnny Rebs, who had set up camp just over the river in Virginia. With her friends, Julia visited camps and hospitals, and even the Massachusetts Heavy Artillery led by her second cousin. But wherever she went, someone always asked after Laura, be it an injured lieutenant or a bugle boy. Apparently, even during wartime, Laura's star had not completely dimmed in the public firmament.

In November, as Julia was watching a review of the troops at Bailey's Crossroads, Virginia, Confederate troops suddenly descended and a skirmish began. As she headed back into Washington, she could still hear the sounds of battle. On the way they passed some soldiers singing the popular "John Brown's Body," and Mr. Clarke teased her that she should write new lyrics for the tune.

That night, Julia awoke well before dawn, and in the dim light began to write out verses, almost as if from memory, with little of her usual effort. As Sammy and her husband slept, she finished her poem, with its echoes of the violence of the Old Testament, in particular a favorite passage of hers from Isaiah. Two months later, James T. Fields published the revised "Battle Hymn of the Republic" in the *Atlantic*, for which the author received the princely sum of five dollars. And though the average fellow did not read this esteemed publication, because she had set the words to the tune of "John Brown's Body," the song was soon on everyone's lips.

Chev, of course, suffered great agitation at his wife's sudden fame. He had not been granted the command of the Sanitary Commission, though no clear reason was given, and so they soon returned to Boston. His headaches grew worse, and he even took Julia away from Sammy to nurse him, all to no good end. President Lincoln himself first heard Julia's song after the Battle of Gettysburg and reportedly shouted, "Sing it again!" to wild applause. Yet when she was invited to attend Lincoln's second inauguration, Chev forbade her to go to Washington because he had a sick head, though she knew it was because he chafed under the idea of being her guest for the event when he himself had not been invited. He went as far as bringing up divorce again, but for Sammy's sake, Julia quelled his hurtful demands.

Julia would have thought she would be ecstatic to be known as the new poetess of the nation, and yet she began to feel more drawn toward the essay form and the idea of reading out and engaging with the public off the page; however, she knew Chev would fight her tooth and nail on the idea of a speaking tour and that she probably wouldn't be allowed to take Sammy with her.

That would have broken her heart, as he was at the age when he asked about everything, talked about everything, her perfect and intellectually curious redheaded child. She liked to pretend he was Mr. Wallace's son and that he would grow up to be a great philosopher or writer, or ideally both, like his parents.

One chilly May morning, Julia set out for a drive with Sammy, and realized after they'd gone a mile that she'd forgotten his scarf and gaiters, but he proved his usual bright self. That night, however, he came down with fever and chills. Chev was away, so Julia called in their doctor from town, who pronounced the boy ill with diphtheria. Her own words thrummed blackly in her head: *He hath loosed his fateful lightning and his terrible swift sword.* Julia telegraphed Chev and he made it home by the next night. They both stayed up with their son, who seemed to be feeling better. At 5:00 a.m., Sammy died in his mother's arms. He had just turned three.

Chev did not blame her; instead he said nothing, withdrawing to his study and then to his bed. He refused to go to the funeral, even after the other children begged him. Julia stayed a mother to her children throughout her pain, her numbness, the unwillingness of her spirit to go on. Surprisingly, only Laura offered her any real comfort, sitting with her for hours as she wrote poems about Sammy, some of which she signed into Laura's palm. What a strange and unexpected twosome, she thought, as they wept together, her patting dry the tears that leaked from beneath Laura's shade.

Julia turned to the Book of Common Prayer, a favorite since childhood, and again devoted herself to her studies. It was only the second time in her adult life that she had been gripped with such anguish, and in her heart the deaths were connected. For a year afterward, she wrote poems only about Sammy and reams of letters to him, which she never showed a soul. She also wrote poems in honor of Mr. Wallace's memory and composed a series of philosophical lectures, concentrating on his beloved Comte and on Hegel, but she couldn't read his novels. She'd tried, but their violence reminded her of the vicious circumstances of his death. She planned to give readings on particular topics of ethics while also advancing the cause of practical Christianity, which in her recent grief had been a great comfort. *Our God is marching on.*

She thought Chev would battle her about the readings, but he gave in without any argument, insisting only that she not charge for the events, which she had hoped to do. Her parlor readings were a huge success, and she decided she'd try a series in Washington. She was publicly embarrassed when Sumner, whom she'd thought would support, if not attend, the readings in his newly adopted city, railed against her ambitions, telling anyone who'd listen that she was in no way qualified to speak on any of those topics. It was one thing not to be for her, but why was Charlie so adamantly against her? After all, Julia had never intervened in his relationship with her husband, though since Sumner was in Washington, he didn't get to spend much time with his favorite friend anyway. As a matter of fact, she and Chev spent little time together anymore, as if the grief had severed their last ties of true affection.

Yet still she was bewildered that her husband stayed away from her bed for so long. How they could have comforted each other, if he had only allowed it. On the night she returned from Washington, where her tour had been a modest success, she greeted him with a genuine smile when he entered her bedroom. He came to stand behind her dressing table, but he didn't lay a finger on her, only watched her in the mirror.

"Has something happened?" she asked, suddenly afraid.

"There will be no more children," he said and left her before she could speak. But she couldn't have spoken anyway. There would be no argument. But then why didn't he push to divorce her now, now that Sammy was gone? Perhaps he had found some way, something, someone to keep him happy enough to bear his present situation, though Julia refused to torture herself over the possibilities. She accepted that that part of her life—that part of her heart, which she now realized had been much larger than she'd imagined—was forever closed. She was forty-two.

For her next reading tour, she bought a white lace cap. She would never again appear in public without the cap covering the waves of her still-bright red hair, which had always been her greatest vanity, a true *rosso* being the highest effort of nature.

Chapter 27

Laura, 1863

The house still vibrates with sorrow. I wrote a poem about Sammy, how he liked to juggle oranges and how plump his fingers were, and when I gave it to Julia, she hugged me hard against her, and I felt the rush of tears on my neck. Strange to be holding Julia, patting her gently, stroking her soft hair. At Mount Auburn Cemetery in Cambridge, where I expect I will be buried also someday in the Howes' plot, I felt the crowding of souls around me, behind and before, and I didn't know if it was the living or the dead. It was not my first death, but it was my first funeral, and though it was horribly sad, I found myself in some way oddly pleased by it, in belonging with this group of people all weeping at the edge of the grave. And yet although there was a minister and a service, the ceremony made me feel estranged from my Lord. How could he justify taking a child? These wartime days are full of death, but that I understand as the pitted road of history. Of course, none of my family or close acquaintances, save Cook's son, are doing the fighting, though Doctor and Julia work with wartime committees in Washington. Would it have been better if Sammy had been maimed by fever and lived on as I do? I dare not ask his parents this question for fear of their answers.

Sammy is not gone a year when I am felled by news from home: Mary has died of the same fever. Mary with her tangled hair, tickling me until I gasped; Mary who covered my face in kisses and would not let me die that winter in Hanover. Nine years old then, chubby-cheeked and snaggle-toothed, brilliant as a flame, she danced around the bed, trying anything to lift my spirits. Mary, who lay with me and petted me as much as I petted her. Mary, now twenty-three and about to be married. I was going to be in the wedding party in the spring—my first wedding—wearing my gayest dress and a straw bonnet pinned with nosegays to match the bride's bouquet. But now the dress turns black, the flowers wilt into a veil. I go down on my knees to Doctor asking can I go for the funeral, but he says it is impossible; I could not make it in time.

Doctor has not been the same this whole year, and I have spoken with him only a few times—Jeannette says he will not even talk to Julia—but today he clasps me boldly to his chest, and for a second, I forget about Mary, feeling only his warmth, and then I feel terribly guilty.

"Want to be with your family in mourning?" he asks.

I don't know. My mother's letter did not ask for me to come; doubtless she and Papa think I would be more a hindrance than a help at such a time, so I do not go. My relationship with God has taken another onerous blow, and I don't know if we will survive it. He is obviously not who I thought He was. He has burdened me with great tribulations by the very circumstances of my life, and I have endured, but why did He take one so dear, so innocent? I realize that this is the way most people feel after such a heavy loss, and yet I take it personally nonetheless. I think I have probably been a great deal more intimate with Him than most others manage, because He has imposed upon me this isolation which posits Him as my only true companion. Now I talk, I rail, I shout, I make all my noises, even in the dining room, but I hear nothing from the heavens. Jeannette keeps pushing me down in my chair and finally puts her hand across my mouth. I bite the soft back sides of her fingers. God has turned me again into an animal.

Though we rarely have Exhibition Days, no matter what Doctor promised, we still have Visiting Days. So I sit myself down in the drawing room, in the black crepe dress I have worn since winter, and await the curious. First up, I have a young girl who sorely tries my patience. She has come alone, not in a group like most of the schoolchildren. I give her my hand and she digs into my palm with block letters, the only way those not versed in finger spelling can attempt to communicate with me, and slowly spells out "Laura." I pat her hand in acknowledgment but then she writes my name over and over. We still get a fair load on Visiting Days, so I know a line is forming behind her, but I can't get her off me. She holds on almost desperately, scrawling my name across my knuckles when I finally close my fist. I have no choice but to wave for Jeannette to come and help me, but when Jeannette tries to pull her away, she grabs my skirts, circling my knees, and I can feel the sobs shaking her thin shoulders. Where on earth is her mother? I feel great pity for her, and yes, a certain pride that she seems so devoted to me, or at least to the idea of me, but there is nothing to be done about it. I pat her head as Jeannette lifts her off and am rewarded with a fine mess of curls. That at least is something.

It is savage enough that He comes in the night to steal our children, and yet the nation has now given the dark emperor permission to mount the carnage at Bull Run and Shiloh, the battlefields littered with the corpses of our finest specimens, North and South. Is the emancipation of the Negro really worth all that dying when we've faced the horrors of Antietam, the bloodiest day of the war, over two thousand Union soldiers dead? And not even a clear winner, though General Lee did finally withdraw to Virginia. I don't care what the Constitution and the abolitionists say; we are not, by any stretch of the imagination, *all* created equal—in God's eyes or in man's—and so we must strive to be happy within the respective cells in which our Maker has confined us. I believe I could teach the slaves a thing or two about making do, though it's true that I am not beaten. The tragedy is that I might enjoy it. I remember Julia's shock that I had no interest in crusading for the rights of oppressed women and slaves. I feel a simultaneous affinity and disgust for both, which I do not nurture, but which is nevertheless inscribed in my nature. They all assume on my part a huge and general compassion by virtue of my condition, but I refuse to be anything but myself, whatever *that* is.

At last Doctor's carriage takes me out to Wayland, where Sarah, just back from the islands, is settling with Mr. Bond. I begged to meet her at the pier, but Jeannette convinced me that she would be very tired after a journey of three months with three children. She is right, so I bide my time one week—that is all I can wait!—and now I've traveled the fifteen winding miles to see her, my darling Wightie, after a dozen long years.

She opens the carriage door, and I restrain myself from falling into her arms. She has been weak, she wrote, since the birth of the last child, so I must be as careful with her as she has always been with me. Finest china, my porcelain Wightie. The children paw at my skirts, and so I stop to pet and peck them all, none very tall for their age. The boy's face rings of Sarah's—the straight, thin nose, the slight dimple in the chin—and all their hair is fine and slightly wavy like hers. Like Mr. Bond's. She says they are all blonde.

I finally loose the children and kiss my darling over and over, but her face seems to have shrunken. I trace the pouches of flesh beneath her eyes and the sunken wells beneath her cheekbones. How much older she feels than forty. Perhaps she is thinking the same of my thirty-three, though I doubt it because I know my skin is still wonderfully soft and smooth. She leads me to a chair by the hearth and pulls up close beside me.

"A present," she says and puts something round my neck. It seems to be a necklace of flowers, but they are long dried. "Lei," she writes. "Island custom." I try to imagine her running along the surf, the circlet blooming between her slight breasts. It is a shock to me how much I have missed her, the touch of her, just knowing she is close by. She fills my hand with notes on the voyage; the girl was sick the whole way. The children miss the island, as does her husband, but she is delirious to be home. Mr. Bond has taken a position as the head of the new Hawaiian Islands Commission in Cambridge and is happy with it. Still, I am glad he is not here.

She did not get my letter about Mary, so I break the tale to her, and she lets me weep against her bony chest, the way she always did. Sammy she knows about. The difference is that she met my Mary, those long weeks she stayed to watch over me in Hanover before she left, when I had turned my heart against her.

"God finished," I tell her, and she is quick to ask my meaning. "No talk, no listen." He is farther away than the moon, less bright than the stars, more dangerous than the sun, and now I know that was always His nature. For myself, I forgave His cruelties, but now that He has loosed His fateful lightning on my family, I cannot forgive. It is a two-way street with God; not only must He forgive me, but I must also forgive Him.

Sarah is shocked, the most shocked she's ever been with me. "God loves," she says. "Rest is life."

"Then why pray?"

"For your soul," she says, "and the souls of others."

"Senseless. Wouldn't have to pray for Mary's soul if He hadn't killed her. Don't you think I've gone easy on God?" I ask her, and she is angry.

"Not only your life hard," she writes, almost scratching my palm. Her nails are ragged. The old Sarah kept her nails neatly filed and was possessed of boundless sympathy; I suppose that becoming a wife and a mother has left her less for me. "Everybody's hard."

Not everybody! Piffle. Until Sammy died, Julia's life was a perfect dream. And all the belles who visit me—they have no idea of suffering.

"Jesus suffered," she says. "For you."

"Then who do I suffer for?" Of course, she can't answer that one.

"How is Julia?"

"Still crying."

"Doctor?"

"Worse than time of John Brown."

"I have a Secret Six," she tells me: three babies lived, three babies died. "Under the volcano." She recites the names of her dead children, Katherine, Augustine, and Clinton, and I write back the names of her living ones: Abigail, Thomas, and Laura. At least my namesake didn't die. People love to name their children after me. I find that flattering but strange, given my condition. I remember the death of one of her children, but I never knew about the others. One of fever at six months, she says; the next boy lived an hour; the last girl the fever at two, a full little person lost.

"If she lived, maybe like you." She asks me: Could she have lived through that or was it better that she died? "The live ones escape me like eels."

What does she mean? They are here, clambering around my chair, annoying the vinegar out of me. She says that her dead children are buried pineapples, and then she tries to tell me about an island priestess walking into a volcano.

I am astonished, not only that she is telling me so much, so oddly, but that she seems more than willing, even eager, to offend me. And then she writes more, signing so erratically that I cannot follow her. This is not the Sarah I know; the years and the islands have changed her. I hold her and pat her, and for the first time since I have known her, we have switched places, and I am the comforter. It feels good, but suddenly, she grows rigid in my arms, as if she just realized where she was, and pulls completely away.

"All right?" I ask.

"Of course," she tells me, and then apologizes. "Headache," she says. "A spell."

I remember her spells; obviously they have gotten far worse over the years. I force myself to let go the topic of religion, and then we are chatting like old times. She puts in my hands the engraved maps Mr. Bond has bought the children to mark the battle territories. A Prussian, Mr. Prang, made the first one after the assault on Fort Sumter, and furnishes the maps with colored pencils—blue for the Confederacy, red for the Union—so that the advances and retreats can be tracked as soon as reported by telegraph in the newspaper. He has sold over forty thousand, though I personally have no interest in tracking the war. Her girl brings a plate of afternoon biscuits, but I can't force more than a nibble or two. I have long given up on trying to taste—what was God playing at?—and there are certainly no occasions to tempt or encourage me. Perhaps it was all a waking dream, a willed delusion, part of the brief, glorious rapture that marked my only union with another human being.

Sarah and I have so much to catch up on that we go on for over two hours, until both our fingers are sore. When it is time to leave, she says she'll pray for me, and I tell her that I'd pray for her too if I were still able. We say our good-byes lightly, and I promise to come again soon. She sends her love to my family and to Doctor and Julia.

All the long ride back in the carriage, I bounce between two terrible thoughts: my Sarah has changed and my God has changed. Where will I be without their constancy? And no one seems to care that Julia Pastrana, "the World's Ugliest Woman," has also passed from the world that titled her so, and I wonder if the Lord will, in the end, find beautiful that which He hath wrought.

Chapter 28

Laura, 1863

Visiting Day again, and I parry a bit with a Methodist minister, keeping my untoward thoughts about his employer to myself, and then we are down to the end of the line. The chapped hand of a young girl. It's been a month, but I remember this one, the one who would not let me go. I feel a moment's gratitude that trouble though she was, she has not flagged in her devotion. Once again, all she writes is my name over and over, until I think that she herself is perhaps in some way enfeebled. But then she places in my other palm a small, hard object, rough and flaky on the outside. I trace the irregular, lumpy circle, and pieces of the skin come off in my fingers. I hold it carefully, feeling the strange contours. A fruit or vegetable. Suddenly, I know it, and almost drop it in my surprise: garlic. The girl has given me a bulb of garlic. I close my fist upon it and time stops. Finally, I reach for her, that halo of curls—red, I'm guessing—and she rests her head in my lap, allowing me to coil and uncoil the ringlets. *Laura.* She has been writing her name! My Laura, after all these barren years. She raises her head and presses an envelope into my hand. I am confused; she knows I can't read it, and she is not able to communicate with me. Wait. This is a letter from— I can't bear to say her name, even in my head, lest all the hope gathers into the storm that has raged so long in me.

The girl rises and I let go of her hair. I pull her to me and kiss her cheek, and she kisses mine in return. I should have known her at once. Poor darling. She pats the letter on my lap, and I nod, though there is no one here that I trust enough to read it to me. Where is her mother? Does the letter contain bitter news? A meeting? Why couldn't her mother come herself? And then I remember: I am also her mother.

At last I let her go, my shade soaked clean through with tears. The day has come at last, though it will take some figuring to discover what wonders or sorrows might lie ahead after all these years. Ten years. I know I must take the letter to Sarah. She is the only one I can trust with the greatest secret of my life.

Two months after my last visit I return to Wayland. I have agitated Doctor for a month, since the day I got the letter, but he has had excuses about the carriage, my health, the weather. I think he doesn't want me to spend time with Wightie; after all, he is the one who tore us apart in the first place. Julia had gone to see her once and wanted to take me with her, but Doctor claimed that I was in a temper that day, which I was not. I am a bit afraid that Wightie will be talking of eels and volcanoes again, but when I arrive, she seems her old self. I bring each of the children a purse I have crocheted, but I can't tell if they like them or not. Perhaps they throw them in the dirt. Sarah natters on about seeing her mother and sister after all these years, but I can't concentrate. The truth is I don't really try. I can't stop for one minute thinking about the letter, pressed into the bosom of my dress, the letter that will open—or perhaps close—my world again.

Finally, I can't take the waiting any longer, and I pull it from its hiding place and hand it to her without explanation. "Read me," is all I say. She's taking a long time to begin, and I believe she is reading it first to herself, perhaps gauging what, if at all, to tell me. I am furious. "Read!" I rap hard, and when another moment passes, I grab her arms and shake them.

"Calm," she writes. "Who gave you this?"

"Just read," I beg her. My head and heart are exploding.

"My beloved Laura," she begins, but my palm is so drenched with sweat that she has to dry it with her handkerchief before she can continue.

Whoever reads this to you does not need to understand, though I pray you trust them.

Only you need to understand and to remember.

I have never stopped thinking of you, but it was impossible to return. Dr. Howe wouldn't allow me on the grounds and swore he would have me jailed.

And then the baby came, and I have worked without ceasing all these years to support us. Now you have met her, our Laura. Isn't she beautiful?

I sent her because I still dare not come to Perkins, though I had to wait until she was old enough to come by herself. She doesn't write much yet, but she is as smart as her mother.

I am not well. All the years as kitchen slave have worn me to a nub. You would hardly recognize me. I am wasting away and cannot work. There is no one to care for us. There has never been. I don't want Laura to end up in the almshouse as I did. It's no place for a young girl.

If you can think of any way to help us, I beg that you do it, and quick. I will send our darling back as soon as I can. She will kiss you for me.

Sarah stops reading and I scratch at her wrist until she continues. It is hard for her. I don't care.

I still long for your touch, and no one has ever replaced you in my heart, where it matters. I pray that you can taste without me.

Yours everlasting,
Kate

My hands are trembling as I loose them from Sarah's. I must see her! How can I see her? She is ill. I could take care of her. Where is she living? Will Laura take me to her? When is Laura coming back? I can't think, even as I can't stop thinking. I have forgotten Sarah's presence until she taps my arm.

"The cook?"

I nod. I had written a bit about Kate in my letters, though not about the passionate circumstances, and certainly not about the baby. I am not sure how much Sarah will understand from what she just read; the less the better, I think.

"She wants money," she says.

"My friend."

"But it's impossible…"

I don't want to hear her opinion on things that are beyond her ken. "I fix," I tell her. "Not you."

"But you don't have…"

I almost slap her palm. "I fix," I write again, though the truth is my mind is tumbling to figure out how to come up with a goodly sum. I have spent most of the last two years knitting only scarves for the Union soldiers, hardly anything just to sell. Generally, I put by about a hundred dollars a year from the sale of my antimacassars, crocheted purses, and lace collars, but I have spent most of the money on gifts for my friends and family. I have been too extravagant, but I didn't know I would be responsible for a child. Maybe I could give her some Laura dolls to sell. There must still be people who want me, the little me. And my mere signature is worth something, if not much anymore, but I could sign reams and reams of Institution pamphlets for her to peddle. How capable is the girl? I reprimand myself for even doubting her—she is our girl, and she is of course clever. Kate says so. Kate. I would recognize her, no matter how worn she is, and I would kiss every beloved inch of her. I would not bite her now, not ever, if she didn't want it. I would worship each mole and rough spot, spend an hour rubbing her feet. She must let me see her. I will push the girl.

Sarah tries one last time. "I don't think..."

"Stop." She is good and dear, but with this she cannot help me, so there is no need to involve her further. I don't believe her love for Mr. Bond could ever match my fire for Kate, and so I don't think it's even possible for her to understand. But I still love my Wightie in a certain fashion, and she does not deserve my dismissal.

"It is God come back," I tell her, and it's true. Through every vein in my body, every breath in my lungs, I feel the return of goodness and rightness to the world. The dead die, and the living live. And Kate and our daughter are just within my reach, my shining angels come back to earth. I weep in Sarah's arms, and ask my Lord to forgive me for ever questioning His wisdom and mercy and the path He has set for me.

She holds me close, and I can feel her warm breath in my ear. She is speaking. Whatever for? She knows better than anyone that I cannot hear. "Write!" I implore on the hand that grasps my shoulder hard, but still she speaks, the velocity and force of her voice only increasing, deep and ragged. Spittle scores my cheek and I realize she must be shouting. And then there is an arm between us, a man's firm advance. Mr. Bond. Gently he pries Sarah off me, though she resists, holding on as if I were Jesus. She struggles and then goes limp. What was she trying to tell me that sent her into a fit? The spell has come and gone so quickly.

Mr. Bond holds Sarah away from me, and pats me awkwardly on the shoulder since we can't communicate. Sarah had always been our translator. It is odd but welcoming to finally feel this man's touch after so many years, and to remember that I considered, even for a moment, that he might prove my champion. I had no genuine feeling for him, only a strong instinct that he was a gentleman, which he has proven to be for my Wightie. To think I might have given my love to him and never known Kate!

Maybe I will taste again. Taste sweetness. Whatever comes, I am forever grateful to have briefly experienced the excitement of that sense, even if it was a lie I told myself. Love, I think, is by necessity constructed of a ladder of lies you climb together. Still, I long for Kate as ardently as I did on that first night, intoxicated by the warmth of her whiskey and her flesh. For the time being, I am left one-sensed, and the rest was perhaps nonsense. We will see. I do not need to know the truth.

There are several church groups here today. The Baptists, as always, want to know if I will ever turn their way, as it's common knowledge through the publicly distributed Annual Reports that I have balked at the strictures of Doctor's Unitarianism.

"Be baptized!" the proselytizer scribbles repeatedly, to which I finally reply, "Might." I have often thought of it, but I know that Doctor would as surely wish me drowned entire than to undertake that ceremony. But his God is too remote from me, and his religion does not encourage me to come closer; nay, even discourages it. Intellect over heart.

The girl does not wait to greet me. She flies straight into my arms and kisses me long on the cheek. My Laura, come again, after a long wait, almost three weeks. It breaks my heart that we cannot easily converse and get to know each other, but that of course will come. I will teach her the finger spelling, and we will hold hands always. Well, except when I am so engaged with her mother. Eventually I will show her the ridged beauty of her own name carved into the choicest flesh of my left inner thigh; her mother's name is carved into the right, so that when I squeeze my legs together, we are all together, warm and secret and safe.

I am ready for her. I slip the tattered purse from my bosom and press it into her hands. "147," I write slowly. Surely she knows her numbers. Yes, she does, for she buries her face in my neck, her hair prickling my cheek. One hundred forty-seven dollars I have scrounged up, and I plan to work hard to give her more. "MORE," I write three times in block letters, and she puts my hand to her face as she nods yes, then kisses my palm. It has taken me years to save up that amount—and it is not much—but it should be enough for them to live on for a while. At least I think so; I do not know much about the prices of things, having never gone shopping by myself. I asked Jeannette how much some items cost—flour, about a nickel a pound; coffee, fifty cents a pound; lard, twenty-five cents to the gallon—and so I think they should have ample monies. Laura's joy seems to indicate it. I have also crocheted two purses, one for each of them, with the word *Love* worked into the center. I pray it is legible, at any rate.

Now that she knows she can trust me, she will take me to her mother. "KATE," I write and then again. I reach for her face, but she shakes her head *no* this time. I hold the cusp of her chin gently and push her head up and down, up and down, but she resists me. I do it a little harder, and she pulls away from me. I am too rough already with my own child, and I begin to cry. After a moment, she strokes my cheek and I rest against her dear palm.

She slips an envelope into my lap. We rock together awhile, and then one last kiss and she is gone. I clutch the letter, rub it over my lips, my nose, press it between my breasts. I can feel Kate's heart beating through the thin paper, her fingers smudging the ink. I calm my breathing and hide the letter in my bodice, then go straight to Doctor to ask when I might have the carriage again to see Sarah. Everything will be explained, and I will know the date and time when I will be reunited with my love.

I have finally finished *Uncle Tom's Cabin*, and I am bloodied to the core. Why didn't Doctor raise this work earlier? I feel its worth is second only to the Bible. Mr. Lincoln has said that this is the book that started the war, and now I understand why. How could I have been so closeted, so naive, about the relentless evils of slavery? Kate could have been black, and I would never have known the difference while loving her just as fiercely. And oh, to be separated from one's children, as I am from Laura. I didn't know they took the slaves' children away. Poor Cassy in her terror and madness even killed her child rather than have her taken. From Uncle Tom down to little Eva, all these things I learned about the treatment of the Negroes now mark me. I am mortally ashamed of my earlier opinions. One in my state should live in an extended universe of compassion, but I was locked in by my arrogance and self-pity. How could I not have recognized their full humanity? Perhaps being a mother has further opened my clamshell of a heart. I will speak out on Exhibition Days and try my best to make amends, as far as I am able, to God and to the Negroes. But still my situation leaves the quandary of my dear Addison, who I've just heard in a letter from Mama has moved South and is fighting under General Joe Johnston on what I now know is absolutely the wrong side, and yet he is my closest blood. God will have to allow my prayers for him, even with a split tongue.

It is two endless weeks before Doctor lets me have the carriage, and I am prepared for polite conversation before springing the letter on Sarah. But instead, as soon as she takes my hand, she asks, "Can you feel my sores?"

Sores? I travel the length and breadth of Wightie's hands, even her wrists, and all is smooth, unblemished, as it has always been. "Nothing there."

"My face," she says. "Check my face."

I am mystified, but I do as she asks, all around that heart-shaped, familiar face, right up to the delicate ears. I find nothing out of the ordinary and tell her so.

"Sure?" she asks and begs me to check one more time.

Maybe she believes she's been bitten by insects. She must have been bitten often in the islands, but here it is not yet even mosquito season. I pat her hand and assure her that all is well.

After a few moments, she calms down and lets me hold her again. I complain to her about the Unitarians. I know, of course, that she is one herself, but she is also my friend, so I feel the subject can be broached. They do not believe in even trying to touch God, and the services seem to be as much about man as about the Creator. Philanthropists, humanists, ralliers for all causes, abolitionism being the latest and now the bloodiest. And yet these do-gooders do not give the Good Book its full due.

"Don't believe all Bible's words?" I ask.

"Acts over words," she tells me.

For me, this makes no sense: the words must be engraved upon the heart before the actions are spent. Doctor hung his reputation upon his presumption that I would know God instinctively and not need instruction or even the Bible. I did have a sense of God, but how could I know of Jesus and the Holy Spirit? I was a child—how could he have left me in darkness, foraging alone for so long? How much I needed the poetry of the Psalms, the common sense of Proverbs, the miracles of the New Testament, even the horrors of Revelation to keep me anchored on the path! Jesus' resurrection became real to me as my fingers traced his fate—and therefore my own—and the warmth of His embrace cannot be equaled by any man, not even Doctor, not even Sarah, *not even Kate*. Doctor has told the world I've failed him miserably by hying to the heart of religion, but he is interested only in the head, where his beloved bumps reside. That he should put phrenology above Christianity cuts me to the marrow. Over and over, my dear mother has asked why I remain a Unitarian if I do not find true solace in its doctrines, and I have told her that Doctor is the one who gave me my religion, and I've clung to it out of loyalty. But now that Mary has died, it seems possible that I should make my catechism match my heart. Mary was a Baptist, my whole family are Baptists, and a hot blood flows through their veins that never touches the formal vessels of Unitarianism.

"I think I'll change," I tell Sarah.

"Into what?"

"Baptist. I want to be baptized."

She waits. "Yes," she says. "You are a born Baptist."

Of course, we're not born anything but children of God, and yet I get her meaning. "So you think it's good?" I would like to have her stamp of approval before I take my case before Doctor.

"Laura under water," she says. That is true; it will be a full immersion, unlike the dainty sprinklings of the Unitarians. I deserve—no, I actually desire—the dunking. I have never been fully underwater. At the beach my attendants have always kept me close to the shore. Once a wave lashed as high as my waist, and I was salted and sanded between the legs, but that was it.

"Doctor," she writes and then she's shaking, and I realize she is laughing merely at the thought of his response. She laughs so hard she falls into my arms, and within moments, the shudders turn to weeping, and she is staining my bodice, her heart thudding like a horse's after a canter. I wanted water, I got water. How did Sarah ever endure my hysterics as a child? I find I am not fit to comfortably endure hers. Suddenly she stops and leaves the room without a word. What change was wrought across the sea in my dear Wightie, what baptism of fire?

Ten minutes and she is back, her hand cold and wet. She has soaked her face apparently, and she does seem present once again.

"The letter?" she asks.

I've been so disciplined at waiting today, though I wanted nothing more than to throw it at her straight out of the carriage. I am grateful she understands my anxiety and anticipation. I wonder does she ever feel replaced in my heart by Kate, but she does not seem jealous, only wary.

Darling,

Thank you with all that I am for your generosity. You are my greatest love from heaven and my fiercest protector from hell.

I miss your touch more than words can ever—, but I cannot bear for you to find me as I am now, so far gone from myself. My heart is stacked with hope that maybe someday I might be strong enough to see you again.

Taste. Taste everything in remembrance of me.

Kate

"That is all?"

Sarah nods.

"Sure?" I ask again. I am reeling. She is not coming to see me, nor will she let the girl take me to her. And Laura! She doesn't even say if she will send her back to me. *Taste... in remembrance?* What rot! Sarah does not add salt to the wound, but only holds me. How quickly she and I change places, again and again, a boundless circle of womanly feeling.

Chapter 29

Chev, 1864

Sherman's March to the Sea was almost complete, and the destruction looked to be finished by year's-end. Having traveled to the South many times to raise money for blind education, Chev had a soft spot for the state of Georgia, and so his gladness at the Union's progress was tempered by a weakness for magnolia trees and the lilting cadences of Southern women. And Lincoln had been reelected, at which he cried foul. Lincoln was a good man, had been a leader of strength and integrity, but he had proven far too lenient in his veto of the Wade-Davis Bill, which required the electoral majority in each Confederate state to swear past and future loyalty to the Union. What could the Union expect if not promised at least that allegiance? Of course, the South believed that a gentleman's loyalty could never be legislated. Chev was wary of what would ultimately come about under the guidance of the lawyer from Illinois.

But at least the nation had Julia's song, however that should help to raise the spirits of the republic. Yes, he understood that the "Battle Hymn of the Republic" was indeed a hum-worthy tune, but it didn't seem to merit all the attention it had so quickly accrued. And he still couldn't believe she'd had the gall to set it to the melody of "John Brown's Body." That was a sword to pierce his side, and it was his own wife who had thrust it in and turned it. The song was indeed a fitting accompaniment to their married life at present: she had trampled on the vineyards where his grapes of wrath were stored.

The week after the reelection, Laura came to the doorway of his office and asked him to take a walk with her. He told her that he didn't have time, but she insisted that it was very important.

"Come in!" he commanded, annoyed that he had to stand in the entrance of his own office to converse, but she shook her head vehemently.

"Parker's brain," she said.

Oh, Lord, the news had spread quickly through the Institution. Recently, his close friend and minister Theodore Parker's brain had arrived from Florence, where he'd died of tuberculosis. Apparently, Elizabeth Barrett Browning, with whom Parker had been staying, had had the brain preserved and left instructions on her death that it be sent to Chev, whom she'd thought might like to keep this gorgeous and much beloved specimen. He had been frankly taken aback by the generous gift. Yes, he'd examined many brains, but he hadn't felt particularly keen to *own* one, especially one of his friends'. But obviously he couldn't get rid of it; Parker's congregation in Boston had over seven thousand members and Julia had loved him dearly. So here it was, prominently displayed in a glass case atop a marble pedestal in the corner of the room, the sunlight dappling the glistening congeries.

"Afraid will knock over brain," Laura said. Well, that would be a fine mess. He certainly didn't want that, so he relented and walked out with her. She still had a bit of pull on his reins, though he'd never admit it, not to her, and least of all to Julia. Laura was in an ambling mood as they strolled arm in arm toward the docks, but Chev got right to it and asked whatever was so urgent that she should call him away from his letters for the Sanitary Commission. The military hospitals were counting forthwith on the report.

She rambled a bit about her sister Mary's death, and that he didn't want to hear.

"Still think of Sammy?" she asked.

"What a ridiculous question," he told her. She made one more try to bind them with overgeneral ties of grief, and he cut her dead. His boy was the one subject that still could not be broached, though it had been over a year. Chev felt as if he were strangling every time he heard his son's name, and he didn't have faith that this knot of sorrow would ever go away. He was also positive, at the rate it was going, that he and Julia would have no more children. Queen Victoria had recently ushered in the age of anesthesia for childbirth, having taken to chloroform with her last birth, so what was left for Julia to be afraid of? If Chev were a woman, he'd have birthed a dozen by now.

"Addison fighting for rebs," Laura said. Jeannette had told Chev this bit of news, and it *was* shocking. Laura's brother had grown up in New Hampshire, gone to medical school at Dartmouth, and yet had changed his stripes just because he happened to marry a belle from Savannah? More proof that there was something terribly amiss with the whole family. What a story that boy's bumps must tell.

"Awful," he told her. "But don't pray for rebs."

"No. Finished *Uncle Tom*. Now I understand."

"You'll speak out?"

She nodded emphatically.

Hallelujah. Julia was right; he should have raised the book as soon as it was published. But before he could congratulate himself, Laura wrote, "But John Brown still wrong."

This was what she'd dragged him out to talk about? "Enough. What is urgent?"

She noodled in his hand and lifted her face toward the sky as if she were examining the cumulus clouds forming on the horizon. It was going to rain soon, and Chev was losing patience. He pecked hard at her palm with his middle finger.

Finally she turned toward him. "Have row with God."

As he'd predicted, this was the fruit of her taking in the Bible before she was ready. Chev had long ago washed his hands of this wreck; he couldn't be held responsible for the damage done by her overweening appetite for religion. She, and the proselytizers who had hounded her, must bear the grave consequences.

"You argue with Him?" she asked.

"No," he told her, which she surely knew was a lie, since he argued with practically everyone.

"Unitarians don't talk to God enough."

The girl—the girl he had made, no less—was going to preach to him? He took her by the shoulders and he wanted to shake her, but he didn't. "What is wrong with you?" Of course, the truest answer was "almost everything," but then they both knew that.

"Change to Baptist," she wrote.

He dropped her hand and moved away. She had the power to rock him still. How could it have come to this? All his work invested for her to dunk her head in a stream and come up a wet and wild Calvinist. He saw the distress on her face deepen as she stepped forward tentatively over the cobblestones, reaching into the air in front of her. She snagged the billowing sleeve of a passing lady, but Chev did not help her. Instead, he walked a few yards away and watched. She wheeled around slowly with both arms outstretched like antennae. She looked like an imbecile, one of the idiots Miss Dix swooned over. She was an idiot, as far as he was concerned. People strolling by gave a wide berth to the crazy, spinning woman on the walkway. He read the panic in her face; she knew she was too far away from the Institution to find her way back. She was asking herself: Could she depend safely on a stranger to escort her? How could he just leave me? Doctor has never left me. She was gasping for air, trying not to cry. She made her sound for him, softly at first, then as a full-throated howl: *"OCKA! OCKA!"* She was counting on his being embarrassed enough to come back for her. After all, most people recognized Laura Bridgman, and wouldn't that make a fine tabloid headline? She let loose again, louder still: *"OCKA!"* Oh, for pity's sake, he couldn't bring himself to leave her, though he'd like to teach her a lesson about who she could actually depend on. Not a Baptist God, that's for certain. And so his hand covered her mouth, the other clamped hard on her arm, and he jerked her around in the direction of the Institution.

When they were safe inside the door, she doubled over, panting, and almost fell. Theatricals worthy of Charlotte Cushman. He caught her, but not gently, and jabbed into the sweating valley of her palm: "You are a disappointment to God and to me. Do what you will. I am done with you." He expected her to collapse, to kneel, to beg, but now she stood up straight. Ah, but she reached for his hand to ask forgiveness.

Her fingers trembled but still she wrote, "My God and I not done with you."

Chev had never been more grateful that Laura couldn't see his face because his jaw had actually dropped. Who *was* this woman? He took the steps two at a time to his office and slammed the door, pressing himself into the wood as if to fuse it with his backbone. He was shaking, and he didn't know if it was with anger or something else. He prayed for strength, the strength to truly be done with her. He could not let these wretched women rule him, or God help him.

Would that he could go to Sumner's comfortable, old flat in the Back Bay, but his man was now ensconced in the capital, having returned to the Senate, and giving his florid and ill-received speeches as heartily as ever. He still had some troubles with his spine from Brooks's beating, but not enough to stop him from courting. Yes, *courting!* Dear Charlie had finally been bitten, and the teeth belonged to one Mrs. Alice Mason Hooper, a socially connected war widow. Chev had yet to meet her, but he couldn't quite imagine the shape, caliber, and qualities of a woman who could genuinely inspire his friend's affections. He'd always pushed for marriage, and yet here his own was currently an exquisite pain, while Sumner seemed poised on the very lip of happiness. How strangely the tides and times change for every man.

Chapter 30

Laura, 1864

The breeze from the pines dries the sweat trickling down my
back as we walk to the river, but by the time we are on the
bank, I am growing sticky again. It seems ridiculous to be wearing a corset and petticoat, much less the heavy ceremonial robes,
but Mama insisted I shine in my full respectable ladyhood for
this occasion. She has made me a new white muslin dress with
satin trimmings. Of course, I helped; no one can thread a needle quick as I can. I can thread even the finest needle by placing
the twisted thread and the eye on the very tip of my tongue.
Every day at Perkins I stop by the girls' afternoon sewing class
and thread their needles for them. Wonder would anything get
made there without me.

This is the most important day of my life, the most important
choice I have ever made, and I have never been so nervous. I have
been over and over all the instructions with Pastor Herrick (Pastor Hyland has gone off to fight the rebels), and he has found me
sound of spirit and ready for baptism and membership into the
Hanover Baptist Church, the church at which my grandfather and
my uncle also preached. I am being born again into my faith and
the faith of my family. It is all right that none of the Howes, whom
I've always considered my other family, are here to support me. I
respect their religious choices, and yet they refuse to respect mine,

as if I am not capable, spiritually or emotionally, of choosing the best vehicle to transport me heavenward. But how I do wish Doctor was here to behold me at my bravest moment—would he not be proud of his little dove in spite of himself?—and my dearest Wightie, who has helped in ushering me toward this day. And if Kate and Laura could watch, then my blessings would be complete.

Mama holds my right arm, Papa my left. I am so thrilled I am finally doing something that makes Papa happy, though he has postponed the ceremony twice, fearing that Doctor would not allow me to return to Perkins if I went through with it. But now he is at peace also with my decision and has not even brought up the fact that I'm still no closer to speaking than a donkey. I know my darling Mary is here, holding court with the other angels above the trees as they wait to applaud me. But it is not for them I come; it is for Jesus Christ, to be baptized in the Holy Spirit. I know that this has already happened in my heart, but the baptism will serve to mark the victory for all. I am still frightened of the water, of having my whole head held under, no matter how many times I have tried to meditate on the moment of immersion. There is nothing left but to do it.

As Mama helps me off with my robe and slippers, I realize that all gathered will probably see the cuts I made last night in remembrance of the nails hammered into my Lord, the greatest sacrifice I have ever given of my body. I knew better than to mark my hands, so I only carved my feet and one a bit deeper in my left side, where the Roman soldier pierced Him with a sword. That one I have covered with a plaster so that the blood won't leak through my dress, but I had forgotten about taking off my shoes. Doubtless I have alarmed them all, but this is no time for an explanation. All I have time to tap into Mama's hand is "No worry" before Reverend Herrick takes me from Papa like a bride, and the ground changes beneath my feet, tiny wet pebbles wobbling between my toes. The river's first lick is icy and I shudder, but I will not turn back. The freezing water slides up my ankles, then soaks my hem, as we walk slowly forward in absolute faith and trust. When the river is up to my waist, we stop, and I try to imagine what we look like to the parishioners and family on the shore: a woman in white, no longer young, a green ribbon tied over her eyes, her brown hair parted in the middle and bunned low, and a tall man with a crooked nose dressed all in black, hat still on, as he places his long-fingered hand on her head, blessing her in the name of the Father, the Son, and the Holy Ghost. And then I am going down and time stops.

At first, all is dark, as I am accustomed, but then a cool blue light rushes in, and I see the water undulating around my out-stretched hands, the brown reeds below bobbing between my bare calves, my skirts aswirl. My hands and feet glow, pearlescent wonders in the new and moving universe. I cannot breathe, but I can see! A fish—what I recognize as a fish from the shape—small and iridescently scaled, swims up to me, close to my chest. Is this the Holy Spirit entering? No, it swims away, tail flashing. I want to stay down here where all life suddenly exists and I am fully part of it, but then I feel the reverend's hands tugging me upward. I resist, bending my knees toward the bottom, my arms thrashing against his. But he is stronger than I am, and I am pulled up, up, up toward the surface of the water, the light ribboned through it as I rise. Just as I reach the luminescent crown, just as my face is fully bathed in the light, I explode from the river, and all is black again. I gasp, fighting for my breath, and look down, but again meet blackness. I shake my head out like a dog and reach for my shade. Still there. It was never off when I was under, so how could I see? Was this vision the Lord's gift to me for just that one mo-ment, plunged into His natural world, His sign that I have done the right thing and that I am now one with Him? I will never know.

We wade through the water, and it leaves me, inch by inch, un-til my toes are again on the rocks. I am shivering violently, and Mama takes me in her arms, and then the pastor and his wife.

Papa leans in and gives me a little pat. Mama covers me with a shawl so the crowd won't see my wet dress stuck to me. Would any find it alluring? How can I have such sinful thoughts after my baptism! As we climb up the bank toward the carriage, I think of the flat, dark eyes of the fish, so close I could've poked them out. If He was going to grant me a brief miracle, then instead of the blasted fish, I would rather have seen the sun and sky or my mother's face, or more than anything, my own. God is a strange and mysterious master, and I no doubt am a strange and mysterious servant, but from this day forward I am His. I am forever changed, by my own *choice*, and I wonder if He is too.

Chapter 31

Laura, 1865

Doctor buys us all Ribbons for Victory for forty cents each. I pin mine to the side of my spoon bonnet, and then we are out the door into the April wind, a procession among processions. I will save my ribbon to give Laura on her next visit; I pray that she and Kate are able to celebrate within their circumstances. So many people we can barely move through the streets, so we hold hands with Doctor at the fore and Jeannette at the rear. We stop so that we can touch the decorations on a shop's windows, and I reach as high as I can until I feel the tip of the flag hung over the awning. Jeannette says that the Stars and Stripes are flying everywhere. Lee has surrendered at last, and though my Addison was on the losing side, he has written that he is safe and on his way back home. Gloria in excelsis Deo. Everyone is laughing and crying, and I am as caught up in the revelry and high hopes as anyone, though I still feel shame at my refusal to speak out against slavery until the eleventh hour. I have tried to right myself, but it is wearing to fight against the extreme conditions that have bent my nature. Forgive me, Lord, for allowing myself this pitiful loophole to a sane and useful personhood.

Tonight all the students are invited to join with the Howes in a celebration banquet. The best of Boston are in attendance: five of the Secret Six; Sumner, unfortunately; the Horace Manns; the

Peabody sisters, who are said to still be among the greatest beauties of the metropolis; and one who gives my heart pause—Julia's dear friend, Mr. Edwin Booth, the actor. I have met him before, and he brought my hand to his lips and kissed me with the very mouth that is said to give the greatest glory to Shakespeare. I have read *Hamlet* and *Romeo and Juliet*, the only two plays that the Perkins press has printed, and stand in awe that Mr. Booth has played the title roles in both. *A rose by any other name would smell as sweet.* I hope that this sentiment includes me, especially in the presence of one so exalted. Tonight in the parlor he kisses my hand again, and I ask Doctor if I may sit beside him, but he says no, that I would take up all his attention. Few men tempt me, but the idea—and maybe it is only an idea—of this man manifesting the depth of love and tragedy stirs something in me, though, of course, I will never know the power of his actual performance. Doctor is right; if I were to sit beside him, I don't think I could stop touching him. He is said to be very handsome, one of the few who can compete with Doctor, so that I would like to get my fingers on him. And tonight I am wearing my new boots in the latest style, with one made for the left foot and a different one for the right. I've only ever worn straights before.

Even all the blind girls are given half glasses of champagne; it has been over ten years since my adventuring with drink. The memory of the first time is relived almost daily. I wonder what Mr. Shakespeare would have made of the story of me and Kate. It is a tragedy, after all, but also a tale that blossoms with beauty, a rose with the thorns twisted into my flesh. Champagne is very different from wine and whiskey. I taste nothing, but still enjoy the fizzing on my tongue and the way it lifts my spirits even higher on this hallowed eve, something I would not have thought possible. We toast to the Union, to President Lincoln, to God's wisdom and bounty. In excelsis Deo. I am surprised with all the blinds that no one breaks a glass. Luck and happiness reign, and it is one of the loveliest evenings of my life.

*　　*　　*

How can the world be so transformed in only five days? President Lincoln has been shot in his box at the theater by John Wilkes Booth. We are doubly in shock, because not only is our savior dead on the heels of victory, but it is our dear Mr. Booth's brother who has performed the unspeakable deed. As soon as we get the news, Julia rushes out to see her friend, but returns in tears. Mr. Edwin had already fled to New York. He is said to be in agony, as he loved the President as much as any of us. Mr. Booth and his brother, now there is a tangled web worthy of Shakespeare. Doctor says that throughout the city, the bright decorations of victory have been draped over with mourning cloth. We all change into our black crepe. The war took so many lives already; why did God feel the need to take this one most holy? Yes, John Wilkes Booth pulled the trigger, but it is always God's decision. In the last years, He has taken Mary, Asa, little Sammy, and now President Lincoln. Every time I think I have regained my trust in His wisdom, He destroys it. I pray that this lapse of faith will pass, and yet it is the one I'm praying to who has betrayed me. Betrayed us all.

Reverend Thomas Wentworth Higginson pays a call today; there is still much visiting in the aftermath of the assassination. Everyone seeks the company of friends more so than usual, as we are stuck together in our grief. He is always much beloved here, though he and Doctor no longer seem close. His hand in mine is very firm, but gentle, as it has always been since he took the time to learn finger spelling to converse with me. I feel him taking stock in that one touch and yet, in the pause before he begins to write, he allows me to take stock of him as well. Most do not intuit well enough to give me those few needed seconds. From this, I know he respects me as an equal. The patronizing tap I know so well, close at home from Julia, as well as the impatient, indelicate, disrespectful pecks of one like Sumner. And best of all, he lets me twirl the waxed ends of his handlebar mustache. It is almost as long as my hand!

I ask if he is going to Washington to see the President laid out, but he says he does not want to talk about that. "Today a surprise for you."

He often brings me little treats, and once even a maple fudge so rich that I thought I could taste its sweetness, just barely. That alone has made me inordinately grateful to him.

"New friend reminds me of you."

"How?" There are so few who are anything like me that I am instantly intrigued, though skeptical.

"Same age. Two sides of coin."

It's startling when a gentleman knows your age, but then again I suppose anyone who is interested knows my years, all thirty-five of them. "In Boston?"

"Amherst."

"Visit me?"

"Does not travel."

"Nor I. Wish."

"Shut in."

"Prisoner? Of husband?" This does not sound like a lady I want myself compared to!

"Of herself."

"Ill?"

"Sometimes."

"Blind or deaf?"

"No."

This I cannot imagine—the girl has all her senses and she doesn't venture from her home? What ingratitude. "Mad?" I should not have written that; Mr. Higginson will doubtless be offended.

Instead, his chuckle shakes his arm. "All poets mad."

A poet. I have liked most of the poets I've met, Longo especially and his good wife. Many have written with me as the subject, but I think pity the object. Or perhaps mainly to glorify Doctor. Poems spelled into my hand are hard to follow. I have found with poetry that I need time to myself to touch the words again and again until they touch me back. Or not. Generally I prefer the poetry of the Psalms, not because of my religiosity, but because, untutored by the muse as I may be, I find them better verses than most of our current crop. And then of course, there are the endless maudlin rhymes of our Julia, poetess of the house and of the nation. I have decided she is a good enough woman, but not a good enough poet. Mine eyes have seen the glory, indeed.

"Like Julia's poetry?" I have caught him off guard, poor fellow. He is such a careful one.

"She has a terrible swift sword."

I love to parry with Mr. Higginson. "And your friend?"

"Mercifully brief. Here—"

He writes very slowly, making sure I understand the pauses that signify the end of each line.

> *Because I could not stop for Death—*
> *He kindly stopped for me—*
> *The carriage held but just Ourselves—*
> *And Immortality.*
>
> *We slowly drove—he knew no haste*
> *And I had put away*
> *My labor, and my leisure too,*
> *For His Civility—*
>
> *We passed the School, where Children strove,*
> *At Recess—in the Ring—*
> *We passed the Fields of Gazing Grain—*
> *We passed the setting sun—*

He stops. Of course we are both thinking of President Lincoln in that slow carriage.

"Hard," he says. "Can rent poem but cannot own."

"If good, reader becomes owner." I am not yet sure that I think this poem is good, however.

"So a good poem can have many owners?"

"Even a bad poem, like a woman or dog."

And so he continues, reading the last three stanzas. I must think before writing. What a profound pity, she seems to me, this lady poet, enraptured with thoughts of the end, instead of the beginning, or for heaven's sake, the middle, where we all reside. She has gone out there on that limb alone, well before her time, and perches there like a sparrow, hopping on one tiny foot, enjoying immensely the hopping. "Obsessed with death."

"In your darkness, as much death as life?"

He presumes far too much of my limitations. "No more death in me than you." I know I am speaking out of turn, out of wits, to so kind and distinguished a gentleman, and a minister no less, but I am helpless to stop. "Christ as full of life as death?"

"Yes, so Miss Dickinson pays court to end."

"And you are comparing her to Christ. Must think very well of her." He withdraws his hand entirely. I have gone too far. Quick, quick to remedy: "Please leave me a poem." I will try to wrap my brains around its heart, for his sake. I have forfeited a last twirl of his mustache apparently.

"As you wish. God blessed with ego to make up for your senses."

He leaves me more than a little sore. But I relish soreness these days.

Chapter 32

Sarah, 1870

Mrs. Bond, you have a visitor."

"I am not dressed, madam. You can see that."

"Don't you want to know who—?"

"I am not dressed, madam."

"The visitor is not..."

"I am not ready today for any person."

Dr. Tergesen's boots clomp down the hallway. The surf foams onto Kaanapali beach, fizzing at my toes like ginger beer, the sun so bright I shut my eyes and wait for it to warm me, the roar so loud it drowns out everything. A hand in mine, pulling me back from the water. Not the doctor's, not Edward's. I know this hand.

"We are so honored to have Miss Bridgman here at McLean today. Could you write that to her please?" Tergesen says, motioning. "Aren't you happy to see your friend, Mrs. Bond?" He doesn't wait for me to respond. "Of course, we often host distinguished visitors because we host the most distinguished patients. Breeding breeds breeding, I always say."

"And madness breeds madness." I do not translate any of this for Laura, though she is knocking at my hand, eager as always to talk. I wrap myself as tightly in my shawl as I am able.

Laura looks old, like a widow, like a useless spider stranded without a web. I suppose she is forty now. Do I look that old?

There are few mirrors here, so the insults are minimal, but of course I have never been vain. Laura has always been far more concerned with appearance than I am—or many women for that matter—an irony I doubt is lost on her. She is dressed impeccably, as always, even adorned with a bustle, which makes it difficult to sit. I am lucky; all I have to wear is my dressing gown and bed coat, no more steel cages or padded bottoms. But look here: a spot on her bodice. She would be so embarrassed in front of Tergesen and the nurses if she knew. Most days at Perkins she has no visitors now that she is no longer a *cause célèbre*, but today she has gotten dressed up and made this journey from South Boston to Charlestown, over fifteen miles. She does not have someone looking after her who cares. She won't know, her caretakers surmise, and it's true that it is hardly noticeable. Should I scrub it off or tell her and suffer through directing her in removing it? I don't have the energy. She doesn't know—why make trouble visible? They don't care what she thinks, her pride, her fastidiousness, her frustration that she must constantly ask, "Am I clean?" Like a baby, though a baby won't aggravate the life out of you for forty years.

Laura perches on the edge of the visiting chair and waves in the doctor's direction. He sits in the other chair, unaware that he has been dismissed.

"How is Dr. Howe?" I might as well get this over with. "Boy died?"

"Years ago."

Well, some child has died lately, I am certain. Probably hundreds. Thousands. Heaven overrun with tiny feet.

"Julia? More children?"

"No. More poems."

Julia did come to see me, jabbering about her suffragist work. I laughed in her face. Why would she talk to me in here about the rights of women? Laura is still scratching away. Sumner, ah yes, the big bumblegoat, I remember him, sniffing around Howe like a dog. Senator Sumner, caned, I recall, on the Senate floor. Almost to death. So tall to reach almost to death.

"Sumner married," Laura is saying. "Six months annulled."

She probably doesn't know what *annulled* means, just parroting the news. Like when she thought she and the Irish were having a baby, and then the girl ran off. I could not bring myself to tell her that her life, as she saw it, was impossible.

"What was her name?"

"Who?" she asks, and I say, not to hurt her, "Your love."

"Kate."

"Come back?"

"I think so."

It is not Laura's way to be evasive; she is as direct as heartbreak. I'd wager she's still feeling up all the ladies in search of her lost sweetheart, even though the wanton took her for every hard-earned penny.

"And the daughter?"

"Sometimes."

"From deck, I watched dolphins and whales," I tell her. "How do they get enough air to stay alive when they go back under?"

She does not answer this, but begins telling me a dream she had about my dead children, how they flew into her arms. I can only stare at her, glad that she can't see my fear, my pity. Is it pity? With her, all other emotions are layered over that sentiment, which is not the same as compassion. This Dr. Tergesen never escorts my family, not even my frail Abigail, but today he lends his arm and time to my esteemed visitor. Laura shrinks away from him; no, she wouldn't like him; she never did most men, except the one she loved overmuch. If she could see Tergesen's dirty white coat and greasy muttonchops, she would like him even less. And the way he stares at her through the ends of his round spectacles roosting on that veiny nose, with no pity *or* compassion, just a gaping, end-less maw of medical curiosity. Dr. Howe could be like that, which Laura would have known if she'd ever seen his eyes, the way he looked at her sometimes. I wish I'd told her, tried to make her understand the truths invested in that cool gaze, but I'm sure she wouldn't have believed me, possibly even hated me for it. That obsession might've come untethered sooner, more mercifully, but it would have broken her heart. Why did God choose me to hold these secrets from her? Heaven knows He has given me enough of my own.

She is still writing, endlessly marching on my palm, when I get up and go to my desk, leaving her to inscribe the air with her gossip and complaints. I pull out the letter I've been laboring over in the last weeks, certain that it is time.

"Here." I press the envelope into her hand. "Give to Edward."

"But he visits..."

"Please, one thing for Wightie."

She nods and I tell her I am tired. I climb into bed, and she tries to kiss me until I push her away. I don't mean to push her hard, but she stumbles back against the visiting chair and almost falls. Tergesen helps her up and she is shaking. She doesn't understand that I am trying to protect her.

The doctor leads Laura out, but at the door she turns back and lifts her shade, and one dazzlingly bright blue eye winks at me.

March 1870, McLean Asylum, Charlestown, Massachusetts

My dear Edward,

The roar is not so loud today, not so wild as on your last visit, and so I seize this precious hour to write, while I am able. They won't let me out of my bed this week, or this month perhaps. I try to rise, but someone I don't know holds me down.

A girl came to see me, maybe Abigail? With a baby. One of them has your green eyes, yes?

My rose shawl I wear for visitors to hide what you were spared, the tassels hanging in my lap so I may clench them in times of need—this is how my shawl gets soiled—so please, sir,

I beg you, do not come again. I long for you, I wait for you, I arrange the gray nest atop my head and pinch my cheeks for you, but once you are here, your beard frightens me. Or worse—the times I am shamed by wanting your comfort in my narrow bed.

Keep your scriptures to yourself, my darling. The words scramble heavenward as I reach for them, and I pull from the air only rhymes and solitary letters.

Lahaina. I think of our years there, but the waves crash in and pull me out again. Not toward you, never toward you. Away.

Sarah

Chapter 33

Laura, 1875–1876

One dollar," Doctor writes. "Sorry."

That is Papa's inheritance to me, his eldest daughter. No remittance to pay for my continued care at Perkins or so that I might have clothes and shoes once a year. I knew he had not loved me as a father should, and in some ways I even understood that sentiment—or lack of it—but I did not know he cared nothing for my health and well-being. To Addison, he gave the house and land, with the stipulation that he and his unpleasant wife, Hattie, allow Mother to live there, in a single small room, and feed her. I am also allowed to visit and will presumably be fed if I do. There was no time to get me to Hanover for the funeral, and I must admit, I am grateful I didn't have to go. Thank God I have had another father since the age of seven, though he of course has also failed me in many ways. And apparently, I him. It is no wonder that I bear so little fondness for men.

"Must go away?" I ask him, holding my breath against the answer, a drum without sound beating in my head. That moment twenty-five years ago when he told me that I had to go home floods back in nauseating specificity. But today, his fingers feel different, a little shaky, but not thrumming with the hard edge of nerves and force that had accompanied my former heartbreak.

"Course not," he says, and I release my breath, so dizzy I grip the arm of the chair with my other hand.

"But no money," I remind him.

"You have some."

"No."

"From needlework," he writes. He would assume, correctly, that I have earned hundreds of dollars over the years, but of course, he doesn't know where it's all gone and I cannot tell him.

"Gone."

"Where?"

He is angry. I don't blame him. "Gifts. Family."

He twiddles his fingers, and I know he is calculating, disbelieving.

"You don't watch me," I say. "For years." My only strategy is to thrust the responsibility back onto his shoulders with a pound of guilt. And it's true, I could have bought a thousand spinning tops and he would have been none the wiser.

"Not good" is all he can come up with.

"I go?"

"We find a way."

I almost leap from my seat and into his arms, the way I used to. He is my dear Doctor again, looking out for his little Laura. Instead, I bring his hand to my lips and kiss it, only once. He accepts.

On the way out of his office, I am so weak with relief that I hold on to the shelves lining the walls for support, and my fingers come upon a tiny foot. I know this foot! It is mine. Doctor has kept a Laura doll this whole time, over thirty years since they were first made. I reach for it carefully, aware that he is watching me, and take her from the shelf. Her gown is covered in dust, but that is all right. He has kept her, seeing her every day, for over three decades. I make sure her eyeshade is still secure—the green must be so faded now—and begin to comb through her hair. It is stiff and brittle, but at least not salted with gray, the way I know mine is. There is a sudden snap, and I am holding her head in one hand and her body in the other. I have taken off my own head. I turn toward Doctor's desk, holding out the head, and he takes it. I set the body gently back on the shelf, and I feel him behind me. He strokes my hair, and I allow my head to touch his shoulder, just for a moment. We stand and all is quiet and still and perfect, the way it has always been, the way it has never been. I pull the door shut behind me.

True to his word, Doctor lets me stay. I have no idea where the money comes from to support me. I do not ask, and he does not say. And anyway, Doctor does not fare well these days, which I suppose is to be expected for one over seventy. He rarely even rides his horses anymore. All sources tell me that he and Julia still look like the prime specimens they have always been, though Julia's fabled auburn locks are now tricked out with gray. Julia Romana's husband, Mr. Anagnos, the scholar Doctor brought from Greece, is helping with the affairs of the Institution and Doctor is obviously grooming him for the chief post. To think he was vibrant enough just a few years ago to return to Greece during the Cretan insurrection to distribute supplies. I do not see him often—"tired," Julia says, "so tired"—and when I do, his touch holds but a tenth of its former vigor. His mind does not appear to lack for clarity, though. He raged against the annexation of Santo Domingo last year, and though I never thought I'd see the day, he and Sumner fell plumb out over the subject. Doctor even abused his dearest friend in print. So hot was the issue that Doctor rallied and set off with Julia to the island to work at politicking.

But while he was away the year, Sumner took ill and died, and the news brought Doctor hurtling back. He is still deeply anguished, Julia tells me, berating himself for his row with his beloved. That is what Julia calls him, and goes as far as saying that her husband should never have married her, but Charles Sumner instead. Though I never liked the man, I think this probably would have been the happier union. Like me and Kate, if we had not been separated.

277

My darling Wightie passed last year, having never set foot out of McLean Asylum again, and I still miss her dreadfully, though she didn't seem to know me at the end. She had told her husband that he could no longer visit, but the hospital let him just the same, as if she had no say. I am not sure I can blame them, but for whose comfort was it? Mr. Bond has become a real friend to me, and he and two of their children, now grown, come to visit more than most. He always takes pains to assure me how dear I was to his wife: "She never stopped speaking of you." I am proud that I left as much of a scar on my teacher's heart as she did on mine. The lei she brought me from the islands is strung across my bedpost, and first thing when I wake every morning, I finger the dried flowers and think on her. I know she is now as lucid as Saint Peter himself and watches over me as carefully as she did in life. I remember when I was young, wishing that I had a cameo of Doctor's face to wear at my neck and to sleep with on my pillow, but now that the years have shown me other kinds of love, it is Sarah's face I would keep pinned at my neck, and Kate's face I would press to mine in the night.

My Laura has not come to me the last two years. She had been visiting annually on my birthday, though it was usually me giving the presents. Sadly, I am certain that her absence is because I told her I have no more money to give her. The last time she brought with her a curly-haired child, a dumpling of a girl, who would not sit still on my lap, even after I gave her a Laura doll, the very last thing I had to offer. She kept jumping off and being put back by her mother. I knew that she was probably afraid of me, repulsed even, though of course it hurts to think it. Maybe Laura did not want to come again either to see my face. I can feel that it has become hollow-cheeked, my bones even birdier than before, and that my skin, which I had prided on its softness, feels now a bit like my boots. I have long given up my bright green shade—by the age of forty, even I knew its gaiety no longer became my station—and replaced it with darkly opaque spectacles, which do seem a bit of a joke. The glass eyes I'd pined for are forever out of reach, now that I have no money of my own.

Kate has never come, and I have almost accepted that she probably never will. At last I forced myself to stop sending letters by Laura since they hadn't been answered in several years, perhaps not even read. Laura finally learned to write decently, at least, and I brought myself to ask her if her mother were dead. "No," she said, "but might as well be." She is a young woman of stolid and sorrowful temperament. When I asked how she lives, if she'd married, she wrote, "You don't want to know." The mystery is far worse than the truth, I think, but that's easy to say when one is not slapped in the face with it. I have certainly done all that I could over the years, and I am sure my Kate has done the best she could under the circumstances, whatever they might have been. I pray that the three of them—Kate, our daughter, and hers—listen to the music box together, the three songs, one for each, over and over, and think of me fondly. I do not complain, but instead thank God for giving me the opportunity, however strange and slant, to fulfill the circle of womanhood. Where would I have been without all those hopes and dreams and memories? Between those and my chatter with the Lord, I am never truly alone. Or so I say.

I am sitting in the front parlor, my chair pulled as close to the fire as caution allows, when there is a tumult, many footsteps, everything shifting. I am up in an instant, hurrying toward the hall, when Jeannette bars my way with one solid arm. "Doctor," is all she writes, and I slide against the wall to the floor.

He is not dead, thank Jesus; he rests in what they say is a coma. The doctors come and go, and tell us that it is something in his brain, a tumor. I think Doctor would make a joke of it himself, the ultimate phrenological display: the biggest bump of all. I reach into the thick masses of his hair and locate each bump on his skull. Ah, there it is: the well-developed veneration bump right at the top between firmness and benevolence, evidencing the faculties of his divine creative spirit and his quest for the sublime. I round the twin bumps of ideality at his temples that denote the disposition toward perfection, toward beauty and refinement in all things, and then notch the bulge of individuality between his eyebrows that sets them so far apart and him so far apart from lesser men. And the prodigious affection bump situated on the upper back of his head, of which I have had my share of its benefits, though far from all. He told the world, told my family, that I was a failed experiment, but still I love him and forgive him all his trespasses as he has surely forgiven mine.

It has been two days now, and he does not speak or open his eyes. Julia is being very kind; she lets me sit with the girls by his bedside, though I am of little help, and they don't leave me alone with him because if he did open his eyes or speak, I would miss the moment. I restrain myself from touching him constantly. I know I must share him with his family, but it still cuts deeply to admit that they have greater claim on him than I do. My namesake sits beside me and we hold hands, rarely talking. The room is warm and time passes strangely, as if in a dream.

On the third day, I am in the dining hall eating what I can of lunch when Julia flies in and takes my hand without a word. Together we climb the three flights to Doctor's room, and she pushes me toward his bed. His forehead is ribboned with sweat, his hands freezing. I trace the lips that I have touched a thousand times, but have never met with mine. I know that Julia is watching, but I can't stop myself, I lean in to kiss those lips, for the first and last time.

"Eph-phatha," I write across the width of Doctor's forehead. "Be opened." Over and over, and yet his spirit remains closed. One last time I reach for his hand, which has held my whole life's conversation, but I can think of nothing to write.

Chapter 34

Chev, 1876

Hands on me, so many hands on me, and voices fluttering in and out. Years have passed—no, decades—since I have been so quiet. It is all right because I am tired, so tired. Julia's hands, worried and sweet, the only hands that traveled the true north and south, east and west of my body. My girls', panicked and damp, pulling at my covers. And the one I refused to see, now I will never know the child's face, half-mine. Sammy does not yet touch me, but he will and without end. He waits, as does my Charlie, just beyond my reach, but soon to be mine.

And then the most familiar fingers, writing in my palm, and then across my forehead, words I cannot follow. Her fingers are enough; I do not need to know their meaning. I have always known their meaning, their endless font of desire, tapping, tapping, always there.

Suddenly, Laura speaks—I know it is her—softly at first, and then so loud that her voice fills the room. Not the noise she made for my name. This is Laura *speaking*, and the voice is different from the one I'd imagined all these years, husky and grave instead of high and light, the most beautiful and solemn sound I have ever heard. "You are mine," she says. "I have always been yours." Now she is laughing, the sweetest laugh, echoing until

I hush her with a kiss. We have finally closed the breach. I can hear the mute speak and be heard by the deaf. I knew this day would come.

I am beginning another life, separating myself limb from limb, thought from thought. In another life, Laura and I—

Chapter 35

Julia, 1876–1877

Julia wreathed her husband's bedstead in her white bridal veil. He hadn't been well for months, but the end had come so suddenly that she was numb with disbelief. Yes, he had been seventy-five, but she had always expected him to outlive her by sheer force of personality. How he must have argued with the Lord when he was called home, and heaven help the angels. His hair and beard had grown bushy and wild—he hadn't let her at him for over a year—so now she trimmed them for the laying-in, careful as always to keep his hair long enough to hide his enormous ears, which he'd always been shy about. She didn't touch the waxy skin or the frozen lips, the stiff limbs in his best suit. Only the hair seemed still alive, that beautiful, thick mane gone gray long ago, and she combed her fingers through the strands, parting and reparting it, fingering his cowlick, grabbing it in greedy handfuls until she realized she'd been sitting there for hours, his hair clutched in her fists.

Chev was buried at Mount Auburn Cemetery in Cambridge beside Sammy, with a plot waiting for Julia on the other side of her son. At the funeral, it was Laura who wailed the loudest, that horrible, unearthly keening as if echoing straight up from hell. She threw herself on his coffin just before it was lowered into the hole, pressing her face into the boughs of white roses, and if Julia hadn't grabbed her, she might have gone down with it. She pulled Laura to her feet, and they all saw the blood streaming down her face from the wounds of the thorns, and yet Julia took the girl in her arms anyway—she still thought of her as a girl, though she was nearly fifty—and Laura's blood spotted Julia's black veil. How she longed to feel the embraces instead of her children, who stood close by, but they were more reserved in their mourning.

At the memorial service later in Boston Music Hall, she read not one of her own poems, but John Greenleaf Whittier's tribute to her husband, "The Hero." Hundreds had turned out, from strangers to the friends they had left who had not preceded Chev. Thank God Sumner had died first; he would have been as helpless as Laura in his grief. The students of Perkins sang hymns and Chev's successor, Michael Anagnos, spoke at length of Dr. Howe's accomplishments. Julia still hadn't recovered from Anagnos's marriage to Julia Romana. The truth was she'd thought the girl lovely but ultimately unmarriageable, cursed as she was with a nervous and melancholic temperament far worse than either of her parents.

At home, Julia did nothing. She was now relieved of all demands and edicts from Chev, and yet she felt no urge to pick up either book or pen. And lately her vision had been going, and at night she could barely read even with the help of a lamp. In her worst moments, she imagined that this was the Lord's punishment for her repulsion for the blind, the children who surrounded her, and for her unkind thoughts—and sometimes actions—toward Laura, the epitome of the damaged and helpless among them. The only thing left to attend to was the reading of the will, which Chev's lawyer would bring in a couple of days.

In the last weeks before her husband's death, she had, at his request, had her double bed carried into his chamber and placed beside his, close enough that they could both stretch out their arms and hold hands until he fell asleep, and his hand released hers. Three nights before he died, she had been in her room at her desk preparing for a lecture, this one on ethical polarities in nature, when she heard him call out for her to rub his feet. It was late, half one, and she was almost finished, so she told one of the servants to attend to him. When she finally came to bed, he was asleep. The next day, when he was taken out for his walk, he went into convulsions and collapsed, never to open those blue eyes again. She knew that it wouldn't have made a difference if she had gone to comfort him in the night, and yet she kept hearing him call her name, over and over, his voice raspy with irritation. She had not gone to him because she was still so angry over what he had told her the week before.

That night, he had reached for her hand in the darkness and said he had something important to tell her. When she tried to get up to turn on the lamp, he pulled her back down. He was still so strong, no matter how he complained. Julia honestly believed this was just another one of his spells, when he would take to his bed and demand to be waited on hand and foot, preferably by his wife, who would then be forced to miss all of her suffragist meetings and lecture appointments.

"There were women," he said, and she tried to wrest her hand away, but he held fast. This she had long suspected, but had never expected for him to confess. She thought of the weanings of her six children, how she had kept him away. Had there been one whore for each of her pregnancies?

"How many?" She craned her head toward him, but in the blackness she could see nothing of his face. Only his voice, steady and sharp as a dagger.

"The details don't matter," he said, and she wanted to leap out of the bed and force him to tell her, her nails on his face, her hands on his neck. But instead she lay still, her hand limp and wet in his.

"Then why are you telling me?"

"It is selfish," he said quietly, "but I am selfish. One I deeply regret, a girl of low station when you were in Rome, who bore a child, my child."

She thanked God she was lying down; otherwise, she might have fainted.

"And there was one I don't regret, an affair of the heart long-standing, which only ended with her death ten years ago."

"Did I know her?"

"Yes."

She combed her memory as if for nits: sidelong glances, interrupted conversations, awkward meetings, but came up with nothing. At least it had not been Laura. She would never have recovered from that. She thought of the final letter she had written to Mr. Wallace; she had learned of his death before she could mail it, but she had saved it and read it again and again over the years, as she did the letters from him, even unto this day.

"My Diva Julia, I knew you'd understand because of your Mr. Wallace," Chev said as if he were reading her thoughts, and abruptly let go of her hand.

She started to protest and then decided she would keep the truth to herself, that she had never actually been unfaithful, only desperately in love. Let her husband believe she was as sin-stained as he was.

Just the year before, Julia had declared in *Woman's Journal* that suffragists were really typical Victorian women, who sought the comforts of home, but also the striving for freedom. She had asked "that the door of human right might open widely enough to allow us to pass through, bearing our babes, not leaving them, assisting our husbands, not forsaking them."

Should she have forsaken him?

Two days later, the lawyer arrived and the family, along with Laura, gathered in the parlor for the reading of the last will and testament of Samuel Gridley Howe. He had left his estate to be divided evenly among his children; his papers to the Perkins Institution, under the guidance of Michael Anagnos; and a two-thousand-dollar bequest to Laura Bridgman. To his wife of over thirty years, he left nothing. Julia wrote the words into Laura's palm even as the pain of it all nailed her to her seat. Was this his way of punishing her for her alleged affair, despite his many? Or was he simply giving her what she had always begged for, the right to earn money on her own from writing and lecturing? *Passion-Flowers*, over the years, had made close to three hundred dollars, the most successful of her poetry collections. She wasn't afraid—her work and, if necessary, her children would support her—but if only he had told her the why of it, the wound would not feel so deep, the infliction so cruel. And she had waited for the revelation of a sum left to his bastard child, but the will mentioned nothing. She would not tell her children that they had a half-sibling somewhere out there in the world, probably poor and bereft, although at that moment how she longed to besmirch her husband's memory, but even more, just to set the truth straight.

At a conference the following year of the New England Woman Suffrage Association, of which Julia was founder and president, she told the assembly, "In my youth, we thought that 'superior' women ought to have been born men. A blessed change is what we have witnessed." Freed from the man who had bestrode her life like a colossus—the man she realized in the end that she had loved above all others—Julia Ward Howe was, at age fifty-eight, finally glad that she had been born a woman.

Chapter 36

Laura, 1883–1887

Another Irish from Tewksbury! And they've stuck her in my cottage, almost as if they know I have an affinity for such. But not this one, alas, even if I could bring my heart to heel once and for all about Kate, which I doubt will ever happen. It's not a beneficent God giving me a second chance at passion, because this girl is only fifteen and practically spits nails. I do know from Kate how much life in an almshouse can crooken a soul, even if it does not break it, but this one has come out fighting like a cock.

"Be patient with her," Anagnos says. "Annie is an orphan," he tells me. "Her brother died in the almshouse, and to boot she has only partial sight." That's why she's gained a bed here; apparently she pleaded her case to Frank Sanborn, head of the State Board of Charities and a close friend of Doctor's, when he visited Tewksbury. She must be pretty. I tried to touch her hair and face, but she actually smacked my hand away. No one has ever done that! I asked Jeannette, "Does she know who I am?" And Jeannette said, "Yes, indeed." I tried again when she was sleeping, or I thought she was sleeping, just to get a feel for her hair, to see if all Irish hair is a dense forest like Kate's, but I'd barely snared a lock when she grabbed my hand. I don't know if I'll ever get to touch that head, a fact that is nettling me much more than I'd like. It is my job to teach her the manual alphabet, and for that she eagerly allows my hand in hers. She is the quickest learner I have ever encountered. Within days, we are conversing as nimbly as I do with Jeannette or any of the older blinds, though her manners are still bad. She is boorish, impatient, and never greets me when she comes into the cottage.

"Lived here all your life?" she asks, and I tell her all but the first seven years.

"Like prison or home?"

What cheek. Of course Perkins is my home.

"Have family?"

I tell her they are far away, and she says at least they're alive. Well, some of them.

Annie confides that at Tewksbury, she was placed in the ward with all the pregnant women, and she learned "everything" from them: of trysts in closets, perversions in alleys, children abandoned on doorsteps, or worse, disposed of. I'm not shocked, but I hadn't truly understood the dark underbelly of the world Kate had come from; now I feel that I am at last gaining entrance into her circumstances, the plot that framed our short romance. It strikes me, hard as a slap, that she could have abandoned our child, but she did not.

Apparently, the deadhouse was still on the grounds of the almshouse, and Annie had seen more dead bodies than she could count, including her own little brother, Jimmie.

"Sister Mary died also," I tell her, and we exchange details about our siblings. I show her the Emily Dickinson poems I have memorized; she has not heard of her, of course, as Miss Dickinson has never published a single book. As I have jousted with mortality, the poems and their obsessions now resonate with a deep and forlorn ferocity, which they didn't hold for me before, and Annie is taken with them right away. It is these particular verses that provide the most comfort to us both:

> *This is the Hour of Lead—*
> *Remembered, if outlived,*

As Freezing persons, recollect the Snow—
First—Chill—then Stupor—then the letting go—

Annie has grown on me—and apparently I on her—because now she lets me stroke her hair, which is not as curly as Kate's, but is still a delight. She allows us but a minute of such intimacies, however. The girl can't brook much tenderness, as if she were afraid it might make her weak. It's just as well; I don't think I could stand a misadventure at my age. Only once has she come to me for genuine physical comfort. About six months after she'd arrived, she pushed her way into my bed in the middle of the night. "Scared," she spelled, quivering against me. She'd had a nightmare about the Horribles, the deformed men who hobbled to the dining hall at Tewksbury to eat alone like animals. Every day at the blast of a whistle, she watched with the others the procession of the burned, the legless, some with faces hideously distorted by tumors or goiters. Annie knew she should feel sorry for them, but still they terrified her. I approve of her moral sense, but at the same time, I wonder how objectionable she finds me. She can see well enough to be disgusted when I remove my glasses to wash my face and clean out my eyes over our little basin in the corner. She has probably even seen the raised scars on my arms and legs, those tiny, jagged relics of my passions, when I change from dressing gown to day gown. I've waited for her to ask, but she hasn't. It has been a long time since I have had anyone to really talk with, and this girl, I know, can handle truths that those twice her age cannot. If I'd had more of my senses—even one—I think I might have been more of the tiger, like Annie.

Annie has been here almost two years now, but the other girls still mock her: she's Irish, Catholic, and from the almshouse—a triptych of the most dismal. Her strategy is to be rude to them and to her teachers, something I well understand. I think Doctor would have enjoyed her, and Anagnos enjoys her until she pushes him to the brink. Last week, he almost expelled her—for the third time—for going to a rally for General Butler, who's making his fifth try at governorship, this time on the Democratic ticket, when she'd said she was going to the Eye and Ear Infirmary. I spoke to Anagnos on her behalf, telling him how learned and insightful the girl is, and what a wonderful boon she's been to me thus far. Annie is the one who sits beside me and translates as the teachers read from the newspapers every night. It had never bothered me before that they read to us only from the *Transcript* and the *Post*, but Annie complains that we are getting only one side of things, their side. Now that she's had an operation, her vision is good enough to read the *Catholic Register*, and she expounds on various political and social issues sometimes until late in the night. She tells me that Alexander Graham Bell, inventor of the recent telephone—a device I cannot even fathom—has successfully devised a system to teach the deaf to speak. He has set up his own School of Vocal Physiology and Mechanics of Speech right here in Boston. Annie says that she will accompany me if I want to attend, but the sad fact is that I gave up that dream long ago—it was far too painful to continue to entertain the fantasy—and it seems impossible to begin its recovery at this late stage. What a breathtaking possibility, though, and so I encourage Annie to learn all she can since she plans to be a teacher.

Annie loathes Julia, who teaches a class in Greek drama. She calls her the "grande dame" and lampoons the way she declaims. As much as Annie makes me laugh, I feel inclined to take Julia's side occasionally. Our friendship, though a slight and twisted skein, has even withstood the shocking news that while Doctor left two thousand dollars for my care, he left his own wife nothing. The betrayal must be remarkably painful. I was so grateful for his bequest, especially since my own father gave me nothing, and yet equally puzzled that he should so dishonor his own wife. Their more than thirty years together must have been much fiercer than even I'd imagined or, frankly, hoped. Julia is forced to go on tours reading from her essays and poetry to support herself, an irony since her desire for public acclaim was the thing Doctor hated most. Once again, I realize I do not understand this man who held dominion over both our lives.

How swiftly the years have passed between me and my needle-work, the occasional worldly visitor, and Annie for entertainment. It is time to graduate her and she has been named valedictorian from her class of eight. Doesn't sound that much of an accomplishment, but Anagnos is making quite the ceremony, with Julia surprisingly at the helm. Hundreds will be coming to the Tremont Temple, including the governor himself. But no one has paid attention to the girl's costume and she has not two pennies to rub together, so she asks to borrow one of my dresses. She is not so thin as I am—no one is—but she comes close; I can tell from our embraces. She has only two calicoes, a dark and a light, and one silk for church, though she despises church and only goes to vespers with the three other Catholic girls. After two years, she refused to go to Mass any longer and told me that she let the priest know she had absolutely nothing to confess. It's not that she prefers the Unitarians or the Baptists, on whose behalf I admit I've tried to proselytize a bit, but that she thinks of God as just one more authority figure on whom she must turn her back. I do not have that option.

I let her go through my dresses—there aren't that many—and tell her she can pick any one she'd like. I sit on the bed while she tries them, my skin prickling at the fact that she is nearly naked before me, only a few feet away. She is not Kate, she is Annie, but she rouses in me something both soft and hard that I must put down. I am, after all, more than twice her age, not that that would matter if I were a man. I wonder if she has any awareness at all that I am trembling so close by as she slides the garments on and off. I doubt it. Finally, she chooses the white muslin, the one I was baptized in, and we take it to Jeannette to add a blue sash.

Her hair is fixed in a high pompadour with ringlets curling at the sides because Anagnos remarked that she favors President Cleveland's young ward, Frances Folsom, recently married at the White House. I'm not sure if Annie is dressing as the famous belle as a joke or if her vanity is truly primed. It's difficult to tell with her, though her manners have vastly improved, or improved at least when she so chooses.

Julia writes Annie's speech out into my hand, and it is more beautiful and impressive than even I had thought she was capable. A few lines make me reflect upon my own case: "To a certain extent our growth is unconscious. We receive impressions and arrive at conclusions without any effort on our part; but also have the power of controlling the course of our lives." I have helped her, this half-blind Irish from Tewksbury, and she has helped me in return, the extent of our growth vast and unconscious.

I enjoy being feted. Though I am not well, keeping to my bed more days than not, it is more than worth it to rise for this occasion. Anagnos I have spoken of perhaps too harshly, for in this he has a splendid idea: a co-celebration of my fiftieth year at Perkins and my fifty-eighth birthday, which also happily coincide with the 1887 Christmas season. The event has been announced in all the papers, and apparently I am the talk of the town again, however briefly. It is not the most appealing that everyone should know a lady's advanced age, but there you have it. Anagnos has even paid for a new dress and bustle for the day, made of the black wool I feel suits me best now, but I did allow for a jaunty silk fanchon with a short veil. And I asked the seamstress please, please, for a feather, for I have never had a feather on a hat. "What color?" And straightaway I said, "Peacock." I've read they have fantastic long plumes topped off by shimmering iridescent eyes. Imagine that: Laura Bridgman sporting a tall, bright feather from which one brilliant eye peers over the crowd. Perfect. My spectacles will still serve me beneath the veil, of course, but when I tried on the fanchon, I felt quite liberated knowing that I presented a more mysterious and perhaps even alluring visage to the world. Would that I had had this hat for Doctor's funeral! But I will be photographed ceaselessly tomorrow at the party, and so my delightful hat will be recorded for posterity. I wonder how many pictures of me already exist. There is no point in me owning any of them because the photographs themselves have no texture, nothing for me to glean at all with my fingers. They should make raised pictures just as they make raised books. I'll bet Doctor would've tried it if I'd had the idea then, but Anagnos is not the risk taker his predecessor was.

He is not bad, I suppose, though he seems to spend most of his time in the pursuit of money for the Institution, and very little time with the children. He has trotted me out to raise funds for printing more books and then again two years ago when he decided to open a kindergarten here. For that one, he asked me to appear with a blind translator—two for the price of one!—to plead with the crowd for donations. Honestly, I did it because I don't have much to fill my days, and I do like to be onstage. I think back to the days when several hundred crowded in here just to see me, to watch me write on the French board or to pick out places on the embossed globe. Those were the loveliest days, although I didn't know it then.

And so tomorrow will probably be the last of such wonders. Anagnos says he is expecting over five hundred, and Julia herself will preside over the ceremonies in the music hall. She has taken much interest in the Institution since Doctor's death. Like me, she has always enjoyed the spotlight, which Doctor had preferred shining brightest on himself.

I sit in the place of honor on the dais, in my favorite velvet chair brought up from the parlor, with Julia on one side and Anagnos on the other. Vibrations all round, not only hundreds of feet, but also the beats of music. A group of blind children

from the kindergarten have come onstage to sing me a song.
Julia writes it out:

The birthday queen we children greet,
And offer roses, fresh and sweet.
May fortune never cease to bless
And crown her days with happiness.

A nice enough song, I suppose, but it could have been written
for anyone. Julia gets up to speak and Anagnos translates, but I
must admit that I am disappointed to find that it is as much a tribute to her husband as it is a celebration of my accomplishments.
Am I never to be seen as separate from him? The speeches continue from ministers and philanthropists—the best of Boston has
shown for me today—and even Edward Everett Hale speaks, saying that my education provided knowledge of "the great unseen."
A good name for me. My own dear minister from South Baptist
speaks of my conversion and my passion for Christ. I know this
does not go down well with all the Unitarian bigwigs assembled,
but he is the one person I insisted be part of the day. He declares
that I am one of the few who can truly be considered "a bride of
Christ." *Ha!* He has no idea that I did not save myself for Jesus,
but let him think that the black spider is a bride draped in white.
I pull my veil a little lower.

The applause is long, and I hope sincere. Many in the crowd
have watched me grow up, pass through all the stages of childhood
and womanhood. What am I to them? A beacon, a curiosity, an
affection, or merely a dark and familiar presence against which all
other shades of humanity seem bright? I have tried, in my own
rocky fashion, to prove an Inspiration, but it has been so hard to
get out of my own way, to know which parts of myself to separate
and which to marry with man and with Maker.

Julia leads me to a Christmas tree and I reach for the prickly
branches—Doctor's mustache. But then she kneels with me, and I

am delighted to find the base of the tree laden with wrapped packages. My fingers flutter over silk ribbons, alight on tissue paper, crinkly paper, slick wrappings. All for me? "Yes," she says, "from Perkins and from guests." I can't even count them, they are piled so high! I have never had this many presents, even my first Christmas here. I know it is not ladylike, but I sit down on the floor and pick up a small one with a velvet bow I rub against my cheek. I'd like to stick it fast atop my hat, but people would doubtless think it looked silly at my age. Still, I would like to be a present for the crowd. That's what I hope they think of me: a present to them all from God, to show how little one can possess of what we think it means to be human while still possessing full humanity. I am a gift, though only one ever dared unwrap me.

The first is a bracelet, gold, Julia tells me, from Anagnos. It is engraved on the front and I can almost make out the tiny etched words: "Our Laura for 50 Years." I rip open another and pull out a long, fuzzy scarf from Jeannette. Julia has given me a raised-letter book of her latest verse (the hubris cannot be vanquished, but that is as it has always been), and Annie has bequeathed me her copy of the *Iliad*. I forget that all are watching me go through my packages and lose myself in the joyful frenzy of the moment, feeling genuinely like that child of fifty years ago, though without any of the fear. Oh, this one is heavy, large, and square. I tear off the paper—cheap and rough, like butcher's paper—surprising. I run my hands over the smooth wooden box until I find the lid and pop it open. At the back I turn a tiny lever and the music begins to hum through my hands. "Who?" I ask Julia, but there's no card.

I stand and turn outward to the crowd, holding the box. Who has brought it, this handsome present? I crank it again and another song plays, one I recognize from its beats, "Johnnie My Boy." The song from my old music box. Is this indeed my own box that I gave Laura years ago? I have never wished for eyes more than at this moment, to scan the crowd before me, sure that I would recognize my Laura, my Kate. Julia takes the box gently from me and says it's time to greet my visitors. I am buzzing, but I allow her to lead me down from the stage, where I stand waiting for all who want to touch me in the last throes of my celebrity. Hand after hand, they go so fast, a few clumsily attempting to write something, but all I can think is: *that's not her hand, that's not her hand.* And then quickly, toward the end, the most familiar fingers close on mine, and I grip them tight, hold on, try to write, but then she is gone. I raise my fingers to my lips. Sweetness. I wheel around, bumping into strangers, grabbing at sleeves, reaching for faces. I make my old noise for Kate, the most beautiful sound I've ever mustered, and I'm sure she will hear me and come running back. I have money now to give her. Does she know that? I will give her everything. I make her noise again, louder, and then Anagnos reins me in, pulls me back to center stage, back to all the hands awaiting me, but not the one I want. I have made a spectacle of myself at my own party, but it must be as God intended. It was Kate, I know in my heart it was Kate. I breathe deeply, in and out, in and out, and tell myself that it is all right that she touched me and fled. I do not pretend to understand, and yet all is still lit with a flame from within that cannot, will not, ever be extinguished. She was here; that is the jewel I must cherish. After all these years, she still wanted to see me, to touch me.

Now it is time for Anagnos to wrap up the festivities, though I can still barely catch my breath. Julia takes my hand again but she is not writing about me. I'd thought there would be a summing up of my accomplishments, but no: she writes two names, Edith Thomas and Helen Keller, whom Anagnos calls the *new* deaf-blind girls. Ah, their long search has finally yielded fresh fruit. He says that Edith will be here at Perkins next month and that Annie will be sent immediately to teach Helen in Alabama. So far for Annie to go! I will miss her spitfire. Anagnos ends by saying what "a singular coincidence that Laura's semicentenary should mark the advent of two little hapless pilgrims to the beneficent care that had given to her life all its brightness." If they are pilgrims, what am I? Apparently, Mrs. Keller read about me in Dickens's *American Notes* and thought her daughter might be helped. "So she sent a letter and a picture," he says, "of the loveliest little girl you've ever seen, smiling, dimpled, a perfectly shaped head." He seems already to have forgotten about Edith in his enthusiasm for describing the beauty of little Miss Helen. I crank the music box again and again, though I know it is rude while he is speaking. I don't know why this news strikes such a hollow and melancholy gong within my heart. Today was meant to be my day, and yet I have been eclipsed by a more radiant sun. Why must the Lord keep making deaf-blind children? Wasn't I enough for the world?

Chapter 37

Laura, 1888

Now I ask Helen again: "Which sense would you have back?"

"Whichever God chooses," she says. The perfect, tiny diplomat to God and man. Oh, she will do fine, this second me; she will do so much better than I did because she understands already—or Annie has made her to understand—what will be expected of her. And she might as well be the second Laura Bridgman because she will never be able to be truly herself. Poor darling child. And yet perhaps I have been too much *myself*—is this possible?

"A delightful answer." I bend close and turn us away from our watchers to allow for a private exchange. She sniffs long and hard against my shoulder. "Speak, speak if you can." I push the air up from my throat and growl a special naming noise for Helen. The normal ones must be shaking in their boots. "And get the glass eyes," I tell her, "the bluest marbles fame can buy to stuff into those dry sockets. It will be worth it."

She taps gently against the glass of my spectacles, and I hold my breath. She traces the prow of my nose and her fingertip rests between my lips. I kiss that finger, and then the palm that she will open to the world.

I want to write out everything—for me, for her—but I am denied the pleasure, or pain, of ever being able to read my own words. You will be able to read them, but I will not. So I write this out into the air, in a grand and looping script, that what is invisible to man may be visible to God.

Epilogue

A year after her meeting with Helen Keller, on May 4, 1889, Laura Bridgman died at Perkins of a streptococcal infection. She was fifty-nine. Her funeral, attended by hundreds, was held in the Exhibition Hall, and her body taken back to New Hampshire for burial near the Bridgmans' farm. Laura's brain was preserved for scientific analysis, and in his 1890 report, Dr. Henry H. Donaldson found no organic traces of disability except for a slightly underdeveloped region of speech and noted only that hers was a "typical female brain." Though Dr. Howe had planned to write a biography of Laura, he never did, and the task was taken up by his daughters, who published *Laura Bridgman: Dr. Howe's Famous Pupil and What He Taught Her* in 1903, a work that centered largely on their father.

Julia Ward Howe continued her work as a writer, suffragist, and pacifist and was also, ironically, the creator of Mother's Day. Her daughters' biography of her won the Pulitzer Prize in 1917. Literary historian Gary Williams recently discovered an unfinished, novel-length manuscript, *The Hermaphrodite*, written between 1846 and 1847, which she had apparently kept hidden, and his resulting book speculates that the novel explores the complex relationships between Julia, her husband, and Charles Sumner.

Annie Sullivan married but still remained the teacher and companion of Helen Keller until her death at the age of seventy in 1936.

Helen Keller quickly emerged, in her own words, as "the best damn poster child the world has ever known." She was the first deaf-blind person to earn a university degree, at Radcliffe College, and became a prolific writer, lecturer, and activist. She learned to speak, though barely intelligibly, and was fitted with artificial blue eyes, which her family strove to keep secret. Helen died in 1968 at the age of eighty-seven.

Dr. Howe's legacy, Perkins Institution, now called Perkins School for the Blind, finally came to embrace Braille, and moved to a larger campus in Watertown, Massachusetts, in 1912. It is the world's preeminent school for the education of both the blind and the deaf-blind, with partner programs in sixty-five countries.

In her 1929 autobiography, *Midstream: My Later Life*, Helen Keller wrote that had Laura Bridgman been blessed with a lifelong teacher and companion like Annie Sullivan, "she would have outshone me."

Afterword

I first read about Laura Bridgman in a 2001 review of her bi-ographies, *The Education of Laura Bridgman* by Ernest Freeberg and *The Imprisoned Guest* by Elisabeth Gitter, both of which have proved invaluable resources. I was astounded that I'd never heard of this remarkable woman, given the extent of her fame in the mid-nineteenth century. Why had she been virtually erased from history, leaving us to believe that Helen Keller was the first deaf-blind person to learn English? While the idea of a deaf-blind woman who also couldn't taste or smell probably conjures for many the narrow cell of a cruelly limited existence, my first thought was that Laura Bridgman must have possessed a most fascinating and complex inner life. I also felt, in some strange and unfathomable way, that on some level, I already knew her.

Over the course of two years of research, both at Perkins and through fellowships at the Houghton Library at Harvard, the Schlesinger Library at Radcliffe, the American Antiquarian Society, and the Massachusetts Historical Society, I really did begin to know and to understand her in historical context and in relation to the other principals in her story. The more I learned, the more questions I had about this woman who became the nineteenth century's greatest educational, philosophical, and theological experiment.

In writing *What Is Visible*, I tried to maintain my balance on what the writer Thomas Mallon has called the "sliding scale of historical fiction," adhering to the "what might have happened *as well*" model as opposed to the "what might have happened *instead*." Besides Oliver Caswell, there were two other deaf-blind persons at Perkins during Laura's stay: Lucy Reed and Julia Brace. I chose not to include them in the novel because neither one made any real educational progress; Lucy wore a bag over her head and never learned the alphabet, while Julia was largely inexpressive and unresponsive, learning only the most rudimentary sign in her single year at Perkins. On this note, there is only one major swerve from Laura's documented life and that is my invention of the character of Kate, the orphaned Irish girl who becomes her lover. There is no record of Laura ever having had a romantic relationship—save her mistaken belief that her teacher's beau was courting *her*—but that doesn't mean, of course, that it didn't happen. As a novelist friend advised, "If you're going to write her whole life, you've got to give her *something*." And so I gave her Kate. I chose a lesbian relationship rather than a heterosexual one because the journals and letters of Dr. Howe and her teachers repeatedly emphasize how much Laura didn't like men and how much she did like women, especially touching them. Dr. Howe's edict that Laura not be allowed into the other girls' beds is true, and quite telling at a time when adolescents, and even adults, of the same sex routinely slept together.

As for my choice to make the sexual relationship a somewhat sadomasochistic one, it seemed natural to me that if one has only the sense of touch, the desire would be to push it to its extreme. It is also noted in Laura's teachers' journals that she often "hurt herself on purpose," though not exactly how, and so the ritual self-cutting seemed to fit also. Laura claimed late in life that she had partially regained the ability to taste, but there were no tests run, and while it is medically possible to regain that sense, it is highly unlikely.

As Kate is my creation, then obviously she did not bear Dr. Howe's child. His romantic life proved a rich area for speculation, however, because of the numerous extant letters mentioning his infidelities, even though his daughters methodically destroyed much of their parents' correspondence, especially to each other. Howe also accused his wife, Julia Ward Howe, of having an affair with Horace Binney Wallace, who indeed committed suicide after she left Rome. It is also true that while Doctor left Laura two thousand dollars, he left his wife nothing. The exact reasons are unknown, but his dismay at her possible adultery and her continued work as a writer seem to have been enough, in his mind, to merit this final act of hostility. As for Doctor's relationship with Charles Sumner, two recent academic works, *Diva Julia* by Valarie H. Ziegler and *Hungry Heart: The Literary Emergence of Julia Ward Howe* by Gary Williams, explore the possibility of an affair between them. Both scholars come to the conclusion that while Sumner seemed to push for a physical relationship, it was probably never consummated due to Howe's reluctance.

Dr. Howe's involvement with John Brown and the Secret Six is entirely factual, including Brown's visit to Boston and Howe's flight to Canada. While it is not known whether Laura Bridgman actually met Brown when he was at Perkins, she did encounter all of the other real-life historical figures in the novel, most significantly Charles Dickens, who devoted an entire chapter of *American Notes* to her. There is no proof that she was introduced to Emily Dickinson's poetry, but it is entirely feasible since Thomas Wentworth Higginson, Miss Dickinson's mentor, was a frequent visitor at Perkins. The versions of the poems used in the text are taken from *The Collected Poems of Emily Dickinson*, edited by Thomas H. Johnson, which restored them to the original versions that Higginson would have had before he edited them years later for publication. The letters in chapters 5 and 7 are fictionalized, but they are based on factual events that occurred during that time period among all the characters. The poems attributed in the text to Julia Ward Howe were indeed all written by her.

While Julia Ward Howe and Sarah Wight became friends, there

was enduring friction between Laura and Julia. The ear-thrusting incident is fabricated, though Laura was known to have slapped her teachers, fellow students, and even once bitten Charles Sumner. Though the use of gloves to punish her is my invention, it was suggested by the repeated handcuffing of Lucy Reed by Dr. Howe during her short time at Perkins. Laura was also highly discouraged from making her noises, including being asked by Howe to do so only in the kitchen closet. Laura's use as a pawn to advance the causes of both phrenology and anti-Calvinism is well documented, as is Laura's decision to be baptized and Howe's rage and disappointment with her decision. The scene at the fund-raiser is fictional, though Howe did keep a vast collection of phrenological specimens on the premises.

Dr. Howe sent Laura home to New Hampshire in 1850, where she almost starved to death, and his quotes denigrating both her and her family are taken directly from his Annual Report. After he allowed her to return to Perkins, the *Boston Evening Transcript* proposed sending Laura to the London Exhibition as America's greatest accomplishment, but Doctor declined, as he did Dorothea Dix's offer to fund a lifelong companion for her. Whether or not he refused Laura artificial eyes is not known, though it's clear that if he'd wanted her to have them, she would have had them.

As for Sarah Wight, I was blessed to discover her husband Edward Bond's shipboard journal in the Houghton Library, where I was told I was the only one who'd ever read it. Bond wrote of how "the one sin of his youth" had ruined his life, his chances with Sarah, and possibly even threatened his sanity. He was not allowed to be a missionary, but sent to the Sandwich Islands in a purely administrative capacity. Though Sarah had previously refused his offer of marriage, she joined him when she was let go from Perkins. I was fascinated by the question of whether he told her about the syphilis; however, his anguished journal revealed him to be possessed of such goodness and moral clarity that I felt sure he had given her a choice. We know that she chose to stay with him and bear his children and that she died in McLean Asylum, though whether from syphilis or an inherited mental condition is unclear.

After her rescue from the almshouse, Annie Sullivan lived in a cottage at Perkins with Laura for several years and Laura helped teach her the manual alphabet, which augments current American Sign Language, and which Annie then taught to Helen Keller.

The search for a "second Laura Bridgman" was conducted in earnest by Michael Anagnos, Howe's successor, in what one historian termed "essentially a deaf-blind beauty pageant," and Helen Keller was chosen because she was judged to be the prettiest, and therefore the potentially best "poster child." Luckily for Perkins—and for the world—Helen also turned out to be a genius. And yet it is clear, as William James wrote in an essay for the *Atlantic*, "that without Laura Bridgman there could never have been a Helen Keller." There is no record of what transpired at the meeting between Laura and Helen, save the fact that Helen stepped on Laura's foot.

"The novelist," said E. L. Doctorow, "has to break through the facts to get at the truth."

It is my greatest hope that I have broken through in my search for the real Laura Bridgman, the *realest* Laura Bridgman.

About the Author

Kimberly Elkins's fiction and nonfiction have been published in the *Atlantic, Best New American Voices, The Iowa Review,* the *Village Voice,* the *Chicago Tribune, Maisonneuve, Glamour,* and *Slice,* among others. She was a finalist for the 2004 National Magazine Award in fiction, and this is her first novel. Kimberly lives in New York City. Visit her website at www.kimberlyelkins.com.